THE GEISHA WITH THE GREEN EYES

THE GEISHA WITH THE GREEN EYES

SECRETS FROM THE HIDDEN HOUSE
BOOK ONE

INDIA MILLAR

Red Empress Publishing
www.RedEmpressPublishing.com

Copyright © India Millar 2016
www.IndiaMillar.co.uk

Cover Design by Cherith Vaughan
www.CoversByCherith.com

ALSO BY INDIA MILLAR

Secrets from the Hidden House

The Geisha with the Green Eyes

The Geisha Who Could Feel No Pain

The Dragon Geisha

The Geisha Who Ran Away

The Song of the Wild Geese

The Red Thread of Fate

This World is Ours

Warrior Woman of the Samurai

Firefly

Mantis

Chameleon

Spider

Dragonfly

Scorpion

Cricket

Moth

Daughter of the Yakuza

Wild Iris

Midnight Sakura

Haiku Collections

Dreams from the Hidden House

Song of the Samurai

This book is humbly dedicated to Benzaiten, the Japanese goddess of good luck for both writers and geisha. May both she and you enjoy the words herein!

FOREWORD

The Geisha with the Green Eyes is a romance, a pinch of fairy dust, and has only the tips of its roots in fact. The Floating World in Edo (now Tokyo) existed, but the Hidden House is a figment of my imagination. What is true is the way that women in general, and particularly "kept" women like geisha and courtesans, were treated. They were not so much second class citizens as goods; they were owned, and their owners could do as they liked with them. Wives, though technically free, were prisoners of their husbands just as the girls in the brothels and tea houses were prisoners of their Auntie. Wives were rarely treated with any affection; they were there to bear children and do as they were told. When they had boy children, they were bullied by them as well. Men who could afford mistresses kept them; those who could not, visited the various classes of courtesans.

Bizarre as it seems to us now, this was accepted as normal behavior.

In general, geisha were not expected to provide sex for their customers. They were high-priced entertainers who sang and danced and played the samisen and made amusing conversation. Courtesans were for sex, and it was normal for a geisha's customer to move on from the geisha to a selected courtesan. In this novel, the girls in the Hidden House were...different. But then again, that was part of their allure.

Both geisha and courtesans were virtually slaves. Girl children were often sold by impoverished parents, and it was commonplace for attractive children to be kidnapped and sold to tea houses and brothels. The girls were expected to pay back their debts to their Auntie – debts that piled up with every new kimono bought for them, every meal they ate, every night they had a roof over their heads. A fortunate few were able to buy themselves out by their own thrift. Lucky geisha and courtesans were bought out by a wealthy patron to be his mistress. No one wanted to be an unvalued wife, bullied by her husband, sons, and her dragon of a mother-in-law!

The mizuage ceremony (the ritualistic paid deflowering of geisha and courtesans from the age of thirteen) was a fact of life and continued to take place as late as the mid-twentieth century.

Those who know the period well will find faint echoes of the life of the Nine-Fingered Geisha in *The Geisha with the Green Eyes*. It is also a fact that a troop of kabuki actors – amongst them women – toured America in the late nineteenth and early twentieth century, to great critical acclaim. Needless to say, *The Geisha with the Green Eyes* is pure fiction.

Tanoshimu!

PREFACE

"Living only for the moment, giving all our time to the pleasures
of the moon,
the snow, cherry blossoms and maple leaves. Singing songs,
drinking
sake, caressing each other, just drifting, drifting. Never giving
a care
if we had no money, never sad in our hearts. Only like a plant
moving
on the river's current; this is what is called The Floating World."

Tales of the Floating World
Asai Ryoi, 1661

PROLOGUE

The other girls had enticing names. Carpi (*Koi*). Masaki
(*Blossom*). Kiku (*Chrysanthemum Blossom*). Naruko (*Chirping
Child*).
My own mother was called Terue (*Shining Blessing*). But me?
I was just Midori No Me.
Green Eyes.

1

Blossoms tremble
At the approach of winter.
As do I.

The first time I was with a man I was only thirteen years old.

But of course, this was normal for any geisha. After all, until one has undergone the ceremony of mizuage – which in English means "hoisting from water" – one is still only a half-jewel, a hangyouku, as we were called in Edo. Elsewhere, the term was maiko, and this is the word I shall use from now on, as I know it is easier for your Western tongue to pronounce.

Sometimes maiko undergo the mizuage ceremony a little later; it all depends on the girl. Occasionally, a maiko would not have her mizuage ceremony until she was as old as sixteen or even seventeen, quite elderly for a maiko! But of course, those were the girls who came late in life to Yoshi-wara - the Floating World in Edo, Japan's capital city.

I was born in the Floating World.

I cannot remember a time when I did not expect to undergo the mizuage. After all, how else did I expect to pay back my Okaasan – my Auntie – for all the years she had fed me, clothed me, kept me warm, kept me safe? How else was I going to start to pay her back for my clothes and my samisen? Apart from all of those important matters, if I declined – if I should dare! – to undergo my mizuage, where would I go? What would become of me? The Floating World was *my* world, *my* family. I knew nothing else. Knew nowhere else.

Of course I would undergo the mizuage.

One heard tales, of course, from the other girls who had undergone their mizuage. Both from the girls who shared the Hidden House with me and occasionally those geisha who lived in the Green Tea House across the courtyard. Some laughed about it, said it was nothing at all. I now think those girls were either lying or had had the good fortune to have an extremely thoughtful danna for their first time. Kiku even had *two* mizuage! She wasn't that unusual, either; if Auntie thought she might get away with it, some girls had two or three deflowering ceremonies. Kiku had two because she was so very fat. On the first occasion her danna didn't actually get what he paid for, though she made sure that he thought that he had. That is the way of the Floating World, after all. It is all shadow and illusion. As long as pleasure is sought and found, nothing else matters. Even on the second occasion she said that it really wasn't too bad. Other girls shrugged and said it was done with, and that was all there was to it. Others refused to talk about it. Inevitably, it was those who would not speak about it at all that we all wanted to hear from. Was it really bad? Would we hate it? Did it hurt?

Those girls shrugged and looked away, lowering their eyes as if to say, "You will find out."

And I did, of course.

I could say I remember it well, but that would only be a half-truth. I not only remember it, I dream of it sometimes, even now, after Danjuro came into my life and everything changed.

The banquet was finished. Teruki-san, my danna, burped loudly, and the girls tittered behind their fans politely. Auntie inclined her head regally and all of the girls immediately got to their feet. Two maids had to help Kiku stand. For a second I thought that Teruki-san was diverted by Kiku as he watched her with covetous eyes, but I was only being silly. He had paid an enormous sum to deflower me, he would not be distracted now. The girls – and Auntie – made their bows to my danna and filed out, one behind the other.

The maids scurried to remove the dishes and would have taken the sake flasks as well, but Teruki-san gestured for them to leave the charcoal burner and the flasks. I kneeled with my eyes lowered, waiting. Bedding was laid on the mats and then the maids approached me and stood on each side, waiting for my danna's signal. I watched the shadows flickering on the screens. It seemed to me that they had grown much longer before he finally clapped his hands. Instantly, the girls helped me to my feet and began to ceremonially disrobe me.

It took them even longer to remove my obi and kimono and undergarments than it had to put them on. Finally, I was naked except for my tabi, my white socks. I don't suppose Teruki-san was prolonging the moment, no doubt it just felt that way to me, but I thought it was an age before he clapped his hands again and the girls wrapped me in a loose, comfortable robe before bowing themselves out of the room.

I was very glad to sink to my knees on the mat. If another second had passed, I think I would have simply folded gracelessly to the floor.

My danna was an old man. A very old man. He still had some hair, but not a great deal of it. The crown of his head was completely bare, and what was left was gathered and tied at the nape of his neck. Oddly, his bald head was as smooth as an egg, in cruel contrast to his face, which was a nest of wrinkles. His eyebrows were very bushy and vigorous, as though all the life of his hair had somehow taken possession of them. He was a heavy pipe smoker, as his upper lip was a darker brown than the rest of his face. I stared at the mat and forced a smile to my lips.

The silence was so profound I could hear Teruki-san breathing. A sudden thought made me feel physically sick: what if Teruki-san decided he didn't want me after all? What if he demanded his money back? What if he complained to Auntie that I was inept? What would become of me then? Would Auntie sell me to one of the cheap houses of prostitution, where men could leer at me through the bars and I would be at every passerby's disposal? I almost wailed in fear at the thought.

The sound of my own breathing in my ears was so deafening that for a second I did not realize that Teruki-san had spoken to me. He had to repeat his words and I could hear from his voice that he was not pleased. I was so terrified that suddenly I was desperate to pee. What if I did? There, on the tatami matting in front of this man who had paid so well for me? I couldn't help myself. I moaned out loud with fear and worry.

My obvious distress seemed to please Teruki-san. He didn't speak again, but patted the matting at his side. I shuffled over on my knees and bowed deeply to him, more worried about my bladder than my patron.

"Closer," he said. Obediently, I inched a little nearer, close enough for him to touch me.

He wafted his hands at me, indicating that I should straighten up from my abject crouch. I did so, keeping my eyes deferentially lowered. I thought that he was going to loosen my robe to see what he had paid for, and I clenched my buttocks tight to stop myself from flinching. At least the insane desire to pee had receded, for which I gave thanks.

But he did not loosen my robe. Not at all. He reached out and poked at my wig. "Take that off."

I stared at him, unable to believe he was talking about my beautiful wig, or rather, Carpi's wig. But he nodded at it, and so I reached up and tugged it free. He waved his hand at the side of the matting, so I placed it where he had indicated, reverently. If any damage came to that wig, Carpi would skin me. He leaned forward and patted my hair, which was pinned up carefully to contain it under the wig. Pursing his lips, he began to pull out the pins.

Strands of auburn hair began to fall with each pin that came out. Finally, it was all down, trailing nearly to my waist. I heard Teruki-san clear his throat, a small noise of evident satisfaction.

He spat on his fingers and took a tendril of hair in his fist, first tugging it and then rubbing it between his wet fingers. He glanced at his fingers, and then repeated the process with another lock of hair. Appearing satisfied, he let the hair fall loose and then leaned forward, pushing my chin up with his thumb.

"Open your eyes, wide."

I did so, and Teruki-san leaned forward and pulled my left eye wide open, holding the eyelid tightly between his thumb and first finger. With his free hand, he rubbed the ball of his thumb across my eye, quite hard. It hurt and I tried to blink, but could not as his grip was too tight.

He inspected his thumb carefully, and then repeated the process with my other eye.

Curiously, this strange inspection quelled my terror. He was making sure that he had got what he had paid for; that my strange, reddish hair and green eyes were natural, not tinted in some way. He had no doubt paid a huge sum to deflower me, and it was only fair that he inspect his purchase. Yet this irreverent inspection made me feel as if I was some sort of exotic fruit on a market stall, not a person at all. I gritted my teeth hard to prevent myself from telling him to stop, to get on with what he had paid for. Had I done so, then it would have been a matter of hours before I was, indeed, behind one of the barred prisons for prostitutes in the slum areas of the Floating World. And although I knew it, it did nothing to diminish my fury; rather, it seemed to increase it.

I sent up a silent prayer to any god who might be listening to make me keep my temper. To stop me striking out at this horrible old man, this man who smelled like the inside of a chest that has not been opened for years. To stop me from telling him exactly what I thought of him. I took a deep breath and made myself wait silently for him to finish his inspection.

Teruki-san finally finished rubbing my eyeballs and was ready to accept that I was genuine. A real half-breed. He smiled at me. His teeth were horrible, brown and yellow and most of them little more than stumps. Perhaps it was those dreadfully neglected teeth that did it, but the fury that had risen far enough to bubble as insults in my throat unexpectedly turned to bitter contempt for my danna. My eyes hurt where he had rubbed them and I was suddenly deeply envious of those geisha outside the Hidden House, those who never had to suffer humiliation like this in their mizuage. But I was just as much a geisha as they were, so I smiled as coquettishly as I could manage. I lowered my eyes and peeped at this horrible old man from under my eyelashes.

This was my mizuage, and no matter what, I was determined it would be done in true geisha style. My danna had paid a fortune for me. I was not going to disappoint him – or Auntie. I raised my eyes and smiled. Properly. Not flirtatiously or shyly. Properly.

Teruki-san seemed quite amused at my boldness. He tapped my breastbone sharply and grinned. I smiled back.

"Well, it's good to see you really are a foreign Barbarian." He chuckled, and I realized that this was his way of trying to flirt. "Stand up, dear, and take that robe off."

I did as I was told, of course – but not how he had expected. I undid the sash slowly, and let it fall to the floor. I shrugged the robe off my shoulders and let it hang for the space of a second before it followed the sash. I stood before this horrible old man naked and unashamed, not even pretending to stoop to hide my height, still less cover my breasts and black moss.

Suddenly, I was worried that I had gone too far in the opposite direction in my new-found daring. Teruki-san drew in a deep breath, and I could see he was shuddering with excitement. He reached forward abruptly and thrust his fingers into my black moss. Not that it was black; in my case it was much, much redder than the hair on my head. This seemed to excite my danna immensely, and for one truly glorious moment I thought perhaps the stimulation might be too much for his aging heart and he might fall over with a seizure.

Alas, no. He parted my moss with eager fingers and then split my sex with his hand. His face fell, and he probed still further.

"Aie." He scowled. "I had thought that foreign Barbarian women's sex was different from that of Japanese women. I have heard tales that they were crossways. Yours is perfectly normal."

Even as he spoke, his index finger was flicking in and out of my opening. His fingernail was long and ragged, and it caught on my moss uncomfortably. I raised my shoulders in bewilderment. What could I say? I was sure that I could hear a hiss of breath from the other side of the screen and I knew that Auntie was listening, and probably watching, from the other side. She was not pleased with me.

My fear of Auntie was far greater than my contempt for Teruki-san. Auntie held my life in her very hands. I licked my lips and words suddenly spilled out.

"Teruki-san, I am only half foreign Barbarian. I think that the half that is Japanese lives behind my black moss and the Barbarian half is in my eyes and my hair."

He paused in his groping and probing for a second and then shrugged. "That may be so. Well, we shall see what you can do for me, child."

He sat back comfortably and loosened his robe. He was propped on one elbow, waiting for me, and I thought, *oh, let's get this over with.* It was a very brave thought, but of course I had no idea what was about to happen.

I kneeled down and bowed. Anything was better than having to look at him. He clapped his hands and nodded at his tree of flesh. Or at least, where his tree of flesh should have been. But I could see nothing except the twin swellings of his testicles and something that looked exactly like the mouth parts of a sea slug. I swallowed, my new found confidence evaporating as quickly as it had arisen. What was I supposed to do? What did he expect of me?

His hand closed around the mouth part of the sea slug and he tugged at it. I realized with dismay that this limp, disgusting thing was his tree of flesh. He waggled it at me and gestured with his head. I realized he wanted me to touch it, to bring it to life. Or at least, that's what I thought he wanted.

I was wrong.

I reached out cautiously, and he let me fondle it for a few moments. It was even more disgusting than I had expected. It was slightly moist and quite cold. I rubbed it between my fingers and looked at him hopefully, to see if that was what he wanted.

Apparently not.

His lips were pursed like a button. He reached out and grabbed my hair, forcing my head down to his groin. I had a moment to think, *oh no!* and then he was mashing my head against his limp tree.

I had two choices. I could keep my mouth obstinately shut, in which case he would no doubt beat me until I did what he wanted anyway, or I could open my lips now and try and coax some life into his tree. I chose the latter. Really I had no choice in the matter. Even sucking at this disgusting bit of withered flesh was better than facing Auntie's anger. If I refused to obey my danna, tomorrow would find me in a low-class whorehouse, at the whim of any man who fancied me.

So I folded my lips around his sad little organ and nibbled at it with my teeth. Abruptly, I stopped nibbling and bit, quite hard. I do not remember consciously thinking that I would do it, so perhaps instinct took over.

I immediately feared I had made a bad mistake. I braced myself, expecting at the very least a hard slap or even a punch from my danna. Instead, he inhaled sharply and suddenly his tree of flesh was no longer a wilting sapling, ready to be blown away by any stray breeze, but a vigorous, hard pine of a tree. He thrust it hard into my mouth and almost down my throat, nearly cutting off my breath.

I couldn't even bite the disgusting thing. It filled my mouth and left no room for me to do anything. I could feel it brushing the back of my throat and I retched, worried anew that I might not be able to prevent myself from vomiting.

So I did the only thing I could, under the circumstances. I sucked that horrible old tree of flesh. Sucked it as if my very life depended on it, which was not far from the truth. I could hear Teruki-san moaning, even over the drumming of blood in my ears. He began to thrust his hips forward and I thought, *please, no!* I thought his fruit was about to burst. In my mouth.

I moaned in my turn at the thought, and perhaps the god who had heard me earlier took pity on me yet again, as Teruki-san suddenly fastened his hand in my hair and pulled me up. He did it so unexpectedly that I was unable to give his tree of flesh a parting nip. I regretted that, but it was very much secondary to the relief of being able to breathe again.

He was leaning back on his elbows, panting. I pushed

the hair out of my eyes and fastened my gaze, modestly, as was proper, on the mat. For an instant, I had a surge of hope. Was that it? Was my danna satisfied? He was, after all, a very old man. Perhaps he was not capable of more? Hard on the heels of the thought came another; if that really was the case, then I would have to go through this all over again, with another danna. I reached out hurriedly to his tree, worried it would shrink without my attentions.

I had no need to worry.

Teruki-san allowed me to grasp his tree. I gripped it with my fingers and moved my hand back and forth, no doubt clumsily. He paused, silent, for a moment or two and then wrapped his hand around my fingers, clenching my grip on him. He grunted. I took this to be approval and worked a bit quicker.

After what seemed like hours, Teruki-san slapped my hand bruskly. I stared at him hopefully, waiting for some sort of signal. Faster? Slower? Let go? Harder? He spoke harshly.

"Enough. On your hands and knees, woman."

I did as he asked – or rather commanded. In any event, anything, anything at all that would bring my mizuage to an end was welcomed. My hair swung across my face, and I was glad of that, as it meant I did not even have to try to look happy.

I heard Teruki-san scrambling to his feet, and then he was behind me, squatting on the mat. For one horrible instant, I was sure he was going to ram himself into my behind, to "split the melon." He did finger my bottom, running his fingers up and down the cleft and pushed an enquiring finger into my anus. I bared my teeth so hard that the tendons of my neck hurt. But no, he made his mind up and next second his tree of flesh was exploring the entrance to my sex.

I was rigid with fear and anticipation. My private parts were as dry as an old, sun-weathered canvas with terror. I could hear him muttering to himself as he tried to thrust into me, but I was so tense and dry that he could make no progress. He sat back. I had no idea what he was about to do, even what he was thinking. I was trembling so hard I could barely keep my balance. My mind was blank, apart from one thought, one thought that repeated over and over again, like a never-ending circle: this old man, this horrible, wrinkled old man, with his yellow flesh and bald head and long fingernails, was going to put himself inside me. I had no say in the matter. None at all. I was nothing. Less than nothing. He had paid to do this to me.

Teruki-san suddenly got tired of playing the waiting game. I felt him move away from me, and tears of relief came to my eyes. He couldn't manage it. I would have to go through this again, undoubtedly. Even more certainly, Auntie would be furious with me. But perhaps – just perhaps – when she found me another danna, he might be a younger man? A man who did not make me feel sick at the thought of having him inside me? I had raised my head, about to apologize to Teruki-san, when he hit me.

He hit me hard, just at the base of my skull, at the point where the head meets the neck. He must have used his clenched fist. In spite of the fact that he was an old man, he still had a sinewy strength to his arms, and the blow felt like a rock thrown with deadly accuracy. It was not quite hard enough to knock me unconscious – more the pity! – but it was hard enough to make my vision spin. Suddenly, my world was filled with pain and I lost my balance, falling forward onto my elbows. With the strange clarity of pain, I could hear Teruki-san grunting with satisfaction. He placed his hands on each side of my hips and lugged my bottom into the air. When I was positioned to his final satisfaction, he simply leaned into me, pushing his tree of flesh into my dryness.

I shrieked out loud at the pain, which was much worse than the pain in my head. Teruki-san seemed to take it as encouragement. He leaned back, almost withdrawing from me, and then thrust down again hard, hard, hard. I tried to hold my breath, hoping that I would pass out from lack of air, but my body wouldn't obey me and after a minute or so I found myself panting for breath, whether I wanted to or not.

I could do nothing. The more I shouted in pain, the more Teruki-san's vigor seemed to increase. I thought it would never end, that I would live in pain and indignity and shame for the rest of my life, which I prayed would end quickly.

I was almost at the stage of fainting with pain and horror when he finally burst his fruit. At least, I assumed that that was what had happened. All I knew was that he slowed and finally stopped, sliding out of me and falling back on the matting.

I could not move. I stayed where I was, my head touching the matting, my bottom pointing toward the ceiling. Teruki-san finally rose. He gave my bottom a playful slap and I could hear him moving about. Then the screen door opened and closed. A moment later there was the faintest of rustles from the other room. Auntie, taking herself off to her own futon, satisfied that all had gone well. Eventually I persuaded my unwilling bones to move and crawled beneath the bedding. Slowly, like a very, very old woman.

I hurt. Everywhere. My skin shuddered with the memory of his touch. I would dearly have liked to have gone to the bath, to cleanse my private parts and wash away his seed, but I dared not leave the room. My danna had bought me for the whole of the night. Although it was unlikely that he would return, if he came back I had to be here for him. Ready and waiting. And willing. At least I was spared the worry of becoming pregnant by him. We girls were too precious to risk that. Tomorrow, Auntie would give me special tea that would kill his seed.

Yet until morning, I would be left where I was. Undisturbed. I cried, alone and without comfort, until sleep finally claimed me. I then dreamed of Teruki-san shoving his tree of flesh into me. Over and over again.

The morning bought no relief. I heard the little maid come in, heard her bustling about the room. Smelled the charcoal burner as she made tea. Heard her calling a cheerful good morning to me.

I couldn't move.

Couldn't so much as open my eyes. I tried so very hard, but the more I tried, the more impossible it was. Eventually, the maid crouched by my side – I heard her knees crack, quite distinctly – and I felt her touch my face and then pull the bedding back. But still I could not move. I could tell from her movements that she was leaning across me, putting her ear to my mouth – probably to see if I was actually breathing – but still I could not move. Could not make a sound.

It was terrible. I felt as if I had been buried alive. Then the thought came to me that perhaps I *was* dead, that this was my karma. That I was fated to be like this, perhaps forever. Alive yet dead. Feeling nothing, but hearing everything. Perhaps even more dreadful, I could not even move enough muscles to cry at the thought.

The maid had scurried off, but returned quickly. I knew from the rhythm of the footsteps that she had returned with Auntie. As the maid had done, Auntie leaned across and I felt her breath on my face. She immediately shouted orders and within a few seconds there were more people in the room. I was lifted to my feet and dragged out, supported by many hands. My head lolled on my neck; I lacked the ability to lift it up.

"Throw her in."

Auntie gave the order briskly, and all at once I was lifted and found myself flying through thin air.

The bath water was very hot. The splash as I hit the water hurt, then I was sinking to the bottom of the sulfurous pool. I inhaled water, and the shock restored life to my petrified limbs. I thrashed out, rising to the surface and then falling back. I gulped more scalding water, and it seemed to me that the water revived me from the inside out. I opened my eyes and managed to stagger to my feet.

Auntie, Kiku, Carpi, Naruko and three of the maids ringed the bath, all staring down at me as I sputtered and fought for balance. Auntie and Carpi exchanged a glance and then Auntie clapped her hands, dismissing the other girls. When they had gone, she leaned over the bath and peered down at me.

"Midori. Do you hear me now?"

I nodded.

"Then listen, and listen well. You are no different from any of the other girls here. I will not stand for this sort of dramatic nonsense. If you try to play your silly tricks once more, then I will let the boys play with you. Do you understand?"

I stood in the bath, stark naked, bewildered, in pain, yet I nodded.

"Yes, Auntie," I said, quietly enough. But something in my tone must have been wrong because Auntie frowned and glared at me before deciding that she had imagined it and turned away.

Once she was gone, I scrubbed myself until my skin burned. I still could not get rid of Teruki-san.

Just as I could never wash away all the others that followed him.

2

The sun shines somewhere.
But I do not see.
I am bereft.

So there I was. Thirteen years old and soon to be no longer an innocent. Soon, I would be not a maiko, but a geisha. The same as every other geisha who inhabited the Green Tea House and the rest of the Floating World.

And I would be even more deeply in debt to my Auntie than I was at present, just like every other geisha. Auntie owned the Green Tea House as well as the Hidden House. She was a rich woman, but no one would ever have known from the way she moaned constantly about the price of everything. Both houses shared a courtyard, but our plain, discreet building could have been a private house. Very few of the Green Tea House's patrons were even aware that we existed. Both Houses were very expensive, very high-class.

But the Green Tea House was open to anybody who had enough money to pay to be entertained by the singing and dancing and wit of the resident geisha. *Our* clients were not only rich, but had to be introduced by an existing patron. All were carefully vetted by Auntie before they were even allowed through the door. Unlike our sisters in the Green Tea House, we were available only to the selected few who would truly appreciate our unique qualities. Although our duties went far beyond singing and dancing.

The geisha in the Green Tea House knew about us, of course. We were all geisha, after all. But our lives barely touched. We girls in the Hidden House were different from ordinary geisha. Apart from anything else, we were shielded from the outside world. Even so, it would be impossible to live in the Hidden House for the whole of your life and not understand men and their desires. From the moment that I could first walk and talk, I knew my place in life. Unlike most of the girls, I at least understood why my life was as it was – I was expected to expiate my mother's sins, as well as all the other sins I had committed in lives I could not remember.

We all understood that being born women made us lesser beings. Just as we understood that the samurai were allowed to cut down any peasant they chose to test the edge of their swords, we knew and accepted the fact that having the misfortune to be born as female made us inferior to men. We were subservient. At least we were not burakumin - outcasts. Burakumin were an unfortunate caste who did the jobs that nobody else would do. They emptied the night soil into wagons and took it away, worked as butchers of flesh, and did other disgusting things. Their women, of course, were of an even lower state. Compared to women of the burakumin, we were fortunate! As Auntie never tired of telling me, both Naruko and I were especially lucky. Were we not under the protection of Auntie, we would both have been regarded with loathing as foreign Barbarians and would have had no option but to live as burakumin ourselves.

Because I was so deformed, I thought for a long time that perhaps I would never have a mizuage. Auntie had kept me hidden from the world as much as possible for a very good reason. She had explained to me over and over again that the world outside the Floating World was not for me. That I was so ugly, so disfigured by my mother's sins and those of my unknown ancestors, that if I ventured into Edo, outside the Floating World, people would turn away from me in disgust. Even the women would be made sick at the sight of me. The men would certainly shout abuse at me or throw things. Even within the Floating World, people would at the very least consider me unlucky and try and drive me away. No, she chose to keep me in the Hidden House for my own good, and I was grateful to her for it.

By the time of my thirteenth birthday, there were only two of us in the Hidden House who had not had their mizuage – me and Naruko, the Chinese girl. She was a quiet, sweet-natured girl who spoke Japanese with a shockingly bad accent and a strange sing-song rhythm, hence her name – Chirping Child. Both of us being gaijin – foreigners – it was only natural that we should be friends, but we were not. Perhaps our origins were just too different. In any case, close friendships were not encouraged by Auntie. Naruko was nowhere near as ugly as I was and could even be mistaken for Japanese when she had her full makeup in place. Her bound feet were the giveaway, but there was not a lot she could do about them. In fact, Auntie seemed pleased with her feet and told the rest of us that we should try and copy the way Naruko walked, as her hobbled gait made her appear pleasingly subservient, like a horse that has been crippled and could only walk at the whim of its master. I think that she actually meant that Naruko had no chance of getting away from any man who fancied her. Our kimonos meant we could all only take very small, mincing steps anyway, albeit not with the pain that Naruko suffered when she walked.

I was amazed to learn that I was to have my mizuage before Naruko. Auntie told me arrangements had been made about a week after my birthday, and I was very excited. Innocence is a fine thing, to be sure. As the days went past and nothing more was said, my excitement began to change to intense nervousness. I was not, you understand, exactly looking forward to the event, but it did make me feel – for once! – as if I *belonged.* As if I was the same as everybody else. All the rest of the girls fussed around me. At that time, there were five of us "special" girls in the Hidden House. Over the years there had been as many as ten and sometimes as few as three. Girls came and went, some remaining longer than others. Some of the lucky ones found a permanent danna very quickly and disappeared to be his mistresses. Others were less favored and lingered with us, sometimes for years. Of course, once a girl got past her prime and into her mid-twenties, she was no longer fresh. No longer able to attract clients very well. Auntie was very generous toward such girls. Other houses would simply have thrown them out to manage as best they could in the Floating World, but our Auntie allowed them to stay, often acting as maids for the younger girls. This in itself was a sort of perversion, an inversion of the natural order of things. In the rest of the Floating World the maids were very young girls who were often maiko in training to be geisha. These older maids were not paid, but did expect to share the tips earned by the geisha.

Kiku had had her mizuage not long before, and she reassured me.

"Don't worry about it," she advised. "My first one was so much of a nothing that I was actually disappointed. In fact, it hurt more when Auntie examined me afterward and found I was still whole."

That didn't sound so bad, I thought.

Kiku started to laugh at the memory, and her whole body shook like water when it just begins to congeal into ice. As usual, she was naked, apart from her tabi, which one of the maids had helped her put on because she could never hope to reach her own feet. She wore a kimono and obi only when there were patrons present since even the softest of silk robes rubbed against her folds of fat and made her hot and sore. Now, she slopped on the tatami mat in front of me, looking as wide as she was high. That was how she had gotten her name, as Auntie said she was actually two chrysanthemum flowers, one blossom for her head atop another huge blossom for her body. She leaned forward to reach for a cup of tea and I hurried to pass it to her as I realized she would never be able to bend far enough to grasp it herself.

She nodded her thanks and drank deeply, draining the cup and graciously allowing me to pass it to one of the hovering maids to replace on the tray of tea things. Today, both of the maids were young girls, both relative newcomers to the Hidden House. Replete, Kiku sat back with her hands laced beneath where her breasts merged seamlessly into her massive belly.

"And the second one?" I asked timidly.

"Oh, well. He was better. He took me from behind in the

end and managed to get his tree of flesh into me." She shrugged and her body shuddered in time with the motion. "I was expecting it to hurt, and it did a bit, but not too much. I made sure, of course, that he thought he had pierced me to the core. I gasped a lot and cried out at what I thought was the right bit. He seemed very pleased. After we had finished, he called for food and sake and sat for ages dangling bits of fish and meat from his chopsticks, just out of reach of my mouth. Every time I parted my lips and tried to take anything, he would jerk it away a little and then bring it back and then take it away again. I pouted and sighed as though I was starving and eventually he relented and let me eat. In fact, he didn't just let me eat, he stuffed me like a pig being fattened for a feast. They nearly all do that," she added with a sigh. "I do wish they wouldn't. I like a drink of tea, or sake occasionally, but you know that I don't eat a lot."

She didn't, either. Unless it was to please a client, she just picked at her food most of the time. A little rice with vegetables, a bit of fish, occasionally some meat, and that was as much as Kiku ever wanted. How she came to be the size she was, none of us could work out. Carpi said it was her karma. Perhaps one of her ancestors had died of starvation and this was the way imposed on her to help her find nirvana by suffering in reverse. That seemed a bit deep to me, but then again, I couldn't find another answer so I daresay Carpi was right after all.

"You'll be fine," she reassured me. I signaled to the maid to prepare me a cup of tea and watched as the girl whisked the tea powder with boiling water. This maid was new – a raw young girl – and amazingly clumsy. Only the day before, she had managed to burn herself on the charcoal burner while making tea and she appeared to have learned nothing from her experience as now she trailed the sleeve of her plain white kimono dangerously near the coals. I called out to her to be careful, and she promptly snatched her hand away, slopping the tea on her hand. To my amazement, she simply shook the scalding liquid off her hand and presented the cup to me, crouching down on her haunches in the proper position. She had filled the cup too full, so I took the fine porcelain gingerly in my fingertips, wary that I would follow her example and scald myself.

"Doesn't your hand hurt?" I asked.

She shook her head, looking down bashfully at the tatami matting.

"I don't think she feels pain," Carpi said. "I noticed the other day when she tripped and banged her knee on the door frame she just carried on. Watch." Carpi reached out with her left foot and pinched the maid hard on the exposed flesh of her wrist. An angry red mark was left on the girl's flesh, but she simply continued to look down, as if she felt nothing at all. "See? Told you so. Did that hurt you?"

The maid appeared not to realize that Carpi had spoken to her, and did not reply. Exasperated, Carpi gave her a kick and repeated her question.

"I said, didn't that hurt you? Cat stolen your tongue?"

I frowned, wanting to tell Carpi not to be horrible to the girl, but I bit the words back. Carpi was senior to me, and I had no right to argue with anything she did. Besides, she was Auntie's favorite, and nobody – not even Masaki, who had been in the Hidden House longer than anybody except me – dared to defy her.

The maid spoke – or rather, mumbled – still looking down at the mat. "No, geisha. It did not hurt me."

"See?" Carpi crowed. "I told you so."

Carpi hopped nimbly to her feet with an athletic grace

that was in no way restrained by her kimono. The girl remained crouching subserviently as Carpi circled her, pausing now and then to raise her foot, as if she would kick her, only to put her foot down again and continue circling. Kiku raised her eyes to the heavens but did not speak. I dared do no more than watch. As she came behind the maid, Carpi appeared to tire of her game and raised her foot again, but this time did not put it down. Instead, she struck out with her slippered foot and slammed it into the nape of the maid's neck. The girl went sprawling on the tatami matting but almost immediately sat up again. I winced for her.

"Alright then. Did *that* hurt?"

The maid stared at her numbly, her expression bewildered. Her lips moved as if she was about to speak, but eventually she did no more than shake her head.

Carpi sat down again, the movement impossibly elegant, like watching the finest silk being folded.

"You do know what pain is, don't you?" she enquired. Carpi was like that. Once she got something into her head, she never let go until she was satisfied, like a cat worrying the life out of a mouse. The girl kept her head down, but stared at her tormentor from beneath her eyelashes.

Eventually, with obvious reluctance, she shook her head mutely. Carpi hissed triumphantly.

"Pain," she said, as if talking to someone who was very stupid or very deaf. "Pain. You know what pain is, don't you?"

Again, that reluctant, mute shake of the head from the maid. Carpi howled with laughter, and even Kiku giggled.

"Didn't I tell you? Oh, she will do so well! You just watch. As soon as Auntie teaches her some manners, she'll have her on display here in the Hidden House so quickly her feet won't even feel the mat!"

I didn't know whether to envy the little maid or feel sorry for her, but decided in the end that it didn't matter. If she really could not feel pain, she would, indeed, do very well. And would probably be very happy with her lot. At any rate, better than being a peasant, constantly wondering where your next meal was coming from.

Tired of her tormenting, Carpi suddenly turned on me for sport. "Looking forward to your mizuage, are you, Midori?"

I shrugged. Better not to annoy Carpi when she was in this mood.

"When I had mine, Auntie told me that there were so many bidders who wanted to be my danna that she could name her own price." She sat back smugly and sipped her tea. "Of course, I'm unique. There will never be another maiko like me."

"Oh, I don't know," Kiku said thoughtfully. I had noticed before that she was less afraid of Carpi than the rest of us were. In fact, I sometimes thought that there was not a lot that Kiku was frightened of. "I bet there's some more like you, somewhere. The patrons like you, but if one of them likes you enough to buy you out, I bet Auntie would find somebody to take your place in no time."

Carpi glared at her, but Kiku met her gaze and Carpi tossed her head indignantly, pretending to take a sudden interest in the shrine niche.

"Fat lot you know," she said, and howled at her own inadvertent witticism. Kiku raised her eyes and tutted, holding her hand out to the maids to signal them to help her to her feet. Both girls rushed forward, one grasping Kiku's hand and the other her wrist. Kiku groped blindly behind herself and placed her other hand flat on the floor. Once she was satisfied, she snapped, "Now!" and both maids tugged at the same time as she pushed. About halfway up, Kiku tottered for a moment, but then the instant of danger passed and she made it safely to her feet. As soon as she was sure of her balance, she clapped her hands and her tiny pet spaniel awoke and shook itself briskly, trotting over the mats to fawn around her mistress's ankles.

In spite of the fact that she was naked apart from her socks, she walked out of the room with a curious grace. Her belly and buttocks ballooned almost to her knees, but Kiku had her own beauty, and her rolls of fat were as lovely in their way, like the bell of a jellyfish. As it followed her, the spaniel looked as tiny as a kitten compared to her mistress.

In spite of the fact that I was wary of upsetting Carpi, as soon as Kiku had pulled the frame closed behind her, I leaned forward to satisfy my curiosity.

"Carpi, is it true that some danna has made an offer to buy Kiku?"

Carpi rolled her lips and pulled a sour face. I waited silently; if Carpi chose not to reply, I would not push the issue. I was, I knew, on dangerous ground. Carpi was not Auntie's favorite for nothing. Carpi had the most clients, made the most in tips and presents, brought the most money into the house. We all knew that a number of potential danna had bid for Carpi, but had been turned down by Auntie. Carpi was simply too precious to let go, at least until she was well past her prime.

Auntie might find a replacement for the rest of us, but in spite of what Kiku had said, there was surely only one Carpi.

"She's had two bids recently." Carpi shrugged. "Auntie's

thinking about the most generous one. You know who it is – that chap who looks like a big dinner would do him good."

I nodded. It was odd, I thought. It was always the small, scrawny men who were entranced by the opulence of Kiku. The big, swaggering kind – the ones who resembled Sumo wrestlers – invariably wanted little Masaki. I often worried for Masaki's welfare. I could see her being broken or smothered inadvertently by one of her massive clients. Masaki herself was unconcerned. She said it didn't matter how big they were, they all treated her like some sort of precious doll. In fact, she said, she would really enjoy a man who treated her like a woman occasionally.

Carpi and I both fell silent as we considered Kiku's fate. Lucky, lucky Kiku! I knew the man Carpi meant. He had been haunting the Hidden House for nearly a year. From the very first, it had been Kiku, and no other, for him. Normally, he made an assignation. If by some mischance he did not and turned up unannounced and found Kiku was unavailable, his face would fall to his feet and he would retreat, inconsolable by the charms of another girl. Now he had made his mind up; Kiku was to be his mistress. Lucky Kiku!

Not his wife, of course. That would never be the way. Not that any of us would want to be a mere wife, oh no! Not even me. Being a wife meant enduring the hell of a mother-in-law who had waited for years to have somebody of lower status in the family than she was herself. A daughter-in-law to bully and demean at any and every opportunity. Although thinking about it, I had to admit that I really could not see Kiku being bullied by anybody, not even the worst of mothers-in-law. No, she would simply stare through the turbulent in-law, and not allow her new relative to bother her at all. Lucky, lucky Kiku!

And anyway, being a mistress carried other advantages. A wife could be divorced with little or no fuss. Virtually cast into the street at will, thrown out with little more than the clothes on her back. I remember one such unfortunate wife who had come to the Green Tea House some years before. A dramatically beautiful woman, skilled on the samisen and a most graceful dancer. A woman of great wit and learning as well. I spoke to her a little when she arrived; the poor thing desperately needed someone to talk to and was willing to settle even for me, a resident of the Hidden House. She could not, naturally, criticize her husband. She insisted the divorce was her fault because her husband had become deeply enamored of a younger woman who was herself a courtesan in the Floating World and she had dared to criticize him for it. Even her own children were ashamed of her, she said. Her sons refused to talk to her after the divorce. In any event, she did very well in the Green Tea House, and it was not long at all before somebody made an offer for her, and off she went to be a mistress. I believe she was very happy about it, particularly since the man who became her danna was a business rival of her ex-husband. I wonder what kind of pillow talk went on there!

A mistress could never be thrown off like a patched coat as a wife could. If a man should become tired of his mistress, then he was expected to pay her generous compensation. And there was always another man to be found. Even if a man patronized the same courtesan more than three times, he was expected to offer her a generous parting gift if he decided he was tired of her. Woe betide the man who did not if he tried to show his face again in the Floating World!

I sighed, thinking that I would miss Kiku. Carpi hissed

at me and I realized with a start that she was waggling her hands at me. Generally, Carpi only did that when she was either very agitated or one of her clients had tipped her exceptionally well to do so. I sat up straight and lowered my head quickly, making it clear that I was listening. To my relief, Carpi stopped waggling and leaned toward me.

"Listen, Midori. Your mizuage is tomorrow."

Just "Green," you notice. Not even my full name. Even though my heart started beating like a horse at a canter, I felt the snub. Still, I kept my eyes lowered and listened with every appearance of quiet courtesy. It would not do to anger Carpi. She had been well named. The Japanese love koi carp, they are appreciated for their color, their slender elegance, their sinuous movements. Carpi was as slender and supple as any koi. She could also be vicious, flashing out with her legs and feet at the slightest provocation. I had seen her try it once with Kiku, but Kiku was having none of it. She had grabbed Carpi's foot with surprising speed and flipped the other girl on her back like a tortoise dropped by an eagle, looming over her and daring her to rise until Kiku was ready to allow her to do so. I knew that Carpi had hated Kiku ever since, but somehow Kiku was simply invulnerable. I was not.

"Yes, Carpi?"

"Yes. Auntie told me. I am going to be your Older Sister for the ceremony, so listen carefully to me."

"Yes, Carpi."

I sat humbly, my eyes fixed on the tatami as she spoke. Carpi was going to be my Older Sister. I had hoped that it might be Masaki, or even Kiku, but thinking about it, I suppose neither would have been a very practical choice. Masaki was too small to be of much help to anybody – she barely came up to my waist even when she was dressed to go out in high wooden geti. In bare feet, she was less than three feet tall. Kiku was so fat she could not get dressed without the help of a maid, not even her own tabi. A sensation of relief stole over me; at least Auntie had not decided that she herself was going to be my Older Sister. Anything, anybody was better than that. Even Carpi.

Carpi was rambling on, and I did try to listen to what she was telling me, but my mind seemed to have gone somewhere else entirely. Tomorrow. Tomorrow was my mizuage. It was here, at last. Tomorrow. My mouth was suddenly very dry, and I signaled to the maid for tea. The little girl who Carpi had decided could feel no pain jumped up to her feet and made my tea at once, crouching down and looking adoringly at me from under her eyelashes. I was quite touched, it appeared I had made a new friend. Although what good I could do for the poor child, I had no idea.

"So there you are," Carpi finished. "Your danna will be here at six, but you must be ready for him well before, in case he is early."

Taking my courage in both hands – and praying to any god who might be listening – I asked, "Who is my danna, Carpi? Do I know him?"

"You will have seen him. He's been in a few times recently, but never settled on one girl. He must have a taste for Barbarians. Auntie told me that he was sniffing around Naruko for a while but eventually he decided on you instead."

I cudgeled my brains, trying to remember a particular man who had shown me some attention. In spite of my extreme ugliness and, as Auntie was fond of reminding me, my deformities, many of the men who visited the Hidden House took an interest in me. I always hoped that it was because of my skill with the samisen or my singing voice – which even Auntie grudgingly admitted was exceptionally good – but I never deceived myself for long. No, these men were enthralled by my very strangeness. It was my deformity that appealed to them, not any sort of talent that I might have. In that way, at least, Carpi and I were sisters. Carpi could sing, she was a witty companion, and she was very beautiful. But none of her many admirers were in the least interested in any of her accomplishments. They simply wanted her because she was different.

Because nobody else in the whole of the Floating World was like her. Not even me.

In spite of her beauty and her accomplishments, it was Carpi's malformation that lured the patrons back, time after time. She had no arms. She had hands, perfectly normal hands. But they sprouted straight from her shoulders. If one looked carefully, it was possible to see that she did have wrists. Not that any of us dared look. Carpi's temper saw to that!

"It's nowhere near your time of the month, is it?" Trust Carpi to think of the practicalities. I shook my head. "Good. Teruki-san probably wouldn't mind too much if it was, but you never know. Better not to risk it. Not when he's paying good money for you."

Teruki-san. Did the name mean anything to me? Try as I might, I couldn't put a face to the name. Carpi was rattling on, and I pushed my thoughts away, concentrating on listening to her carefully.

"You'll need a decent wig, of course." She stared disdainfully at my hair. I shrugged apologetically, but there was nothing I could do about it. No matter how it was combed, my hair curled extravagantly. And – even worse – it wasn't black. In some lights it appeared almost black, but let the sun or lamplight catch it and it was obvious that it was actually dark brown with the strangest red sheen. Even Naruko had proper hair, black as pitch and straight. But not me. "You can borrow my divided peach wig. I haven't worn it since I was a maiko myself. But after your mizuage, Auntie will probably buy you a proper wig. Unless the customers like your hair as it is. It has novelty value, I suppose. If she does buy you a wig, she'll take the money out of what Teruki-san pays for your mizuage, of course. A taka shimada will do for you nicely. You'll need a new kimono for the ceremony as well. Not that your mizuage fee will cover all of that, not to mention what you already owe her for your keep all these years, but it's a start, I suppose. After your mizuage, you can start earning real money instead of just tips and presents."

I nodded in agreement. No matter how long I worked at the Hidden House, I could never hope to pay Auntie back for all I owed her. Perhaps, one day, I would be as lucky as Kiku and have a man who wanted me for his mistress. That fee would also go to Auntie, but at least then I would be free.

Free as a caged bird.

3

The birds on my roof
Fly away. Would that I
Could follow.

*C*arpi had collected me and taken me to the bathhouse earlier that afternoon. She had supervised critically as the maids poured hot water over me, soaped me from head to foot, and rinsed time and again until she was satisfied. Eventually, she had discarded her own kimono and gestured at me to climb into the bath with her, even grudgingly allowing me to help her climb down the rather slippery steps.

Both of us stood chin deep in the hot water. Within seconds, my skin had turned lobster red from the unrelenting heat. Carpi sighed luxuriantly, stretched, and turned to stare at me.

"Anything you need to know?"

I shook my head. In my stupidity, I had no idea what

questions even to ask. What was there to know, I wondered? Auntie had already explained to me what was to happen. When my danna arrived, he would be taken to the bathhouse and would be bathed carefully by the maids. Once he was ready, he would proceed to the Hidden House itself and would be plied with sake by Auntie prior to the feast. Carpi, Kiku, and Masaki would enter the room with me. Naruko, still being a maiko, would follow later on her own.

We would all bow to my danna and would sit at his command. Food would be brought in when he requested it. Masaki would probably be chosen to play the samisen. Kiku and Carpi would flirt politely with my danna. We would all eat and drink, at his signal.

At this stage, nothing would be expected of me except to sit and giggle at any witticism he might make. I could look at him with reverent adoration, of course, and if he wanted me to dance or play the samisen or sing, I could do so, but not unless he asked.

Either when Auntie thought the time was right or my danna became impatient for his money's worth and made it clear that he wished us to be alone, Auntie would stand and she and the other girls would make their farewells. The maids would clear away the dishes and charcoal burners and bring in the bedding to change the room from a banqueting hall to a bedroom.

Then my mizuage would begin.

Although at least in principle we would be alone, I was well aware that Auntie would be outside the room, somewhere very close. She would certainly be able to hear everything. Knowing Auntie, I would guess that she would make sure that she could also see everything as well. I could only pray that she was alone and had not invited some favored patron to watch my deflowering. I would never know if she had, of course, but the thought made me feel sick.

Satisfied that we were clean, Carpi scrambled out of the bath, leaving me to follow. The maids dried us carefully, and then Carpi hustled me off to her room to attend to my makeup.

I was used to the thick, white makeup required of a maiko, but today's was even more concealing than usual. I suppressed a hysterical giggle as I wondered if my danna would even recognize me underneath the coating.

Carpi sat me down on the matting and pursed her lips as she looked at the assortment of jars and bottles set out on the tatami.

"Sit still," she commanded. I nodded, without thinking, and got a brisk slap from her left foot as a reward for daring to move.

I hated Carpi touching me anywhere, but especially on my face. I closed my eyes and tried to pretend it was Kiku, or Auntie, who was dabbing at my skin. It didn't work, I still felt slightly sick. But I kept still, as instructed.

Carpi nodded at the bottle of camellia oil and the maid picked it up quickly, patting the oil on my face and neck and then rubbing it in gently. None of the incredibly expensive courtesan's nightingale dung face cream for me! It was said – by those who could afford it – that the potions made from nightingale dung lightened and brightened the skin like nothing else could. I was grateful I wasn't rich enough for it be used on me. The thought of rubbing unguent made from bird droppings into my skin did nothing for my queasy stomach. Satisfied that my skin was ready, Carpi grunted and the maid stepped back but hovered nearby, ready for Carpi's commands.

Carpi leaned forward, a tiny bottle clasped between her

finger and thumb. With the other fingers, she pried my eyelids wide apart. The bottle was tipped slowly toward my eye, and a single drop of thick liquid dripped out. It felt icy cold and stung. The action was repeated with my other eye. Within a minute, everything at any distance became blurred. I blinked.

"It's a distillation made from a flower," Carpi said briskly. "Don't worry, it will wear off by morning. In the meantime, it makes your pupils look huge. I think it makes your eyes look even more green, if that's possible."

She sat back on her haunches and nodded in evident satisfaction.

The pink undercoating came next. Carpi put that on herself, and I closed my eyes as I felt her touch, trying not to squirm. A white topcoat followed, brushed on quickly before it could set. For one insane moment, I thought about telling Carpi that I would do it myself, but my tongue refused to speak the words and I simply sat mute, suffering her touch.

I heard her grunt with satisfaction and I opened my lips and drew a deep breath.

Rouge followed, highlighting my cheeks. In spite of the fact that my eyes were tightly shut, Carpi snapped at me to keep them closed as she puffed white powder on my eyebrows and eyelids. My own eyebrows were hidden completely by the powder and I could feel Carpi's breath on my face as she leaned forward to draw my new brows in place. Red paint first, then black over the top, with just the tiniest hint of red allowed to show through.

"Open," Carpi said, and I hurriedly opened my eyes, trying not to blink in the sudden light. With the tiniest of brushes, she outlined my eyes with red, which was – like my brows – then covered in black.

"Pout." In a second or two, my lips were bright red. Carpi sat back to consider her work and nodded. "You'll do. You can still tell you're a Barbarian, but then again I suppose that's what your danna is paying for. Put your head back."

I did as I was told and Carpi took up the large brush again to stroke the white paste over my throat and bosom, down as far as my undergarment. I turned automatically, praying that I was getting it right.

Finally, she gestured for me to turn around and painted me from my shoulders to my hairline at the nape of my neck, leaving only a strip of my own flesh showing down my spine. Japanese men find the nape of the neck to be especially erotic, often more so than a woman's breasts, so this piece of painting had to be correct.

Finally satisfied, Carpi nodded at the maid to bring me a mirror. I stared into its depths wonderingly. Was this really me? Was this painted, anonymous doll that looked back at me from the mirror truly my own face? Fascinated, I reached up to touch my cheeks and got a sharp hiss from Carpi for my trouble.

"Don't you dare! Do you really think I've gone to all that trouble for you to mess it up?"

I mumbled my apologies.

"Come on. Let's get you dressed."

I stood, naked and still pink from the heat of the bath, as Carpi shouted at the maids to get me properly dressed.

First, the tabi socks. I felt clumsy, and it took an age for the maid to get my big toe properly inserted in the divided sock. I remember laughing the first time I saw a Western sock and thinking it strange that there was no separate place for the big toe. Did foreign Barbarians not have a separate big toe, I wondered. But on that day I would have given a great deal for a pair of Western socks; they would have been so very much easier. Carpi tutted at my clumsiness, and I was suddenly all thumbs.

The maid helped me into the red-patterned undershirt and skirt and tied them around with a waist tie to keep them in place. A wide under sash followed. Then my lovely, silken kimono.

This was the first time I had seen it, and it was quite beautiful. Auntie had gone for simplicity – green silk with a subtle pattern of intricate embroidery in a slightly lighter shade. Whether the color choice was to enhance my eyes or was a play on my name, I had no idea. All I knew was that the kimono was by far the most beautiful thing I had ever owned. At that moment, I didn't even care that I would spend the rest of my working life paying for it, and all the kimonos that were to follow. It was mine!

The maid slipped it around me, patting the right side under the left, and closing it off with another waist tie. An under sash followed, and then a wide obi that went around my waist twice with a knot tied at the back and the ends of the obi sash brought around to the front where they were tied off so tightly I had to fight to draw a deep breath.

And that was it. I was dressed. I was ready.

I looked at Carpi, desperate for her approval.

She rose and stretched lazily, walking around me. She pushed and tugged at the obi and tweaked my kimono at the neck. I stood stock still, trying not to show my distaste. Finally, to my relief, she shrugged.

"Your breasts are still far too big, even in the kimono." I looked down at myself. She was right, they were. "And we can't do anything at all about you being so tall. No, don't slump. It just makes your breasts look even bigger. Your nose is too big, as well. And as for your eyes! Never mind. Your danna knows what he's getting."

From anybody else, the words would have been heart-breakingly rude, but from Carpi, they were simply matter of fact. No one, of course, would ever have dared make the same sort of comment to her. As if she had read my mind, she added, "We are all the same, here in the Hidden House. All of us are wrong."

From Carpi, it was almost a comfort.

The feast was spread out on the tatami mats. The feast must have cost my danna a huge amount, not to mention the fee for me, of course. The matting was full and over-flowing with dishes, grilled squid, seaweed, fruit, noodles of every description, beef, and – dominating everything – a huge platter of fugu fish, sliced so thinly that when it was picked up, you could see right through it. Teruki-san gestured at me munificently and I picked up a slice of the fish, bowing my head in gratitude for his generosity, although really I could never see a great deal in the stuff. It could, of course, kill you if it had not been prepared very well, but the only thing it did to me was to make my lips slightly numb.

I ate as slowly as I could, as if by doing so I could put off the moment when the food would be finished and Teruki-san decided the time had come to get his money's worth.

The screens had been pushed back to make a large, twelve-mat room so that there was plenty of space for all of us. Auntie had taken her place at the side of my danna and was leaning toward him, chuckling richly at some witticism he had made.

I was flanked on each side by Carpi and Kiku, both dressed in their best kimonos and obi. As Teruki-san glanced at Kiku, she shook out her fan and retreated behind it, tittering politely. Even though Kiku's eyes were almost hidden in folds of fat, they really were remarkably beautiful, perfectly almond-shaped and gleaming with a light that seemed to come from some source that only Kiku was aware of. Teruki-san beamed at her and shook his finger roguishly. I wondered how much sake he had drunk before he had come to us; already he was making inroads on his second flask, and even as I thought about it he glanced at his cup and held it out. Masaki reached out and plucked the flask from the charcoal burner to refill it for him. A maid immediately placed another flask into another warming vessel to be sure it would be ready when he needed it. With great dignity, Teruki-san gestured at Masaki to fill a cup for me.

Taking his gesture as a signal, Auntie curled her fingers at me urgently, flicking me forward with her fingers. My legs were trembling so hard I knew that standing would be beyond my power, and so I shuffled forward on my knees, my head tucked down. Teruki-san seemed to like this, as he applauded and nodded.

As I approached, Masaki turned to Teruki-san and bowed, presenting the cup she had filled for me to him. With what I guessed was drunken dignity, he grasped the cup and took three deliberate, rather noisy sips. Auntie smiled widely. She leaned forward and took the cup from him, presenting it to me. In my turn, I took three careful sips, which emptied the cup.

Unsure what to do next, I simply remained crouching, clutching the cup in my fingers. It seemed to me that silence fell, and that everybody was staring at me.

I will not speak of what followed again.

It is done, and what is done can never be undone, no more than time can be turned back. I will never be a maiko again. Never an innocent. But at least I will never have to suffer another mizuage.

4

Time is like water.
I try to grasp it, and
It is gone

The sun was shining very brightly on the day that Carpi was ill. Only she and I were inside.

The rest of the girls were outside in the courtyard, lolling about in the warmth, lifting their faces to the sun with pleasure. I longed to join them, but did not dare. Even if I had done, Auntie would have chased me back inside, thwacking my legs with her stick as a reminder that I had disobeyed her.

I remembered very well the only time I had sat in the sun.

It had been years before, when I was still quite a small child. Just as today, the other girls had gone outside. It had been a different set of girls then, six of them, if I remember correctly. As always, each of them was...distinctive. One had strange, white eyes and had to be escorted everywhere as she could not see. Another had a club foot, which made her lurch when she walked. Another was a hunchback. She was especially popular with the clients for some reason. And so on.

Anyway, I went out with them on that day. We sat in the sun for hours, talking and gossiping. I remember I could hear the world going about its business outside and made up stories to myself about the people I could hear. A couple of lovers, walking slowly and languishing in each other's gaze. An older woman, pushing a cart. A couple of wealthy men, talking and laughing. I dozed, and when I opened my eyes the other girls had gone and I realized I had been outside all day.

I could hear Auntie calling for me, crossly, and I ran inside, anticipating a slap. Auntie barely glanced at me when I came in. She wanted her hair combed. I was bending forward to grasp her comb when she screamed. I was so surprised, I dropped the comb and was scrabbling for it when she grabbed my hair and pulled my head back. In the next second, she had let me go and was pushing me away from her as she scrabbled backward. She crossed her arms over her breasts as if she was warding off a demon.

"Child! What has happened to you! What is the matter with you? Do you have a fever? Are you ill? What have you done?"

She was shrieking and I looked at her in bewilderment.

"I am well, Auntie," I reassured her. "I have done noth-ing. I have been sitting in the sun with the other girls."

She continued to stare at me in horror. Alarmed by her shouts, two of the other girls came in, and both started back in shock as they looked at me. Their revulsion was infec-tious, and I burst into tears without knowing why.

"Have you dared bring smallpox into my house?"

Auntie was still almost shouting, her voice shrill. Smallpox? She thought I had smallpox? I raised my hands and rubbed my face, terrified I would find the pustules that accompanied the dreaded disease. But there was nothing. My skin was smooth as normal. A little hot from the sun, but that was all.

One of the girls leaned forward toward me, her mouth agape in wonder. "Auntie, I don't think Midori has the pox."

Auntie stared at her, her eyes bulging. "What's wrong with her face, then?"

"I don't know." The girl puckered her lips in thought. I stared from one to the other, swaying between hope and terror. "I remember a few years ago seeing one of the foreign Barbarians with marks on his skin like that. He had red hair, much redder than hers, and very pale skin. He had marks all over his face and arms, just like Midori has. He was Dutch, I think."

Both girls and Auntie stared at me intently. I stared at the floor, wishing somebody would just tell me what was wrong with me. I felt well and nobody had noticed anything odd earlier in the day. What illness could possibly come on so quickly and disfigure my skin yet not make me feel ill?

"Come here, child." Auntie spoke reluctantly, in the tone of one who knew her duty, no matter how distasteful it was. Obediently, I walked across and squatted at her feet. She reached out and pushed my chin up with her cane.

"See?" the girl said. "I told you, that's not smallpox. She's just got a lot of funny marks on her face and neck. I think it's the sun that's done it."

Auntie hissed and spat on her finger before running it over my cheek.

"Lemons," she snapped. "One of you go to the kitchen

and get me a couple of lemons cut in half. And some rice vinegar."

When the lemons arrived, she rubbed them all over my face and neck. They stung my eyes terribly, but I dared not protest. She shook the vinegar into her palms and patted my skin with it.

"Leave the juice and the vinegar on, and stay out of the sun," she said. "In fact, keep to your room for the rest of the day. I'll have a look at you first thing in the morning."

I did as I was told, and stayed alone in my room for the rest of the day. I had a caged cricket as a pet at the time, a fine, male insect, and I spent hours chirruping at him, hoping for a response but got none.

By morning, the strange marks had faded a little. Auntie repeated her lemon wash, following it up with vinegar to be on the safe side, and did it again the next day. Eventually, the marks went away completely, but I had learned my lesson. No more sun for me.

As long as I was in the Hidden House, I would keep to the shadows. So instead of going outside, I went along to Carpi's room. I tapped on the screen door and then stood awkwardly, unsure what to say now I was here.

Carpi must have been feeling very low because she did not even snarl at me for hovering without greeting her and immediately asking her how she was. She told me, anyway.

"My stomach hurts."

I arranged my features in a suitable expression of sympathy, but I was surprised. Carpi never complained that she had pain. She glared at me, as if reading my thoughts.

"My period was well overdue, so Auntie gave me some medicine to make it start. I feel as though I have been kicked in the belly by a mule. Make me some tea."

I scurried to do as she said. The kettle was already on

the charcoal burner, so it was only a few seconds before I could whisk the green tea powder into the hot water. I kneeled down to help Carpi sit up and she grasped my shoulder with her hand to steady herself. I managed not to shudder, but I swear to this day that she knew how much I hated her touching me and that she did it on purpose.

I held the teacup so she could sip from it, and she nodded her thanks. Another first!

"You know, in this light and crouching down, you could pass for Japanese," she said grudgingly. "Of course, as soon as you stand up anybody can see you're as tall as a man, and those breasts are grotesque."

I wanted to shrug. What could I do about it? But I didn't. Even when she was in low spirits, it was not a good idea to annoy Carpi. Instead, I directed my glance at the tatami matting, making sure that my expression was neutral. Nothing she could do about my thoughts. Strangely, ever since my mizuage, I had found myself wanting to answer back. To argue. To question. Some days, I gave myself a headache wondering why and what for. I shared a little of my confusion with Kiku, who I trusted, but she just looked at me and told me it was better not to worry about the way things were. After all, what did I think I could do about it?

She was right, of course, but it didn't help. Not at all.

"You just don't know how lucky you are, Midori."

I blinked at the bitterness in Carpi's voice. Me? Lucky? Lucky to be ugly and deformed? Lucky to resemble a foreign Barbarian? What was so lucky about that? I risked a glance at her face and blinked in surprise.

Carpi was crying.

Or at least, tears were rolling down her face. She made no noise, nor did her expression change, but she was definitely crying. Thinking she must be in great pain, I stood up.

"Shall I get Auntie for you?" I asked.

Carpi shook her head so hard that the tears flung themselves onto her robe. "No. Just sit down for a minute, will you?"

I did as I was told and sat silently, too shocked for words. Eventually, curiosity got the better of me.

"Why am I lucky, Carpi?"

I thought she was not going to bother to reply, she was silent for so long. When she spoke, her voice was weary.

"You were upset by your mizuage, weren't you?"

Upset? Well, that was one way of putting it. I still dreaded sleep, knowing that I would dream of Teruki-san. Dream of what he was going to do to me, time after time after time. And every time, it was as sharp and degrading and awful as the actual act had been. I nodded, not bothering to try and explain.

"I suppose you think it was worse for you than the rest of us?"

I frowned. Oddly, the idea had never occurred to me. None of the girls – except Kiku, who had made light of it – ever wanted to talk about their mizuage. I suppose I had thought they had simply taken it in their stride and got on with life. I shrugged.

"You're a fool, Midori. It's always dreadful. Degrading. Something we all have to live with. Oh, I know Kiku pretends to shrug it off, but that's her way. Don't you go thinking you're so different from the rest of us because you're not."

Carpi paused, seeming to stare through me. A particularly bad cramp made her suck in air and I quickly offered her more tea.

"Why am I lucky, Carpi?" I asked again.

She waggled her hands at me. "Rather be like me, would you? At least you're whole. Oh, you look strange, foreign, but at least you're not a freak, are you? Someday, somebody is going to like you enough to offer Auntie a good price for you, and you'll go off to be a respectable mistress. But me! I'll be here until I get old and wrinkled and nobody is willing to pay good money for me anymore."

She spoke bitterly, and I stared at her in surprise.

"I thought Auntie had already had offers for you," I blurted.

"Well, she hasn't. Would you want to pay a good price for somebody who was nothing more than a trained monkey? I tell you, Midori, there are days when I would take poison if I could get hold of some. Commit seppuku if I could. See what I mean? I'm not even capable of giving myself an honorable death."

For one horrified second, I thought Carpi was going to ask me to help her kill herself. I must have flinched because she laughed. An ugly, bitter sound.

"Oh, don't worry. I'm not going to do it. Not yet, anyway. Not for a long while. I should have done it years ago, but I never had the chance."

She turned her head from side to side, staring at her hands where they joined on to her shoulders. They were remarkably beautiful hands, the fingers long and slim, and the nails beautifully shaped. I had never thought about it before, but I suddenly realized that their beauty made their horror all the worse.

Carpi had no arms at all. Her wrists were barely more than stumps so it appeared that her hands were growing straight out of her shoulders. Those beautiful hands were fully functional, she could use them just as anybody else would use their hands, but she had little chance of doing so. She could not eat with her hands, she could not write with them. Lacking arms, it was impossible. She couldn't even put her makeup on with them. Instead, she used her feet and her toes. Used them exactly as the rest of us used our hands.

I had a sudden, unwanted vision of what Carpi could do for her clients with her feet and felt ill. As if she had read my mind, Carpi grimaced.

"I suppose I should be used to it. I was born like this."

We had all wondered about that. When we were sure that Carpi could not hear us, we discussed the matter between ourselves. Some thought that a strange illness had caused Carpi's disfigurement. Others said that a jealous lover had cut off her arms and then sewn her hands back onto her shoulders. Masaki insisted that her own parents had done it, when she was a baby, to get a living out of her. We were all wrong, it appeared.

"My mother was an aristocrat by birth. My father was a high-ranking civil servant. I was their first child." Once started, I guessed that Carpi was unable to stop. I desperately wanted to cover my ears, or just get up and walk out, but I knew that I could not. If nothing else, politeness held me fast. "In fact, I was their only child. I was told that my mother said that my father took one look at me and told my mother that I was not his. That it was not possible for something like me to come from him. My mother begged and pleaded with him, but he wouldn't listen. Of course he wouldn't. Who would want a monster for a child? A freak? He turned his back on my mother – and me, of course – and sent one of the servants around to collect her belongings in a bundle for her. The servant told her she was to leave immediately and to take me with her. My mother offered to expose me on Mount Fuji, anything to be allowed to stay, but my father was adamant. We were both to leave.

"My mother was still bleeding from giving birth, but somehow she got up and walked out of the house. She took me with her. I think she was going to expose me anyway, but she fell down in the street from weakness and loss of blood, and a family of burakumin found her and took us both in. Even for burakumin, those people were low caste. They were traveling gypsies who made their living juggling and doing tricks in the street. All they had they carried on their backs with them, like tortoises.

"My mother never got over the shame of it. First there was me, half a child. The devil's own spawn. And then to be forced to owe a debt of gratitude to burakumin – she who had once been a rich woman with servants at her beck and call. A woman born to an aristocratic family. It was all too much for her. The burakumin who took us in told me the tale when I was old enough to understand. My mother simply refused to eat. She died quite soon, so they left her where she had died, in a field somewhere. That was her choice, they said. Nothing they could do about it.

"But me? I was their salvation, their treasure. As soon as I could toddle, they began to teach me to use my feet like hands. One of them could write, and he taught me to hold a pen in my toes. Chopsticks took me an age to master, but whenever I tried to eat straight off the plate with my mouth, my new family slapped me and made me try again with chopsticks clasped in my toes. For a while, I found it so diffi-cult that I thought I was going to follow my mother and simply starve to death.

"Yet I learned. And I lived...after a fashion. The burakumin locked me in a cage at night so I could not run away. During the day, they exhibited me at any village or town they came across. Sometimes I just sat and let people look at me. Now and then I was taken to a rich man's house and made to eat in front of him. Nearly always the people who were paying my new family to look at me wanted to see me naked, to ensure that it wasn't all just a trick. Quite often, the rich men wanted to play with me. Or wanted me to touch them. With my feet, of course. That's where I learned to be skillful with my feet. Learned to make any man burst his fruit with just a touch of my toes.

"I might still be living that life if Auntie hadn't heard about me. I must have been about ten or eleven, I think." I nodded. I could clearly remember Carpi arriving at the Hidden House. Auntie had kept her tucked away for months until she had taught her manners and how to speak nicely to the clients. "Anyway, as soon as Auntie laid eyes on me, she offered the burakumin a purse for me. They argued and pretended that they couldn't bear to be parted from me, but when she actually tipped the gold out in front of my 'father,' greed got the better of him. And so here I am."

"That must have been better than being kept in a cage," I said.

Carpi looked at me contemptuously. "What do you know about it?"

The words came suddenly, and I could not stop them. Even if Carpi had said she would tell Auntie, even if I was threatened with the Boys, I could not have stopped.

"Aren't I in a cage just as much as you were?" I asked. "I can't go anywhere. Can't do anything. I was born here. Every day, I suffer for the sins of my mother just the same as you do." I was so agitated, I got to my feet and started to pace about the room. "I'm not allowed even to sit in the sun. I have to stay in the darkness all the time."

"At least you're whole!" Carpi said. "At least you stand a chance of getting out of here."

She leaped to her feet, supple as the fish she was named for. As always, I stared at her in fascination – watching Carpi get to her feet was a thing of great beauty. We glared at each other, almost head to head.

"Oh, go away." Carpi suddenly seemed tired of me. "Go on, push off. Leave me alone. You're only making me feel worse."

I went, not at all reluctantly.

5

Laughter is not always
As you might think.
It can hide tears.

ou may, if you know the ways of the Floating World, think that I am lying when I describe myself and my companions as geisha. Geisha do not sell their bodies for sex. Geisha sing and dance and entertain. Courtesans – if the man has enough money – are for sensual pleasure. For the lower type of man, there are common prostitutes. For those who have very little money, there are always the women behind the lattices, women who can be inspected from the street by every passerby and claimed by anybody who fancies them and has a copper coin in their purse.

But you must understand, even by the standards of Edo's Floating World, the Hidden House was extraordinary.

Auntie called us geisha, as did the men whom we entertained. And that is what we considered ourselves to be. And the men were vetted very carefully. No one was allowed to enter the Hidden House without being introduced by somebody who was already a client. And, to be sure, they all had one thing in common – they all had very large purses. For us girls in the Hidden House were nothing if not expensive.

We attracted the wealthy. The important. Hidden from the world as we were, yet we were aware that many of the men who visited us were important politicians, often nobility. Samurai, very often.

Geisha could, of course, have lovers. Men whom they chose for themselves. We did not have that good fortune. Our men were chosen for us by Auntie very carefully. But did it matter? All geisha were captives, all in debt to their Auntie. All expected to be nice to the patrons. One way or another. We girls in the Hidden House were not just expected to have sexual talents. No, indeed. Each of us could play the samisen, except for Carpi, of course. We could all sing and dance, make witty conversation. We knew how to make our men feel even more important than they were. So, do not tell me that we were not geisha. We were. We were exceptionally talented geisha, at that.

It was sometimes the case that men came to us purely for those social skills. They would eat with us, enjoy our singing and playing, and then move on to another house somewhere else in the Floating World to the courtesans of their choice. When this happened, Auntie would still make her money as the courtesans would, of course, be suggested by her, and she would expect a share of their fee for the introduction. But this did not happen often.

The Hidden House was also odd in that we were only open to clients in the evening. Most tea houses and houses of assignation were open to visitors in the afternoon as well. But not us.

We were special. Or so we told ourselves.

That evening, Auntie told me we were to hold a party. It was the first time that my services had been called for since my mizuage. I looked at her pleadingly, but Auntie was stone. Had she not given me many weeks to recover? Had I no gratitude at all? Where would I be if she had not taken me in when my mother had disgraced herself by running off with her Barbarian? She would have done better to have exposed me on Mount Fuji at birth. And so on. And on. And on. Finally exhausting herself, Auntie gave me a brisk thwack around the back of the knees with her cane and told me to get to the bathhouse.

The maid who felt no pain helped me. Auntie had named her Suzume - Sparrow. Small and chirpy as she was, the name suited her. I thought she was rather a nice child and that it was a shame that she was doomed to lead the sort of life I anticipated for her. Oddly, it seemed to bother her not at all, and I wondered what her background was that she was happy in the Hidden House. She chattered on cheerfully as she soaped me and then poured buckets of water over me before I climbed in the bath. The other girls followed very quickly, apart from Carpi, who was still ill, and I realized that this was to be an important event if we were all to participate. A very expensive event.

I huddled on my side of the bath, seriously considering

ducking beneath the water and not coming up again. The other girls chattered on happily, even Naruko, who had had her mizuage just after me. I lowered my head until just my nose was above the steaming water. I didn't think I could do it. If every encounter with a man was like my mizuage, I would rather never see a man again. I would rather die.

"What's the matter with you, Midori?" Kiku swung her head from side to side, causing ripples. "You look positively sick."

"I'm not exactly looking forward to this evening."

Kiku raised her eyes heavenward.

"She's at it again!" she tutted. "Look, Midori, what makes you think you're so special? We all have to do it. Why not be sensible and try and enjoy it? It's going to be a special occasion tonight. Auntie told me we have some special guests who will probably give us all a nice present afterward. Unless you ruin it with your sour face, that is."

All of the girls stopped talking at once and turned to glare at me. Even tiny Masaki, who was perched comfortably on the steps so as not to drown, looked angry. Just as they could not understand me, I was bewildered by them. Enjoy it? Enjoy having your body ravaged by a strange man? By old men? By ugly men? Men who could do exactly what they wanted to do to you again and again until you were too old and too worn out to be of any further use. A fine future to look forward to that was!

"How are you supposed to enjoy it?" It wasn't what I wanted to say, but those were the words that popped out. "We have no choice in it at all. We're just sold to anybody who wants us. We might just as well be on the street, common whores."

I heard an intake of breath that was so shocked, the silence afterward was profound. Then all the girls spoke at once, and I have never – then or since – felt so *hated*. I was stupid, they said. I was going to ruin things for everybody. Who did I think I was, to give myself such airs and graces? Of all people, I had been born here! I should know how things worked. I flinched back from the torrent of anger. At first, I thought I had hit a sore spot, that they were genuinely upset to hear their own hidden feelings dragged into the light. I was wrong.

Kiku restored order by slapping the bath water, hard. She rose up so that her shoulders and breasts were exposed, streaming water, and wagged a finger at me.

"Midori, shut up. You're no different from any of us, from any woman in the Floating World or out of it. What do you want? A single man to *love* you?" She put such an ironic tilt on the word "love" that it sounded frankly pathetic. "And where, in the whole of Japan, are you going to find such a creature? Men don't love their wives, that's why they take mistresses. Even mistresses, who may be cared for, are still at the beck and call of their owner. That's the fate of women in our world, all of us. We have to be owned by a man or we belong nowhere. Without a man, we are nothing."

I writhed in the water. I understood what Kiku was saying, and of course she was right. No man married for love; the aristocrats married for money and position. Peasants often married because the object of their interest had slightly more than they did, albeit "more" might mean a cooking pot or – lucky man! – a donkey.

"I know," I muttered. "I know all that. But at least if you are married, you only have one man. And you know him. You...you don't have to service anybody who pops up with the money in their pocket to buy you."

For a moment, I thought Kiku might hit me she looked so angry. But she did not, and her sarcasm was worse.

"One man. Two men. A dozen men. What difference does it make? If you were out there, *Midori*, exactly who would want to marry you, looking like you do?" The other girls giggled their agreement. "And if somebody did marry you, how much do you want to bet that he wouldn't spend all his free time – and money – somewhere like the Hidden House? Isn't it better to be the one who gets paid, and well looked after, the one who enjoys themselves with somebody else's husband? Eh? You know perfectly well that Auntie would never let just any man in here. They are all introduced. She makes sure that they are all right."

I lowered my eyes and muttered agreement. I could see that Kiku was right. Still, the thought of having to smile and pretend to enjoy myself with total strangers made me feel sick.

Satisfied they had convinced me, the other girls resumed their normal chatter. When Kiku said she had heard that the Boys were to be present tonight, even I began to wonder who we were entertaining.

*A*untie had decided that I wasn't to wear a wig. My own hair was simply piled up and allowed to curl. The evening was very warm, and I felt quite smug as I saw Kiku immediately begin to run with sweat beneath her huge wig.

The men were waiting as we bowed our way in. Three screens had been pushed back to make one huge room.

Looking from under my eyelashes, I counted six men lounging about on the matting. The sake was already warming, and from the level of noise I guessed that a lot had already been consumed.

We all filed in, heads bowed, and kneeled on the mats. The noise level rose immediately. Some of the girls were already acquainted with the patrons. One of them called out Kiku's name and she hid behind her fan and giggled respectfully. I stared at the customers carefully from beneath my eyelashes. All of them were prosperous, obviously. Three were middle-aged, verging on fat and looking like successful merchants. Two were much older and my heart sank as I realized they were both looking at me with undisguised interest. The last man I could hardly see as he was right on the edge of my field of vision.

But I felt him. I could feel him in my bones, my skin, my stomach. He had an aura about him that reached out and demanded my whole attention. I felt tranquility radiating from him, peace and gentleness. And power. All that before I had even seen him! *Please, please, please*, I shouted silently. *Choose me! Me!* I wanted him. Wanted him to stroke my skin. Touch my hair. Fondle my breasts. Part my black moss with his fingers and – yes! – put his tree of flesh in me. I didn't care that there were other men in the room or that my sisters were here. I just wanted him, this stranger.

This man I had not even seen.

I was suddenly worried that I would be disappointed when I did see him. What if his aura was completely at odds with his body? What if he was old? As old as my danna? What if he was so ugly I could hardly bear to look at him? What if he was fat and bald? My heart was wrung with disappointment as quickly as my body had been roused. It was nonsense, of course. How could my senses betray me like that? But still, I would look, I decided. I must know!

Before I could peep out from behind my fan, the Boys made their entrance and the moment was lost. Unlike us girls, who crept in as if we were afraid of disturbing our audience, the Boys tumbled in with as much noise as they could manage. They shouted. They whooped. They whistled. And to add to the show, they did somersaults and walked on their hands and pretended to kick at each other.

The patrons loved it. They applauded and laughed and the Boys turned to each other and grinned before they sat down and clapped their hands for sake, just as if they were paying customers themselves. I glanced at Auntie, expecting her to shout at the Boys, tell them to behave themselves, but no such thing. She was smiling and nodding her head in encouragement. The Boys were *male* geisha. They were not at all the same as us girls.

The Boys had been around the Hidden House – and the Green Tea House – for as long as I could remember. When I had been much smaller, they had puzzled me greatly. They seemed to have the run of both establishments and were Auntie's pets. I had asked Carpi about it – Carpi being the fount of all knowledge – and she had laughed at me. They were, she explained, geisha. Same as we were. I frowned at her, frightened to disagree but at the same time sure she was wrong. Geisha were girls, not men! But Carpi had insisted.

"Hundreds of years ago, the first geisha were all men," she said firmly. "They didn't do the same sort of things as we do now, but they were still entertainers. They did acrobatics and juggled and sang, and I suppose they entertained the men who liked other men and not women."

I gasped with my hand to my mouth. Even at that age I

knew that matching the bird to the nest between men was not only against the law but was frowned upon as socially unacceptable. Carpi just shrugged and continued.

"I know, it's not supposed to happen these days, but it does. Sometimes Auntie gets clients who like something a bit different. That's all it is, you know. The same thing, but different. Some men like girls, some men like other men. Some prefer dogs or even sheep. Other men don't want to know about any of it and just keep themselves for themselves. It's the way of the world."

I nodded, but I was still doubtful. I knew to keep well clear of the Boys, though. They might call themselves geisha, but they also had other functions.

None of us knew what their real names were. They were just called Big and Bigger. At first sight, the names might have sounded ironic, as neither was particularly tall and both were slim. But I had seen them in the bath and knew that their slimness disguised wiry muscles. And that was not all I had seen in the bath. The Boys always bathed together, and we girls bunched to one side to give them plenty of room.

The Boys would nod at us disdainfully and then set about the process of cleansing each other. Just as they did for us girls, the maids soaped and rinsed them carefully before they got into the water. However, that was not enough for the Boys. They each took a large sponge into the bath and as soon as they were comfortable, commenced washing each other. Or at least, that was what they pretended to do. Actually, they used the sponges and their hands to excite each other, rubbing and caressing each other's bodies, all the time ignoring us girls who chattered like sparrows as we pretended not to watch them. Especially when they got to work on their trees of flesh. At that stage, it became obvious where the Boys got their names from. Bigger was perhaps an inch or so larger than Big, but both of their trees were gigantic. Just like us girls, the Boys were freaks. They were so large we all wondered whether they would one day faint from the amount of blood that passed from their body to their tree. They never did. Or at least, if they did, we were never there to see it.

When their act of dew mingling was obviously near, one of the girls would decide we had had enough of the bath and we would all climb out. We made sure that no part of our naked bodies got close to the Boys. The Boys had been known to reach out and spitefully pinch any female flesh that came close enough for them to grab.

And the Boys were not just feared for their physical attributes.

Auntie used them as correctors, to administer punishment to the geisha.

Normally, even the threat of the Boys was more than enough to cure an advanced case of the sulks or a disinclination to perform. Yet every once in a while, one of the girls in the Hidden House or even the geisha in the Green Tea House would go too far and the threat of punishment turned into reality.

I stared at the Boys now, trying not to think of the last time they had meted out punishment. Bigger was leaning against one of the plump merchants, tickling him under his chin and laughing. The man was trying to pretend he wasn't happy with Bigger's attentions, but he clearly was. He was chuckling and only feigning pushing Bigger away from him. The more he acted as if he wasn't interested, the more daring Bigger became. As I watched, I saw Bigger's hand snake into the merchant's loose robe. I looked away quickly before he caught me looking.

Big I could not see. He had not left the room, so I guessed he was with the man who had excited me with his very presence. Even the idea of Big being close to *him* made my stomach clench. I had to know what they were doing. Greatly daring, I used my fan as a screen and swiveled my eyes past Auntie, who was scolding poor Suzume about something, and so missed my insolence, to seek him – them – out.

I was right. Big was curled up beside my stranger, his head on the man's shoulder. Oddly – for the Boys were usually unerring in their choices – the man was paying no attention at all to him. In fact, Big might as well have not been there.

Instead, the man was staring across the room. At me. I was so shocked, I almost dropped my fan. For a moment, I didn't care if I had or not. I gave up all pretense at flirtation and simply stared back. He smiled, and my world changed.

He had a pleasant, open face. A gentle expression. He was slimly built beneath his loose robe and I thought he must be quite tall when standing. Not young, not old – perhaps in his early thirties. I thought I heard Big hiss with anger, so I dragged my gaze away quickly, pretending a sudden interest in one of the other men.

As soon as I looked away, I could not have told you what the man looked like. Considering the emotions and physical excitement he was causing me, this was beyond strange, but at that moment I thought nothing of it. Would I know him again if I saw him in a month, or six months, or even a year hence? I would. I would recognize his presence in an instant. That was all that mattered to me.

Well, not quite all. I wanted him, quite desperately. I couldn't understand it for a second. He hadn't even touched me, had done no more than look at me, and yet if he had signaled to me, I would have crawled across the floor on my belly and prostrated myself in front of him, ready to do anything he asked of me. And whatever it was, I would have loved it and begged for more. I wouldn't have cared if everybody else in the room had stopped to watch, I would still have wanted him.

Quite suddenly, someone – and I think it was Big – clapped their hands and called out "Statues!" As if the word was contagious, all of the other men laughed, and also began to chant, "Statues! Statues!" Bewildered, I followed the other girls' lead. Kiku signaled that she wanted to be helped up, and Naruko and I went to her aid. When she was on her feet, we formed a line in front of the men and began to dance as Auntie struck up her samisen.

So far, everything was going well, but then the music stopped suddenly and I was the only one that continued to dance. The men howled with laughter and slapped their legs with glee.

"Off!" someone shouted. "You were last. Off!"

I stared modestly at the floor, totally uncomprehending. My confusion seemed to delight the men, as they all began to chant, "off, off, off!" together.

Kiku tittered behind her hand and took the opportunity to hiss at me, "If you're the last one to stop when the music finishes, you have to take something off as a forfeit. Quick!"

I flushed as red as my black moss and fumbled quickly with the knot on my obi. It seemed to take an age to get it undone, but as soon as it came loose, Suzume darted forward and took it away for me. All the men applauded wildly.

After that, I was ready for it. As soon as Auntie gave any hint that she might stop, I froze. Very quickly, Naruko was down to her under-robes and Masaki had also lost her chemise. I was congratulating myself on my quickness when I suddenly realized that at this rate, I would be the only one dancing. That all eyes would be on me alone as I finally stripped naked. Horrified, I mended my ways as fast as I could and was the first to disrobe for the next three pauses.

That got rid of my under-sash, my kimono, and my under-skirt. At that point, I made an attempt not to be last again, and before long it was Kiku who was naked except for her tabi. At that point, she subsided gracefully to the matting, and one of the men promptly grabbed for her, putting his arms around her and pretending to pant with the effort of enclosing her. Kiku giggled charmingly; I wanted to go and kick him as hard as I could in his tree of flesh. Masaki was the last person still dancing at the next pause, which rendered her naked, so she too was grabbed by one of the men, who perched her on his knee like the doll she was.

So it was down to Naruko and me. As if the men sensed that there was suddenly some competition going on, they began to clap and shout, hissing their pleasure. I clenched my teeth to keep the smile frozen on my lips and glanced at Auntie. She was clearly delighted, nodding and smiling happily.

One of the men reached into the sleeve of his robe and produced some money.

"A hundred yen on the red-haired Barbarian to win!" he shouted. Auntie played on. Naruko and I continued to dance. After a beat or two, the man who had clutched Kiku threw some money on the pile.

"Match you on the other one!" he yelled.

When the music stopped again, Naruko and I froze at the same moment. The room exploded. All the men were shouting at once, a couple of them getting to their feet in their excitement. More money went on the pile. Auntie's smile expanded into a grin; of course, she would take her share from the pot.

Over the chaos, I heard Big's mocking voice. "Come on, what do you say we make this really interesting?" A couple of the fat merchants mopped their faces and turned to look at him eagerly. "Whichever of them is last next time, the money's shared between those that bet on the other one." The men looked at each other. What was so interesting about that? "And just to add a bit of sauce to the dish, what do you say to me taking the one who loses? You could all take bets on how long it takes before I make her scream."

If I thought the men had been excited before, it was nothing to the chaos that ensued at Big's words. More money was flung onto the pile. I exchanged a glance with Naruko and thought I saw the fear in her eyes. I looked pleadingly at Auntie, begging her to stop this game before it began, but she was caught up in the excitement and was laughing as loudly as her customers. Not that she would ever have taken any notice of me anyway. She began to play again.

I felt as if I was moving with the grace of a wooden doll. I was sure I could hear my joints creak. Naruko would win, I knew. She had to. My hands felt as if they were being pricked with needles. Big. Big was going to have me. Here. On the floor in front of everybody. In front of *him*. Even the pain would not be worse than that.

And there would be pain. Oh yes. More pain than I was capable of imagining.

I realized the music had stopped while my thoughts were still focused on what was to come. My hands fumbled at my chemise, but I stopped as I saw that Naruko was already naked, her last garment lying on the floor at her feet. A couple of the men who had bet on her stood up and lurched across, both of them laying claim to her, as well as the money in the pot. I stood helpless, hardly able to breathe.

"No." Just the one word, but said with such authority! I turned my head slowly – slowly was all I could manage – and stared at the man who had enchanted me. He was getting to his feet, tugging his robe around him. He moved with a grace that was almost feline, and – even in the extremity of my fear – I wanted him. Without meaning to, without even realizing I was doing it, my body swayed toward him.

There was a mumble of disappointment from the other men. Bigger tutted and I heard Big snarl a profanity.

"Danjuro! No, you cannot spoil the gentlemen's fun!" Big said.

The man raised his hands, put them together at chest height, and then parted them slowly, palms pointing down. Such was his presence that the whole room instantly became quiet.

"Get the young lady a robe," he said, his voice level. Neither angry nor amused, just...masterful. Suzume instantly darted over and helped me into a loose, comfortable robe. I stood, having no idea what I was supposed to do.

For once, Auntie helped me. "Midori No Me, what are you thinking of, girl?" Her voice was a strange mixture of scolding and simpering. I stared at her in shocked surprise. "Danjuro is waiting for you. Get a move on."

Hardly able to believe what was happening, I moved across to the man she had called Danjuro. He patted me gently on the arm and gestured for me to sit down beside him.

Big was still sitting on the floor, but as I sat, he rose. He made a stiff bow to Danjuro and sneered at me. I was too happy, too relieved, to even react. Danjuro put a protective arm around my shoulders and for a long moment he and Big stared at each other. I shivered. Overjoyed as I was, both to be rescued from Big and to be actually caressed by Danjuro, worry made my stomach go cold as I tried to interpret the look.

Big shrugged and turned away, and every bone, every muscle in my body relaxed.

The noise level rose suddenly as the tension broke. Kiku laughed, and at her signal the rest of the girls began to chatter and giggle. Auntie resumed playing her samisen and Suzume began to circulate with the sake flasks. All at once, normalcy resumed.

I leaned against Danjuro, trying to get as close to him as I possibly could. His body was warm, and I could feel the muscles beneath his robe. He patted my shoulder almost as if he was patting a little animal. Either following my instinctive longings or because I had been trained so very well for so many years, I slid my hand inside his robe and groped for his tree of flesh.

He was erect, I discovered. Quite beautifully so. Nowhere near as large as the Boys, for which I thanked my ancestors, but still substantial enough to be thrilling. I circled my hand around his tree and began to rub the hardness up and down, slowly at first, and then a little faster. My heart was beating so fast, I felt that it must be rocking my entire body. It would, I thought, have been so much better if we had been together in a private room, but no matter. By this time, there were knots of bodies all over the room, tumbling together like autumn leaves tossed by a playful breeze.

For the first time, I found myself sexually aroused. I had never even considered that watching people enjoy each other's bodies could be stimulating; in the past, I had simply tried not to think about it. Perhaps it was the strangeness of the evening, coupled with my sudden feelings for Danjuro, but now I felt lust flow through me like hot lava. The more I watched the play in the room before me, the more aroused I became.

One of the merchants was taking Kiku from behind. His tree was completely hidden in her bulk, yet still he was thrusting at her until I thought that most of his lower body might disappear. Kiku was either a better actress than I had given her credit for or she was truly enjoying herself. Certainly, the little yips of sound she was making were far removed from the giggles and assumed noises of pleasure she usually made.

Another man was sitting with legs akimbo, his knees almost knocking on the matting. Masaki was sitting on his lap, facing him, looking as if she really was an exquisite porcelain doll. Naked, she was perfectly beautiful, her skin unmarred in any way, her tiny breasts just big enough to be grasped. I had often wondered how tiny Masaki managed to take any man's tree, but she appeared perfectly unconcerned and was juddering up and down in time to her patron's movements. Unlike Kiku, her exclamations I recognized as practiced rather than pleasure.

Naruko was on top of one of the other men, riding him as if he was a donkey. I gawped foolishly as she raised herself up, up, up, until only the very tip of his tree was still inside her. Just as it seemed he would pop out, she slammed herself down on him and leaned forward, dangling her breasts in his face. The man raised his head and tried to take her nipples in his mouth, but she swayed away teasingly.

I leaned back against Danjuro, my breath coming in short pants. Even the antics of the Boys were deeply erotic. Both of them were engaged with the remaining two men. I stared in mingled fascination and horror. Big had his man pinned down to the floor, as much of his tree as he could manage jammed into his patron's gaping mouth. For a horrified second, I thought the man was choking to death – hardly surprising, given the size of Big's tree – but then I realized that he was still managing to gasp encouragement and the plum color of his face was caused by excitement rather than pain. Or possibly both. In any event, he was clearly deeply excited, as his own tree loomed rigidly. As I watched, Big glanced at me – or did he actually look at Danjuro? He leaned casually back to pluck at the penis of the man beneath, sliding it back and forth almost idly in his grip. The man's voice rose in a scream of pleasure and Big's grip tightened until the organ in his grasp was almost the same plum color as the man's face.

Bigger had his head buried in his client's lap. The man was laying back, his robe flung open, and he, in his turn, had Bigger's tree of flesh in his hand. The pair had all the grace of a dance. As Bigger's head bobbed back and forth, the man's hand moved up and down Bigger's tree in time to music I could not hear. Bigger's lips were drawn back from his teeth in an expression that was more snarl than smile, and as I watched, fascinated and unable to look away, I saw his mouth open wide and bite down so hard that blood spurted from his patron's penis and dribbled down Bigger's chin. I expected his patron to scream, to hit him, to call a halt to proceedings and cause chaos, but there was none of that. Instead, he gave a breathy wheeze and flung his head back, his mouth wide open as if he was gasping for air. At the same time, I saw Bigger swallow deeply, and I realized that the patron had burst his fruit in Bigger's mouth.

My own mouth parted in shock.

Danjuro gestured at Suzume, and the maid came at a run, clutching a flask of sake. Danjuro asked her for two cups, as quietly as if we were alone somewhere, as if we were not surrounded by bodies coupling and breaking and coupling again, sometimes in the same combination, sometimes moving on to another partner. He gulped down his sake and held his cup out for more. I sipped mine, but still the cup was soon empty. Suzume refilled both and then trotted off for another flask.

The sake went straight to my head. I had rarely had more than a sip or two of the liquor before, and now I had downed two cups in a couple of minutes. And I was on fire. The sake was making the room spin around me. Danjuro at my side was making me even hotter. His tree of flesh was still in my hand. I drank my third cup of sake and put the cup down, determined to concentrate on Danjuro.

I leaned across him, brushing my hair against his chest. Moving as slowly, as deliberately as I could, I lowered my head to his penis, taking it in my mouth and moving back and forth as slowly as I could make myself. I wanted, desperately, to gulp him down. To take as much of him as I could manage in my mouth. I pressed my breasts against him, and – try as I might – I could not stop myself rubbing against him, as blatant as a cat in heat. I could hear his heart beating against my ear. The skin on his chest and belly was smooth as silk, but in my state of heightened awareness, my flesh felt inflamed where I was rubbing against him. Abandoning all pretense, I threw myself against him, oozing like oil across him.

He was breathing heavily, and his eyes were half closed, his lips parted. Greatly daring, I rose to my knees and pushed my nipple in his mouth. He sucked on it so gently, I wanted to scream. I wanted him to suckle it greedily, to bite, to nibble. Most of all, I wanted him to put his engorged tree of flesh inside me. To pound his body on me. To find my hidden parts and to drench my fire with his waters.

The noise of complicated copulations washed over us in a wave of eroticism. The girls were trained to please, as were the Boys, and that was exactly what they were doing. I had eyes and ears and senses for nobody but Danjuro, but I could not help but hear the moans and shouts of mingled pleasure and pain that filled the room and drowned out the music of Auntie's samisen.

Danjuro's fingers fixed themselves in my hair and he dragged my head away. At the same time, he leaned back and tugged me up his body, dragging me up by his grip on my curls. My scalp was on fire, and I rejoiced in the pain. I felt that every sense was heightened, that noise was louder, colors brighter, even pain more exquisite than anything I had ever known, had ever imagined. He put his hands on my breasts, pulling me down, and I slid on top of his tree of flesh with a scream of pleasure.

Since my mizuage, I had dreaded having sex with another patron. I had dreamed of the horror of it, in my waking moments I had felt nauseous at the thought of it. But never, awake or asleep, had I imagined anything like this.

Danjuro lay still, allowing me to do the work for him. I rejoiced in it, dictating my own speed, my own rhythm. Now slow, now faster. As soon as I felt him rising up to meet me, I slowed down. When he subsided beneath me, I bucked my hips and tightened my muscles, drawing him into me as tightly as I could. When I thought he might be ready to burst his fruit, I slowed to a crawl, pulling myself as far away from him as I could, without actually allowing him to withdraw from me. Finally unable to bear my own torture any longer, I began to bang up and down on him more fiercely, desperate to get as much of him inside me as I possibly could.

The final mingling of juices was a glorious thing for me. Danjuro was panting like a donkey on a hot day, and I cooled him with my own sweat, for the night was hot. Suddenly, he grabbed my bucking hips with his hands, and forced me down onto him, raising his own body to meet me. A final, hitherto undiscovered, part of his tree of flesh found me and pleasure erupted from my private parts, echoing round and round and round and finally receding slowly, leaving me languid and content.

I fell forward on Danjuro, and he lay beneath me, supine and still. After a moment, he rolled me over and pulled my robe around me. I found the gesture desperately tender, as if our coupling had been uniquely caring, and now he was shielding me from the grosser activities that were still going on all around us.

He put his head against my hair and leaned against me, neither moving nor speaking. After a while, he began to sing, very quietly, and I listened, enthralled. His speaking voice was beautiful, his singing voice even more so. The only way I could describe it was to think of a caged bird that had somehow managed to escape and was singing for pure joy. I closed my eyes, praying that another patron would not fancy a change and come and demand my attention.

After a while, Danjuro finished his song and fell silent.

He beckoned Suzume for more sake, which I refused. My head was already spinning with excitement and pleasure and alcohol. He finished the cup, and, to my intense disappointment, stood, pulling his robe around him. He bowed politely to Auntie and then to me, though not as deeply, and was gone.

I could have cried. Although I had been satiated once, having him so close had already started to make my juices flow again. I had hoped that he would stay, that I would arouse him again, and we could find new ways to please each other. Suddenly I dreaded the moment when one of the other patrons would realize that I was alone and I would be called upon to perform with one of them.

But I was in luck. It was as if Danjuro's exit had broken a spell. Gradually, the noise level fell. When the couplings broke, they did not resume. Patrons stretched and yawned and called for sake rather than glancing around eagerly in search of another partner, another way of satiating bored desires. Even the Boys went and sat with each other, ignoring their former partners quite rudely.

Big stared at me deliberately, sneering. I was drooping with mingled pleasure and a sense of amazement, still barely able to comprehend that this evening that I had dreaded so deeply had turned out so delightfully well. I rubbed my thighs together, and felt Danjuro's bodily fluid, mingled with my own, sliding between them. The sensation made me shudder with pleasure. Without thinking, I smiled at Big. For a second, naked fury peeped out from behind his well-trained expression, and even in my dreamy, pleasurable state I was frightened. Then Bigger laughed and put his hand on the other man's arm, and Big was smiling as well. I decided I had imagined it.

6

Clouds pass across the sun.
When will I see
Its light again?

*B*igger leaned back on my tatami matting and tickled Nekko under his chin. The kitten hissed and slapped out playfully with his claws. Fearless kitten! Bigger laughed and pushed the cat away with his finger, really quite tenderly.

I watched Bigger carefully, watching for any change of mood, ready to respond immediately to whatever he asked for. The kitten seemed to amuse him, and I was grateful for that. Suddenly, I worried that Bigger might really take a fancy to Nekko and claim him from me. Even the thought of losing my pet was hurtful. I had never had anything to call my own before, other than the odd cricket or firefly in a cage, and they were never terribly good companions. Nekko had been a present from the little maid, Suzume, and I treasured him all the more because of the gift. He was a sweet little boy, very playful, very clean. And the kitten was devoted to me, much as Suzume herself seemed to be. I wondered if I had suddenly gone from having no pets at all to having two.

I hid a sigh of relief as Bigger decided he was bored with Nekko and abruptly stopped playing with him. Instead, he sat back on his elbows and grinned at me.

Since the evening of the party, Bigger seemed to have taken to me. I was torn between puzzlement and fear at his attention, but gradually – as the weeks passed and he did no more than talk to me – the fear began to abate a little. Even so, I was always very careful to treat him with immense respect and to ensure that I matched my conversation to his mood.

One could not be too careful with the Boys.

At least Big ignored me, and I decided that I had imagined that hateful look I thought I had seen after Danjuro left the party. After Danjuro left me.

I know, you would have thought that I, I who had been born and raised in the Floating World, would have known better. What was I thinking, hoping that a patron might actually *like* me? The other girls teased me endlessly about it. Where was my handsome young man, they demanded. They had all thought he had taken a shine to me, the way he had singled me out. What had I done to him? Or rather, what hadn't I done? And on, and on, and on.

I refused to rise to the bait. I just shrugged. These things happened, I had told Kiku. As it turned out, neither of the patrons who we had thought were going to make an offer for her had done so, and she was still in the Hidden House.

Catching my meaning immediately, Kiku laughed, as good-natured as ever.

"At least you're not moping about the place, bemoaning your fate anymore." Kiku grinned.

The girls said I was lucky, and I knew that they were right. My patrons tended to be the middle-aged men, the ones who were fascinated by my foreign looks. Sometimes, they didn't even want to mingle dew with me, but preferred to allow me to wind my hair around their tree of flesh, and tighten it until their fruit burst. Even the ones who did want to match the bird to the nest were rarely unreasonably demanding. Not always, of course. I had my share of the strange ones. I learned to forget quickly.

But I could not forget Danjuro.

I knew I was being silly. I knew it was likely that the one time he had singled me out had been nothing but a whim. After all, I had never seen him at the Hidden House before. And months had passed since the party and he had never been back.

But still, I could not forget him.

I used his memory whenever I was with a patron. It didn't help greatly with the ones who just wanted to achieve bursting fruit with my hair, nor with those who favored just a bit of twirling the stem. But the others, those who wanted to put their tree of flesh inside me, those, I pretended were Danjuro.

Often, it didn't work. Often, I went through the motions and giggled and panted and pretended that they were causing me pain. It was strange, all the girls agreed, that every single one of our patrons, even the ones with trees like bent fingers, were all delighted to think they were causing us such ecstasy that it hurt. Still, we agreed, if it kept them happy we would moan to order, without as much as a single spasm of real pleasure.

Other times, it helped to play act to myself, to try and pretend it was Danjuro who was riding me. Strangely, it didn't seem to matter in the least whether the patron remotely resembled Danjuro – or at least my memory of him, which seemed to become hazier and more formless by the day – it was more a case of how much I could pretend to myself that they were Danjuro. This was easier when the patron wanted to take me from behind; then, I closed my eyes and tried to conjure up the memory of his features, the warm strength of his body, the feel of his hands sliding on my flesh. When it worked, I sometimes even managed to achieve bursting of the fruit myself with the patron. Never like my ecstasy had been with Danjuro, of course, but still pleasurable, in a way.

Especially did I concentrate on my memories of Danjuro when it became obvious that my patron wanted to split the melon. Some of the girls actually preferred this. The doll-like Masaki, of all people, admitted that she actually found it exciting when a man went for her backside rather than her black moss. Kiku said she wasn't bothered greatly either way. Carpi said wryly that she rarely got the chance to find out which she preferred; all of her patrons invariably wanted her to twirl their stem with her feet. Naruko simply lowered her eyes and giggled, not expressing an opinion either way.

The first time a patron wanted to split the melon with me, I was too terrified that I might disgrace myself and shit on him to worry about anything else. I confided this to Kiku afterward, and she roared with laughter, advising me not to worry about it.

"Some of them love that," she said. "In fact, I once had a patron who came to me regularly and he actually wanted me to do just that – shit on him. Nothing else, just mess on him."

"No!" I said.

She nodded vigorously. "He did. He didn't want anything else at all. He would come in, drink a flask of sake and then lie down on the matting without a word. He had to explain to me what he wanted the first time, but after that, it was always the same. He would lie down, and I would squat over him and shit on his tree. As soon as I did that, he would play with his mucky tree himself and his fruit would burst without me doing anything else at all. Auntie always charged him extra as she had to throw the matting away. Or at least, she threw it away in the first place, but then he said if he was paying for it, he wanted it, and so she started rolling it up for him and he would take it away under his arm afterward. I often wondered what he did with it."

We all looked at one another, fascinated.

At least I never had a patron who wanted me to do that. I was fairly sure I would not have been able to manage it, but Kiku said I would because that was my job. To do whatever the patron wanted. I made a face.

"Haven't you had those that wanted you to make golden rain on them and nothing else?" she asked.

"Well, yes. But that wasn't as bad as all that." Or at least, not always. Reluctantly, I thought of one man who had demanded not only that I pee on his naked body, laid out on a matless floor, but then had pulled me down on top of him and rolled me over and over in it until we were both sopping wet. My thick makeup caked like snowy mud all over both of us. Only then had he parted my black moss and entered me. Once comfortably inside me, he slowed down and I could hear him grunting with effort. I was puzzled at first, but soon realized that he was trying his best to pee inside me. I have no idea whether he managed it or not. As soon as he finished, he got to his feet, bowed and went off to the bathhouse. I waited until I was sure he must have finished before I followed him, and on that particular occasion I insisted that I have the bath to myself. Even the other girls seemed to understand why.

Funnily enough, it was while I was sitting in the bath, after Suzume had soaped me and poured hot water over me until I was clean, that I started to see the silly side of it and giggled. Once I started, I couldn't stop. Here was this man – by his bearing and his clothes he was possibly a minor noble, but certainly someone important – paying a huge sum to Auntie to do something that no doubt his mother had slapped him for when he was a little boy. I would have bet my lovely kimono that he had a polite, compliant wife at home, and probably a mistress as well. The more I thought about it, the funnier it seemed.

Any desire to laugh at the memory fled as Bigger suddenly got to his feet, pacing back and forth. My small bedroom did not give him much space, and he almost tripped over Nekko. The kitten hissed at him and dug his claws in Bigger's ankle. I held my breath for fear he would kick the kitten, but he did not. Instead, he bent down and detached the claws from his leg quite tenderly. A rivulet of blood ran down Bigger's ankle. He reached down and rubbed it with his fingers, licking the blood off his hand lazily.

He was restless, and I watched him warily. A tranquil Bigger was bad enough, a nervous Bigger was terrifying. All at once, he clapped his hands and shouted for the maid.

Suzume popped her head around the screen and scurried off at his instructions, returning a moment later with a lacquered tray in her hands. Bigger nodded to her to put it on the floor, and I watched him looking at the outline of Suzume's body through her thin kimono. I winced inside for the girl.

Bigger would know, of course – the Boys knew everything – that Suzume could not feel pain. Until her mizuage, Auntie would make sure that neither of the Boys could have fun testing just how much she would be able to endure. But of course, there were a multitude of ways that the Boys could enjoy themselves with poor little Suzume that did not include deflowering her. I shuddered at the thought, then prayed that Bigger had not noticed.

He picked up the pipe off the tray and ran his finger appreciatively down the long, ivory stem before fitting the ceramic pipe bowl into its mounting. Suzume had left a pot of opium, already rolled into neat balls, and Bigger picked one up carefully, prodding it into place in the bowl with a sliver of metal. The pipe lamp was lit and he leaned forward, all his attention on the pipe bowl as he turned it too and fro in the heat. When the opium was vaporizing to his satisfaction, he sat back and – to my surprise – offered the pipe to me. I bowed low, but shook my head. I had tried a pipe once and had been so sick afterward I thought my insides had come loose. Carpi, I had noticed, seemed to be smoking opium more often these days, and I did not like the look of the effect it was having on her.

Bigger shrugged at my refusal and took a long draw at the pipe stem himself. He held his breath for ages and then exhaled slowly.

"Big hates you, you know." His normally sharp voice was

mellowed by the opium. I looked at him in confusion and waited until he had inhaled again before I dared ask.

"Why?"

I was even more terrified of Big than I was of Bigger. On the rare occasions that I met him in the corridors of the Hidden House, I invariably made sure to flatten myself against the wall and bow as low as I could without coming into contact with him. But still I could feel intense dislike radiating off him like a black cloud. In spite of the fact that I had wondered since the night I had met Danjuro why Big had decided he disliked me, if it had not been for the opium, I would never have dared question Bigger.

"Don't you know?" His voice had slowed to a lazy drawl. I shook my head. "He couldn't believe that you took Danjuro away from him. Big's been in love with him for years. And of course, Big was very fond of Terue. Your mother."

Bigger yawned and I prayed he would not fall asleep too soon. My mother. Big had been fond of my mother. No one ever spoke about her, at least not when I was listening. Now Bigger was telling me that Big, of all people, had been fond of her? I was beyond amazed. I wanted to know about my mother, but I knew I must tread very carefully. Bigger was obviously more interested in Danjuro, so I risked asking him about that.

"Does Danjuro feel the same about Big?" I asked, feeling my way carefully.

Bigger shook his head lazily. "I don't think Danjuro cares about anything except his art." He yawned again, exposing his teeth and his gums. Through the fog of opium, he must still have seen my bewildered expression because he laughed. "You don't know anything at all, do you? Do you even know who Danjuro is?"

I shook my head. He had been well dressed, but his bearing had none of the arrogance of a samurai, still less a noble. Neither could I believe that he was a merchant. Truth to tell, Danjuro had been a mystery I had been picking at from the moment I had laid eyes on him.

"Danjuro is...Danjuro!" Bigger laughed uproariously at his own wit. Like the well-trained geisha I was, I giggled with him. Bigger sucked on the pipe again. "He's the lead actor with the Edo kabuki," he said finally. "The lead actor is always called Danjuro, at least he is if he's considered good enough and he comes from that family of actors. It's a great honor. Danjuro must be the seventh or eighth actor to bear the family name."

He put the pipe down with great care, smiling at me beatifically. I could tell he was falling asleep even though he hadn't told me anything about my mother. My need to know overcame my fear, and I slid across the matting to Bigger, inching my hand into his partly open robe. It was a huge risk; as far as I knew, Bigger was not interested in women. It was quite likely that he would, if I was very lucky, shrug me aside. If he took offense, he was likely to slap me so hard that I hit the floor. But it was a chance I had to take.

I smiled up at him, and my hand found his tree of flesh. I was bitterly disappointed to discover that he was completely flaccid, and for a few moments nothing I could do seemed to make any difference. And then, suddenly, Bigger became interested.

"What are you up to, little Midori?" he slurred, the words clearly an effort.

"I hoped to please you, Bigger-san," I murmured, as shyly as I could. Bigger grunted and began to grow under my fingers. I was glad my face was hidden from his view or he would have seen the astonishment – and fear – in my expression. Seeing the Boys aroused in the bath or with a patron was one thing. Having that arousal under your own hand was different. Very shortly, I understood only too well why Bigger had his name.

His tree of flesh was like nothing I had ever imagined. It was not only huge – it must have easily reached to beyond his belly-button – but was also thick and solid. What tiger had I roused? But at the same time as I felt fear, a slow snake of excitement began to uncoil in my belly. Could I, could any woman, take this inside her? Ride this snake and live to tell the tale? I licked my lips and slid my fingers, which barely met, around his thickness. Slowly, slowly, slowly, I began to move my hand back and forth, expecting every second that Bigger would get tired of my nervous efforts and would knock me aside.

But he did not. Instead, he seemed amused. Moment by moment, it seemed that the effect of the pipe was wearing off.

"What a brave little Midori No Me you are," he snickered. "Don't you know what I do to little girls like you? Why, I break them in two!"

I was breathing heavily. I couldn't help it. Part of me was terrified at the thought of trying to take all this inside me. Another part was as deeply excited. What would it feel like? Could I do it? Could I?

Bigger settled the question for me. He laced his fingers in my hair and dragged me up, level with his face. Very deliberately, he pushed the tip of his tongue between his lips and licked my face, starting between my eyebrows and ending up at my mouth. His tongue traced the outline of my lips with an absurd delicacy. When he spoke, his lips were so close to me that I felt the puff of his breath on my skin.

"Do you want me to break you, Midori? Is that what you

want? Do you want to feel me inside you? Do you think you are woman enough to take me? Do you?"

I was screaming inside. Fear was telling me to say, No, Bigger, no, of course not. I am so sorry I disturbed you. I don't know what came over me.

My lips said yes.

Bigger was laughing at me silently, his lips parted, his teeth bared in almost a snarl. I was reminded of an alpha wolf, growling at his pack to keep them in order.

"Yes," I whispered. "Yes."

Bigger slouched onto his back and threw his robe open. He gestured at his tree of flesh. A gesture that said, *Go on, then. If you dare.*

I was wet with desire, but even so I dared not accept his invitation. Not yet. Instead, I bent and took the engorged bulb of his tree of flesh in my mouth, licking and sucking until he was slippery wet. And all the time, Bigger lay back and watched me, his expression unreadable.

When I finally thought I was ready – or as ready as I was ever going to be – I raised my head and took a deep breath. Very carefully, I slid across and put one leg over his belly. Bigger lay still, neither helping nor hindering. I raised myself onto my knees and then began to lower myself, as slowly as I could. After a lifetime, I felt his erection nudging my sex. I stretched myself wide with my fingers and took the plunge before I could change my mind, taking him inside me.

Bigger laughed.

I was lost. Suddenly, I was a greedy child. I wanted as much of him as I could take, no matter how it hurt. I forced myself down onto him, perhaps halfway down his tree, and then raised myself up again. Down another half inch. *No more*, I thought. *I could take no more.* Bigger had other ideas.

"If you sow the wind, you must expect to reap the typhoon, Midori No Me."

His voice was hoarse and rough. I stared at him with my mouth wide open, shaking my head slightly from side to side. Bigger moved fluidly, rolling me onto my back so that he was looking down at me. And from that moment on, his gaze never left my face.

His erection was so enormous that he had not fallen out of me as we turned over. Ignoring my squeaks, he began to force himself inside me. I was almost relieved. I was no longer in charge. I had no option. What I had started, Bigger was going to finish. No matter what.

I slid my hands beneath him and stretched my sex as wide as I could, hanging on to his tree of flesh to try and control his movement. I might as well have tried to stop Mount Fuji from erupting. Bigger was iron, his flesh not flesh at all but something harder than any man had a right to. He pushed and pushed and pushed, and suddenly he was fully inside me.

I moved with him, hardly able to believe that I had been able to take this giant of a man. He gave me incredible pain with every thrust, but alongside the pain was equally huge pleasure. I screamed out loud, pain and pleasure mingling into one indescribable whole. And still Bigger watched my face, his gaze never wavering.

Had he stopped, I would have crawled on my knees to him. Done anything, anything at all to entice him back inside me. He was not a man, he was a god. Suddenly, my world began to spin and I screamed again with pure pleasure.

Bigger did not burst his fruit inside me. When he withdrew, he was still fully erect. I looked at him dizzily, hardly able to believe what had happened.

"Midori No Me, you would not have been able to do that had I wanted to punish you."

I shook my head and blinked at him fuzzily, still deep, deep in pleasure.

"If you tell anyone, anyone at all, that you took me and lived to tell the tale without screaming every time you thought about it, then I will punish you. Punish you worse than anything you could ever imagine."

A shudder rippled my flesh like a cold wind had blown over me as I realized how insane I had been to tempt this man. And how lucky I had been to get away with it. It would not, I knew, ever happen again. I bowed my head in unfeigned humility.

"Yes, Bigger," I whispered.

I felt him staring at me and wondered if, after all, I was going to be punished for my insolence. I was, but not how I expected.

"You look nothing like your mother, you know," Bigger said.

I froze. A few minutes ago I would have given anything for him to tell me about Terue, the mother I had never known, but now I did not want to hear. It seemed to me to be a blasphemy to her memory that this man should speak about her, especially after what we had just done. I felt absurdly guilty and offered a prayer of apology to my unknown mother. I lowered my head and tried not to look interested, but Bigger was relentless.

"Terue was very beautiful. The perfect geisha, she was called. Tiny, much smaller than you, and slender as a willow branch. To hear her sing a sad song was to bring tears to your eyes."

I closed my own eyes. Bigger poked me in the ribs hard enough to bruise and I opened my eyes.

"She had not just the patrons of the Green Tea House at her feet, but the whole of Edo. Could even have had a nobleman for a husband, if she wanted. But what did the silly bitch do? Run off with a foreign devil. You get your looks from your father."

My father? Strange, I had rarely spared a thought for him. He was just too much of an unknown. I had no concept of what he looked like, how he thought. I kept my gaze modestly lowered.

"He was tall, like you. And he had hair the color of a red fox." Bigger had known him, I realized with astonishment. He actually knew my father! The knowledge was a revelation. "Same color eyes as you as well. He was as ugly as sin, should have been in a circus side show as a freak, if you ask me. What Terue ever saw in him, none of us could understand. But that's women for you. The gods only know how they think. If they think at all. We hardly saw any foreign Barbarians in Edo in those days, so he stuck out like the monster he was. He was a merchant, imported opium and exported silk and porcelain. I'll give him his due, he actually bothered to learn Japanese. If you didn't look at his ugly face, you would have thought you were speaking to a native of Edo."

I stayed silent. I couldn't have spoken if I had wanted to. A sliver of mucous slipped down the inside of my leg, distracting me. I tried to ignore it.

"Of course, we all knew why Terue ran off with him." Bigger was jeering at me. He stopped, and I bit my tongue hard enough to draw blood rather than ask him to go on. He pulled a sour face and went on anyway. "The stupid bitch had got herself pregnant by him. There would have been no place for her in the Floating World, nowhere in Edo, if she had produced a half-breed deformed freak like you. She could have exposed you and left you to die on Mount Fuji, of course, but word would soon have got round as to whose little monkey you were. So she was merciful, and left you here when she ran off with her foreign devil."

He smiled at me, almost lovingly, and I tried not to shiver. As he rose to his feet and fastened his robe, he added casually, "If you really want to know about Terue-san, you should have a chat with Big. He knew your mother better than anybody. Except her foreign Barbarian, of course."

Bigger swaggered off, pulling the screen closed behind him with exaggerated courtesy.

I sat silently. Nekko climbed onto my knee, purring to himself. That was the barb on the arrow, then. Big. Big had known my mother well. Big, the one man out of the whole of the Floating World who I could never hope to talk to. Big, who had hated me simply because I was my mother's daughter and now hated me even more because of Danjuro.

I lifted Nekko off my lap and rubbed my face in his fur. I blew on his neck and he mewed, whether in pleasure or indignation I had no idea.

When I was sure that Bigger had gone, I changed my robe and went to the bathhouse. Nekko sat at the edge of the bath and tried to bat the steam with his paw. As I sunk into the hot water and felt it cleanse me, I wondered if my mother, the famous geisha, would have been ashamed of my conduct with Bigger. Suddenly, as certainly as if I heard her voice whispering in the echoing bathhouse, I thought not. She had taken her chance, had done the unthinkable. Had done what she wanted to do. Had taken her life and shaken it and reformed it in the pattern she wanted. It was a life that did not include me, but so be it. Few, if any, Japanese women would have had the courage to do what

she had done. At least she hadn't exposed me on a moun-
taintop. I was alive!

In just the same way as Terue had done, I had followed
my impulse and done what I wanted with Bigger. I had
decided that I would have what I wanted at that moment.

No, I decided. Mother would not have been ashamed of
her daughter. In fact, she might even have been proud
of me.

7

*Blossoms skip at the
Caress of spring.
I share their pleasure.*

I had never seen Auntie ruffled before. Had never dreamed that anything could get her even the least bit excited. But here she was, clucking like a mother hen rounding up her chicks.

"Should I wear a wig, Auntie?" A totally irrelevant question, of course, but I was so ecstatic myself, I hardly knew what I was saying or doing. Auntie actually thought about the answer for a second as well. Truly, a day of the strangest happenings!

"No, I don't think so. We'll put your hair up, of course, and style it properly for you. I recollect that he liked your hair, so no wig. Your green kimono, of course." As if I had another one that was fit to go out in! "And full makeup. One of my girls is not going to be seen out improperly styled."

I almost laughed out loud at the last comment. When, I wondered, had one of the Hidden House girls ever been "seen out," either properly or improperly styled? We were hidden gems, blossoms too strange to be seen by the light of day. On the rare occasions that one or two of us had been sent for to attend an especially important occasion inside the Floating World, we were put into a closed carriage and escorted by the Boys. It had never happened to me, but Carpi had gone once, in company with a girl who had since been bought out by a danna. I couldn't remember her name, but she had been mute. I asked Carpi about it afterward, and she had simply shrugged, her mouth turning down sourly at the corners.

"It was nothing." My face fell and she shrugged again, almost apologetically. "Auntie put us in the carriage straight from the door and closed the curtains on us. The Boys traveled inside with us and handed us out when we got there. I don't even know where 'there' was. When the patron had finished with us, we were put back in the carriage and delivered to the door of the Hidden House. And that was it. A patron is a patron, after all. Here or there."

Now the moment had arrived and I was so excited I found it difficult to breathe. I gave thanks to the gods on my knees. It was exactly as if Danjuro had heard Bigger talking to me about him and about Big. For the moment, I was too excited to even worry about either of the Boys.

After months and months of thinking about Danjuro, wondering about him at every possible moment, dreaming about him, it seemed that he had suddenly awoken from a sleep of his own and had taken it into his head to send for me. I was to attend a performance of the kabuki! And – if it was possible for things to get any better – he had even said that I was *not* to be escorted by the Boys, but was to be allowed to go to the kabuki on my own, accompanied, as was only proper, by little Suzume, who would act as my maid.

He would, of course, be happy to pay the fee for me for the whole evening, and there would be a nice present for Suzume.

Although I had not seen Big, I could almost feel his loathing simmering.

Bigger came and poked his head into my bedroom. Wicked as ever, he did not speak but simply shook his head sadly and sucked his teeth in a shocked manner, crossing his eyes in an affectation of great sadness. I don't know to this day what possessed me to do it, but suddenly I found myself shuffling across the matting on my knees. I flung my arms around his knees and buried my head in his robe.

"Oh, Bigger!" I wailed. "I don't know what to do. I know Big will hate me if I go, but if I don't, Auntie will give me to Big to be punished anyway, so I'm caught in the middle. Oh, help me, Bigger, please!"

I could tell he was pleased by my appeal to him. He patted my head as if I was a puppy and I felt him shrug.

"Well, looks to me as if you've no way to turn, have you?"

A memory came to me of this terrible man caressing my tiny, helpless kitten and I wailed even louder.

"I only have you, Bigger! I have no one else in the whole world to turn to!"

For a horrible moment, I thought he was going to kick me away and go to tell Big how unhappy I was. But he did not.

"Mmm. Well, I suppose I could keep an eye open for you. If I wanted to. If you made it worth my while."

Made it worth his while? How could I? I had nothing of my own. And I held no attraction for him, he had made that obvious already. I might have amused him the one time, but I did not fool myself that he would welcome another performance. My stomach contracted so hard that I felt as if I had been kicked.

"Bigger, I have nothing. I owe Auntie everything." Even in my distress, I realized it was better not to try to offer my services to Bigger. One wrong word and I could find myself committed to something even worse than any patron wanted to inflict on me.

"Shush, little Midori, shush." Bigger sounded so pleased, I began to feel quite ill. In spite of my caution, had I let myself in for something that I would regret forever more? Oh, Danjuro. What have you done to me? Even as I thought it, I knew I didn't mean it. There was nothing I could imagine that I would not do for Danjuro. "There is something you can do for me. A very easy something. Something that I think you will enjoy greatly."

Throwing caution to the wind, I bawled, "Anything!"

"Make Danjuro fall in love with you."

I was so surprised that I actually rocked back on my heels and stared up at Bigger. I thought he must have been mocking me, but his face was deadly serious. He gripped my shoulders in his hands and shook me quite gently.

"Can you do that, Midori? Think carefully before you answer. Don't tell me that you will try or that you will do your best. Tell me the truth. Can you do it?"

"Yes." The word slipped out between my lips before I could stop it. I knew the enormity of what I was saying. Japanese men did not *love* women. They used them. When they married, it was to produce sons or to gain kudos with people who mattered. They did not love their wives; very rarely did they profess to love their mistresses. Perhaps one man in ten thousand loved a woman intensely enough to kill himself for her, but even that was no consolation since the woman was expected to kill herself at the same time. And I now knew that Danjuro was a famous man. A wealthy man. A man who must be worshiped by thousands of women, and men.

A man who was loved by Big. Once that thought came to me, I understood everything. Bigger loved Big, just as Big loved Danjuro. He would do anything to come between them. Did Danjuro also love Big, I wondered? The thought was abhorrent, and I shoved it away. Of course he didn't. Why would he have protected me at the party if he did? Why was he sending for me now, asking that I came to him all alone? I could see Bigger watching these thoughts go through my mind and knew if I committed now I would be risking everything. Probably even my life. Even so, I said it again.

"Yes. I will make Danjuro love me. I will take him away from Big. I promise. I will make him forget that Big ever existed for him."

Bigger nodded and inhaled deeply. He delved into the sleeve of his robe and produced a small knife. The blade glinted wickedly as it caught the light. He reached down and caught my hand and I gasped as he slit my middle finger deeply. Blood dripped out immediately, but before it could fall to the floor Bigger had cut his own finger and was pressing it against my wound.

"There. The promise is made, and sealed in blood. If you do not do it, I don't care what Auntie says. If I have to do it to get to you, I will kill Auntie myself. If you fail, I will make your life a living hell for as long as I can bear to keep you alive. Every day, I will come to you, Midori. Do you understand?"

I nodded. His words filled my mind. I had no doubt at all that he would do it.

But I would not fail.

Danjuro was going to be mine. I knew it. That was going to hurt Big, at the same time as it pleased Bigger. What a tangle it all was! But I didn't care. At least I would please one of the Boys, as well as myself. And, I hoped and prayed, I would please Danjuro as well.

I smiled.

Auntie fussed around me so long, I began to think the performance would be finished before I got to the kabuki. My makeup was perfect. My hair pinned up, with each curl placed carefully. My obi and kimono were fastened by Auntie herself.

Finally, she expressed herself satisfied and shooed me out of the door. Suzume knew where the Ichimura-za Kabuki Theater was. It was not far, still well within the Floating World. I was itching to ask how Suzume knew where the kabuki theater was located, but I was even more anxious to be off so I stayed silent.

Even though it was very early evening and a cloudy day, Auntie had insisted that I take a parasol to shade my skin from any sun that might peek out. I did as I was told. After all, I had never in my entire life stepped outside the confines of the Hidden House compound before.

I could hardly breathe for terror. The outer door was pulled shut behind me and I had to take a deep breath before I could even move. For once, I was thankful for my kimono's tight embrace around my legs, for without it I think my knees would have buckled. I could hear them knocking together. Suzume tugged at my sleeve and urged me forward.

"This way," she said confidently and set off. I had to

follow. If I did not, I would have turned back to the door of the Hidden House and beaten on it, demanding to be allowed back in. The idea was still all too appealing, but with it came the memory of Bigger's wicked little penknife. I was between a rock and a hard place. I could either follow Suzume into unimaginable terrors or retreat back into the safety of the Hidden House and face the all-too-real terrors of Bigger.

Fear of Bigger won. Suzume had come back to me and was peering into my face, her expression concerned.

"Come," she coaxed gently. I realized that she understood at least some of my abject panic.

"I've never been outside before," I croaked.

Suzume's mouth fell open in disbelief. "Never?" she echoed. I shook my head miserably. She stared at me and then nodded briskly. If I hadn't been so frightened, I would have been amused at the little maid's sudden confidence.

"Don't worry," she said decisively. "I know the Floating World well. I was born here, and I know every twist and turn. I will look after you. Can you walk?"

I made a face. Could I? I didn't really know if my legs would support me or not. I was clutching the corner of the wall of the Hidden House as if my life depended on it. I let go very carefully, to see if I could still stand and was surprised to find that I could.

"I think I can."

"You must." Suzume's little face was earnest. "If you don't go to the theater, Auntie will be very angry with you." Auntie would be angry? That would be nothing, nothing at all, compared to Bigger's reaction! The knowledge gave me the impetus I needed. I took a deep breath and shook out my fan, hiding my face behind it in the approved manner.

"Go on." I spoke quickly, trying to convince myself that I

could do this. After all, Danjuro had sent for me, hadn't he? My beautiful Danjuro was waiting for me. Danjuro, who I had waited for in my turn for so long. What would he think if I did not have the courage to go to him? He would never think of me again, simple as that. Big would have won, and Bigger would probably – eventually – kill me.

"Go," I said again. I had no choice, did I? Suzume was shaking her head.

"No," she said firmly. "You are the geisha; you must walk in front of me. I will follow behind you and make sure your kimono does not trail in the mud. I will speak quietly and tell you which direction to turn. Keep your parasol up – it looks as if it may rain, nobody will think it odd – and your fan in front of your face."

I took courage from little Suzume's confidence and took a step. For the first time in the whole of my life, I left the Hidden House. I walked the streets of the Floating World amongst people who had not paid to use me. Amongst strangers. I had to open my eyes very wide to stop myself from crying.

As Suzume had said, the evening was overcast. Not cold, but not warm either. I barely noticed – it could have been raining frogs and I would not have been aware of it. I took my first tottering steps in my wooden geti and waited. Waited for the uproar that I knew would come as soon as the first person noticed my deformities. Waited for the people of the Floating World to crowd around me, to stare at me. Perhaps to spit on my hair, as my first danna had done. To pinch and nip at me, just to see if I was real. Perhaps to back away from me, muttering a prayer in case I was an evil spirit walking amongst them. At the very least, to laugh at and make fun of me. Just as Auntie had always said that they would.

Suddenly, a sense of shock hit me like a wave of cold water. Why, why had Auntie let me venture out now? Why, when she had always guarded me from harm? Did Auntie, as well as Big, hate me? Did she want rid of me? Self-pity mingled with fear to leave me almost fainting. All at once, I felt that I hated Danjuro. This was all his fault. If he had never taken a fancy to me in the first place, I would have been safe. Safe in the Hidden House.

Then the moment passed, and I wanted, desperately, to be safe. But not in the Hidden House. No, rather with Danjuro. With Danjuro, who I was risking so much for.

The streets were crowded. I had never seen, never imagined, so many people together. I kept my head down, my face hidden by my fan. Suzume trotted behind me, quite close. I stared at the cobbles beneath my feet. A few steps further, and I heard Suzume say quietly, "Turn left in five steps." I did as I was told.

The next street seemed even more crowded than the first. My senses reeled from the attack on them. So much noise, voices shouting and laughing, calling out wares and attractions. I could hear animals, somewhere close. A cock crowed and a donkey brayed repeatedly. Nobody seemed to be just speaking, they were all talking at a shout. And the smells, they were even worse. I was fresh from the bath, and my own skin smelled sweet and clean. But some of the bodies around me reeked. They stank of sweat and clothes that had been worn for too long. Some of the smells I did not even try and place, they were just plain dirty. The streets themselves ran with filth so I was forced to hold my parasol in the crook of my arm and hitch up my kimono away from the cobbles. I held my fan closer to my face in an attempt to ward off the stink.

"Left again, now." Suzume's soft voice was almost lost in

the uproar. I turned and found myself almost face to face with a man, himself coming round the corner at a swagger. This was it, then. The abuse, the scorn, was about to begin. If I was very lucky and the gods were with me, I would not suffer physical abuse.

I kept my eyes downcast and stopped dead. I could see from his robes and swords that the man I had bumped into was a samurai. It could hardly have been worse. I braced myself for the slash of one of his two short swords and prayed silently that his aim would be true and the next incarnation would be better than this one. After all, if a samurai was allowed to strike down a peasant simply because he fancied trying the edge of one of his swords, what chance did I have, a deformed woman who had had the temerity to actually jostle the gentleman? It was almost a relief; the worst had happened. Auntie had been right all along.

"Now then." His tone was jocular. *Please, no.* He was going to tease me before he finished me. I stood still, petrified. "What do we have here? Lost your voice, girl?"

I managed what was supposed to be a giggle, but my throat was so dry the sound emerged as a husky sigh. Still no sound of a sword being drawn.

A finger pushed my fan down. I kept my eyes lowered, modestly. The finger ran down my face and inserted itself under my chin, pushing my head up.

"Well, well, well. An exotic little flower, to be sure. What is your name, geisha?"

Geisha? He was actually calling me *geisha?* In spite of all the many times I had assured myself that I was a geisha, I delighted in hearing this strange man say it. My heart began to beat at such a rate I felt sure that it must have sounded like a drum.

"Midori No Me, sir," I managed to whisper.

"Aye?" He thrust his head forward. "Appropriate enough. Well, you're no classic beauty, are you, Midori No Me? But you are different, I'll give you that."

He stood back and surveyed me critically. I leaned against the wall, as unobtrusively as I could. It was either that or collapse in a heap on the cobbles.

"No, sir," I whispered.

He stroked his chin thoughtfully. "Where do you live, Midori No Me?"

I was about to blurt out the name of the Hidden House when little Suzume spoke up. "My mistress lives at the Green Tea House on Willow Road, my lord," she chirped.

"Does she now? And where is your mistress going tonight, little one?" The samurai sounded amused. I was deeply grateful for Suzume's courage in speaking, as I doubted I could have gotten any sensible words out.

"We are going to the Ichimura-za Kabuki Theater, sir. Danjuro has requested my mistress's presence."

I could sense a change in the samurai's attitude. He was still, suddenly, and seemed to stiffen.

"Danjuro?" I nodded. "Aie. You have a very distinguished patron, Midori No Me. Does he own you?"

"No, sir." I had managed to get those two words out before, so I decided to stick to them.

"And you live on Willow Road? Well, Midori No Me, I may well come and visit with you in the future. Would you like that?"

"Yes, sir. Very much." I hoped that the crow's croak that emerged from between my lips sounded throaty rather than terrified. It must have passed muster because the samurai chucked me under my chin and swaggered off. As soon as he had gone, Suzume tugged at my kimono and levered me off the wall, almost pushing me to get me moving.

"Just keep on walking," she hissed.

I did as she instructed, hardly able to believe that I was still alive. After a few moments, a thought occurred to me.

"Why didn't you tell him that I was from the Hidden House? Why did you lie?"

"If I had told him the name of the Hidden House, he would have treated you like a common prostitute," Suzume said quietly. "Even with Danjuro named as your patron, he could easily have made you go with him. He would have thought he could do as he liked with you. In fact, he would have done for sure, because he would have thought you had tricked him and he would have lost face. As it is, he thought you were a free geisha and was interested."

I was bewildered. Auntie had always insisted we *were* geisha. We could all sing and dance, we had all been trained in the arts of a true geisha. We were all very talented. If we were not, Auntie would never have tolerated us for a day. Unlike a geisha in the free world, we were expected to be intimate with our clients, but those clients were very well chosen by Auntie. And everybody knew that geisha took lovers. Hadn't my own mother, who was still spoken of as the most beautiful, most talented geisha of her generation, hadn't she taken a lover? Of course she had, that was how I had come to be born into the Floating World, after she dared to elope with her lover and left the both the Green Tea House and Edo far behind her. I opened my mouth to explain this to innocent little Suzume, but she forestalled me.

"You are *hidden*," she said patiently. "Everybody at the Hidden House is expected to be kept from the world. You are not allowed to walk the streets like normal geisha."

I thought about this for a moment as we walked on.

"But geisha are just as much slaves as we are," I said doubtfully. "Unless they can find a danna to buy them out, they can never expect to pay back their debts. They have no more freedom than we do."

I could feel Suzume's impatience, but I was intrigued. I really could not understand what she meant. Auntie protected us Hidden House geisha for our own well-being. How often had she explained to us that we could not go out, not even into the Floating World, as to do so would sign our own death warrant? She had told us, over and over again, that *normal* people would find us repugnant. That they would revile us, spit on us, probably treat us with less respect than they would an animal. Hadn't Carpi told me that she had been kept in a cage by the burakumin when she was a child? That she had been exhibited, just like some freakish wild beast? That was why our patrons were selected so very carefully. Auntie was careful to allow entrance only those who had a taste for the bizarre, as well as a very well-filled purse.

Yes, we were still geisha. Just...different.

I stopped suddenly, so suddenly that Suzume stumbled into my back.

"Please, Midori No Me," she said. "Please, just carry on walking. If you keep stopping like that, you will attract more attention. And if you do that, Auntie will be angry with me."

I raised my eyes over my fan, and watched the people go past us. For all my ugliness. for all my huge breasts and enormous nose and extreme height and red hair and bizarre eyes. in spite of all my deformities, no one was giving me a second glance. Even the samurai who had bumped into me had been interested rather than repulsed.

I was bewildered.

Why hadn't I been attacked? Had things thrown at me? At the very least been ridiculed by the crowds of people who surged past us? As I glanced around me, a man – walking with what I thought must be his wife, as she wore a very plain kimono and tottered on very high geti, keeping her gaze screwed to the ground beneath an older-woman's wig – glanced at me with obvious interest. In fact, I thought for a second that he was going to walk away from his wife to come across to me. It was only Suzume's soft groan of terror that got me moving again.

I walked on, turning to Suzume's directions. Slowly, my initial terror began to ebb away and was replaced by a curiosity so intense it was almost wonderment. Although I kept my eyes down like any other woman in Edo, I risked a glance around me whenever I thought it was safe.

For years, I had dreamed of what the world looked like outside the Hidden House. When I got the chance, I had, of course, spoken of it to the girls in the Green Tea House who were free to go out into the Floating World. But it was commonplace to them, and nothing they had said could have prepared me for this wonder. The amazement of it all even pushed out my confusion over my own reception, to the extent that I was almost able to forget that I had no real place here, that I was a freak who belonged in the Hidden House.

Didn't I?

It was the people who fascinated me. To begin, there were so many of them. Every inch of roadway seemed to be blocked by bodies. Mainly men, of course, but with a fair sprinkling of women amongst them. A few of the women I decided were wives. They looked even more subservient than I felt myself to be. Some were geisha, dressed in beautiful kimonos and accompanied by one or two maids. In spite of the tottering gait imposed by their kimonos and high geti, these were obviously women who were simply out to enjoy the evening, happy to be alone. The courtesans were dressed more lavishly than the geishas. Their wigs were even bigger and they wore their obi fastened at the back not the front. Their eyes were...restless. One was approached by a man – a middle-aged man, not a peasant, but not very well off either, judging by his clothes. Auntie would never have allowed him into the Hidden House. The woman was beautiful and elegant, but the man immediately put his arm around her and began to feel her breasts. She lowered her eyes and giggled at his attention, and after a second or two of conversation, she walked off with him. I must have stopped to stare because I heard Suzume urging me on.

Then I saw the caged women. The other girls had spoken of these poor women often and always with sympathy, but I had not really understood what they were talking about.

Now I did.

We passed two cages in buildings that were almost next to each other. Both houses looked as if they had seen much better days, but the cages gleamed with gilding and light reflected from inside. I slowed as much as I dared to get a better look.

I was certainly not alone in my interest. The road in front of the houses was thronged with men. Some stood a few feet away from the lattices, as if the women within were monkeys who might attack them if they ventured too close. I could hardly blame them. Auntie had had a monkey as a pet, once. A tiny, sweet-faced animal with a vicious streak as big as its body. It had bitten one of the patrons once and disappeared the same day. Here, other braver souls actually

lounged against the latticework, inspecting the women clustered behind with pursed lips. I thought that they looked
like men who were inspecting a banquet laid out for them,
pausing before they ate to decide which was the tastiest
morsel.

The women behind the bars flirted with their eyes, their
fans, their bodies. They leaned forward and called out. As I
passed, a man in front of one of the cages made his mind up
and went in. I passed by too quickly to see which woman he
had selected.

I was suddenly grateful for Auntie's constant protection.
Our patrons were invariably wealthy men. Men who were
vetted by Auntie and were introduced by an existing patron.
Men who, if they overstepped the unwritten rules and went
too far with the girls, would rapidly be "educated" by the
Boys.

For the Hidden House was our world, and no matter
how high-born or wealthy a patron was, the basic rule was
always the same. The girls were not to be harmed. Or at
least not harmed permanently, or in any way that showed.

These poor girls had nothing, and no one, to look out
for them.

"Midori No Me. Stop. We are here." Suzume's voice
broke in on my wandering thoughts.

We were in front of a huge building, a building that glit-
tered and shined with light like the sun itself. I wondered if
Suzume was mistaken. Had we stopped in front of the
Shogun's palace? Or in front of some wealthy nobleman's
home? But no, this was the theater. People were wandering
in and out of the wide entrance doors, and I watched them
in fascination.

Suzume said something that was lost in the uproar of
conversation, shouted rather than spoken, and I waved my

hand at her in acknowledgment. I barely noticed her disappear. It seemed to me that the whole world was busily engaged in going in and out of the theater. The vast majority were men, but not – as I had naively expected – only wealthy men. The obviously rich literally rubbed shoulders with the very poor, with a good sprinkling of what looked like middle-class men. There were women as well. Some obviously geisha, tottering in tight kimonos and wooden geti. Others were courtesans, both grand and well dressed and some no more than common tarts in cheap cotton robes. Even some perfectly respectable groups of married women, entering in groups of four or five and all giggling happily amongst themselves.

The strange thing about all these women was that it was obvious that they were here to enjoy themselves, not to attract customers or to act as companions to their men. They were simply here as themselves.

Many of them stared at me, but with rising joy I realized that they were not staring because of my outlandish appearance, but simply because I was standing alone. *That,* it appeared, was not done outside the kabuki theater.

I looked around wildly for Suzume and was immensely relieved to see her trotting along with an elderly man following in her brisk wake. When she reached me, she bowed deeply and apologized for taking so long. A couple of women who had been staring at me curiously immediately lost interest and returned to their conversation.

Elation bubbled in my throat. For a moment, I forgot that I was a freak. That I was a slave of the Hidden House, where I would have to return after my moment of freedom. For this evening, I was simply Midori No Me. A lucky geisha who had been invited to the theater by Danjuro, the star of the production.

If it hadn't been so strictly against protocol, I would have loved to have shouted it out loud. Raised my voice above the hub-hub and called Danjuro's name. Brimming and over-flowing with happiness as I was, I was not quite mad enough to do that. In any event, the man with Suzume was bowing deeply to me. Bowing! To me!

"Midori No Me-san. Welcome to the kabuki! Danjuro has reserved a box for you. Please, follow me."

The man turned and I followed, with Suzume behind me. Once inside, I stopped and gasped, lost in this amazing new world. Of all the shocks that I had suffered on this strangest of days, this was perhaps the most amazing. I heard Suzume tut impatiently, and her hand on the small of my back urged me forward relentlessly.

The stage jutted out into the body of the theater like a square tongue. The performance was already well under way, with a group of actors pacing about in the midst of all the theater patrons. All around, spectators were arranged on the ground floor in little boxes. Tiers of enclosed boxes rose on each side of the stage, and it seemed to my dazzled eyes that every single space was taken. As I paused, desperate to drink in every detail of this miraculous place, a roar of laughter rose from a hundred, a thousand throats, male and female alike.

Suzume's companion picked his way between the boxes on the floor, and I followed as best I could. I was sure I would trip over somebody, and was grateful for Suzume's helping hand. It didn't help that I could not take my eyes off the stage for fear of missing a single syllable, a single gesture.

By the time our guide had handed us into our enclosed box, close to the stage and lightly hidden behind a wide cross-lattice of gilded wood, I was enthralled.

The man bowed deeply to me again. "Should you require anything, Midori No Me-san, just ask your maid to get it for you. Danjuro has left instructions that you are to have the best this poor house can offer. Could I recommend the sake? It is the best to be found in the whole of Edo."

I nodded vaguely, and a few moments later a flask of sake already heated in a burner was bought to our box. Suzume poured a cup for me and looked shocked when I told her to pour some for herself. It occurred to me that I had been too nervous to eat anything all day and that I would soon be drunk.

"Do you think we could get something to eat?" I asked hopefully. Suzume nodded and beckoned to a man who was passing below us with a tray full of bowls of noodles. The tray smelled delicious, and I was instantly ravenous.

The man was at our box immediately. Suzume leaned down and gestured for two bowls, calling that we were guests of Danjuro. The heaped bowls, together with chop-sticks, were passed up at once and the man bowed so deeply I thought he was going to lose the rest of his display.

They were fat udon noodles, and I had always thought I did not greatly care for them. On this day, I loved them. I even drank more sake to wash them down.

But I was still fixated on the stage, even more hungry and thirsty for the action beneath us than I was for food and drink. A number of actors were on stage, all wearing heavy makeup and wigs. As I watched, an old woman, bent almost in two, hobbled on to the stage, pushing a younger woman before her. The young woman hid her face behind a fan and giggled. I realized quickly that the crone was trying to sell her daughter to what appeared to be a rich noble. This man's clothes were so opulent that they gleamed in the torchlight. After some prolonged bargaining, the young woman was propelled into her purchaser's arms and her mother left the stage.

Both of the actors who were left burst into song and were then interrupted by a newcomer, a young, vigorous man who began to argue heatedly with the noble, trying to tug the woman from his arms. The audience obviously loved it, as they began to shout and hiss, waving their fists in the air. After a moment or two, I picked up on the plot. The old woman had sold her daughter to the noble, against the younger woman's will, and this handsome young man was her lover, who was trying to take her back and marry her himself. Alas, he had neither money nor family and it seemed obvious that his intentions were doomed.

I watched enthralled, with Suzume leaning over at my side to get a better view.

The only thing that stopped the whole thing from being absolutely perfect was that I could not see Danjuro anywhere. I whispered my disappointment to Suzume.

"I thought he was the star of the theater? Why isn't he here?"

She looked at me strangely and then started to giggle. "Can't you see him?" she asked. I glanced around the theater, wondering how Suzume had picked him out amongst this huge throng when I could not. She giggled again, and pointed at the stage. "There! Look, Danjuro is the young suitor. He was the old mother as well."

"No!" I exclaimed in disbelief. I stared intently at the young man on stage and then caught my breath in disbelief. Now that I knew, I could see it *was* Danjuro beneath the heavy, white makeup. But could he possibly have also been the old woman?

"He'll probably take another part as well," Suzume said confidently.

I spared her a glance. How, exactly, did little Suzume know all this? And come to that, what had happened to the quiet, timid little maid that was Suzume in the Hidden House? I would have a long conversation with her when we got back.

The thought of going back to the Hidden House depressed my spirits for a moment, but such was the exuberance of the kabuki that the sadness was gone in a flash. Yes, I would have to go back. Yes, Bigger would demand I keep my side of the bargain. Yes, there would be other patrons on other nights, but that was then. Tonight, I had walked the streets of the Floating World as my own woman. For the moment, I was watching the kabuki as the honored guest of the great Danjuro. I would live for this moment, this night. And, I hoped with all my heart, for the rest of the night that was to come.

Now that I knew what to look for, I was able to pick Danjuro out quite easily. The production was one that tugged at my heart. It was a tale of two lovers who were parted by circumstances and eventually ran away together. Rather than be parted again, they committed suicide. Just as Suzume had said, Danjuro also played the part of a samurai and then came back as the young lover. When the two lovers committed seppuku together, the whole theater erupted in a roar of approval. It was so realistic, with what looked like blood all over the place, that I was horrified. It was only when the dead lovers got to their feet and made their bows that I was able to breathe again.

Behind me, Suzume breathed a sigh of contentment.

Another production followed, but Danjuro did not appear. After a while, the man who had escorted us to our box appeared. Bowing deeply, he said, "Midori No Me-san, Danjuro has requested you."

I was on my feet in an instant, the play suddenly losing its attraction. Suzume hid a smile and said she would stay where she was, if the theater employee would be kind enough to send for her when she was wanted.

I kept my eyes on the man's back. My head was still full of the wonders of the play, and as much as I wanted to see Danjuro, to thank him for sending for me and to touch him, to have him touch me, I wanted more than anything to tell him how much I had loved the play. How breathtaking it had been.

He was pacing up and down in what I assumed was his dressing room as restless as a caged tiger. He still had his heavy stage makeup on and the robes he had been wearing as the young lover. My mouth dried at the sight of him and my legs began to shake. How could I not have recognized him?

I bowed deeply. He nodded at me, but carried on with his restless movement. I waited, having no idea whether I should speak or remain silent. As he continued to pace, my stomach knotted itself. Had he forgotten me? Was he regretting inviting me here? He stopped abruptly, right in front of me.

"How was it?" he demanded. "Did you enjoy the play?"

His voice was urgent, and I realized with amazement that my opinion actually mattered to him, the great Danjuro. I thought carefully before I answered.

"Danjuro-san. I have never been to the kabuki before." He thrust his face forward, watching my expression intently. "But if I never see it again, I will always remember this as the greatest night of my life."

He began to nod, and I could almost see the tension leaving his body. But he was still overflowing with excitement. He threw his head back and laughed and then reached out, grabbing my shoulders tightly. I felt the buzz coming from his fingers as if I had been stung by a bee. My legs finally gave way and I sank to my knees in front of him.

Even through his robes, I could see clearly the shape of his tree of flesh, so vigorous that I thought it was pulsing with a life of its own. I moaned out loud and reached forward, parting his robes and taking his tree in my hand.

I rubbed it gently back and forward. It was as if Danjuro's excitement had concentrated itself in his stem. As soon as I touched it, he jerked back and forward with his whole body, immediately in rhythm with my movement. Much as I was desperate to feel him inside me, I made myself lean forward and placed my lips around his hood, licking and nibbling softly. I heard him moan out loud and suddenly reveled in the power I held in my hands, in my mouth.

I teased him with my tongue, my lips. First biting very gently, then darting forward to sink my teeth hard into his flesh. With his hood in my mouth, I rubbed his stalk back and forward with my fingers, allowing my hand to meander down to his testicles and slide back to the slit of his delicious bum. He arched against me and I let him slip out of my mouth.

His hips were bucking as he searched for me again. Instead of taking him between my lips, I caught his tree of flesh in my fingers and licked the length of him, coming back to run my tongue around the head of his hood. I could hear – above the pounding of my own blood – him moaning out loud.

Suddenly confident, I leaned back and stood up. His eyes were wide, his face, even beneath his stage makeup, intensely hungry. The white makeup attracted me immensely. It was as if while I was making love to the

Danjuro I knew, I was also making love to a complete stranger. I found the thought deeply arousing even though the irony of it took me aback. How often had I raged when a complete stranger took me? How often had I headed quickly for the bath afterward to try and wash every trace of the man away from my body? And now, I was not just welcoming a man who might as well have been a complete stranger, I was longing for him. Desperate for him.

The strangeness of it made me tremble with excitement. I stood back a step, then another. I tugged at my obi and it came away obediently. Tonight nothing would go wrong. Nothing would come between me and Danjuro and whoever was living in Danjuro's body and mind with him. The under sash followed and I untied my kimono and shrugged out of it. I would have taken off my chemise and under-skirt, but I had no time.

Danjuro lunged for me with a roar of pure lust and bore me to the floor beneath his weight. He fumbled to push my under-skirt aside and I helped him, crumpling the supple silk recklessly. His fingers found my black moss and were then probing inside me. I think I shouted with pleasure, and the sound seemed to make him lose whatever control he still had as he plunged his tree into me with the ease of a sword seeking a familiar scabbard.

This was not the Danjuro I remembered from the Hidden House. That man had been tender, almost hesitant. This Danjuro was hard and strong and demanding. Taking rather than giving. And I reveled in it.

I met his every movement, not bothering to tease or even to try and slow him down, instead raising my own body to meet him as he pounded me. Our movements were perfectly synchronized, perfectly *right* and it was no surprise to me at all when I felt him coming to his climax seconds after I had already come to the bursting of the fruit myself. How could it have been otherwise?

Afterward, Danjuro talked to me. Talked *with* me. And I realized that this great man, this amazing actor who held the whole of Edo in the palm of his hand, was hiding behind his makeup and his costumes. On stage, he was the character he was playing – male or female, young or old. At that moment, in front of an audience roaring its approval, the character was Danjuro. The real Danjuro was a frightened little boy, always worried that even his best was not going to be quite good enough.

He had, he said, been adopted by the Danjuro family, not born into it. Because of that, he always felt that he was not good enough. That no matter how he tried, no matter how much he gave of himself, he would never be quite as great as those who had been born to be Danjuro.

He paused, his head down, and I stared at him in amazement. All the years of subservience, all the carefully instilled manners and instructions were forgotten in a flash. Instead, I was a woman talking to my lover as if we were equals. As if that could ever be!

I shook my head in frustration, searching for the right words. "Danjuro," I blurted. "That is all wrong. Don't you understand? If you had been born into the family, it would not matter whether you were a good actor or not. People would simply assume that you were a great performer because you were Danjuro as of right." He did not raise his head, not by so much as a fraction, but I could see from the tense set of his shoulders that he was listening carefully to me. "But you were adopted. You were *chosen* to be Danjuro because you are the best. If you were not, then somebody else would be in your place. Don't you see that?"

I stopped, suddenly breathless. If this had been a patron

in the Hidden House and I had spoken to him like that, he would have been within his rights to strike me. He would certainly complain to Auntie, and it was entirely likely that she would hand me over to the Boys to be punished. All at once, I realized what I was risking by my daring.

Danjuro – the great Danjuro – had asked for me. For Midori No Me. Green Eyes. Not only asked for me, but taken me out of the Hidden House to share his world. And what was I doing? Talking to him as if I was his equal. I trembled. Lowered my eyes. Waited for him to tell me curtly to get out. Or for him to beat me.

But he did not. I held my breath for what seemed like an age. When Danjuro spoke, he sounded very young. His voice shook.

"Midori No Me-san. Do you really think that? Or are you just trying to reassure me?"

I let my breath go in a long sigh, so relieved I could have cried. "You must know it is true," I said quickly "The crowd loved you. I have never seen anything like it. I didn't even recognize you at first. I really thought that you were an old woman."

Danjuro laughed at my words, a strangely innocent sound. He climbed to his feet, bent his back, and hunched his shoulders. Suddenly he was the old crone again. I gasped, my hand in front of my mouth, and then applauded wildly.

For the next ten minutes, Danjuro gave me a private performance. He made me laugh and cry by turns. My hands were sore from clapping. Eventually, he stopped and shook himself. Abruptly, he was Danjuro again.

He bowed and then leaned toward me, patting my face, my shoulders, my neck very gently with his hands. It was an odd gesture, but very tender. I melted.

"Danjuro," I whispered. "I would do anything, anything at all, to be part of this. Please, is there a place here for me? Make me the smallest, the most insignificant. I will clean for you. Empty the night soil. Anything at all to belong here."

Even as I pleaded, I realized what I had said. Why, I wondered, had I not begged to be with Danjuro rather than asking to be part of his world? He was my lover, wasn't he? I would do anything he asked and love it. Why, suddenly, was I asking to be part of the kabuki rather than part of Danjuro's life?

I bit my lip hard enough to hurt, sure that he would be the one man in a thousand who was sensitive enough to pick up on what I had said. Mentally, I pummeled myself. How could I be so stupid? Why was I choosing to deliberately turn my back on the greatest chance any girl could long for? Stupid, stupid, stupid.

"You feel it too?" He was smiling. I almost fainted with relief. "When I first came to the kabuki, I was a small child. I had come from a village in the north. I had never seen a play or a theater. Not even a town. My parents sold me to a merchant who was in need of somebody with a good memory to keep a tally of the wares he had sold. Even as a child, I could remember everything. My father stood me in front of the merchant and begged the man to recite something to me. Anything, he said, it didn't matter. I would remember it. The merchant laughed at him, but then reeled off a long list of goods, each with its own price. He had a huge grin on his face when he stopped and nodded at me to repeat it. It was easy. I rattled it off without even thinking. The merchant was so impressed, he paid the price my father wanted without haggling and took me off with him then and there."

He paused for so long I became impatient. "But how did

you come to be Danjuro?" I demanded. Oh, dear. There I
was again, showing no respect at all. If Auntie could see me,
I would be dead, or as good as. If Danjuro noticed my rude-
ness, he gave no sign of it.

"The merchant brought me here, to Edo. He taught me
to read and write and he was pleased with me. I worked for
him for two years before he ran into misfortune and had to
sell his business. I was sold with it, and it turned out that
my new patron had an interest in the kabuki. I don't mean
he liked the theater, I mean he owned part of it. Of course,
he came often to make sure his investment was performing
properly, and I came with him. I fell in love with the kabuki
as soon as I first walked through the door. There was a
performance going on, and my master stayed to watch it. By
the time we went home, I had memorized every line that
had been spoken. I was so enchanted I began to perform for
the other servants, taking every part myself. One day, my
master caught me, and rather than beating me as I
expected, he gestured for me to continue. When I had
finished, he demanded to know how I had learned the play.
I told him I had remembered it from when I went to the
theater with him. He didn't believe me, so to punish me, to
make me feel silly and lose face, the next time he went to
the kabuki on business, he took me with him and told me to
get up on the stage with the actors and perform. My master
was an important man, so the actors accepted me." He
paused, his eyes shining. "Midori No Me-san, it was
wonderful. As soon as I began to speak my lines, I felt as if I
belonged here. As if I had found something inside me that I
never dreamed existed. I forgot my master was there, forgot
everything except the play. When we had finished the
scene, I could see that my master was furious. But I was very
lucky. The actors told him that I was good, that I had a

future in the theater. One of them was from the greatest of the theater families, although I didn't know it at the time, and he took my master aside to talk to him and persuaded him that it would be a very good investment in the theater if I was allowed to perform with them, that I could be truly a great actor. I learned afterward that this man was Danjuro Ichikawa, a very great actor. From that day on, I was part of the kabuki. In the beginning, I was not allowed on the stage. I worked on the scenery, fetched things for the actors, helped with their makeup. Ichikawa-san allowed me to perform very small parts eventually, and I knew that this was what I wanted to do. When Ichikawa-san retired, I was adopted into the great family and eventually took on his title." Danjuro stopped and shook his head, as if he could still hardly believe his own good fortune.

I realized I had been holding my breath and exhaled noisily. I understood perfectly. I too would have done anything to be allowed to remain here and become part of this make believe world. After all, I thought bitterly, hadn't I been acting a part the whole of my life?

"You feel it too, don't you?"

I nodded, lost for words. Danjuro took my hand and patted it gently, smiling at me. "You cannot perform on stage, Midori No Me. The stage is only for men."

I smiled, but shouted inside, Why? Why must everything be denied to us women? Why?

"The only places for women in the kabuki are very lowly. Women clean and sell food. They make our costumes. Sometimes, if they are very skilled, they are allowed to help paint the scenery. That is not for you, Midori No Me-chan."

Midori No Me-chan! I noticed the endearment and was thrilled.

"Come. I am very tired." He yawned and stretched, and I wondered if this was Danjuro the man or Danjuro the actor. "I must take a bath and then I need to sleep. It is time you were on your way."

I lowered my head submissively. At the same time, I lingered as long as I dared, hoping against hope for one word to indicate that Danjuro wanted to see me again.

Danjuro was on his feet, waiting courteously for me to rise. I stood rather stiffly. I had sat for too long, amongst much else! Suzume was outside the door, and Danjuro nodded to her pleasantly.

"Take good care of your mistress." I saw the glint of gold pass between them, then Suzume was bowing and bobbing and fussing around me and the screen door was closing, closing Danjuro away from me.

8

Do flowers love the sun when
They raise their heads
To the light?

*S*uzume scurried along behind me. Even hobbled by my kimono, my stride was much longer than hers, so she had problems keeping up. I heard her panting, so I apologized and slowed my pace.

Only hours before, everything had been foreign to me, now everything was fascinating. It was not commonplace exactly, but it had lost its allure. I had seen the kabuki, had spent the evening with the man I already thought of as my lover. I felt that nothing in my life would ever be the same again.

My heart sank at the knowledge that I was heading for imprisonment. In the space of a few short hours, the Hidden House had ceased to be a place of safety, of protection, and had suddenly become a jail. I thought about the other girls and realized with a dawning sense of shock that they had no need of Auntie's vigorous protection either. All of us – except for poor Carpi – could survive in the Floating World. After all, I had walked the streets in safety, hadn't I? Nobody had shrunk from my deformities; nobody had thrown stones at me or spat on me. In fact, the samurai, no doubt a man of wealth and importance, had made an assignation with me. Or at least, he thought he had. Above all, Danjuro had honored me. Danjuro had called me Midori No Me-chan. I raised my eyes from the cobbles and looked at the stars. It seemed to me that I saw them for the first time. And that they shined for me and me alone.

I heard a noise coming from somewhere close. Above the sound of people talking at the top of their voices, animals braying and hooting and chirping, and the inevitable drunk singing, there was something else. I could hear what sounded like tables being overturned, shouting, and even louder laughter. Suzume tugged at my sleeve, trying to pull me toward the wall. She was mouthing something and her face was alarmed, but I could not make out her words over the din. I shook my head, lost in my world of wonder.

A gang of men swaggered around the corner, coming directly toward us. The crowd parted in front of them, but they still shouldered aside an old man and a young woman just for the fun of it. They all wore swords, they were all laughing. To my eyes they were all nothing more than riff-raff. Auntie would never let the likes of them into the Hidden House, I thought.

Suzume gave one last, despairing tug to my sleeve. Catching her urgency, I moved back against the wall. But it was too late. The man leading the gang was already nearly in front of me. I looked at him with interest. And why not?

Everything in the Floating World was fascinating to me. I knew nothing, nobody, and nobody – apart from Danjuro – knew me. I was an unlikely innocent in this bewildering, bewitching world and thought myself invisible.

I soon learned that I was not.

"Oh, now then, boys. What have we got here? Is it a foreign devil, do you think?"

The leader stopped across from us and was now leering at me. He was quite ugly. He was tall, a good deal taller than I was, and broadly built. Even through the lines of his expensive robe, I could see that he was very muscular, unlike my lovely, slender Danjuro. And his face! I glared at him. *He* had the cheek to call *me* a foreign devil? Although his hair was jet black and straight, and his skin the color of very weak tea, his features were pronounced. His nose jutted fiercely, and his lips were very full. His cheek bones were even higher than mine and his eyes were grey, not black.

Suzume moaned softly. I glanced at her and was surprised to see that her face had gone the color of tofu. A sense of unease began to rise up my body. I had been so buoyed by the lack of reaction to me on this amazing day that I had become almost confident. But Suzume knew far more about this world than I did, and if she was concerned, then probably I should be as well. I was so elated by the time I had spent at the kabuki with Danjuro, I felt that at this moment I was invincible. Surely, no god could wish me harm, today of all days? I squared my shoulders and stared back at the gang leader.

"And who are you to go calling other people foreign devils?" I demanded. "Looked in the mirror recently, have you?"

Suzume stuffed her hand in her mouth and wailed with

terror. Suddenly aware that the whole street around us had gone quiet, I began to shudder. Perhaps I wasn't quite as invincible as I thought. But I had already gone too far to back away. I lifted my chin and looked the gang leader full in the face.

The hush in the street around us was so intense it could have been sliced and served like rice cake. The man's eyes bulged and I began to whisper a silent prayer for me and for Suzume, who had done nothing. I saw his hand fall to the hilt of his sword and noticed in an odd moment of total clarity that the little finger on that hand had been chopped in half. *Typical*, I thought irrelevantly. Peasant and noble alike were supposed to leave their weapons at the gate before they entered the Floating World. But first the samurai and now this ruffian were fully armed. The gods had obviously decided that I had used my full quota of luck today. Oh well. If I was going to die, then at least I would die having tasted very great happiness.

"On your knees, geisha," the man hissed.

I thought about it. I really did. I was looking death quite literally in the face, and my thoughts were ordered and clear and unflinching. I decided that if tonight was the choice of the gods for my death, then I would not die on my knees. I, who had never had any choice in my life, would have a choice in the manner of my death.

"No," I said quite simply. "If you are going to kill me, then get on with it. But I am not going to kneel in this filthy street and spoil my kimono."

"It will get soiled when it gets your blood all over it," the man snarled. I was reminded of the wicked character in Danjuro's play, the one who scowled all the time and strutted about the stage as though he owned it. The likeness was so appropriate that I felt laughter building up in my throat. That man had been nothing but a bully, his character greatly exaggerated so the audience knew he was the villain. They also knew that he would not triumph, but would eventually get his comeuppance and be exposed for the blustering fool he really was.

"I shall be dead by then, so I will not care greatly," I said crisply, trying desperately not to laugh, though by this time there really was an edge of hysteria to my words. I hoped beyond hope that Suzume would be spared, and that she would get word of my tragedy to Danjuro. Perhaps, if I was very lucky indeed, he might be so moved that he would commission a play about my terrible end.

I watched as the gang leader started to draw his sword, and then hesitated. I would not look away, I decided. I would see the blow coming. I lifted my chin.

Without warning, he slammed the sword back into the scabbard and let loose with a great bellow of laughter. All those around us joined in sycophantically, though I was fairly certain that some of the street people were disappointed at being cheated of their spectacle.

I continued to stare at him. He leaned forward so that the end of his nose touched mine. His eyes, so close, were very strange. The irises were light grey, but the pupils were huge and the deepest black I had ever seen. His eyelashes were so long and thick they seemed almost feminine.

For a long moment, grey eyes met green eyes.

"Well, now. As one foreign devil to another, what do I call you, geisha?" He was laughing at me. Although not one feature in his face moved, he was laughing at me.

"My name is Midori No Me," I said with as much dignity as I could manage. Abruptly, my treacherous bladder was threatening to betray me and I desperately needed to pass water.

"Suits you." He grinned and stepped back. "My own name, alas, does me no such justice. I am Yoshida Akira. If I wanted to pay my humble respects to Midori No Me-san, where would I find her?"

I sucked in air through my nose. It turned out I wasn't due to die, after all! Truly, a miraculous day.

"If Akira-san wished to find me, then he need only come to the Green Tea House on Willow Road. Of course, he would first need to make an appointment, but I am sure that for a man of Akira-san's position, that would not prove to be a problem."

His lips writhed as if he was trying to control either laughter or anger.

I watched him with interest rather than fear. Today, it seemed I was the pet of the gods and not even this strutting cockerel was going to harm me.

"I think that it is time my little bird got herself back to her nest," he said.

Yes, he was definitely trying not to laugh. He stood a little to one side, and I bowed my head graciously as I moved away from the wall and passed him. I heard him whisper something to one of his gang, and I am sure that the man followed us all the way back to the Hidden House.

Suzume followed me into my room and began to prepare tea for me. I noticed her hands were shaking. Had that posturing gangster really upset her so much? She spoke very quietly as she waited for the water to boil.

"You were lucky, mistress. Akira-san could have struck you down in the street and walked away without punishment. He must have taken a fancy to you."

"That ruffian?" I smiled, thinking she was exaggerating. Suzume glanced up from the tea tray and I frowned. My little maid looked terrified. It was so unlike her, I began to worry myself. "Who is he, anyway?"

"Akira-san is the leader of the Ishikawa-ikka yakuza." I bit my lip. Even in the Hidden House, we knew about the yakuza gangs. Criminals who wielded immense power and were feared throughout Edo. This particular gang was said to be the most terrible of them all. And I, a mere girl, had defied its leader, caused him to lose face in public. Just as well I was unlikely to see him again.

I took the tea cup from her and sipped the contents. I decided that I didn't care. In the space of a few hours, I had tasted glamor and love. Had hovered between life and death itself. In fact, I had taken part in my very own kabuki performance.

How could some low-life gangster compete with that?

9

When the snow leaves the
Ground, does the
Earth remember its kiss?

had a visit from Bigger very early the next morning. I was barely awake when he barged in, prowling around my room and tickling Nekko with his toe. The kitten spat and tried to bite his foot. I lowered my gaze and tried not to look happy. After all, no one was entitled to more than one day of immortality, and back in the real world of the Hidden House, I had no desire to annoy Bigger.

I had dreamed, but I could barely remember what of. Danjuro's face mingled with the samurai who had stopped me in the street. Then the rough man's features appeared suddenly, coated with the white makeup of the kabuki. Only his grey eyes blazed at me. Was he laughing or lusting? I had no idea. At one point, I seemed to be on stage in the theater, acting out the part of a young man. Strangely, that was the one bit of my dream that I could remember clearly. If only! Even though Danjuro had made it brutally clear that I could never be a kabuki actor, it was the one thing above all that I wanted. Even above Danjuro himself? At that moment, I just didn't know. Later in the day, when my brain had woken up a little, I would have poured scorn on the idea. Me? A woman? On stage at the kabuki? What nonsense! What a crazy thing to even dream about! Of course it was Danjuro, my talented, wonderful Danjuro, that I wanted.

Bigger mooching about my room put all my skittering thoughts in order. I took a deep breath and ordered myself to concentrate.

"Well? How was it?" Bigger demanded. I bit back a suicidal desire to blurt "wonderful!" and lowered my eyes to the floor modestly.

"I think Danjuro was happy with me," I said.

"Did he mention Big?"

I didn't even need to think about it. The answer was no, and I said so firmly.

"You're sure?" Big used his foot to poke me.

I nodded. "Quite sure. I watched him perform in the kabuki, and afterward he took me. All he wanted to talk about was the play and his part in it."

Bigger grunted. I kept my eyes down, willing him to go. Eventually, I thought he was going to leave, but instead he squatted down in front of me, his eyes level with mine.

"Did he say he wanted to see you again?"

"No…no. But I'm sure he will. He called me Midori No Me-chan!" I said desperately.

Bigger stared at me, hard, as if his gaze could penetrate my mind. I looked back at him unflinchingly. I was not going to lie. If I did, I felt certain that Bigger would see through the lie and punish me for it.

"We'll see. I'll find out soon enough from Auntie if he wants you again. If he does – *when* he does – remember, I want to hear about it. Immediately."

Before I could even say yes, Bigger stood up and left. It seemed to me that the very screen walls breathed a sigh of relief as he went out. I wanted to summon Suzume and ask her how she knew so much about the Floating World. About the kabuki. It was a mystery to me how the shy, biddable little maid that existed in the Hidden House could be transformed into such a confident, talkative creature as soon as she was free of this place. It was as if my Suzume's body had been taken over by somebody else entirely, one of the mischievous spirits from a fairy tale perhaps. And how did she come to know so much about the kabuki? It suddenly occurred to me that when she had left me at the entrance, she had darted off to find our guide without a second thought, as if she knew exactly where she was going. And then, when we were back in our own courtyard, the new Suzume was gone in a flash, and the quiet, timid little maid was back in her place. Before I could shout for Suzume, there was a soft rap on the door frame, which startled me to no end. Who in the Hidden House ever bothered to knock on a door before they entered? Particularly my door? I called out "come in" in some confusion, and all of the girls piled through. Kiku first, her spaniel at her heels, with Carpi behind her. Tiny Masaki sandwiched between Carpi and Naruko.

I stared at them in surprise, which deepened into something very like horror as I glanced at Carpi. I had been so wrapped up in the surprising turn of events that were taking place in my own life that I had not really *looked* at

Carpi for many weeks. I was vaguely aware that she had lost weight recently. In fact, I had meant to talk to her about it, but it seemed that Carpi was keeping to herself much more these days, and I had never dared to intrude into her room without being invited. Now, I saw that she had not just lost weight; rather, it appeared that she was fading away to nothing. Never fat at the best of times, now she was as thin as a reed, and just like a reed it seemed to me that the slightest puff of breeze would bend her in two. She seemed to move without any of her old, vigorous grace, almost as if she was a tired old woman rather than a young and vigorous one.

But Kiku was talking to me, so I tore my gaze away from Carpi.

"Go on, then. Tell us. What happened? What was it like? Did you really go to the kabuki? What was Danjuro like? What play was it?"

In spite of my worries over Carpi, I was forced to laugh. All of the girls were talking at once, echoing Kiku's questions.

"Curiosity killed the cat," I said smugly.

"That's not at all it will kill if you don't tell!" Kiku tried to snap, but her face was alight with genuine interest. "Shut up, all of you. Let Midori No Me tell it in her own fashion."

I stared at the ring of avid faces surrounding me and blinked. Where did they want me to start?

"At the beginning, of course. As soon as you stepped out of the door."

That was Carpi, back to her old, acerbic self. Thank the gods.

So I started at the beginning, and told them everything. Or at least, almost everything. For some reason, I omitted the rough, villainous man who had accosted me on the way home. He didn't matter, anyway. Perhaps that was why I left him out.

The girls were an excellent audience. They oohed and aahed when I told them about the samurai and were greedy for details of the performance. What was the theater like? I had had a private box, all to myself. Near the stage? No! I only had to mention Danjuro's name, and food and drink appeared. Anything I wanted? I hardly liked to disillusion them by adding that I was too nervous to eat anything except a bowl of noodles. And – with many a sly glance between them – how had Danjuro's performance been? Afterward, as well as in the kabuki!

I talked myself hoarse. Finally, the girls were satisfied and sat back, looking at me as if I was an exotic creature who had wandered into their midst unnoticed. I decided to take my chance and ask the question that had been bothering me from the moment I had stepped outside the Hidden House and taken my first steps into the Floating World.

"Kiku, there's something I don't understand."

Kiku sipped at the green tea Suzume had bought unbidden and waved her hand in a grand gesture. "Ask," she said benignly.

"I don't understand why everything was all right. I don't mean with Danjuro. I mean outside the Hidden House."

The girls exchanged glances and then looked at me, obviously puzzled. Kiku raised her eyebrows and shrugged.

"Why shouldn't it be alright? You walked modestly, didn't you? Kept your head down? Made sure Suzume was behind you?"

"Yes, of course I did. But Auntie always told me I was so deformed that if I went outside, the people would spit on me to avoid bad luck. That I would probably have things thrown at me. At the very least, they would all jeer and laugh at me. But they didn't. The honorable samurai was even interested in me. And I know I was in a box at the kabuki, but nobody paid any attention to me there. Auntie has always said that the Hidden House was the only place where I would be safe. That not even the Floating World would ever be safe for me. For any of us."

I looked hopefully from face to face. At first, their faces were expressionless, then a strange uneasiness began to appear on all of them. More and more puzzled, I stared fiercely at Kiku.

"Kiku, why wasn't it like Auntie said it would be?"

Kiku licked her lips and looked around at the other girls. Obviously having elected her spokeswoman, they all nodded encouragement, but remained silent.

"You were born here, weren't you?" I nodded, perplexed. What did that have to do with it? "The rest of us started life out there, Midori. We've got a bit of an advantage over you. Auntie tells us all the same thing. That we are safe here. That the Floating World is no place for us. That the people out there would treat us as freaks. But the difference is, we know Auntie isn't exactly telling the whole truth."

She paused and the girls nodded. I shook my head, even more bewildered now than I was before she had spoken. Kiku rolled her eyes in desperation and Carpi took over.

"Auntie needs to keep us here," she said bluntly. "She says these things to make us frightened. To make us depend on her. She can't see that we *want* to be here. That life inside the Hidden House is far easier, much more pleasant than it ever was for us outside. So she tells us all fairy tales about how bad it is out there. The only problem is, she doesn't realize that *we know*. We just let her tell her horror stories to humor her."

I was shocked. Auntie, the one stable person in my entire life, the only mother I had ever really known, had told me lies? I shook my head.

"Carpi, that can't be right. You told me yourself how you were locked up in a cage and exhibited for small change. Wouldn't the same thing happen to you if you went out now?"

Carpi bit her lip and waggled her hands. The forlorn little gesture broke the tension and we all laughed, more from relief than humor.

"I don't think it would. It's difficult to explain, but you have to remember I was put on show in tiny, out of the way villages. Half of them thought the burakumin were devils anyway, so I was just a little extra tidbit. Let's face it, if you put a monkey in a cage, people stop and stare just because it's behind bars. You saw how the men clustered around the whores behind the bars, didn't you? Saw how they stared at them?"

"Well, yes. But that's not the same thing, is it?"

The ring of faces around me nodded. Naruko leaned forward and spoke hesitatingly, her odd Japanese strangely charming.

"Midori-chan. Where I was born in China, a strange woman lived in one of the local villages. She had two heads. She did!" Naruko insisted, even though nobody was disagreeing with her. "She was born like that. Two heads, two bodies, four legs, but they both sort of joined together from her breasts to her hips. She had four arms as well, but two of them were always kept behind her back. She always said that she wasn't one person, she was two. She said the other one was her sister. But the other one never spoke. It was all most odd. But anyway, this woman actually married. Two brothers in the village married her, or them, however you want to think about it. And she, *they*, had babies. They both did, a couple of weeks apart. The babies were perfectly normal babies. Big strong boy children they were." Naruko nodded vigorously. "But the thing is, nobody thought twice about her – about them – after a while. Strangers marveled at her, but nobody in the village cared. I think that's the same with us. We might not be quite like everybody else, but in the Floating World, I don't think anybody would greatly care."

"They care enough to part with good money for us," Carpi said bluntly. "And that's the only thing that matters. Look, Midori. If I were you, I wouldn't believe everything Auntie tells you. We're all safe here, we're well looked after. That's the main thing. If your Danjuro wants to take you out of this place, then all well and good. If he doesn't, eventually somebody else will."

Her voice was oddly bitter, at odds with what she was saying. But all the other girls were nodding and smiling, so I decided it was me who was just imagining the bitterness. I was still deeply shocked to think that Auntie had lied to me all these years.

It was Kiku, as usual, who had the common sense to finish the discussion.

"Auntie's probably trying to protect you from the same fate as your mother," she said quietly. "After all, none of us have heard a word about her since she left the Floating World. I don't want to upset you, Midori, but if you think the Floating World is bad, what must it be like outside? Outside Edo itself? In another country, even?"

We all fell silent, considering her words, and I shuddered. She was right, of course. Japan had been sealed away from the outside world for many hundreds of years. We knew little about the foreign Barbarians, and what we did know was brutal. They were not like us. They were not just foreign, but strange in ways we could not begin to comprehend. Everything about them was strange; their languages were barbaric, their morals even worse. Not for the first time, I wondered what could have convinced my beautiful, talented mother to run away with one of those monsters. I would never know, I supposed. Only Auntie and the Boys had been here when I was born, and they never spoke about my mother's flight from the Green Tea House. Not even Big, who would torment me in any way he possibly could, ever referred to my mother.

Suddenly, I felt very glad for the girls who were ringed around me. They – and Auntie, despite her well-meaning fibs – were my family. I felt a rush of gratitude for them all and smiled my thanks.

Obviously relieved to be at the end of the serious discussion, the girls stretched and yawned and got to their feet. Carpi stood up with her usual athletic grace and Kiku was pulled up by Naruko in front and a push from the back by tiny Masaki. They filed out, grumbling good-naturedly that nothing of any interest ever happened to them. Some people, Masaki said, were unduly favored by the gods.

In the doorway, Kiku paused for a final word. She spoke very quietly, for my ears alone.

"It's not so bad here, Midori. Not so bad at all. We have Auntie and the Boys to protect us. We are well fed and warm. All of the geisha and courtesans in the whole of the Floating World are no better off than we are, remember that. We are all slaves. But at least our cage is made of silk."

She smiled, clicked her fingers at her spaniel, and glided away silently with her usual grace.

I waited until the girls' voices died away before I clapped my hands for Suzume. If today was the time for curiosity to be satisfied, then let Suzume explain to me what had happened to her the moment she had stepped outside the Hidden House.

She came at her usual trot, a tray with a charcoal burner, teapot, and a cup in her hands. She placed it in front of me and kneeled, her head bowed. Once again, I was baffled by the change in her. Was this really the girl who had led me through the maze of the Floating World so deftly? So very confidently?

"Suzume, stop it."

She kept her head bowed, but wound her hands around each other in a humble gesture. I was having none of it. I wanted to know which Suzume – if either of them – was the real one.

"Suzume, you were not at all meek yesterday when we were outside. Tell me about yourself. How you came to be here." I saw she was peeking at me from beneath her eyelashes and I realized that she was actually a very pretty girl. It was not that I had simply not noticed, rather she was normally so self-effacing that she simply escaped attention. Was she trying not to laugh? I rather thought she was.

"I'm sorry, Midori No Me-san. Did I do wrong yesterday?"

"You know you didn't. I wouldn't even have found my way to the kabuki theater without you." I saw her eyes light up at mention of the kabuki and seized my chance. "You've been to the kabuki before, haven't you?"

"I worked there, when I was a child," she said simply. I stared at her in surprise and, *yes*, jealousy. Suzume had actually worked in the wonderful kabuki? It was as if mere thought of the theater had unlocked a hidden place deep within her and she began to speak without further prompting.

I poured myself a cup of green tea. Suzume should have done it for me, but I was reluctant to interrupt her flow of words. The more she spoke, the more fascinated I became. Truly, I thought, Kiku had been right when she had said that there were worse places than the Hidden House.

"I was born in the Floating World." Suzume sat back on her haunches and spoke to the corner of the room, somewhere behind my left shoulder. "My father was a calligrapher, one of the best in the whole of Edo. His handwriting was very beautiful, and he always had more work than he could manage. People paid him very well to write letters for them, to compose scrolls. Even the nobles came to him, he was so well known.

"I was the third daughter born to him and my mother. He had no sons, which of course was a great sorrow to both of them. Father would have been within his rights to put mother away for her inability to bear him sons, but he would never consider it. He said he had known Mother was the only one for him the moment he had seen her, and if it was her karma not to have sons, then it was his as well."

I must have gasped in surprise at that because Suzume nodded her head vigorously.

"He was a good man when I was very small. He did not even take a mistress. Mother told him that he should, of course, and then if his mistress had a son by him, the boy could be adopted into the family. But he would not hear of it. As I grew, my father's hands began to bend. He started to get much pain in his fingers, and eventually his hands became so clawed that his handwriting began to suffer. He visited the doctor, of course, and he prescribed bitter herbs and barks for Father, both to rub into his hands and to drink. But it did no good. Day by day, his hands became more and more useless. His clients began to look elsewhere and our income diminished. We were not poor exactly, because Mother had always been very careful, so we had some savings put aside.

"But as he began to lose his skill, it seemed that Father also began to change. He started to berate Mother, telling her that it was she who had bought bad luck on the family. He beat her as well. He beat us girls, too. I think it was the shouting and taunting that upset Mother more than the beating. After all, wives must expect to be beaten at least occasionally. Eventually, it all became too much for Mother and she committed suicide by jumping into the river. She had bound her legs together first, to make sure she could not try and swim and to keep her body tidy when it was found. She left a note for Father, apologizing for being a bad wife to him and bringing bad luck on the whole family. She urged him to take another wife, saying it was not yet too late for him to have sons."

Suzume straightened her back and fell silent for a moment. I wanted to urge her to carry on, but then saw she had tears in her eyes, so I waited. Now that she had started, she would tell her tale in her own good time. Besides, if I spoke, she might realize she was speaking to me as to an equal again and stop. I was intensely curious to hear the rest of her story.

"We all thought Father would take another wife or a mistress. But he did not. Talking about it between ourselves, we decided that Mother's death had been the breaking of the final branch that had supported Father. It was only with her death that he remembered how much he had once loved her. So instead of bringing in a woman from outside, he took my eldest sister to his bed as his wife.

"She was proud to be chosen, of course, and did her best. But she was not Mother, even though she looked very much like her. Father kept on being angry with us all, nothing we did was right. He had taught us all to read and write, and before Mother died he had even said that if I had been a boy, I could have followed him in the family business, my calligraphy was so good. But I was only a girl, so there was no chance of that happening. I tried to help, and for a while it seemed as if everything was going to be all right. Father instructed me on how to write in the same style as him, and he began to pass my efforts off as his own. Some of his old patrons began to come back to him, and we were prosperous again.

"Everything finally went wrong when my sister became pregnant. She lost the child when she was almost eight months pregnant, and died herself of a fever soon after. It was a boy child, and that seemed to be the end for Father. He ranted and raved and screamed. Said it was all us women about the house that had bought bad luck on him. That it was all our fault he could have no sons. Eventually, he said that we had cursed him. We were terrified, frightened for our lives. My sister and I tried to run and hide, but he found us and beat us until we could hardly stand."

Suzume fell silent again, and it was no good, I had to ask.

"Carpi says you can't feel pain. Is that true? Did it hurt when your father beat you?"

She looked at me curiously and then shrugged. Her face was bewildered.

"My sister cried when Father beat us." She frowned. "I asked her why she was crying, and she said she was crying because she hurt. I didn't understand what she meant. I found it difficult to walk, as my legs seemed not to want to straighten where Father had taken a stick to my knees, but that was all. I asked her again, 'Why are you crying?' and she held her arms out to me. They were black and green with bruises, but I had the same colors on my arms and back and legs, so I thought she was upset because her skin had been disfigured. 'Don't worry,' I said, 'they will fade.' 'I know!' she whimpered. 'But I *hurt*.'

"I still didn't understand what she meant. I remembered when I had broken my wrist years before, and the doctor had said what a brave little girl I was when I didn't cry. But why should I have cried? Why was my sister crying now?"

Suzume looked at me in puzzlement, and I took a deep breath. "It's true, then. You really don't feel pain. Carpi was right."

"I don't know." Suzume frowned. "I don't know what pain is. Is it bad? If it is, why would I want to feel it?"

I blew out my cheeks, bewildered. "You must at least know what it is!" I said firmly. "How did you feel when you broke your wrist?"

Suzume thought for a long time, and then said, "My arm felt very odd. I couldn't make my hand move like it should, and the bone stuck out of my skin. Is that what pain means?"

I stared at her, lost for words, and shook my head. Seeing my confusion, Suzume leaned forward and inspected my face, sucking at her bottom lip. Finally, she said, "If I had been born blind, how would you describe colors to me?"

She was right, of course. I wouldn't be able to. So it was true. Little Suzume could not feel pain. I felt a sudden spasm of compassion for her. It might appear that she would do very well in the Hidden House, but knowing what some of our patrons were capable of, I feared for her. Sometimes a very loud scream was the only thing that could stop them. How would Suzume ever know when the time to scream had come?

We both fell silent for a moment, lost in our thoughts. Then I realized I still did not know how Suzume had known the Floating World so well, so I asked her to continue. "What happened to you, Suzume? How did you end up here?"

"We both – my remaining sister and I – thought that Father would take her next, in place of our mother and dead sister. But it didn't happen that way. Father began to drink, very heavily, and he was rude to the customers we had left. Well, nobody was going to stand for that, so it wasn't long before he had used up all the money I had made and nearly all his savings as well. I remember the day he sold my sister very well.

"He had been sober for a couple of days, and then one afternoon he disappeared and came back with an old woman. She inspected both of us – me and my sister – and then went off and talked to Father for some time. When he came back in, he told my sister that she was to go with the old woman. I found out later – when I saw my sister behind the lattice of one of the brothels on the main street of the Floating World – that he had sold her for a whore.

"After my sister went, Father was drunk for a week solid. When he sobered up a bit, he started looking at me in a strange way, and I realized he intended for me to take Mother's place. I suppose I should have stayed and did my duty by him, but some demon got into me and the more I thought about it the more I decided I didn't want to end up like my poor eldest sister. So I ran away."

I gasped. Suzume, little more than a child, and a girl child at that, had run away? Questions boiled in my mouth. Where did she go? How did she survive? Why didn't she starve to death or end up in a brothel herself? Guessing my questions, Suzume continued.

"You have to remember, I was born and brought up in the Floating World. I had run errands for Father ever since I could walk. I knew my way about well enough. I had no money, but I found a place to shelter near the kabuki. For the first few days, I begged. That gave me enough to buy noodles and water. Then somebody left the door open at the back of the kabuki, and I slipped in. At first, I just wanted to get warm. But then I saw the actors rehearsing, and I fell in love with it. The color, the sound, just the whole *life* of the thing. It was wonderful."

I nodded vigorously, understanding perfectly. I had felt just the same.

"Well, there were plenty of places for a small child to hide in the kabuki. I hid there for days, pilfering from the kitchens when I could, begging outside when I couldn't. Of course, somebody caught me in the end, but I burst into tears and sank to my knees, imploring them to let me stay. I could help, I said. I could wash and clean. Repair the costumes. Cook. Help write the playbills. The man who had found me – I later discovered that he was an official of the theater, an assistant to the manager – laughed when I said that I could read and write. But I insisted that I could, and as a joke he gave me a playbill advertising the latest production and told me to copy it out. I can remember the play clearly; it was *Kanadehon Chushingura – The Revenge of the Forty-Seven Ronin*. I copied it in my very best calligraphy, and the man was astonished. He dragged me off to see his boss, and he in his turn told me to copy a playbill out. I did so, and the two men looked at each other. 'Well, Mineko,' he said. Mineko was my name then, you understand. 'It seems you are not telling lies.' Both men looked at me for so long that I became uncomfortable. 'Where is your family?' I took a deep breath and lied. 'My mother is dead, lords,' I said. 'She committed suicide last year. My father died of a fever not long ago, along with my sister. I am all alone in the world.' The manager had very long earlobes, which he was in the habit of stroking when he was thoughtful. He did so then. 'Well, if you have nowhere else to go to, it seems to me that you could be useful to us here.' He raised his eyebrows at the under-manager, who nodded vigorously. 'In return for as much calligraphy as we need from you, I will allow you to live here, and be fed from the theater kitchens. What do you say to that?'

"I fell to my knees and kissed the hem of his robe. I felt as if all my dreams had come true. I was given a cubby-hole to sleep in and allowed to eat and drink in the kitchen whenever I wanted to. I was happy to copy playbills for them, and after a while I was even allowed to make alterations to the scripts for new plays, as the actors often wanted changes made after the first rehearsals. And whenever I had a moment to spare, I would watch the kabuki. I loved every moment of the plays, no matter whether it was a tragedy or a comedy. I had a very good memory, and often when I was on my own I would act out one of the plays in my little private space."

For the first time, Suzume – or, as I supposed I should now call her, Mineko – looked uncomfortable. I realized that she thought I would laugh at her for doing something as silly as that, but I understood perfectly. I had run through the words of the play I had seen a hundred times in my own mind, but each time, it was me who was on the stage, me who was taking the bows and pleasing the crowd. I nodded.

"Yes," I said. "I know. I understand how you feel. Oh,

Mineko. If only we had been born men. What could we have done!"

We both sighed at the thought.

"You must have seen Danjuro perform?" I asked.

Mineko nodded. "Many times. He didn't notice me, of course. In fact, I always doubted that Danjuro saw anything at all beyond the theater. The other actors often spoke of him. They said he was so dedicated, if somebody didn't make sure that he ate, he would have starved to death because he would forget anything that didn't concern the kabuki."

I glowed with pride. This wonderful actor, this dedicated man, had noticed me, the ugly half-barbarian Midori No Me! He had been interested enough to send for me to watch him perform. I sighed happily.

"I saw Big, as well," Mineko said quietly. I stared at her and put my finger to my lips in warning. She nodded and spoke very softly. "He would often watch the performances and then go backstage to see Danjuro. Sometimes, he would persuade Danjuro to go out to a tea house with him or somewhere to drink sake. Big always pretended he was mad about the kabuki, but I think he lied. He was only interested in Danjuro. I think he was in love with Danjuro from the start."

"And Danjuro?" I whispered urgently. "How did he feel about Big?"

Mineko shrugged. "I think he was vaguely flattered that this handsome man was so besotted by him. But I also think that as soon as Big walked out the door, he forgot he even existed. Did you know that it was Big who introduced Danjuro to the Hidden House?"

I stared at her in astonishment, shaking my head.

"It was. I was nearby when Big tried to be friendly with Danjuro after a new performance. Danjuro had been playing both of the main female roles, and he felt his performances were not as realistic as he would like, which upset him. Big tried to coax him out of his mood, but nothing worked. Eventually, I heard Big say to him that he needed to mingle with some real women, women who had known true sorrow in their lives, to get inspiration, and that he would take him somewhere that would interest him. I heard the name of the Hidden House spoken, but then I was chased out."

She frowned and I was nearly frantic with curiosity. "Go on," I urged. "Finish your tale. How did you go from the kabuki to here?"

"It was my father." Mineko's mouth turned down at the corners. "I heard that he was very ill, on the verge of death, and was calling for me. So, like a fool, I felt I had to go home, to see him before he died. There was nothing wrong with him, apart from the fact that he had no money to buy sake and was in a foul mood. As soon as I got home, he grabbed me and locked me in a cupboard. Next thing I knew, Auntie was opening the door and Father was urging her to pinch me, hard as she liked. She did, and then followed it up with a hefty whack from her cane. I just stared at her, and she laughed. She turned to my father, looking pleased. 'It seems that you are right,' she said. 'She does not feel pain. How old is she?' 'Twelve, mistress. She can read and write, as well.' 'No good to me. Can she play an instrument?' Father shook his head reluctantly, but then brightened. 'She has a good voice, though. And she can dance. Show the lady, Mineko.'

"I crawled out of the cupboard and did as I was told. I danced a few steps and sang the chorus from one of the kabuki plays. Auntie grinned and said I would do. She asked if I was whole, and Father said that I was.

"And that was that. She took me by the arm and bought me here to the Hidden House. She said I would work as a maid at first, and then – when I had learned a little of the ways of the House – I could become a geisha, like the rest of the girls."

Did Mineko know exactly what that meant? She stared at me scornfully. Of course she did.

"I will learn to sing and dance like a geisha should. I will flirt behind my fan and make the patrons feel witty and handsome. And when I have had my mizuage, I will learn to pant and moan when they put their tree of flesh into me as though they are breaking me in two with their wilting sapling."

I was torn between amusement and annoyance. No matter what Mineko had gone through, she had no right to talk to me like this, as though we were equals. But suddenly, Mineko was Suzume again, her gaze on the floor.

"When it is time for my mizuage, will you be my Older Sister, Midori-chan?" She spoke humbly. I smiled, knowing then that I would never be able to stay angry with Mineko for long.

"Of course I will," I said. "Of course I will."

10

Clouds blow across the sky.
Stars smile at them.
But what of me?

It had been six weeks since Danjuro had sent for me. I was beside myself with anxiety. From one minute to the next, I veered from being sure that he had forgotten all about me to being equally sure that something terrible had happened to him. Perhaps he had moved to another kabuki theater far away. It didn't help at all that Bigger kept up his visits and was beginning to drop strong hints that I hadn't done enough to entice Danjuro, to keep him by my side and away from Big. Between my own worries about Danjuro and Bigger's implicit threats, I began to get headaches and stop eating.

Mineko was only somewhat reassuring. In all the time she had spent at the kabuki, she said, she had never known Danjuro take more than a passing interest in a woman. He was always too devoted to the theater to really notice them. And he had never – and she would certainly have heard should it have been so, for there was nothing worse than the kabuki for gossip – sent for a woman to come to the theater. I shouldn't worry, she said. He would be back. Once he could drag his attention away from the play, he would send for me.

Oh, how I hoped she was right!

As it was, I had no option but to carry on as if nothing was wrong in my life. I knew the other girls were snickering and nudging each other behind my back. There were even some barbed comments made to my face about Danjuro's absence, but I just smiled and shrugged, as if it was nothing. "Well," I said, "Spilled water cannot return to the tray, as the saying has it." I even managed to laugh. The girls laughed with me, and no more was said.

We all had our dreams, after all, even if we knew they were never going to come true.

I had spent the evening with one of my favorite patrons. That was outstanding in itself, as truly I had very few favorites. But this patron was very nice, causing the other girls to be envious. He was a middle-aged goldsmith who had come to the Hidden House a few months before. He was not handsome exactly, but he had a very pleasant face and his body had not run to fat like most of the patrons. His sponsor was a loud braggart, a nobleman who spent a lot of money but was not liked by any of us. If we did not please him completely to his liking, this man was very handy with his fists and had once given poor Naruko a black eye. Auntie had, of course, charged him extra, but it didn't alter his behavior at all.

Mori-san took a shine to me on his first visit. I was very wary of him, as I assumed that he would be like his sponsor, but I need not have worried. He turned out to be the gentlest of men, one who genuinely enjoyed my playing on the samisen and was very complimentary about my singing. In fact, on that first visit he did nothing at all except listen to me play and sing. Oh, he chatted to me, and actually listened to what I said, but nothing else. He left around midnight and that was that. I was convinced that he had simply not fancied me and would no doubt complain to Auntie and demand that my fee be drastically reduced, but no such thing. He came back the next week and Auntie said he asked for me, and that if I was not available, he didn't want another girl.

On that occasion, he seemed to me to be nervous. He drank his sake and nibbled at some sweet rice cakes, and after half an hour I was at my wits end to know what to do to entertain this strangest of patrons. Surely, he would not be happy to just talk to me again! After a flask of sake, he became quite frisky and asked me – very shyly – if I would undress in front of him. Nothing unusual there. I took my clothes off as enticingly as I could and was deeply relieved when I saw that his tree of flesh was very much in evidence beneath his loose robe.

I squatted down in front of him and was about to reach for his tree when he put his hand around my wrist and stopped me. His gaze was fastened on my breasts, and he put his fingers out very hesitatingly, as if he was doing something very daring, and fastened his hand around my right breast, pulling me toward him. He suckled at my nipple as if he was a very, very hungry baby and then pulled back, breathing heavily.

But still he did not want me to touch him. I was puzzled. What *did* he want me to do? By this stage, most patrons were only too happy to tell us girls what they wanted, whether it be twirling the stem, splitting the melon, or simply matching the bird to the nest. But not Mori-san.

He asked me, quite hesitatingly, if I would stand up straight in front of him. I obliged, of course, and then simply stood, awaiting instruction. To say I was surprised by what happened next would be putting it mildly. Mori-san shuffled toward me on his knees. He dipped his head toward my black moss and parted my sex with his nose. It tickled, and I almost laughed. Then, when I was parted to his satisfaction, he rubbed his face inside my slit, up and down, up and down. All desire to laugh left me, and was suddenly replaced by growing desire, pure and simple. That in itself was surprising. Normally there was very little – if any – pleasure involved in pleasing a patron for us girls. In fact, since my evening with Danjuro, I had felt nothing but distaste for the men who paid to take me. To use me. Perhaps, then, it was the surprise that did it. In any event, before I could think about it, I reached down and grabbed his head, pushing his face as far as I could into me.

Mori-san immediately opened his mouth and started to seek the seed, licking and mouthing at me with his lips, using his teeth to nibble at me, but very gently. After a few minutes, I was dripping with longing. I groaned out loud and, apparently taking it as a signal, Mori-san slid his tongue up until he was licking my pearl.

I could take no more. Lust won out over all my careful training, and I pulled away, literally pushing Mori-san on to his back. He fell on the matting with a soft thud, and I had a momentary vision of his face, eyes wide and tongue protruding, before I slid down on to him, my legs on each side of his hips. I searched for his tree with my hand, and positioned myself carefully, poking his hood just inside the entrance to my sex. I wanted to tease him a little, but could not, all my self-restraint had gone.

Instead, I pistoned down on him, forcing as much of his tree inside me as I possibly could. Almost immediately, I realized that I was close to bursting my fruit already, and it took a huge effort of will to make myself slow down. I raised myself so high that he was in danger of popping out of me, and then lowered myself down again, bit by bit by bit. And, oh, so very slowly.

Mori-san reached for my breasts and I leaned forward so that he could clutch me and take both nipples in his mouth. His eyes were closed in intense pleasure, and I smiled. I allowed him to suckle at my nipples for a few moments and then resumed taking as much pleasure as I could extract from him. His tree was not quite as vigorous as some of the younger men who visited us, but it was enough. I squeezed him hard with my internal muscles, muscles that had been honed by the use of love globes.

A patron had given me a set once as a present, and the other girls had laughed at me when I said that I didn't know what they were. In spite of the fact that the patron had leered at me when he handed them over, I was under the impression that they were some sort of jewelry, although how I was supposed to wear them, I had no idea.

The girls had taken them away from me, and little Masaki dangled them from her fingers.

"Lay down," she instructed. I looked suspiciously from face to face, but did as I was told, curiosity blossoming. "Hitch up your robe, and open your legs. No," she tutted, and the other girls giggled. "A lot wider than that. Pretend I'm a patron who wants to put his tree in you."

I raised my head and frowned at her, and she grinned.

"Trust me. You will be happy with it. I promise."

She weighed the balls in her hand. They were made of silver, each about the size of a large cherry and very heavy for their size. There was some sort of liquid inside one, and I could hear it sloshing about lazily. Each cherry was tied to the other with a length of what looked like plaited gold thread.

"Goodness me," Masaki said seriously. "You must have pleased your patron greatly. These are very expensive ones."

She leaned forward and I felt her cold little fingers probing at my black moss. I was about to ask what on earth she was doing when her whole fist shoved inside me, forcing me wide open. The other girls shouted with laughter. Obviously anticipating that I would wriggle about, or even try and get away, Kiku and Naruko grabbed my shoulders and shoved me back down on the matting.

Kiku laughed right in my indignant face. "Pretend we're patrons, out for a good time!" she giggled.

I was too breathless from trying to get away to say anything. Masaki was still trying to keep my sex open and at the same time seemed to be pushing something into me. Something very cold and heavy. Although I still wriggled, it was hardly unpleasant. We in the Hidden House – and I strongly suspected elsewhere, both in the Floating World and outside it – were used to each other in the way that only women who live together constantly can be, and we were very aware of each other's bodies. After all, it was by no means unknown for a patron to want to watch a couple of girls enjoying each other rather than taking them himself. Quite often, a patron would demand to see two girls seeking the seed for each other or we would be told to perform a little mutual dew mingling for him. We were always happy to oblige. After all, who but a woman knows how to really please another woman? It also had the advantage that more often than not, the patron would get so excited watching us that he would either burst his fruit on his own, without us so much as laying a finger on him, or at the most only a little twirling of the stem would be required to see him happy and satisfied.

When it came to two or more of us girls performing together for the enjoyment of a patron, naturally we never let it be obvious that we were enjoying ourselves by our own efforts. Oh, no. That would never do. The order of the day was to keep a straight face, to wince occasionally as if it was all distasteful in the extreme, and we were only doing it to enhance the happiness of the respected patron. The more we winced and disguised our groans of pleasure as mews of disgust, the more they loved it.

Strange things, men.

Anyway, there I was, flat on my back, legs spread wide, while Masaki fiddled about inside me.

"Keep still," she scolded. I tried, but whatever she was doing tickled, and whatever she was putting inside me was very cold. "There. Done it."

The girls let me go, and Masaki rubbed her palms together briskly. She was grinning widely.

"Go on, stand up."

I looked at all of them suspiciously. They were all trying to hide huge grins. I stood up carefully, wondering what on earth Masaki had been up to. I got as far as a crouch, and then stopped as suddenly as if I had been turned to stone.

"Oh!" I gasped.

The girls erupted into laughter, literally hanging on to each other for support.

"Told you!" Kiku crowed. "Isn't that nice?"

I moved slowly, feeling the love globes moving sluggishly inside me. The weights in the globes were slightly uneven, and with each movement they moved up and down, up and down. I was sure I could hear a faint click each time they moved. My mouth dropped open in disbelief.

"How long do I leave them in for?" I croaked.

"Long as you like." Kiku laughed. "As long as you can stand it!"

It was no good; I started to laugh with them. And the more I laughed, the more the love orbs continued their subtle motion until I felt I was on the very verge of a constant orgasm, as though at any minute my fruit might burst and it would go on and on and on. It was a delicious sensation. I scrambled into my clothes, carefully. And still the love globes rocked to and fro, to and fro.

"They're not just for pleasure." Masaki grinned. "Keep yourself nice and tight whenever you're wearing them, and you'll find that your muscles get stronger and stronger. After a while, you'll be able to tense and flex and move them about even when you're sitting perfectly still. If I were you, I would thank the patron who gave them to you very nicely the next time you see him."

I did, too.

Anyway, I digress. To return to Mori-san. As I say, on that second occasion I more or less made him take me. Once I had his tree nicely inside me, he seemed content to let me set the pace, and so I did. I had never had a patron before who had been interested in anything at all except satisfying his own pleasure, and so Mori-san was a very pleasant change. He burst his fruit long before I was really ready, of course, and as soon as he was gone I grabbed for the consolation of my love globes. All of us girls used them like that. Few of the patrons ever came near to satisfying us, but often left us in a state of such arousal that it was the love globes or scream. On occasions like that, Naruko and Masaki often took pleasure in each other, as they were particularly fond of each other's company. Often, if one was wandering about the Hidden House at night – and there was always somebody moving during the night to answer a call of nature or to see a patron off the premises – it was noticeable that either Masaki's or Noruka's screen door was left ajar, and when this happened we knew that they were seeking comfort and satisfaction in each other's arms. We made a point of keeping it hidden from Auntie, as she would not have been pleased. Not, you understand, that she would have thought it immoral in any way, rather because strong friendships between the girls were discouraged. Auntie was of the opinion that it distracted the girls' minds from their true duties, and it was always difficult if one girl was bought out by a danna and left the House, leaving her friend behind.

I was worried that Mori-san had not appreciated my aggression. We were supposed to be supremely compliant, always alert to our patron's needs, to the total disregard of our own. I had to admit, I had actually used Mori-san far more than he had used me. And it was Mori-san who was paying the bill! But I had no need to worry. He came back the following week, and again the week after. On both occasions, he ordered food for us both, even asking what I liked. When seaweed, sliced lotus root with ginger, ramen noodles, and thinly sliced fish cooked with mushrooms and vegetables appeared on the matting on his fourth visit, I was astonished. Every single one of my favorites! He even *fed* the food to me. I could hardly believe it. Once the maids had left the room, Mori-san took up his chopsticks and selected a morsel of fish. I was about to reach for my own chopsticks when instead of eating himself, he leaned over and presented the fish to my lips. And he did that every time! Before he ate anything himself, he fed me first. He even poured sake for me before filling his own cup. I tried to protest that I should be serving him, but he would have none of it.

I should, I suppose, have enjoyed the attention, but instead it made me uncomfortable. Delicious as the food was – and the Hidden House shared its kitchen with the Green Tea House, a kitchen that was famous throughout the Floating World – I would have been much happier had our roles been reversed and I had fed him before taking so much as a mouthful for myself. That was traditional behavior for any geisha. This was unheard of. But what could I do? Mori-san was the patron, he was paying.

Once the food was cleared away, it got worse. Mori-san invariably sat back on the bedding that had been spread on the mats and smiled at me. He clapped his hands softly and then – I have never told anybody this before, because if I did, they would not believe me – asked me what I wanted *him* to do to please *me*. The first time it happened, I thought I had simply misheard him, and naturally asked him what he would like.

He shook his head. "No, no, Midori-chan. Nothing would give me greater pleasure than to give pleasure to you. Please, tell me what you would like me to do. Anything at all."

Even as he spoke, I could see that his tree of flesh was wagging at me through his robe. He was beginning to breathe heavily and his face was red. He was on his knees already, but now he put his hands together in the prayer position and bent his head almost to the floor in an attitude of abject submission.

I had kneeled in front of a man so many times in exactly

the same way. Suddenly I saw my own helpless obedience mirrored in his gesture, and I trembled with fury. It was not fair, of course, to take my anger out on this nice man, but that is exactly what I did. I simply could not help myself.

"Sit up," I snapped. He did so, his expression as eager as a spaniel, waiting to please. "Touch yourself. Touch your tree. Pretend it's me that's doing it."

I could hardly believe it when he immediately grasped his erection in his fingers and began to rub it up and down quickly. And a real mess of it he made, too. I could see that his grip was far too tight, and he was moving too rapidly. At this rate, he would achieve bursting of the fruit in no time at all.

"I would never do it like that. Stop it," I jeered. He stopped immediately and looked at me humbly. "Put your hand fully around your stem. Move your hand slowly. No, not as tightly as that. Slower. That's better."

I watched him for a while. His face was sweating and he was beginning to pant. I was becoming excited myself, watching him. Was this, I wondered, what the patrons found so exciting when they asked us girls to touch ourselves in front of them? I had often wondered why they seemed to like it so much. Now I knew.

"Stop," I snapped. "Take your hand away and come here."

Mori-san released his grip at once and shuffled across to me on his knees. I held my hand up to signal him to stop just before his face was close enough to touch me. Even so, I could feel his breath on my black moss. I had taken very little sake, but I still felt drunk. Perhaps for the first time I was drunk with power! I decided I would carry on pushing this strangest of patrons until he protested. At that point, of course, I would cast myself at his feet and humbly beg his pardon. But in the meantime, it was such fun!

I swayed toward him, brushing my black moss against his nose. Mori-san moaned. Hardly able to contain my own excitement, I moved forward again, but this time, I did not withdraw. Very slowly, very deliberately, I leaned against him until his lips were buried in my black moss.

I do not remember telling him to do anything, although so great was my need by this time that I may have barked some instruction to him. In any event, Mori-san did not hesitate. He buried his whole face in my black moss and I bent backward, opening my sex to him like a flower. His lips slid up and down my sex, making me moan out loud. His tongue flicked in and out of me like a snake, wet and warm.

"Up!" I hissed. "Up!"

Mori-san obeyed instantly, moving his head up so that his tongue could caress my seed. My tender bud felt as if it was on fire, and the touch of the tip of his tongue was like the softest touch of fine silk. Gentle as it was, it ignited my fire and I felt the waves of pleasure beginning to radiate from my belly down to my sex. I shouted out loud, and in response Mori-san bit down on my pearl - not hard, but sufficient to nip.

I exploded. When the fireworks had faded from my vision and I could draw breath again, I looked down at Mori-san. His face was shiny with my juices, and his expression glazed. He was breathing so hard, it was as if he had just run a race.

I put my hands on his shoulders to steady myself, and he instantly threw himself at my feet, covering my toes with kisses. I was so dazed, so full of satisfied pleasure, that I could do nothing.

Mori-san sat up eventually. His tree, I saw, was still

rearing and in spite of my sudden languor, I took pity on him. Gesturing to him to sit up, I took his tree in my hand and rubbed it up and down, up and down. It took no time at all, I was pleased to see.

That night, Mori-san curled up beside me on the futon and only left at dawn. I would have loved to have asked the other girls if anything similar had ever happened to them, but I didn't dare, in case they accused me of making it up.

In any event, Mori-san's incredible behavior and what followed was one of the reasons why I remember that particular day so well. The other reason was Danjuro.

Once Mori-san had left, and I had had my bath, Auntie sent for me.

Being summoned by Auntie was always an occasion for concern, and I sped to her as quickly as I could. Auntie was sitting on the raised platform in the room she used as a sitting room in her suite. Her knees hurt her greatly, and she found it impossible to sit on the floor like the rest of us. In later years, when the foreign Barbarians made the fashion for high furniture all the craze, Auntie immediately bought a chair and a Western-style bed and was much more comfortable. I could never get used to them.

I bowed deeply and waited. Had Mori-san complained about me after all, I wondered? And what on earth could I say if he had? By the time Auntie spoke, I was trembling with fear.

"Midori No Me." Bad! My whole name, not just Midori. My stomach churned.

"Auntie, you sent for me?" Stupid! Of course Auntie had sent for me. Why would I have been here otherwise?

Auntie leaned forward and rested her chin on the handle of her stick. She puckered her mouth and stared at me.

"Midori No Me. I had a visit from Mori-san this morning. As soon as he left you, he came to see me. He took tea with me."

I swallowed, with difficulty. I felt as if a hastily swallowed piece of meat was lodged in my throat. This was it, then. I had overstepped the mark with Mori-san. He had complained to Auntie. No use in telling her I had only done what my patron had asked of me. If he had complained about me, he was in the right. That was the way of it. Was my disobedience so bad it would merit a visit from Big, or Bigger? Or – and my vision began to cloud at the thought – both of them? Not quite a death sentence if it was one, but both...

"What, exactly, did you do to him, Midori No Me?"

My mouth opened and closed. I tried to speak, but nothing emerged but a croak. I cleared my throat and tried again.

"Only exactly what he asked me to do, Auntie." Not quite the truth, but near enough. I had certainly acted in the spirit of what Mori-san had wanted.

Auntie stared at me. When she spoke, I was so surprised I thought I had misheard her.

"He told me that his wife died last year." I was almost sure that Auntie was trying to keep her face composed, and that she was hiding – surely not! – laughter rather than anger. The tiniest firefly of hope began to glow in my shaking body. I bowed my head in polite interest. Mori-san had already told me that, and I had commiserated with him, as was only proper. "I knew that already, of course."

Of course she did. Auntie knew everything and everybody in the Floating World. She knew who was married to whom, who had been born, who had died, who her patrons were interested in, which tea house was prospering, which was going downhill. If it had – or could have – any bearing on Auntie's business, then she knew about it.

But suddenly, I was slightly less terrified. Auntie had no doubt expressed polite surprise and sorrow at Mori-san's "news," but why was she telling me?

"Has Mori-san spoken to you about his wife?"

"No, Auntie, except to tell me she had died quite recently."

"I knew of his wife. Then again, most of the Floating World knew of his wife. She was..." Auntie paused and sucked her lips. "She was an unusual woman. She was much higher class than Mori-san. She came to him with a very good dowry, I understand. Enough to set him up in his own business."

This *was* interesting. A high-class woman marrying beneath herself and still coming to her husband with a good dowry? That was unheard of! There had been, in the past, women of the samurai class who had, for some terrible transgression or other, been sold into virtual slavery as courtesans by their honorable family. But even those women were enslaved for only five or perhaps seven years, until it was considered that the stain on the family honor had been cleansed. Then they were welcomed back into their clan, and their period of absence was simply forgotten. Generally, they married well and continued with their lives as if nothing had ever interrupted it. Some said it still happened, but I had my doubts. For a woman of a high-class family to marry beneath her generally meant being disowned by her family, treated as an outcast. Forever.

Auntie must have seen the surprise on my face, as she nodded and continued. And yes, she *was* struggling not to laugh. "Mori-san's wife was generally known as a very commanding sort of woman. To be blunt about it, she was bossy. It was generally thought that she wore the sword in the family and that her husband simply did as he was told. In fact, she was so bad that many swore she was not a woman at all, but a man who had been born in a woman's body. That was why she could not marry into her own class, her reputation was so bad. Her father was actually Mori-san's patron, and the gossip at the time was that he offered his daughter to Taruko-san with a good dowry, giving him the choice of taking her or of having his business destroyed before it could even begin to flourish. Being a sensible man, Mori-san took the woman and the dowry. And flourish he did. His wife brought not only a substantial dowry, but a good business head and even better connections. I heard that many of his patron's friends flocked to him simply because they were so relieved that they were no longer in fear of being offered his wife in marriage."

I struggled not to laugh myself. My poor Mori-san! Had his wife treated him as a servant for years, I wondered? But, again, why Auntie had sent for me? All desire to laugh died.

"Anyway, that is all history. Mori-san came to me this morning to make an offer for you, Midori No Me."

My mouth fell open in disbelief. Mori-san had made an offer for me? Auntie glanced at me shrewdly, and then continued.

"He wants to marry you," she said bluntly.

Well, I didn't know whether to laugh or cry. Marriage? Mori-san wanted to marry me? Not take me as a mistress, but *marry* me? Take me out of the Hidden House and turn me into a respectable woman? A woman who could have everything she asked for? And no mother-in-law about the place to make my life hell?

"What do you think about that, Midori?"

I swallowed, trying to focus my thoughts. I should be

hopping about the place in delight. This was unheard of! The likes of me, who had been born and raised in the Hidden House as a freak to be taken by any man who had the money and the credentials to be allowed in, to actually be offered for as wife by a well-off man, and a kind, gentle man at that. A man who I was even quite fond of, albeit in the same way I might have been fond of a helpless puppy. Why, I should be on my knees, banging my head on the mat in front of Auntie in thankfulness for my good fortune.

Why, then, was I not?

Thoughts jostled in my brain. I knew Auntie was watching me carefully, so I gritted my teeth, forcing my face to remain neutral.

I did not dislike Mori-san. He was *truly* a nice man. But I was not the wife he had lost. It was amusing to be able to order him about, but – oh, that word yet again! – but did I really want to live the rest of my life with a man I knew I would soon come to despise for his very weakness? A milksop? No, I did not want that. I wanted a man who was a man. A man who would tell me what to do. I may not always want to do as I was told, of course, but at least I would have a man with some resilience. A real man, not one who wanted to hide his head in my black moss. A man I could respect.

I wanted Danjuro. I wanted him so badly that I was prepared to stay in the Hidden House if that was what it took. Suddenly, the thought of poor Mori-san and his eagerness to please and his lost-puppy-dog look made me feel quite sick.

I spoke slowly, choosing my words with great care. Auntie was offering me the world on a plate; it would not do to anger her.

"I am lost for words, Auntie. Mori-san has truly done me great honor."

"I turned him down."

The words took some time to penetrate my leaping thoughts, but when they did, I could have fallen on my knees and embraced Auntie. Instead, I bowed my head and tried to pin an expression of deep sorrow on my face.

"It was a reasonable offer, but not enough. I daresay he might come back with something better, and if he does, then I will consider it. But that is not the only reason I turned him down, Midori."

I fixed my eyes on the floor, waiting for whatever was to come.

"While you were occupied with Mori-san last night, Danjuro came." Somebody took my heart in their hand and squeezed it tightly. Danjuro! Had my thoughts summoned him at last? Auntie was frowning, pursing her lips so that the wrinkles on her upper lip stood out as if they were carved. "It seems, Midori, that you are very favored at the moment. Danjuro came to see you. Suzume let him in, and when he demanded you, she brought him to me, as was right."

I nodded vigorously. *Get on with it, Auntie!* I begged silently.

"I explained to him that not even for the great Danjuro, not even for the shogun himself, could I take you away from a patron." She paused and wrinkled her brow, "Well, perhaps for the shogun. Or one of the very great nobles." I very nearly reached out to shake her, to make her get on with it. Danjuro! Suzume had been right, all along. He had not forgotten me! "I explained to him that you were with a patron, and that I could not disturb you. That it would be a gross breach of manners and could not be done. The reputation of my house would have been lost in an instant."

She paused again, nodding to herself in satisfaction. I cursed Mori-san and myself. While I was pleasuring myself with my insignificant little patron, I could have been with Danjuro! Truly, sometimes the gods displayed a perverse sense of humor. Why, oh why, hadn't Suzume gotten word to me? Even as I thought it, I shrugged the idea away. As Auntie had said, for the shogun, I could have been diverted. Most certainly would have been, if Auntie did not want to find herself cut in two. But no, not for any lesser man, no matter what my own thoughts on the matter were.

Suzume would not have dared. Mad as I was for Danjuro, *I* would not have dared. Would I?

"Was Danjuro angry, Auntie?"

"He was furious. He paced my rooms like a caged tiger. I offered him his choice of the other girls – as luck would have it, you were the only one with a patron so late – but he would have none of it. I offered him the bathhouse and the attentions of *all* the other girls, but I might as well have saved my breath. I even offered him Big or Bigger, or both, in case his tastes might be diverted by them, but I might as well have not spoken." Deeply thankful, I nodded vigorously. Finally I would have something to tell Bigger the next time he asked me about Danjuro! "In the end, he calmed down enough to drink tea with me. I had to tell him that it was no good him just turning up and demanding you. That Danjuro or not, I could not keep you sitting about the place waiting for him."

I goggled at her. Truly, Auntie was a brave woman! Would anybody else have dared to have spoken to the great Danjuro like that? I doubted it. Although even as I doubted it, I did wonder, deep inside, if I might also have argued with him. The thought pleased me greatly. I would like Danjuro prowling about my room, like a caged beast. A beast who might not be tamed, but oh, the delights of trying!

"What did he say to that, Auntie?"

"He was not happy. I thought he was going to throw his teacup at me and leave for a moment. But his manners are too good to allow that kind of thing." She smirked like a young girl and I realized that Danjuro had worked his magic, even on the adamantine Auntie. "Eventually, we agreed. You will be available for him on the third day of each week. He will either come here to you or he will send for you to go the kabuki. If he cannot come or for some reason he does not want you to go to him, he will still pay the negotiated fee."

I could feel happiness radiating out of me like a beacon fire. Had Auntie touched me at that moment, I would have burned her hand. I tried and tried to keep my face composed, but I knew that I had not achieved it. Auntie looked at me shrewdly.

"And that is another reason why I will not sell you to Mori-san, child. When it is known that Danjuro has bestowed such honor on my humble house, we will be turning the customers away." She cackled gleefully. "Please him, Midori. Whatever he asks of you, give him double."

I said, "I will do my best, Auntie."

She grinned, showing her uneven teeth. "Truly, the gods are favoring you, Midori-chan. What a pity I did not know about Mori-san's kind offer before I spoke to Danjuro. It would have been interesting to share the news with him. To have seen his reaction."

For once, I agreed with her.

11

The bone moon watches
Without interest.
Does it see us?

*T*ruly is it said that the gods do not like us mere humans to have too much good fortune. Too much happiness is not good for us. It makes us inflated with pride and too god-like for our own good.

I realized this the same week that Mori-san asked for me and Danjuro came to see me but did not find me.

The girls were anxious to know what had happened. They knew, of course, that Danjuro had come and was turned away by Auntie. Someone was always awake in the Hidden House, always listening, no matter what the hour of the day. Kiku said his face had been like thunder when he left. I was delighted and didn't bother to hide my pleasure.

Oh, that I had only known what was to come. How humble would I have been then! Even though I gave thanks to the gods for my good fortune, if I had known how annoyed they were getting with me, I would have been on my knees in front of the house shrine, offering incense and praying for forgiveness for my own happiness.

But I did not. How could I? How could any mere human know the ways of the gods? And if I had known, it would have been a false face I presented to them. For the first time in my life, I felt I had value. That I was wanted. That the man I loved wanted me. Could even the gods have expected me to be truly less than happy?

The girls crowded around as soon as I came out of Auntie's rooms. They hustled me off to the bath and surrounded me. Even little Suzume was allowed in beside us after she had scrubbed our backs and poured water over us.

Proudly, I told them the story of how Mori-san had made an offer for me. Not as his mistress, but as his wife. It was, I think, the only time in its whole history that the bath-house in the Hidden House had been totally silent.

Then all the girls started talking at once. I let them ramble on, smug in my own joy. Until Masaki – perched on the steps, as usual – asked, "What about Danjuro? We all heard him come in, and Suzume took him straight to Auntie. Didn't you, Suzume?"

Puffed up with importance at being included in the conversation, Suzume nodded vigorously. "I did. He wanted Midori-chan, and when I said she was engaged with a patron, I thought he was going to explode he was so angry. He wanted me to go get Midori-chan at once. Straight away. And when I said I couldn't, he said he was going to get her himself."

The girls all drew in deep breaths, their eyes huge. I was

so inflated with self-importance, I was quite surprised I didn't float to the top of the steaming water.

"No!" Kiku gasped. "What did you say?"

"I bowed and told him that I couldn't do that, that if I did, Auntie would take my skin off. I managed to sound really terrified, and he calmed down a bit, said he understood it wasn't my fault. So I said I would take him to talk to Auntie. He really is the most attractive man, isn't he? So tall and commanding."

I looked at Suzume through the steam and gave her a glance to tell her not to overdo things. She caught on immediately and lowered her eyes modestly to the water.

It didn't matter. She could have said Danjuro was eight feet tall and had devil's horns and no one would have contradicted her. They were all too eager to share in my moment of romance. I didn't blame them, not for a minute. I would have been just the same.

"What did Auntie say about him?" Naruko asked in her chirping Japanese.

"She said he was furious that I was with a patron," I said. "He wanted me to leave Mori-san straight away and go with him." A sharp intake of breath all around. "Auntie said she couldn't do that, of course, and that made him even more angry. Eventually, she calmed him down and they agreed that I would be reserved for him on every third day of each week, no matter who else wanted me. He will either send for me to go to the kabuki or he will come here."

I stopped and shrugged, as if it was all of no real importance. The girls sat in a ring around me, each of their faces – with the exception of Suzume, who simply looked gleeful – looking as if they were so hungry they wanted eat me. It was Masaki who put her finger on the nub of the thing.

"What are you going to do if Mori-san comes back with an offer that Auntie can't refuse?"

I squirmed. "I don't know," I admitted. "Mori-san is a nice man, and he wants me to be his wife. I am deeply honored, of course..." I trailed off, some of my happiness draining away as I realized that this was no fairy tale with a happy ending. This was real life, where things did not always go entirely as one would want them to.

"You could always marry him and take Danjuro as your lover," Kiku said helpfully. The girls nodded their agreement, but the idea left me numb. How could I possibly do that? To begin with, how could I betray a man who had taken me out of the Hidden House, not to make me a mistress but an honorable wife? It was unthinkable. Although I guessed that if I told Mori-san that those were the terms I would marry him under, he would probably be happy to agree. But that thought did not please me either. How could I possibly submit to my husband's caresses when all the while I was thinking of my lover, wishing I was lying in his arms, kissing his lips, feeling his tree of flesh seeking entrance to my black moss?

No. The idea was repugnant. Knowing I could never make the girls understand my stupid objections, I smiled. "Oh well. I'll worry about that if and when it happens."

They all nodded, clearly pleased. What else could a woman in the Floating World do but take whatever chance of happiness she could grab? Especially a woman like me, a woman that the gods were smiling upon.

Or so I thought.

It was only when we climbed out of the bath that I came out of my trance of happiness long enough to realize that, out of all the girls, Carpi was missing. I asked Kiku where she was. She shrugged.

"She says she's not feeling well again. I don't know what's the matter with her. If she doesn't pull herself together she's going to stop smiling at the patrons and Auntie is going to get really annoyed with her. Even Carpi isn't above having the Boys inflicted on her if it comes to it."

Now that I thought of it, it must have been a week – no, more than a week, perhaps a fortnight – since I had seen Carpi. She had stopped joining us all in the bath and had been conspicuous by her absence when we girls got together for our regular tea and chat times. I would, I decided virtuously, go and see her. Tell her all my news. Cheer her up. After all, Carpi had been my Older Sister for my mizuage. We were supposed to be special to each other.

I tapped on Carpi's screen door gently. When there was no reply, I knocked again, harder. I was about to turn away, thinking she was perhaps asleep, when her voice called out, asking who it was. I said it was me, cheerfully, and was a little hurt when Carpi took her time to answer, and even then sounded reluctant.

The smile faded from my lips when I entered. Carpi nodded to me to close the door, and I was glad to turn my back to hide my face, to give me time to adjust my expression.

How had Carpi come to look like this in the space of a few weeks? As I walked across the tatami, my mind was working furiously. It hadn't just been a few weeks, had it? Hadn't I thought months ago that Carpi was looking very thin, not just in her body, but in her face? That she seemed to have lost some of her animation? But my own adventures, my own pleasures, had pushed any concern for poor Carpi out of my mind and I had simply forgotten about my Older Sister. That was when I began to suspect that the gods themselves were jealous of me and had decided to make a mockery of my sudden good luck.

I had no words to say to Carpi. I could not bring myself to ask how she was, or – even worse – to lie and comment that she was looking well. Because she was not looking well, not at all. She looked as if she was suddenly an old woman, as though she had aged thirty years in only a few days.

Her face had always been remarkably pretty, in a way that was almost perfection to Japanese eyes. She had lovely, almond-shaped eyes, a small nose, broad cheekbones, and wonderful, smooth skin. As her patrons were wont to say, a "face like a melon seed." But now, Carpi was no longer pretty. She had lost weight in her face and her cheekbones dominated her expression. Even her eyes seemed to have sunken in. And even worse, her face had none of its normal animation, the devil-may-care look that had made her so very vivacious. Her skin was taut over her bones and seemed to have changed color from her old, deeply attractive tea-rose pink to a distinctly unattractive spoiled milk hue.

"Sit down." Even Carpi's voice was a dull echo of her old, full-of-bravado tones.

I sat on the tatami at her feet. "Carpi, what is it? What's the matter?" No point in pretending I had not seen the changes in my Older Sister. She would not have appreciated my lies anyway.

"I don't know." Her voice was flat. Hopeless. I wanted to weep for her.

"You need to see the doctor. I'll tell Auntie." I had half risen to my feet, but Carpi waved at me to sit down.

"She knows. I've seen the doctor. In fact, I've seen two doctors."

I blinked in shock. Auntie had actually paid for two doctors to see Carpi? She must be worried!

"What did they say? What's wrong?"

Carpi laughed shortly and shrugged her shoulders. "Auntie was worried that one of the patrons had given me something horrible. She kept patrons away from me for a month to be safe." My eyes widened in shock. A month, a whole month, without a patron? No money coming in, and doctor´s fees going out? Auntie must have been so distraught. "Then when I didn't start showing horrible pustules, she decided at least it wasn't that. Do you know," she added almost conversationally, "I think I would have been happier if it had been the pox. At least that way the doctor could have given me mercury and I would have had a chance at getting better."

I shook my head. "Don't be silly. They say the mercury cure is almost as bad as the disease. Anyway, it's obvious you haven't got anything like that. But what did the doctors say was the matter?"

"The first one said my vital energies were out of balance." Carpi smiled ruefully and I saw her teeth had turned yellow. Her disease or just neglect? "He said I needed to eat more vegetables and no meat. He also gave me some powder to burn. I had to inhale the fumes. They made me sick. When that cure did no good, Auntie got a different doctor to see me. One from Edo. Outside the Floating World."

"No!"

Carpi nodded, her expression wry. "I know," she said. "When she did that, I really started to worry. I thought I must be very near death if Auntie was prepared to go to that sort of expense. I needn't have worried. It turned out that this physician was a regular at the Green Tea House and an old friend of Auntie. I think he owed her a favor or two, and I was one of them. Anyway, he said it was definitely not the pox. He agreed with the first doctor and said it was my entire balance that was out of sorts. He prescribed more foul herbs – only these ones I had to swallow – and said I was to rest. And drink sake three times a day. And not to take any spices in my food. And to take a pipe when I felt really out of sorts. The sake gave me a headache, but the pipe is good."

"Do you feel better?" An inane thing to ask, but what else could I say?

Carpi stared at me for so long, I began to feel uncomfortable.

She climbed to her feet with a total absence of her usual, sinuous grace. I was about to put out my hand to help her, then realized helplessly that there was nothing I could grasp to help her up. Embarrassed, I changed the gesture into one of pretending to push back my hair. Carpi was not fooled, I knew. Not at all. But politely she pretended she had not noticed. Once on her feet, she loosened her robe with her teeth and tugged it aside. "Look," she said.

I stared. I couldn't help it. She was naked under the loose robe. I had seen Carpi naked many times, in the bath or when a group of us was entertaining clients. But this was not Carpi's body. She was more like a living skeleton than a young woman. Her breasts had shrunk until they were barely more than empty bags on her chest. I could count each one of her ribs. Her hips stuck out like the handles on a cooking pot. Even her rounded little belly was now concave, as if it was slowly but surely being sucked toward her backbone.

"Oh, Carpi!" I whispered. "Have you stopped eating? Is it the herbs?"

She shook her head and I rose and pulled her robe around her tenderly, fastening the sash as if she was a child.

"I don't feel like eating, but I do. In fact, I'm eating more than I used to do. And drink! No matter how much tea I drink, I'm still thirsty all the time. I seem to pee more than I drink, as well. I can't go more than a couple of hours without reaching for the pot. And Midori..." She hesitated, and I guessed that whatever she was about to say worried her more than anything. "Midori, I can't see properly. Everything is blurred. I can't even read a scroll anymore. I think I'm going blind. And I'm tired. It doesn't matter how long I sleep for, I can't seem to wake up. I just feel awful, Midori. What is it? What's the matter with me?"

"I don't know, Carpi. I'm sorry, I just don't know. Can we ask Auntie to get another doctor? Perhaps one of the foreign Barbarians might have some knowledge that we don't possess?"

"I've asked her," Carpi said miserably. "But she says that whatever I have, it's a Japanese disease and the foreign devils would have no idea how to treat it. I suppose she's right."

We both fell silent, tied in our own thoughts. Carpi looked and sounded so unlike her normal, ebullient self, was clearly so very ill, I had no idea what to say to her. What to do that might help her.

"Can I do anything?" I asked lamely.

To my surprise, Carpi nodded. Very slowly. "Yes. Yes, you can help me, Little Sister. You are probably the only one in the Hidden House that can help me. If you will."

I stared at her. Her tone was very serious, and I was bewildered. What could I possibly do to help her that none of the others could? I held my hands out in a gesture that said, *Tell me!*

"Midori, I am not going to get any better." The words *of course you are* died in my mouth. If Carpi, with her iron will, had decided that she was not going to recover from this mysterious ailment, then she would not. I blinked back tears.

"Do not die, Older Sister," I whimpered. "Please, do not die."

"I am going to die, Midori. If I carry on like this, then I will either go to sleep and stay in my dreams forever or my flesh will fall from my bones entirely and I will starve to death. I do not welcome either of those ends, Little Sister. If I am to die, then I want it to be at a time of my own choosing. In a way of my own choosing. That is why you are the only one who can help me."

Already, I was shaking my head. I knew, now, why Carpi had said I was the only one who could help her. Because of Danjuro, I was the only one of the girls in the Hidden House who was allowed to venture outside, into the Floating World.

"Help me, Midori." Carpi reached out and grabbed my shoulders in her hands. I had never felt her grip before, and it was shockingly strong. I did not recoil, as I might have done at any time before, but felt rather nothing but intense pity. "Help me, Little Sister. I want to leave this world in my own good time, by my own hands." She laughed bitterly at the irony of her words. "I can hardly commit seppuku, but I can take poison. You remember, when it was your mizuage? The drops I put in your eyes to make them sparkle, to make your pupils bigger?" I nodded reluctantly. "That drug, in large enough quantities, will kill. It is easily available from any apothecary. Next time Danjuro sends for you, stop at an apothecary and tell him you want some. He will hand it over without a second thought. It is something a geisha will always have use for. I ask nothing else of you. I will put the drug in my tea, or perhaps the sake. And then...I will find peace. Do this for me, Little Sister. Please."

I swallowed and shook my head again. I could not. Suicide was an honorable thing, but surely Carpi could see that she might get better. That she still had years of life to look forward to. I could not help her kill herself. Not while there was still a chance of life. Perhaps it was the half of me that was truly a foreign Barbarian that was stopping me, but I could not. I just could not do what she was asking of me.

While I was trying to find the words to explain my feelings to Carpi, she closed her eyes and sighed. "You will not help me," she said flatly.

"I cannot. You will get better, Carpi. Auntie must find you another doctor. You are too young to think of death."

"You think so? Oh well. Perhaps you are right." Was it just my imagination or did she sound less defeated, a little like the old, strong, Carpi? "Don't tell anybody what we've been discussing, will you?"

"No, of course not. Is there anything...anything else I can do for you?"

"Prepare me a pipe, please." Carpi nodded at the tray beside her. Eager to help, I rolled a ball of opium between my fingers carefully and held it over the flame of the lamp on the end of a long pin, until it began to go sticky. With equal care, I pushed it in the bowl of the pipe and then heated that over the flame. As soon as the fumes began to ripple the air with their sweetness, I placed the pipe between Carpi's eager lips. She inhaled deeply once, twice, three times and then nodded her head. I took the pipe away, set it back on the tray, and waited until Carpi laid down and her eyes closed. Then I sneaked away and closed her screen door, shielding her from the world.

I thought that our little chat really had done Carpi some good. The next day, just after the noon meal, she appeared in Kiku's room and sat for a while with the rest of us girls. And she did, she really did, seem like the acerbic, witty Carpi of old. The girls were so obviously pleased to see her that I felt certain it had done her good. That she would get better, no matter what the gods had chosen to inflict her with.

We discussed it amongst ourselves, after Carpi had pleaded sleepiness and left us. We all agreed that none of us had ever seen anything like it before, but that it was definitely not the pox, for which we were all deeply thankful.

And anyway, all thoughts of Carpi soon left my mind. It was the third day of the week, and Danjuro had sent for me.

I hustled my way through the Floating World on winged feet, little Suzume trotting at my heels. This time, there were no nervous steps with Suzume hissing directions at me. This time, I knew where I was bound and was eager to get there. To my lover.

The only thing that gave me the slightest pang of unease on the walk was the apothecary shops we passed. I could not help but recall Carpi's plea and was so glad I had refused that it added an extra frisson to my excursion. Unlike last time, nobody stopped us. Neither samurai nor yakuza showed the slightest bit of interest in us girls, and I guessed that it was because we were walking as though we belonged in this world, with neither nerves nor fears.

The male servant was waiting for us at the door of the theater and bowed us to what I had already begun to think of us as "our" box. Even the noodle seller seemed to be hovering, waiting for us, and I took it all as fortunate signs. How lucky I was! Who among those who lived in my world could ask for more? And then Danjuro – in the character of a young man – leaped eagerly on the stage. I forgot all about my luck and the fact that I would have to return to the Hidden House in a matter of hours and simply lost myself in the magic of the kabuki.

This was a new play, a tragedy recounting the story of two young lovers who had eloped and been discovered. Brought home and separated by the girl's father, who intended his daughter for a rich merchant, the two resolved to commit suicide together. This aspect of the play gave me a distinct twinge of unease, but it was soon submerged by the make-believe world of the theater. I sighed and brushed away tears and hissed and booed with the rest of the theater as the action unwound. As the two young lovers ran from the stage, with Danjuro as the man, I held my breath with the rest of the audience until the sound of a loud splash came from behind the scenes, and we knew, with total and complete satisfaction, that the lovers had drowned themselves together and were now as inseparable in the next life as they had wanted to be in this one.

Perhaps it was because I was becoming a little more used to the drama of the kabuki, but just the tiniest thread of criticism rose in my mind. Not of Danjuro, of course. Never Danjuro. He was always sublime, no matter what part he took. Whether it was a withered old crone, a young lover, or a commanding shogun, Danjuro was always the character he was taking. Something elusive about that thought, something important, danced just out of my reach and I shrugged it away, annoyed that it dared to try to belittle my joy in this evening.

No, it was not Danjuro I was criticizing. Certainly not. And it was barely *criticism* anyway. It was just...the actor who had played the part of the young girl. He had been excellent, certainly. Of course he had. He would have had no place in the Edo kabuki if he had not been a wonderful actor. And yet there was just something about the way he had walked that was not quite right. His use of the fan was just slightly unconvincing. Suddenly, I knew what it was.

I could have done better. If I had been playing the part of the young girl, then I would have had the audience weeping with me, shouting for me. As it was, the greater part of the applause – as was only right – had been for Danjuro.

But if it had been me on the stage. Me in his arms. Me playing the part of the lover that I was in real life...I drew a huge sigh.

Not possible, of course. All the parts in the kabuki were taken by men. Women were not so much as allowed on the stage. I glanced at Suzume and knew instinctively from the tension in her body, the expression on her face, that she shared my longing. Oh, what a pair we were, shaking off our amazing good fortune and longing for what we could not have. But then, that is the nature of woman, and there is nothing to be done about it.

And yet, Carpi had told me that once, many hundreds of years ago, all geisha were men. That women geisha were unheard of. And I was sure, although I could not remember how I knew, that once upon a time it was women who took center stage in the kabuki and men who were unheard of as actors. But that was all years ago, many lives ago.

I shook off such impossible dreams. *Count your blessings, woman*, I scolded myself, *for they are many*.

Suzume and I were escorted backstage. By that time, I was on fire. Not for the kabuki, but for Danjuro.

He was sitting down when I entered his room, but he leaped to his feet at once. His eyes were shining and his face animated, as if he had taken the first puff from an opium pipe. Although he had wiped off his thick stage makeup, I could still see traces of it around his hairline and in the creases of his nose. Suddenly, I thought, *we are both the same, Danjuro. You and I. We both hide behind our makeup. We are both actors. And neither of us, no matter what the outside world sees, is comfortable in the skin that karma has given us to wear.*

"Well? What did you think of it, Midori-chan?"

"It was wonderful," I told him. "I was deeply moved. Moved to tears." In spite of my enthusiasm, something in my voice betrayed me. He moved toward me and took my shoulders in his hands, staring into my face. Perhaps, after all, I wasn't such a good actor as I thought myself to be. Or was it that Danjuro knew me better than I knew myself?

"It wasn't right, was it? Tell me. Tell me what was wrong. I know the crowd loved it, but I felt in my blood that something wasn't quite right. Was it me?"

I bit my lip in confusion. I wasn't here to criticize, I was here to applaud the great man. To offer him my body – oh yes! – and bring him down gently from the tension of his performance. I was a geisha, not a critic. Should I lie? Heap on the praise until my lover was happy? I glanced at him and decided he wanted the truth.

"It was the young man who took the part of the girl," I

blurted. "He was very good, please don't think he wasn't, it was just that I still knew he was a man. Not a woman."

Danjuro let out his breath in a long hiss and loosed his grip from my shoulders. I immediately felt the lack of his touch.

"Yes. Yes, you're right. I felt it myself. What was it? What was wrong?"

I told him, explaining about the walk, the way he held his fan. And for good measure – Danjuro was my lover, after all – told him that there was something lacking in the way the young man looked at the object of his desire.

He looked at me intently and then nodded brusquely. "Show me." He held his arms wide and then stood back. Abruptly, he was no longer Danjuro, my lover. He was back in character. He was Danjuro, the great actor. "You have come to tell me that your father is going to marry you off to an old man. That there is no hope for us. Show me your face, your walk."

It was quite ridiculously easy. I could even remember the dialogue from that particular scene. I turned my back on Danjuro, took a deep breath, and when I turned to face him, I was no longer Midori No Me. I was the doomed lover, come to tell her man that everything was lost.

He made me act the scene out three, four, five times. Eventually, he nodded and I saw the tension leave his body.

"Yes, you have it. I will try and explain it to him, but I don't know. Did many others see what you saw?"

"I don't think so." I was elated, full of the pure joy of being somebody else. Although, I had to admit, why would I not be good at it? After all, it was what I did almost every day. "Suzume noticed. I know she did. But I don't think anybody else in the audience realized it. Not even the women."

Danjuro sighed and finally took me in his arms. He spoke softly, right in my ear. "Ah, Midori-chan. What a shame you are a woman!" Before I had time to bristle at his words, he added, "If you had been born a man, what an actor you would have made. You would have been the shining light of the kabuki, alongside me."

I was delighted. It was as if Danjuro had read my inner most thoughts. "I would love it," I admitted candidly.

Danjuro laughed in my ear. "That I cannot give you. I am sorry."

I felt him begin to rub against me and all thought of acting in the kabuki gave way to more urgent needs.

Danjuro was as excited as I was. It took him only moments to yank off my obi, and my kimono and undergarments followed quickly. In common with all geisha, I had not worn my tabi outside the house, so in what seemed like seconds I stood before him naked.

He slid his hands down my body, wrapping his fingers around my breasts and fondling them. I pressed against him, wanting him to hurry up. Alas, he did, but not how I anticipated. Instead, he forced me onto my knees and jerked his tree of flesh toward me. Obediently, I took him in my mouth, teasing with tongue and lips. So wrought up was Danjuro that it was less than a minute before he was thrusting hard into my mouth and barely a moment later that he achieved bursting of the fruit. So vigorous was his orgasm that I could not contain it. I could feel his juices trickling out of the side of my mouth and down my chin. I could not bring myself to wipe it away, but licked at it with my tongue, determined that I would have every last trace of him inside me. One way or another.

As soon as he was finished, he sat down and put his hand over his face. I rocked back on my heels, torn between worry that I had disappointed him, and disappointment for my own unsatisfied state. I had looked forward to being with him all day, had reached a pitch where I thought I would scream with pleasure if he so much as touched me, and now it was finished. So quickly. So very quickly. I hoped that I would be able to arouse him again, but even that was denied to me. I thought bitterly that even Mori-san had taken the time to give me more pleasure than my lover.

Danjuro wiped his face with his hands and smiled at me. I was relieved that at least he was not angry with me.

"Midori-chan. You have my thanks. Not just for this," he waved his hand at my discarded clothes and naked body, "but for telling me what was wrong with the play. I am eternally grateful for that. Forgive me, I have given you no pleasure at all. But I have certain things on my mind that I cannot share with you yet. Important things. As soon as I can tell you, I will do so. For now, you should go back to the Hidden House. I will come to you as soon as I can, do not doubt it."

He smiled, I believe in a tender way, and I scuttled to gather my clothes, obedient to his wishes. He pressed his lips to my forehead before I left, and gently told me to travel safely. He asked if I needed an attendant with me, to see me safe. I shook my head. I would be perfectly safe with Suzume. If it had not been for the fire raging in my sex, I would have walked home on the very air. As it was, I took my bath quickly and closed my door. As soon as the screen was shut, I lay down and reached for my love globes. I rocked myself to sleep, and to satisfaction. It was not Danjuro, but it would have to do.

12

If sleep is the
Sweet friend of life,
Then why do we fear death?

I had hoped to sleep late the next day. But like so many things in this life, it was not to be. I – the whole house, actually – was roused early.

Auntie was stomping around, braying like an annoyed donkey. She shook all our doors in turn. I could hear her banging her way down the corridor and bellowing at us all to get up. Now! This minute!

We tumbled out, wrapped in nothing but our sleeping robes and the remains of sleep itself, pushing our hair out of our faces and rubbing our eyes in an attempt to at least appear awake. Only the maids, who were always up first, were properly dressed, and they looked terrified. Even Suzume seemed upset.

Auntie shooed us all into one of the big reception rooms

and we sat on the tatami, looking at each other curiously. Never did Auntie allow herself to be seen in such a state. Not only was she clearly agitated, but she had not even bothered to put on a wig, and her grey hair hung down her back in her sleeping plait. I think it was that irregularity that disturbed me more than anything and I felt fear clutch at my innards.

Finally certain that she had us all together and had our full attention, Auntie lowered herself down carefully on a pile of futons and stared at us all. Each of us in turn was subject to her stare. I cannot speak for the other girls, but I immediately felt guilty, as though Auntie had found something out that I would rather have kept hidden. My tendresse for Danjuro, perhaps? Or my contempt for poor Mori-san and his fumbling efforts to please me? Whatever it was, I lowered my eyes before Auntie's glare.

She spoke suddenly, making us all jump. "Carpi is not here."

We all looked around us and all stared in surprise. No, Carpi was not here. Anxiety clutched me. Surely Carpi had not died. No, Auntie would hardly be carrying on like this if she had. But something had obviously happened to her. Kiku spoke all our thoughts out loud, but softly, as if she feared the answer.

"Has something happened to her, Auntie?"

In the silence, the sound of Auntie grinding her teeth was clearly audible. It was a horrible sound, worse than somebody clicking their knuckle bones, and I set my own teeth in response.

"I have no idea," Auntie snapped. "Carpi has gone. She has run away."

The room erupted as everybody started to speak together. No, she couldn't have! She was too ill! Why would she run away? Where would she go? I sat silently, thinking that it had happened again, that the past had come back to haunt me. I glanced at the others, expecting their faces to mirror my horror, but they were all simply looking amazed.

Did none of them remember poor Fumie? Surely, I could not be the only one who thought of her? But is seemed so. Then I remembered that Fumie had been my friend and had little contact with the other girls.

Auntie clapped her hands together sharply, and obediently as schoolchildren, we all fell silent. I kept my eyes on the tatami, suddenly sure that this was all my fault. Was I the only one who knew that Carpi wanted to commit suicide? Was I the only one who had refused to help her? What was it she had said? *Don't tell anybody else.* Yes, I was the only one. I was the only one she had asked to help her, the only one who had betrayed her. Just as I had betrayed Fumie. Now she had run away. And it was all my fault. Again. How much guilt could I live with?

Auntie spoke into the silence. "When did you all see her last?"

"Yesterday afternoon." Kiku looked around at us, and we all nodded. "She came to see us all for a chat, and she seemed happy then. Much more like her old self. She even said she felt better."

We all nodded vigorously.

"Nobody saw her any later?" Auntie looked from one to the other of us. We all shook our heads. "Midori!" I jumped and tried not to look guilty. "Midori, when you came in last night from the kabuki, did you notice if Carpi's door was closed?"

Relief swept over me. I closed my eyes and tried to concentrate. I had been in a hurry to get to the bathhouse, but even so, I was sure I would have noticed if Carpi's door had been open or if a lamp had been lit in her room.

"No." I shook my head firmly. "I'm sure her door was closed, and the room was in darkness. Did you notice anything, Suzume?"

The maid shook her head. "No, mistress. There was a light in the little reception room, but that was all."

Masaki nodded and reminded Auntie that she had been entertaining a patron.

Auntie blew out her cheeks. "I was the last one to see her, then. I spoke to her in the late afternoon and made her drink some sake. She said she was going to sleep for a while when I left."

We all waited, not knowing what to say. Carpi had run away from the Hidden House? Where did she think she was going to go? Who was going to hide her? If Fumie hadn't escaped, what prayer did Carpi have?

"She has taken her jewelry with her, and the money she had hidden in her room that she had received from her patrons over the years." Auntie pursed her lips, talking more to herself than to us. "I told her to give it to me so I could put it away safely for her. She must have been planning this for some time."

"But why, Auntie?" Naruko blurted. "Why would she run away? She was not well, why go now?"

I could tell you that, I thought. But I'm not going to. Although it would be nice to be able to share my guilt this time, to make all of you feel bad that you didn't notice how ill Carpi really was. Just the same as I hadn't noticed.

"Perhaps it was her illness that turned her mind." Auntie frowned. "I don't know. None of us will know until we get her back. I have already set the Boys to look for her. They will bring her back."

The unspoken words "and punish her" hung in the air like icicles. We all clutched our robes a little tighter, wondering how we would feel if the Boys were on our trail. I shuddered, suddenly cold.

Auntie dismissed us briskly. Life in the Hidden House would continue as normal, she instructed. Fortunately, because of her ill health, Carpi had no patrons booked. The rest of us would not talk of it, even amongst ourselves. We would not mention it to anybody. Until Carpi returned, she had ceased to exist.

In spite of Auntie's firm instructions, I could not bring myself to believe life could go on as normal. I returned to my room and sat, staring at the wall. Kiku stuck her head around the door and said something to me, but I didn't catch her words and didn't answer. She sighed at me, stuck out her tongue, and left me alone.

Carpi. Carpi had run away. She had asked for my help, and I had denied her. Just as I had denied Fumie. Fumie, whose name was the most beautiful of all the geisha: Poem of Glory.

Fumie was not one of us. She lived in the Green Tea House. She played the samisen and sang and prepared the tea ceremony and whispered witticisms in the ears of enchanted patrons. Of course, she had had her mizuage, just the same as the rest of us, but apart from that, no patron could buy Fumie. Their money could buy her wit, her elegance, but never her body. Unlike us. She was dazzlingly beautiful. At the time, I envied her beauty, but nothing else. She was as much a captive bird as the rest of us geisha, whether in the Green Tea House or the Hidden House. We were all enslaved. All in debt to Auntie, a debt that would never be paid unless some man bought us out.

And if that happened, we would simply be owned by a new master.

To this day, I have no idea what brought Fumie into the Hidden House. Perhaps she was bored, perhaps she had heard of the geisha in the Hidden House and wanted to take a look at us, rather like going to the zoo to inspect the caged exotics there. Anyway, I found her standing uncertainly in the corridor outside my room one afternoon and I stared at her with as much interest as she was staring at me.

"Who on earth are you?" Fumie tittered. I was certain that she had changed to "who" from "what" at the last possible moment. I glanced at her expensive kimono and elegant wig and decided that she had wandered in by accident. I don't know what possessed me, but my first thought was that I had to get her out of the Hidden House before Auntie found her and was furious.

I bowed low. "I think you do not belong here, geisha," I said politely. "Please allow me to show you out."

Fumie just giggled. "Well, no. I don't exactly belong here. I live in the Green Tea House. My name is Fumie. What's yours?"

"Midori No Me."

She peered at me with huge, unaffected interest. I was bewildered. How had she found her way across the courtyard to us? None of the Green Tea House girls ever came to see us. Occasionally, on a fine day, they might sit in the inner courtyard with us, but that was it. Otherwise, our worlds did not touch.

That was before I knew Fumie better, and realized she always got her own way. By turns she was innocent, irritating, and fascinating. She was beautiful and witty and talented. And she knew it. Of course she did. Her patrons told her so every single day, and she had no reason to disbelieve them. She even had Auntie under her spell.

When I tried to explain to her that she should not be here, that Auntie would be angry if she found her, she simply giggled. Auntie loved her, she said. She would not mind, whatever she did.

I goggled at her. *Auntie* loved her? But Fumie was taking my arm and steering me back into my own room. Once inside, she sat down on the tatami, making the simple movement resemble nothing more than a flower head unfolding in the morning sun. She waved her hand for me to sit with her, and I did as I was instructed. I was so fascinated by her, it never even occurred to me to be annoyed that she had walked in and taken over my room as if she owned it.

Fumie was like that, I learned. She was so used to getting everything and anything that she wanted, it was second nature to her. She did not even realize that she might be giving offense. If anybody had tried to tell her off, she would just have giggled at them.

Once seated, she stared at me far more intently than politeness indicated. After a second or two, her beautiful features creased in discontent.

"Are all the girls here like you?" she demanded.

Bewildered, I shook my head. "No. We are all different."

"Ah." Fumie seemed pleased. "Good. Which one of you has two heads, then?"

My mouth fell open in disbelief. Who on earth was this rude girl, this one who thought she could walk in here and take over my room and insult us all?

"None of us," I said indignantly. "What are you talking about?"

Fumie pouted. I daresay that look would conquer any patron, but I am not a man and am not stupid.

"We've heard tales in the Green Tea House that all you... *geisha* in the Hidden House are different from the rest of us. But you look almost normal. Are the rest of them like you? Not much point keeping you locked up if they are."

Fury gradually turned to amusement. I wondered how old she was. She looked a few years older than me, perhaps fifteen or sixteen at the most, but there was something about her that was essentially childlike. I hid a smile and thought, *right, Fumie. You've coming looking for freaks, then freaks I will give you.*

"Oh, it's the bits you can't see that are different." She looked at me with wide eyes and eager lips. "Not me, you understand, but some of the girls are...different." I licked my lips, wondering just how much nonsense she would believe. "Some of them have both male and female parts."

"No!" Fumie was trying to look horrified, but only succeeding in looking fascinated.

I nodded vigorously. "Oh, yes. And one of us has three breasts. And...and," I racked my brains for something even more bizarre. "And, well, I hesitate to go into personal details when we have only just met, but I myself am not the same as other women." I tried to look knowing. Fumie's gaze ran down the front of my loose robe, and she nodded earnestly.

"You're the one that's half foreign Barbarian, aren't you? Yes, I've heard tales about the Barbarians."

I was very grateful she was polite enough not to enquire further. I was fascinated by her, this tiny, beautiful doll of a girl with her perfect features and slender body. She asked if I would like her to sing for me. I nodded, and she stood up immediately and sang a few verses of a popular song. Her singing voice was as sweet and perfect as the rest of her. She smiled at me condescendingly, and I wanted to dislike her, but it was impossible.

Everybody loved Fumie. It was impossible not to. Or at least, so I thought.

For some reason, she seemed to have taken a fancy to me, and after that first day she wandered over often when she did not have a patron. As she had said, Auntie did not seem to mind at all, just instructed me to make sure that Fumie did not visit when any of us Hidden House geisha had our own patrons present.

The other girls regarded her with as much curiosity as she paid to them. I could see her wondering, *Is that the one with three breasts? Is she one of the unfortunates with male and female private parts?* I would have explained that I had only been teasing, but I soon realized it would do no good at all. Once Fumie got something into her head, there was no dislodging it.

Oddly, none of the other girls seemed in the least bit interested in my new friend. She did not belong to our world, and if I chose to amuse myself with her, then that was my business. In any event, it would not have mattered if they had tried to be friendly with Fumie. She was the most single-minded person I had ever met. She had decided that I was to be her friend, and that was all there was to it. Apart from avid curiosity, she had no interest at all in the other girls. With the exception of Carpi, who fascinated her.

Fumie would not go near Carpi. When she saw her, she did everything but hide behind my back, and it was only ingrained politeness that stopped her from doing that. But she asked me about Carpi constantly. *Had she been born like that? How did she eat, dress, wipe herself when she went to the toilet? Was anything else about her...strange?* I answered

abruptly. Carpi bore her malformations with immense
dignity, and Fumie should honor her and do the same.
Fumie sulked for an hour or two and then went back to
trying to guess which of the girls had three breasts. She
finally decided it was Kiku, and nothing I said could make
her change her mind.

In spite of her beauty and apparent freedom, Fumie was
just as much a slave as the rest of us. She was always happy
to talk about herself, and it did not take long for her to tell
me her story. I had a strong sense that some of it was richly
embroidered, but Fumie was nothing if not convincing, and
it was impossible to untangle truth from pure fiction.

She had, she said, been born on a country estate in
Kyoto. Her father had been a high-ranking civil servant, and
she had been the only girl amongst four brothers. She did
not have to say that she had been a spoiled child, that was
obvious. As a child, she had enjoyed the best of everything.
She had a naturally good singing voice – stated as a fact,
with no false modesty – and her father had had her taught
the samisen so she could sing and play to him in the
evening. She was amazed that I could read and write; her
father never saw any need for such unfeminine accomplishments, but Fumie didn't bother to question that. After all, it
was her we were talking about, and that was always Fumie's
favorite subject.

Her mother died after giving birth to her youngest
brother. I stared at her in disbelief as she stated the fact
baldly and then rattled on with the rest of her tale. I often
thought of my own mother. Wondered where she was. If she
was still with her foreign Barbarian – my unknown father. If
she was happy. If she ever wondered about me, her abandoned daughter. Occasionally, if I was very sure I would not
be interrupted, I held imaginary conversations with her,

asking her all the questions I had asked myself. Strangely, she gave me different answers each time. But Fumie seemed to be totally unconcerned about her own mother. Perhaps it was because she was dead. Fumie didn't have to wonder where she was, what had become of her. I doubted if Fumie ever really spared a thought for anybody but herself. Of course, that was something else I was wrong about, but at the time I had no idea.

Anyway, there Fumie was with a father and four brothers but no mother. Her father soon took another wife, as was only natural, and it was that wife who was Fumie's downfall. That woman, as Fumie referred to her, was from a much lower class than her father. She was the young widow of a rich merchant who brought not only wealth to the union but two daughters of her own. According to Fumie, her new sisters were plain and untalented. Her new mother was bitterly jealous of her beautiful, clever new child.

Soon after her father married again, Fumie found her life changing. Her father no longer had time to listen to her play and sing. In fact, he appeared to have lost all interest in his only daughter. Bewildered, Fumie began to hang around him, as she put it, "trying to make him love me again," but I guess she just managed to irritate him with her continued cries for attention. In any event, after a few months Fumie was summoned by her father and was introduced to an older woman she had never seen before.

"She was very well dressed," Fumie said. "But in a terribly showy sort of way, and she wore too many pins in her wig. Father said she was to be my new mother and I must be sure to do as she said. I was bewildered. I already had my own mother and father's new wife, so why did I need yet another mother? The woman waved at me to come to her and she put her face so close to mine that I could feel her breath. She was very rude, but father had said I was to do as I was told, so I stood still while she prodded and poked at me. She finally asked Father if I was whole, and he was very angry and said of course I was. I had no idea what she meant. Anyway, she said that I would do and Father told me I was to go with her, that I was going to be trained as a geisha, and I would become very famous and have lots of men who wanted to marry me." Fumie smirked and lifted her chin, playing to an invisible audience. "So I went with the woman and she brought me to Edo. I didn't stay with her long. After a couple of weeks, Auntie came to have a look at me and took me to the Green Tea House, and here I am. Father was right, of course. I am a geisha, I am famous, and lots of patrons want me for themselves." She touched her face in an odd gesture, as if her fingers could confirm what she already knew – that she was indeed beautiful. The same fingers wandered to her wig and stroked a beautiful red comb. Seeing me watching her, she smiled, but not too widely. It was important not to crack her carefully made up face.

"My red combs are made of kingfisher beaks. They're terribly expensive. A patron gave me a set, two for each day of the week. Aren't they gorgeous?"

I nodded, although privately I felt that the kingfisher beaks would have looked much better if they were still attached to the kingfishers. I did not envy Fumie her trophy. Had they been mine I would always have felt guilty about the beautiful birds that had been slaughtered for my whim.

Mistaking my lack of enthusiasm for her combs for doubt, Fumie pouted and repeated her words. "I am very famous, you know. Patrons come from all of Edo for me. Auntie said I got the highest fee *ever* for my mizuage."

She seemed totally untroubled by any memories of her

mizuage. Nor, I thought sadly, did she appear to understand that having many patrons was not quite the same thing as men queuing to marry her. But Fumie was so shallow, I wondered if she even understood the difference. She certainly seemed less than heartbroken at being parted from her family.

Strangely, Fumie suddenly stopped visiting me. I was surprised at first, but then shrugged it off. No doubt Fumie had gotten tired of me or perhaps had been given a pet puppy or monkey that had taken my place.

I was wrong about that, too.

When Fumie did come back to the Hidden House, a blind man could have seen that something had happened to her. Always beautiful, now she was radiant and could hardly contain her happiness. As soon as my screen was closed, she blurted out that she was in love. My heart sank.

"One of your patrons?" I asked hopefully.

Fumie laughed at me. "Those old men? Of course not! He's a student. Barely older than me. From a really good family. And so handsome, Midori! I fell in love with him the moment I saw him, and he feels the same about me."

I could have shaken the silly bitch. Not that it would have done any good, of course. Once Fumie's idiotic mind was made up, nothing could dissuade her.

"Well, that's lovely for you," I said cautiously. "But there's not a lot you can do about it, is there? I mean, you owe Auntie everything. The only way you can get out of the Green Tea House is if a danna buys you out." A sudden thought struck me, and I asked hopefully, "You say he's from a good family? Is he wealthy enough to buy you out?"

Fumie giggled. Charmingly, of course. "Oh, no. He's got no money himself. Only what his father gives him. He's not going to have much money at all until he leaves university."

I stared at her in disbelief. Could even Fumie be this stupid? But apparently she could. She rattled on happily.

"We met by the river when I was on a trip with a patron. I felt him watching me, and he followed us back to the Green Tea House. He couldn't afford a geisha, of course, certainly not me, but he sneaked about, waiting until I saw him through the window, and that was that. We chatted and I loaned him some money so that he could come in the front door and he bought me for the evening."

Even for Fumie, this was too much. She had paid the boy to buy her services? I wanted to bang my head on the floor.

"We're going to elope, Midori. Once we've been together for a few days, Auntie will have to accept it, and so will his father. When we're married, his father will let him have his inheritance early, so we'll have plenty to live on. I've got it all worked out."

I went from exasperated to horrified in the space of a few words. "No, Fumie, no. That is not going to work. Auntie will never let you go. She will find you and bring you back and punish you. And your boy's father will never allow him to marry a geisha. This is the stuff of the kabuki, not real life. Listen to me, please."

But Fumie would not listen. She shrugged aside all my worries and said I was jealous of her. I hid my head in my hands and wept, but still Fumie would not listen. Worse still, she wanted me to help her.

She had hatched a hare-brained scheme whereby she was to hide in my room until the Green Tea House was shut up for the night. Once it was safe, I was to let her out of the Hidden House and her boy would be waiting for her. They would then run away together, out of the Floating World. In vain did I tell her that it would not work. That even if I could get her out of the Hidden House without being seen, she would not get out of the Floating World. The gates were shut at midnight and only opened to let late-leaving patrons out. A geisha would be marched sharply back to her Tea House.

She simply looked at me mulishly. "I don't care what you say. I'm going to do it. Whether you help me or not." She stood and stomped out and that was the last I saw of Fumie.

We heard the tale, of course. Somehow she had got herself out of the Green Tea House. But her boy was not waiting for her, and once outside, on her own, Fumie had no idea what to do or where to go. She wandered off, probably looking for her lover, and found herself back at the river, at the same spot where she had first seen him. She simply stayed there, all night. That was where the Boys caught up with her. It must have been true that Auntie loved her, as we heard that the Boys had been instructed to bring Fumie back and to treat her gently. Whether they would have obeyed her instructions or not, nobody was ever to find out.

True to her creed of making sure that everybody noticed her right until the last minute of her life, Fumie saw the Boys approaching her and managed to climb onto the parapet of the bridge, where she teetered, shouting at them to leave her alone or she would jump. By that time, of course, a large crowd had gathered.

Apparently the Boys tried to talk some sense into her, but as soon as they came within touching distance, Fumie carried out her threat and jumped.

I think, to this day, that she had no real intention of committing suicide. She was always the center of attention and enjoyed being a spectacle. But instead of the reasonably shallow water Fumie had anticipated, the river at that point surged into a deep basin. Even worse, the water was choked with sharp-edged trailing weeds, weeds that clutched and kept whatever they caught. Her kimono and under clothes were heavy, and within seconds she had sunk below the water. She couldn't swim, of course, but it would not have made any difference if she could. The river wanted her, and the river took her.

We heard that the Boys dashed down to the river edge and dived in. They must have been truly terrified of Auntie's wrath because they could not swim either. But it was no good. The river wasn't about to give up its prize easily, and it was nearly a week later that poor Fumie's body washed up, well down from the outskirts of Edo.

She had left the Floating World after all, but not as she had expected.

Fumie's death provided gossip for the girls for weeks. Although they had not really known her, I could not under-stand how they could treat it so lightly. I was deeply upset, both for poor, silly Fumie and for what I saw as my part in the tragedy.

Over and over again I wondered, if I had helped her would it have been different? Would she still be alive? The thought would give me no peace. Eventually, I decided it was my fault. I might not have actually killed Fumie, but if I had given way and helped her, then she would not be dead.

My fault. All my fault.

Ironically, as it turned out, it was down-to-earth Carpi who stopped me worrying myself into the grave along with Fumie.

"What are you moping about for? I can't remember when I last saw you smile."

I glared at her indignantly. "You seem to have forgotten that Fumie was my friend. I blame myself that she's dead."

Carpi stared at me, frowning, and then her expression softened the slightest bit. It was enough. I started pouring out the tale of Fumie and how I had ignored her plea for help. When I was finished, Carpi shook her head.

"Nothing to do with you," she said firmly. "If you had managed to keep her hidden and got her out, her boy would still not have been there, would he? And you knew Fumie better than the rest of us. Do you really think it would ever have entered her empty little head to just go back to the Green Tea House? That would have been too tame for her. Oh no. No matter what, she would have made sure to make a feast of it. It's that bastard she thought she was in love with who should be weeping. Did you know he was betrothed to another girl all along?" I shook my head, incredulous. "Well he was. His father had arranged the marriage years ago. He never had any intention of eloping with Fumie. He just couldn't believe his luck when she fell for him."

"The bastard!" I said bitterly.

Carpi shook her head. "What can you expect? We live in a man's world. No matter what, we are at their beck and call. If we were noblewomen and free, we would still be expected to marry whoever our father wanted us to marry, no matter how old and ugly he was. Remember that, Midori No Me. At least we get paid for our services. It's more than most women do."

She leaned forward and rubbed her cheek against mine, and I smiled, albeit sadly. But I was eternally grateful for her common sense.

And now history had repeated itself. I still couldn't

believe that Carpi, of all people, had run away. Nor that –
yet again – I had denied help to a friend.

The Boys found her. Carpi was bought back in the
late afternoon some two days after she vanished.
We were all astonished that she had managed to evade
capture for so long. In spite of all Auntie's warnings, the
gossip filtered down immediately. Carpi had been found
living with a tribe of wandering burakumin on the outskirts
of Edo. Whether she had gotten so far on her own or had
been taken up by the burakumin was not known.

What we did find out was that Auntie had spoken to her
and Carpi had told her that she would run away again as
soon as she had the chance. I heard this from Suzume, who
had been mending a tear in a kimono in Auntie's sitting
room when the Boys brought Carpi back. I was stricken by
guilt. Poor Carpi had gone back to the only people who had
ever looked after her. At least, looked after her better than
I had.

None of us dared leave our rooms. Even though Carpi
was – had been – Auntie's favorite, even though she was ill,
she would have to be punished. Auntie would not, could
not, let her off lightly. Auntie would see it as her duty to
punish Carpi, and nothing would lessen that punishment.

So we all sat in our rooms, our fingers in our ears, our
head buried our futons as we tried not to hear Carpi's
screams. Auntie had let the Boys loose on her. Both of them.

I felt Carpi's pain even more than the rest of the girls. I
sobbed to myself, wishing that I had done as Carpi had

asked. That I had helped her to ease her way painlessly out of a world that had become anathema to her. Wished that I hadn't failed her, just as I had failed Fumie. I felt every cruelty the Boys inflicted on her in my own body.

When Carpi had no breath left to scream and could only sob, I waited until I was sure that the Boys had gone. As much as I wanted to run to Carpi, to shout at the Boys to stop, to leave her alone, I could not make myself move, knowing perfectly well that if I tried to interrupt them the Boys would turn on me, gladly.

I hated them both more than I had ever hated anybody in my life, and I vowed that if it was ever in my power, I would avenge my Older Sister for every moment of hurt they had inflicted on her.

When I heard the Boys leave – laughing together – I forced myself to get up and go to Carpi. I was oddly pleased that I was on my own and that the other girls had not dared to come. Only little Suzume joined me at Carpi's door, and we looked at each other fearfully before we dared enter.

Carpi had rolled herself in her bedding and was as still as death. We kneeled down beside her, one on each side, and I pulled the uppermost futon away from her face gently. For a moment, I thought she was not breathing. And I was glad of it. Glad for her. Then I realized that I was wrong, that she was breathing, but very shallowly. Very carefully.

With Suzume's help, I got the bedding pulled back. Carpi was naked, and tears poured down my face as I saw the hurt that the Boys had inflicted on her poor body. They had been careful to leave no bruises, no cuts, but Carpi was bleeding badly both from her private parts and her rear. Without being asked, Suzume got up and ran to bring a bowl of warm water and cloths, and between us we did our best to clean and soothe Carpi.

Eventually, she opened her eyes a crack and tried to speak. I shushed her and nodded.

"Older Sister. I am sorry. More sorry than I can ever tell you. If I had helped you when you asked me, this would not have happened."

Carpi shook her head slowly and put her hand on my arm. My guilt doubled. Carpi was trying to calm me, to tell me it was not my fault.

"This will not happen again. I promise you. I will not fail you this time."

Carpi closed her eyes and breathed noisily through her mouth. I realized with a sweep of pity and anger that one of her front teeth had been knocked almost out and was thrusting sideways into her gum. One more small hurt in the panoply of great ones.

I looked at Suzume, willing her to help. She glanced at Carpi grimly and nodded.

"Whatever you need, Midori No Me. I will help." She smiled thinly. "After all, it doesn't matter what the Boys do to me, I will not feel it."

I held Carpi's poor, useless little hand and kissed it, and she drew a deep sigh.

I took Suzume into my confidence and explained how I had let Carpi down. She didn't bother to try and make me feel better, but simply said that this time there would be two of us, and between us we would help Carpi to the next world. I was so relieved. I almost cried all over again.

Although the other girls knew I had been to Carpi, they asked me nothing. It was as if Carpi was already dead to them. Perhaps she was. In any event, I prayed on my knees to Auntie's household gods that Suzume and I were doing the right thing and that we would be successful.

I gave Suzume some coins from the little stash I had

been given as presents by my patrons, and she said she would go to the apothecary as soon as she could slip away. I would willingly have gone myself, but Suzume said it would be better if she went. My absence would be noticed, hers would not. In spite of her confident words, I was nearly sick with nerves by the time she got back.

I was determined that – this time – everything would be done correctly, that Carpi would die with dignity and no pain. She had surely suffered enough already.

Suzume and I crept into her room that night, when everybody else had gone to bed. It was very late as a number of the girls had entertained patrons until the early hours. It was probably only my imagination, but I was sure that every single one of them was awake and holding their breaths in the privacy of their own rooms. I spared a quick prayer for my own interests, asking the gods to make them keep whatever knowledge they had to themselves.

Carpi was waiting for us. As I slid her screen door open, I heard her sigh, quiet as a baby snuffling happily in its sleep. Knowing that she was welcoming death more than she had ever welcomed life made tears blur my eyes, but I blinked them away. The greatest gift we could bestow on my Older Sister was that of death, and there could be no turning away now.

Suzume helped me make Carpi comfortable on her futon. So sure was she that we would come that she had left her spare obi at the side of her bedding. We wrapped it carefully around her legs, tying it loosely in an attempt to make it look as if she had managed it herself. It was tradition for a suicide to bind their legs to keep their bodies straight. A courtesy for those who found them. Carpi lay still, watching us calmly.

Suzume prepared an opium pipe for her, and Carpi took

it greedily. As she slipped into sleep – the sleep that would be eternal – I mixed the flower distillate Suzume had bought with sake and held it to Carpi's lips. She swallowed the entire contents in one gulp and lay back with a sigh.

We sat on our haunches and each of us held one of Carpi's hands – the hands I had always found so repugnant in her life – and waited until her grip faltered. When we were sure that she had stopped breathing, we stood and I tipped the empty cup on its side by her shoulder, as if she had drunk from it where it rested on the floor. We left the empty poison bottle by its side.

We crept away like quiet ghosts, and I felt Carpi's spirit – free of its worldly chains – brush past me joyfully in the corridor.

I was very glad.

There was hell to pay the next morning. If I had thought it was bad when Auntie had discovered that Carpi had run away, it was nothing compared to her fury now. One of us, she hissed, had helped Carpi commit suicide. Even if she had managed to do it on her own, she would never have been able to buy the poison. She had had none with her when the Boys bought her back, Auntie made sure of it.

If whoever had done it did not confess now, then she would punish all of us. Each of us would be given to the Boys in turn. They would be delighted to teach us a lesson. Little Masaki burst into tears, no doubt anticipating the pain the Boys would inflict on her tiny body. Even Kiku was biting her lip and looking terrified. It was no good, I decided. I would have to own up. No matter what the Boys did to me, I could not live with myself if I let the rest of the girls suffer for what I had done.

Just as I was about to raise my head and confess, Suzume jumped to her feet. She had her hands clutched in front of her face, her head lowered. Her whole posture was eloquent of terror.

"Auntie, it was me. I am so sorry. I didn't know!" Her voice rose in a wail of sorrow. Auntie looked at her incredulously.

"You, Suzume? You gave Carpi poison? Why? How?"

"No, I didn't give it to her. Or at least, not exactly. Carpi told me that the Boys had hurt her, very badly, and asked me to get her some stuff from the apothecary to sooth the pain. It was the same thing that the geisha wear in their eyes, to make the pupils big, so I didn't think there could be any harm in it. So I bought some for her and gave it to her and now she's dead and it's all my fault."

Suzume's voice rose in a wail. Even knowing what a good actress she was, I almost believed her. Tears were pouring down her face and she fell on her knees in front of Auntie and beat her head against the floor. Auntie's face was a marvel to watch. Disbelief chased anger across her face, both finally giving way to something that looked very like relief. And it was certainly relief that I could feel washing over the rest of the girls.

"I see. What form was the poison in, Suzume?"

Suzume raised her head, an expression of bewilderment peeking out from beneath the tears. "It was in a bottle, Auntie," she said innocently.

Auntie gave her a hard look, and I mentally shouted at Suzume not to overdo it. "And what was in the bottle, child? Powder? Liquid? Bark that had to be rubbed?"

Suzume's face cleared. "It was a liquid, Auntie. I took it to Carpi and she asked me to pour some into a cup with some sake. She told me to put the cup down by her futon and to leave her. And so I did. Oh, and I made a pipe for her, as she asked."

Auntie nodded. Try as I might, I could not tell from her expression whether she believed Suzume or not. If she didn't, then I decided that I would own up. Whether it meant the Boys or not.

"I see. And when you left Carpi, where was her obi?"

I tried to pretend I wasn't staring at Suzume as though my life depended on her answer, which it probably did. Both our lives, come to think of it. Oddly, I felt very calm. If I was to die, then at least Older Sister would be waiting for me. For both of us. Suzume frowned, as if she was giving the strange question serious consideration.

"Carpi was wearing her bed robe, so it wasn't fastened with a sash." She squinted, as if she was trying to recall the scene. Her mouth opened and closed, as if a thought had just occurred to her. "I know. Her kimono was hanging up on the wall, and her obi...her obi was on the floor, not far from the futon. As if it had been hanging by the kimono and had slipped off the hook."

She sat back and looked at Auntie with a hopeful expression. Auntie stared at her in a way that would have had me quivering and confessing my sins but had no effect at all on clever little Suzume.

"I see. Well, it appears that Carpi must somehow have managed to tie her obi around her legs herself. The liquid you gave her was a poison, Suzume, so you helped her to kill herself."

Suzume's mouth fell open and she wailed loudly. Auntie frowned and waved at her to be quiet.

"It was not your fault, child." I closed my eyes in relief. "If Carpi was determined to commit suicide, she would have managed it one way or another. You are sure she said nothing to you?"

Suzume's face was the picture of innocence. She shook

her head vigorously. "She would not have talked to me about it, Auntie," she said simply. "Not to a maid."

"That's true," Auntie admitted. She stared at the rest of us in turn. "She said nothing to the rest of you girls? Nothing at all?"

We all shook our heads firmly. I apologized to any god who might be listening for the lie.

"None of us had the chance to speak to her before last night," Naruko said timidly. "We had no idea. None at all."

Auntie drew a deep breath and stood up, leaning on her stick. "You will forget this. All of you. I will not have Carpi's suicide mourned. This is a house of joy, not sorrow. And you, Suzume. It is your mizuage shortly, is it not?"

Suzume mumbled, "Yes," not lifting her gaze from the tatami.

"Well, I suppose you did not know what you were doing. But in future, you will tell me before you run any errands for the geisha. As it is, I will have to give a great deal of thought to a suitable danna for your mizuage."

She stumped out without another word and we all sat dumb. None of dared one look at the others, but I just knew that they all knew I had helped Carpi depart this world.

I was just intensely grateful that they had all remained silent. It was more than I expected. Faced with the threat of the Boys, I wondered if I would have had as much courage.

13

The peach blossoms dance
In the breeze.
How do they know the steps?

We all thought – even though it was unspoken – that the Hidden House would be different without Carpi. And yet, it was not. We all grieved for her, but at the same time we felt that if she had been so determined to leave this world, that she had done the right thing. I know that all the girls thought that I had done the honorable thing by poor Carpi. No one actually said as much, but it was conveyed by subtle remarks and a certain silent approval. Suzume, also, was suddenly much more part of the family. I guessed that she was pleased. I also wondered and worried about Auntie's remark regarding Suzume's mizuage. Although she appeared to believe in Suzume's innocence, there was no doubt that the maid had to be punished in some way for her mistake. But if Suzume could feel no pain, what could Auntie do? I decided I was worrying without cause and shrugged the niggling doubts away.

In any event, I soon had more to distract me.

Poor Auntie was all of a flutter. First, it was Danjuro popping up, then Mori-san making an offer for me. And then poor Carpi committing suicide. As if all of that wasn't enough to disturb the even pattern of life in the Hidden House, there was yet more. We girls giggled amongst ourselves, saying – when Auntie was well out of earshot, of course – that Auntie must be getting old to allow herself to be upset like this.

The uproar in the Hidden House was a pale reflection of what was about to take place in the whole of the country. Just as our own sealed casket was beginning to be pried open, so was Japan.

Even with Carpi's death casting a pall over my happiness, I could not remember a time when I felt more joyful. True to his word, Danjuro either sent for me to go to the kabuki or visited the Hidden House himself on the appointed day. Better still – if such a thing was possible – he took to sending a messenger for me, and Suzume as escort, on other days. Always either in the late morning or early afternoon, when he knew the Hidden House would not have clients. He must have paid Auntie a fortune for my services considering the way she beamed and clucked every time a summons came. Worldly-wise Suzume was not so sure. Having Danjuro as a devoted patron of the Hidden House was, she pointed out cynically, the sort of recommendation that no amount of money could ever buy.

"He's only an actor in the kabuki," I said, trying not to preen.

Suzume raised her eyebrows. "*Only* an actor? He's

Danjuro, Midori-san. He's the head of the theater. He directs the plays, discusses what he wants with the most famous playwrights in Japan. He no doubt owns part of the theater. And he's been adopted into one of the best families in Edo. Do you know how lucky you are?"

I should, of course, have given her a good slap for her insolence, but I couldn't bring myself to do it. It was strange, but I could not bring myself to think of *my* Danjuro as the same rich and famous man she was talking about. My Danjuro was a man who gave himself totally to the theater, a man who worried constantly that his best was not good enough. A man whom I longed for more and more with every day that passed. Not just when he sent for me, but all the time. As his mistress, if that was what he wanted. As his slave. Anything, as long as I was with him.

Even the ecstatic Auntie was beginning to drop broad hints that it was time for Danjuro to negotiate to buy me out. She asked if he had mentioned such a thing to me. I shook my head dolefully. I could not even try and explain to her that it was unlikely Danjuro had even thought of it. For twenty-three hours of each and every day, he lived for the kabuki. I was fortunate enough to occupy his mind for the other hour. Sometimes.

"Mention Mori-san's offer to him," Auntie instructed. "And be sure to tell me exactly how he responds."

I said that I would, but I knew that Auntie was going to be disappointed. She did not know Danjuro like I did. Or at least, how I thought I did.

Suzume understood, I knew. But then, Suzume loved the kabuki as much as I did. I felt myself come alive every time I entered the theater. When we were watching a performance, it was lucky we were in a latticed box as I started becoming part of the production. I would mouth the words silently, mimic the actors' gestures. And, increasingly often, I made changes to both words and gestures. I longed, almost as much as I longed for Danjuro, to be on that stage, acting alongside him.

Probably without realizing he was doing it, Danjuro encouraged my ambitions. Often when I was summoned to the kabuki when a play was not in progress, Danjuro would rehearse with me, letting me take the part of another actor. Very carefully at first, I began to make suggestions about a slight change in dialogue or a different approach to an entrance. Amazingly, Danjuro listened to what I was saying, and he increasingly agreed with me. Soon, I began to feel as if I was not only part of Danjuro's life, but also part of the kabuki.

I should have been the happiest girl in Edo. And when I was with Danjuro, I was. But being with him only made it more difficult to play my part in the Hidden House. In spite of Danjuro, I was still expected to entertain patrons. It was no longer enough to close my eyes and ears and pretend I was with my lover instead of an old, fat, sweaty merchant. Even – no, I lie, *especially* – poor Mori-san raised my anger more than anybody.

I began to hate it when I heard he was waiting for me. And the more I showed my distaste for him, the more Mori-san kneeled at my feet and worshiped me. Auntie told me with a smirk that he had raised his offer for me three times. Eventually she would have to give in. Unless of course Danjuro was willing to show his hand...?

I would not have done it unless I had been driven to it. I would hardly have dared. But Danjuro had sent for me, and he greeted me in full makeup and costume. He had been rehearsing, he said, with the company. I felt such a spasm of jealousy that my guts hurt.

And truth to tell, Danjuro in makeup and costume was more than I could begin to resist. He was dressed for the part of a great noble, and I could see at once that he was still in character. He was full of the role: tall, handsome, imperious. He waved Suzume away with a gesture, and she took to her heels. My treacherous knees refused to bear me any longer and I sank to the floor on the tatami in front of him, trembling.

Danjuro put his hands on my shoulders, his thumbs digging into the base of my neck. I felt his strength, could almost smell his desire. I trembled, wanting him to take me any way he wished, just so long as it was totally without mercy. Wanting him to tighten his grip on my neck, to give me pain, to make me shriek with pleasure and pain and something more that I could not even name.

I wanted him to master me. To make me his subject.

And I was not disappointed.

Danjuro's voice was not his own when he spoke. Instead, I heard the tones of the great noble, the man who could buy and sell men and women at his smallest whim. "My little Midori No Me, kneeling before me. Who do you worship?"

"You, Danjuro."

"No other?"

"No, Master."

He laughed, a high, vaunting sound that made me shiver. For a moment, I was afraid. This was not the man I thought of as my lover. He was Danjuro, and yet something more. Was this a part of him that he had always hidden from me? Was this the real Danjuro? I had no idea. His grip on my neck tightened, and I felt the world going grey.

He loosed his grip at the moment I was almost unconscious and I swayed, fighting for balance. Danjuro had taken a step back from me and was staring down at my face. He seemed impossibly tall, looming above me.

He clapped his hands together and I searched his face, looking for a clue as to what he wanted. I was prepared to do anything, anything at all, but I sensed that this was part of a new game that we were playing. I was supposed to know what he wanted. If I got it right, I would be rewarded. If I did not...My sex pulsed at the unknown.

I licked my lips and reached for his tree of flesh, hidden in the voluminous robes of his costume. He slapped my hand away and shook his head. He was smiling, but there was little humor in the smile.

"Try again, Midori No Me."

What? What did he want?

He was staring at my breasts. Did he want me to undress? I reached up and loosed the collar of my kimono. He shook his head. I was so wound up, I felt like screaming. In a sudden flare of defiance, I sat back on my heels. Very well, if he wouldn't tell me what he wanted, then I would simply wait until he did.

He walked behind me and I could hear him breathing. He put his hands on my shoulders and leaned down so I was looking at his face upside down. His mouth smothered my lips and he bit me, hard.

"Who is your Master, Midori No Me?" He spoke into my face and I was panting as I replied.

"You are, Danjuro."

"Very well then, please your Master."

"Tell me how."

"You should know." He walked round in front of me and I licked a bead of blood from my lip. It tasted delicious. He watched me, and I could feel his excitement. Suddenly, I knew what *this* Danjuro wanted. I slid to my stomach on the tatami matting in a gesture of worship, my arms outstretched in front of me as I made my obeisance.

Danjuro took me from behind, yanking my kimono and undergarments up without bothering to undress himself. His tree of flesh felt huge as he thrust into me and I prayed as I have never prayed in my life before that his passion would not be so great that he would spend himself quickly.

I need not have worried.

He toyed with me. First fast, urgent. Then slow. He sensed when I was ready to come to orgasm and pulled back so that only the very tip of his tree was playing with the entrance to my sex. I thrust against him, desperate for more. Desperate for all he could give to me. But Danjuro was having none of it. I could have screamed as he actually pulled out of me.

He sat back on his haunches, his erection mocking me as it jutted out from his body. "Who is your Master, Midori No Me?"

This time, I needed no hints, no education. I rolled on my stomach and hitched across the floor like a snake, wrapping my lips around him. I could taste myself and Danjuro in the juices that mingled on his flesh. I sipped our sap and found it delicious.

But still Danjuro teased. I would have taken him in my mouth down to his belly, but he would have none of it. Every time I tried to take more of him between my lips, he pulled back. I ran my tongue around the head of his tree, searching for that exquisitely tender spot that no man can resist. I knew I had found it when I heard him gasp, and refined the subtle torture as only a geisha, a woman who has spent all of her time pleasing men, knows how. I licked, nibbled, and finally bit.

Danjuro laughed. Whether he was laughing with pleasure, or pain, or amusement at my efforts, I had no idea. Nor did I have time to consider it further.

Without freeing himself from my mouth, he lay on his back so that I was partially on top of him. He grasped my shoulders firmly and lifted me up. I was still greedy for his flesh and tried to hang on.

As soon as I was free, Danjuro twisted me around so that our private parts met our mouths. I howled with pleasure as his tongue flicked into me, in and out and in and out. Not like a snake, for snakes are cold blooded and Danjuro's tongue was hot, scalding my sensitive flesh. Like a forest fire, then. A fire that cannot be satiated until it has consumed everything in its path.

I jerked on his mouth, spreading myself against him, forcing as much of his lips and tongue into me as I could get. He sucked at my pearl and I thought I was about to explode. But no, for a second later he had taken his lips away and was running his nose up and down my opening, teasing and arousing at one and the same time. Then his lips came into play again, and his tongue, that eloquent actor's tongue, was forcing itself inside me.

I thought that I could take no more pleasure. But I was wrong. Without removing his lips and tongue for a second, Danjuro slid his hand up my flank and slid his fingers in my anus. I was so slippery with my own juices that the movement was effortless. He worked his fingers in me for a few moments, and then withdrew them slowly, teasingly. They were soon replaced by his fingers and thumb, and then tantalizingly slowly, his whole hand. He clenched his fist and worked it around in me.

It was too much. I felt the heat build in my belly, spreading to my sex like a fast moving fire. I screamed against Danjuro's flesh in my mouth and he laughed again.

It was only when my sensations began to ebb that Danjuro took himself away from my body, and turned himself so that he was half-sitting, half-crouching across my breasts. He began to thrust into my mouth, slowly at first, then so fast that I could do nothing except to try and contain him. When I could hardly breathe for the size of him, he gave one last, great, thrust and his ejaculation spilled down my throat, trickling out of the corner of my mouth since I could not contain it all.

Danjuro watched me dress and tidy myself in silence. This did not worry me at all; most men were quiet afterward. But I realized that I had not mentioned Mori-san to him, and that Auntie would be most displeased with me if I did not.

I left it to the last possible second, when Danjuro had risen and was courteously taking my arm to walk me to the screen door. He was smiling, a gentle, pleasant smile and I wondered who was the real Danjuro? The man who worried he was not good enough to *be* Danjuro? The intense, demanding lover that he sometimes was? The man who often just wanted to talk to me, who treated me as an equal in an unequal world? Or the man I had just seen, who was not just my Master, but reveled in the knowledge of it.

I shook my head at the uncertainty of it all, and then thought, did it matter? Whether the real Danjuro was one of them, or all of them, or somebody I had not yet met, what did it matter to me? I was here. In the kabuki. With my lover. That was all that mattered.

"Auntie has had an offer to buy me out," I blurted, angry with myself for my clumsiness.

Danjuro stopped and his grip on my arm tightened. "You surprise me," he said lightly. "I would have thought that a geisha of your beauty and talents would have had many offers."

He was playing games again. I knew it. Very well, two could play that game, not just one. I smiled up at him, as gaily as I could manage. "Ah, but Mori-san has not offered for me just once, but three times. Each time he has increased the amount he is willing to pay to secure me. I think Auntie is becoming tempted."

"Mori-san." Danjuro was fingering his upper lip in a gesture that was familiar to me. He often did that when he was trying to work on a difficult piece of dialogue, and I was delighted. He didn't know he was doing it, but it meant he was concentrating. "I know the name. He's a goldsmith, isn't he?" His tone was unconcerned, but I knew better.

I nodded, waiting. He was using the silence as only a skilled actor could, waiting for me to falter and be forced to speak again. I did not. Finally, Danjuro spoke slowly.

"You may tell Auntie that I would be very displeased if she accepted an offer for you. From Mori-san or anybody else."

He turned away and held the door open for me. Suzume was waiting outside, and she bowed deeply. Danjuro nodded at both of us, kindly. We could have been honored guests that he had entertained with tea.

I trembled when I gave Auntie Danjuro's message. I thought that she would be furious, but she was delighted. "As good as we could have hoped for!" she crowed. She saw my bewildered expression and wagged a minatory finger at me. "A man like Danjuro knows how the game is played. We could not expect him to make a counter offer for you straight away. He would not do that. But he has indicated that he is interested in you, child. It will do. Oh yes."

I was pleased, and hoped that she might divert Mori-san to somebody else. But she did not. A bit of competition would do Danjuro no end of good, she said.

14

Fireflies share their beauty
With the night.
We are sisters.

*T*he day for Suzume's mizuage had arrived. She had asked Auntie – brave girl that she was! – if she could resume her given name of Mineko once she was no longer a maiko, and Auntie had agreed. I had thought of her as Mineko for so long, I was delighted.

I had gladly agreed to be her Older Sister and had spent weeks answering her avid questions. I explained the order of the day: the visit to the bathhouse, her makeup, putting on her kimono, and finally the feast where she was introduced to her danna. "You were there for my mizuage feast, you saw how it went."

She nodded, her little face very serious. "Will Auntie watch mine in the same way she did yours?"

I frowned. I had always been aware that Auntie had

peepholes everywhere, but I still did not like the idea that she was watching us with the patrons, making sure that we girls performed as she wanted. Mineko must have guessed what I was thinking, as she smiled slyly.

"Perhaps we should think of it as a little kabuki performance?"

We both laughed at the thought and the tension was not so much broken as shattered. We had been through too much together, Mineko and me, to have any secrets between us. We still did not know who Mineko's danna was going to be. Normally, rumors would have been circulating weeks before, and by the week of her mizuage, we would all have had a shrewd idea of who the danna would actually be. I would have been happier if I had known, at least then I would have been able to coach Mineko in the best way to please him. Stranger still, Auntie announced that the danna himself was providing Mineko's kimono, and that she was to keep it as a gift afterward! Now that was almost unheard of. Very occasionally, a girl who was obviously going to be an exceptional geisha was honored in this way, but it had never happened to anybody in the Hidden House.

Stranger and stranger. Even the normally imperturbable Mineko was beginning to jitter. Who is he? We all wondered, turning names over in our heads. But we couldn't come to any conclusion. Even Mori-san, who had given me presents, had never gone so far as to buy me a kimono. Kimonos, with their rich embroidery, were fabulously expensive and were the main reason why so many geisha could never hope to be out of debt to their Auntie.

And Mineko's kimono was sumptuous. Made of the finest silk, it was embroidered with gold thread and tiny seed pearls. We were all deeply envious of it.

I prepared Mineko's makeup with a hand that shook.

Her danna must be an important man, a very rich man, to afford this. Even her undergarments were sheer silk, edged with contrasting colors. I sat back on my heels and looked at her admiringly.

"Mineko, you are truly beautiful. I hope your danna appreciates you."

A sudden thought nearly choked the words in my throat. No, it was not possible. This couldn't, could it, be some sly trick of Danjuro's, to punish me for flaunting Mori-san before him? Other than himself, of course, he had never given me anything more than some nice bits of jewelry, certainly nothing to rival the magnificence of Mineko's kimono. I had seen him a number of times since the day I had told him about Mori-san's offer for me. Though, now that I thought about it, he had chosen to visit the Hidden House rather than summoning me to the kabuki theater. But he had been the same, hadn't he? Or at least the same as Danjuro ever was, this consummate actor who seemed to be half a dozen men all living in the same flesh.

Worry burned like acid in my stomach. I winced and pretended to Mineko that I had been crouching for too long and that my foot had cramped. I don't think she was fooled, she knew me too well.

I adjusted the folds of her kimono, jealousy almost making me want to vomit. Danjuro? Danjuro and Mineko? Had he ever even glanced at her? Not that I had noticed, but now, I began to wonder. He wouldn't, would he? His mocking voice echoed in my head. *Who is your Master, Midori No Me?* He would. Oh, but he would.

I fixed my face into a smile of welcome as I escorted Mineko to the reception room. We paused outside the door, listening to the sound of the samisen and laughter.

"Ready?" I whispered.

Mineko nodded and slipped her hand into mine. Her fingers were deadly cold. "I know he can't hurt me, Midori-chan. But I'm still terrified."

I forgot my own worries and slipped my arms around Mineko, hugging her as tightly as I dared without disturbing her makeup or her kimono.

"Don't worry," I said with more confidence than I felt. "I'll be close by. If it gets too much for you, shout for me. Your danna can have two for the price of one if it comes to it!"

Mineko giggled shakily and we entered the room side by side.

The yakuza who had stopped me on my first visit to the kabuki was lolling on the tatami in the place of honor, his chin cupped in his hand. Three of his henchmen sat across from him. I couldn't remember his name, but Mineko could. She hid her face behind her fan and hissed, "Yoshida Akira. Akira-san."

If I hadn't been so relieved that Mineko's generous patron was not Danjuro, I would have remembered the dreadful man's name. Abruptly, a wave of fear for little Mineko washed over me, drowning any thought of Danjuro. Or perhaps not drowning him, exactly, but putting him aside for the moment in the face of this new worry.

Something was wrong here. Something was very wrong. Akira-san had barely glanced at Mineko that day. His whole attention had been focused on me, or at least I thought it had. And I knew he had never been to the Hidden House before. If I had been absent when he came, the gossip would have found its way to me. I had told him he could find me here, certainly, but he had not sought me out. Now here he was, buying my poor Mineko's virginity. And not only paying for the mizuage, but also paying far more for Mineko's beautiful kimono and undergarments, an unbelievably extravagant gesture.

Suspicion flared brighter than the lamps that illuminated the room, but I kept a smiling face. We – Mineko and I – had our parts to play. No matter what.

Mineko tottered forward and bowed deeply to her yakuza. He smiled and nodded at her, gesturing for her to sit by his side. Deeply courteous, he gestured to one of the maids to pour her a cup of sake. I was left standing, totally ignored.

I glanced at Auntie, who was beaming and nodding like a puppet, manipulated by unskilled hands. Deeply embarrassed and feeling totally out of place in my own home, I was forced to simply stand as the feast progressed. Etiquette demanded that I could not sit down until the guest of honor indicated that I should. Equally, the same politeness dictated that none of the other girls, not even Auntie, could pretend to notice me until then. I smiled and smiled, into thin air, more worried every minute.

The feast was nearly over before Akira-san pretended to see me. He was a terrible actor. He looked startled, his grey eyes wide open with surprise, and he placed his hand over his heart as if to hold back a jolt of shock. Two could play at that game, I thought, and I unfurled my fan, holding it in front of my face as I tittered like the true geisha I was.

If Akira-san was a bad actor, then that night I was a great one. He jumped to his feet, his expression a mask of concern, and took my elbow, ushering me to a suddenly vacant place on his left. I smiled and bowed and fluttered my eyes at him, as though he was doing me the greatest honor by finally acknowledging that I was in the room. I lowered my gaze to the tatami and murmured my thanks for his condescension in noticing my humble presence. I could feel the puzzlement bouncing between the other girls, but they simply carried on as if nothing strange was happening.

Akira-san pressed a cup of sake on me, and I accepted it with fulsome thanks. Would Akira-san like me to play on the samisen for him? Or perhaps dance? I asked. Akira-san said he would be greatly honored to hear me play.

I took the samisen from Auntie – who was nowhere near as good a player as I was – and after I sat behind it, I began to pluck out one of the melodies from the current kabuki performance. I thought I saw Akira-san hide a smile that might have been amusement, but it might equally have been a grimace.

And so the evening wore on. Mineko was getting quite tipsy. Not a bad idea, I thought, as I was beginning to dread whatever Akira-san had in store for her. The Hidden House had never entertained a yakuza before, so none of us had any idea what to expect. As the sake was replenished, Auntie began to beam more and more widely. This must be costing Akira-san a fortune. And for what? To deflower one poor, defenseless little girl. Perhaps I had had more sake than I thought, as once the idea had taken root in my mind, I could not get rid of it. I became angrier and angrier.

How dare this stranger, this low-class gangster, come into the Hidden House and behave as if he owned not just the house, but all of us in it? The more my fury built, the wider I smiled and the deeper I bowed at every witticism uttered by one of the yakuza. The gleam in Akira-san's eyes became ever brighter.

As midnight approached, Akira-san clapped his hands and rose. He bowed deeply to Auntie, and at his signal she got up – shakily, somebody else who had taken too much sake! – and began to usher us all out. But Akira-san stopped her with an oddly elegant gesture of his hand.

"My friends would also like to be amused while I am preoccupied." He smiled widely. Auntie was nearly bent double bowing. I could see the pile of coins mounting in her abacus of a mind.

I knew, just knew, what was going to happen. Even so, I could hardly believe it. Akira-san's thugs rose to their feet quickly. One went over to Kiku and bowed to her. Another chose little Masaki. The third paused by me, but then passed on and put out his hand to Naruko. Even though I guessed instinctively that our earlier meeting was behind all this elaborate play-acting, this final, carefully planned humiliation left me bewildered. This was a rich and powerful man. Head of the most feared yakuza gang in Edo. Why was he spending so much time and money to humble me, a nothing in his world? He had appeared amused by my defiance at our first meeting. But now I wondered, had he decided he had lost too much face by my refusal to kowtow to him in public? Apparently he had.

Within a minute, the room was almost empty. The maids came in to clear the feast and lay down the futons and bedding. I stood and stepped aside to allow them to work. For one terrible second I really thought that Akira-san was going to pile further insult on me and ask me to stay, to watch or even participate.

But at least I was spared that indignity. Once the maids had finished, he bowed with great politeness and simply stood, obviously waiting for me to leave.

I bowed even deeper and backed myself out.

15

Those the gods wish to
Demean, are first
Given great pleasure

*W*e all clustered around Mineko as soon as we could next morning. Akira-san had stayed all night with her, not departing until dawn. His entourage had also stayed with the other girls, and they all presented warm, satisfied faces, their eyes still lazy with sleep. I hated every one of them, and I was sure they were all smirking behind my back.

"Well?" Kiku demanded. "What was he like? We've never had a yakuza before. Do we want one again?"

All the girls giggled happily. I joined in, but each laugh cut my tongue like a sword.

"He was lovely." Mineko was beaming shyly. I stared at her in disbelief. What did she mean "lovely?" The man was a gangster, a ruffian. Surely, he had played some strange games with her? Surely he had wanted his money's worth, not just for the mizuage, but for the incredibly expensive kimono?

"Didn't he try and hurt you?" Naruko demanded bluntly. I was very glad she asked. I was dying to ask, but felt that I couldn't.

Mineko shook her head. "Not at all. He said that I was a dear little flower, and he was glad that it was he who had plucked me."

We all stared at her in astonishment.

"Akira-san said that? But he's a yakuza!" I finally blurted out. "Not just a yakuza, you told me he's boss of the biggest yakuza gang in Edo. They say he's killed more men than I could count!"

Mineko shrugged. "I can't help that," she said smugly. "He wasn't at all like you would expect from his reputation. He was really gentle and patient. He showed me what he wanted me to do for him, and later on he said he was going to make me happy. And he did, too." Mineko's voice was doting. I itched to give her a slap.

Kiku's face was a picture. Her eyebrows rose and she grinned. "Well, there is something new under the sun after all! I must admit, his...associate was a pleasant change as well."

The rest of the girls murmured their agreement. I shrugged and tried to look as if it was all irrelevant to me. As if I couldn't care less.

"There was one thing that was a bit odd." Mineko's little face creased in puzzlement. We all looked at her with avid interest. "Akira-san was very nice. Very...practiced. But he never took his clothes off. Not so much as his robe. Not all night."

We stared at each other with interest.

"Didn't he visit the bathhouse?" I asked. "I was too busy getting Mineko ready to notice. He was already here when we came in. I assumed he had been to the bathhouse first, as customary."

The girls shook their heads.

"No, no he didn't," Masaki said slowly. "I thought it was odd at the time, but I forgot about it after a while. Was he dirty, Mineko?"

"Not at all." Mineko shook her head firmly. "He smelled nice and fresh, he really did. And young. You know what I mean? Some of the old men who come in can sit in the bath for hours and they still smell sour." We all nodded. We understood exactly what she meant. It was as if the smell came from inside them somewhere. Or was perhaps exhaled in their breath. "Akira-san didn't smell like that at all. He just smelled of clean skin. It was nice."

She beamed at us all happily. Nobody wanted to disillusion her, but Kiku obviously felt she should issue a warning.

"You were lucky, Mineko. They're not all like that, trust me."

But Mineko just smiled at us all. "He gave me a present as well," she chirped. We stared at her in disbelief. Wasn't the outrageously expensive kimono gift enough? Mineko held up her right wrist. The exquisite jade and gold bracelet encircling it caught the light and flashed fire. Very, very costly fire.

I excused myself as soon as I could without being rude. Mineko had decided she would like a nap, indicating without saying as much that her danna had kept her very busy all night. The other girls melted away to the bathhouse to continue their gossip.

I sat in my room with Nekko on my lap and wondered, sourly, what game the yakuza was playing. I felt ugly and bitter and unwanted. Never had I felt more like the deformed half-breed Bigger had called me a lifetime ago. Even the knowledge that it was the third day of the week, that I would likely be seeing Danjuro, barely cheered me. Perhaps Danjuro, too, would decide that he had had enough of me, that I no longer attracted him. Just as I had obviously failed to attract Mineko's ugly yakuza.

After a while, even Nekko became bored with my company and wandered off on business of his own. I could have cried, I felt so lonely.

I was hugely relieved when a message came from Danjuro summoning me to the kabuki. I dressed with great care, determined to shrug off the yakuza's disrespect. As Mineko was now a full-fledged geisha, I had a new maid with me, a quiet, pudgy girl who followed in my footsteps as if she was my shadow and said not a word. She irritated me. I wanted Mineko, wanted to be able to chat with her, share hidden laughter as we watched the world swirl past us. The new girl – Taneka, meaning "Classic Beauty," a name completely ill-fitting on her – was so silent she might as well have been dumb. I tried to scold myself for my lack of charity. Taneka was clearly terrified at being told to go with me, but it was no good. I still wanted to shake her when she answered my every remark with nothing more than silence or a nod of her head.

As we made our progress through the crowded streets, I noticed several foreign Barbarians, all men. They fascinated me, and I glanced modestly at each one as I passed them, seeking my own reflection in their features. Did I look at all like one of their women? Did they see anything *different* in me? I couldn´t tell. They were all so ill-mannered they just stared at us blatantly, with no attempt at discreet politeness. My Barbarian father couldn't have been like them, surely!

A year ago, they were so unusual that the sight of a single foreigner would have caused people to stop and stare, fascinated by their strangeness, just as the patrons used to stare at me in the Hidden House. But since the iron Yankee ship had forced its way into the harbor at Edo and the captain demanded an audience with the highest nobles, times had changed. We had heard about it, in the same way that all gossip found its way to the Hidden House, but at the time the patrons had laughed at the insolent foreign devils and had told us not to worry our pretty little heads about it. They were foreign Barbarians, badly brought up children who simply did not know any better. The shogun would deal with their impertinence in his own good time, just wait and see. But the shogun had not dealt with them, it appeared. Or at least not in any way that us lowly beings could understand. Rather, the Barbarians had returned the next year, and this time it appeared that they were here to stay. Suddenly, the mighty shogun was no more, and after centuries of absence, there was once again an emperor on the throne who was not just a puppet, but who wielded real power over Japan.

We were, of course, far too lowly for any of it to mean much to us, but even so, the very air in the Floating World sizzled with rumors of change. Rumor also had it that Barbarian women had even been seen around Edo, poking their way about the streets with an expression on their faces that said they did not like what they saw, not at all.

So now I stared at the foreign Barbarians with as much curiosity as politeness allowed. Did I really look like them? Any man with fair or red hair particularly fascinated me. I couldn't help it. I remembered Bigger's description of my father having hair the color of a red fox, and each time I saw a foreign devil with red hair I wondered, *Could this be my father*? Was it even possible that he and my mother might come back to look for me, now Japan had been forced to open its gates to the outside world?

One man caught my eye. He was tall with very broad shoulders. His hair was fair rather than red, but he had a beard! I had never seen a man with facial hair like that before. The samurai sometimes sported long, drooping mustaches, but a man with hair all over his face? I was fascinated and stopped dead, the better to stare.

The hairy foreign Barbarian must have felt me looking at him because he stopped and turned to glance at me. I saw surprise in his expression, then he was walking toward me. I hid behind my fan quickly, and would have hurried on but the crowd was too thick and I was forced to stand my ground.

Hairy Face walked right up to me, close enough to touch – how rude! – and smiled. He said something in a strange language that meant nothing to me, but I could tell from his tone that he was asking me a question. Confused, I shook my head and managed to force my way into the crowd, with Taneka trotting at my heels.

My face was burning with embarrassment. Had the Hairy Devil tried to make an assignation with me? Did he think I was a Barbarian myself and wonder why I was dressed as a geisha? Surely not. Even in spite of my red hair, beneath my thick makeup, he could never have taken me for a foreigner. A new anguish popped fully flowered into my head. With all these foreign Barbarians about Edo, would I suddenly lose my status in the Hidden House? What would happen to me if I was no longer a novelty? Would Auntie be forced to accept Mori-san's offer for me if I no longer attracted the patrons? I almost wailed out loud.

Danjuro did nothing to help my peace of mind. Taneka

and I sat in our usual box. Had Mineko been with me, we would have discussed the play, enjoyed the action. Taneka was so silent a presence, I could not even throw myself into the production the way I normally would. In any event, I sensed that something was wrong with Danjuro. Oh, the audience loved him, as always. They roared with laughter when he played a decrepit old man courting a young woman. They wept with him when he was the young lover, banned from seeing his girl by ambitious parents. The applause was tumultuous when Danjuro and his lover finally fled the stage, bound for mutual suicide by throwing themselves off a cliff. Of course they applauded. The kabuki patrons loved nothing more than a happy ending with a good suicide. But I knew that the performance was wrong. It was difficult to pin it down to any one thing, but finally I decided that it was Danjuro himself who was wrong. There was the slightest hesitation in his responses, just a hint of disbelief in his own performance. If it was possible for me to become even more depressed than I already was, then I was.

Tonight would not go well, I knew.

Danjuro barely glanced at me when I entered his rooms. Taneka was banished outside. I told her to ask someone to get her some food, and she brightened immediately. So she was interested in something then!

I decided I would not mention tonight's performance unless he asked. Which he did. Immediately.

"I was bad, wasn't I?"

And what response should I make to that? Any Japanese woman would have said *no, you were wonderful*. It was the expected answer. Japanese women did not criticize their men. Ever.

Danjuro was staring at me bleakly.

"You were not bad," I said, choosing my words carefully. "The patrons loved you, as always."

"And you, Midori-chan? Did you love my performance? Did you think it flawless?"

All through the play, I had been longing to pour my woes out to him. To have my lover take me in his arms and tell me it was all nonsense. That I was worrying over nothing. Instead, he was asking me to reassure him simply because one performance out of a thousand was not as perfect as he had expected. Something sparked in my mind and my mouth formed its own words.

"No, you were not flawless. You were not yourself. Your timing was off and you did not have your normal enthusiasm. It was as if I was watching somebody else playing the part of Danjuro. An actor playing the part of an actor."

There, it was said. Let him do what he liked. Say what he liked. I didn't care. Things could hardly get worse.

He bowed his head in his hands, and for a moment I thought he was going to tell me to get out. To leave him to his misery. I half rose, anticipating his words.

When he raised his head, his eyes were gleaming and I sat down abruptly.

"And which Midori No Me is the real one, I wonder?" He put his head on one side and looked me up and down. I said nothing, just...waited. "Being an actor myself, I'm surprised it's taken me so long to see it."

I stared at the floor, silent. *Go on, then*, I thought sullenly. The god of luck had surely deserted me. Perhaps even Mori-san will decide he doesn't want me. Although I couldn't decide if that was good luck or bad.

"Which one, Midori No Me?"

I raised my head and met his gaze. Firmly. Insolently. "I play a part every day of my life, *Master*." He watched me intently. *All or nothing*, I thought. "Just as you perform different roles, so I am different for every patron who has the money and the taste to buy me. I perform nearly every moment of my waking life."

"And in your dreams, Midori No Me?"

I shook my head. "I do not dream, Master. We in the Hidden House have no time for dreams."

"In your dreams, Midori No Me?" he repeated, and I felt tears gather in my eyes. I blinked hard to stop them falling.

"In my dreams, I am at the kabuki." I whispered. "In my dreams, I am on the stage with you."

I felt his surprise. He shook his head. "Ah, Midori No Me. That is one dream that even I cannot give you."

He stood up and stretched, pushing his hands over his head and flexing his back. He beckoned me toward him. I stood and moved in front of him.

"And do you play a part when you are with me, Midori No Me?"

I shook my head.

"Do I believe you?"

I lifted my head and looked at him. He was still wearing full makeup, although he had taken off his stage robes and was wearing a loose gown. The truth was that I wanted him. Wanted him in a way I never, ever felt for anybody else. Especially not the hated Akira-san. I told him so.

"Ah, but is it truly me you want, Midori-chan? Or is it one of the characters I play? Or all of them?"

Abruptly, I had had enough of all this introspection. Danjuro had had a bad performance, so what? There would be many more where he was triumphant. I wanted him. Now.

I sank to my knees and parted his robe. His tree of flesh reared up at me, hot and strong and thrusting. I took it in my mouth and sucked hard. Forgetting he was a great actor in the need that is common to all men, Danjuro grabbed my hair and tried to push further into me. *No*, I thought. *No. This is my time,* Master. *Today, you will perform for me.*

In spite of his grip, which had the roots of my hair screaming in pain, I moved away from him, almost allowing his flesh to slip out of my mouth. Almost, but not quite. He gasped and I allowed him a little way further between my lips. Lick. Nip. Caress. I prayed that Danjuro would not become so excited by my teasing that I lost him before I had even properly begun. At the same time, I couldn't help but prolong the exquisite pleasure I was both giving and taking.

Danjuro jerked away from me abruptly. Before I had time to react, he jerked me to my feet and pushed me against the door, my hands pinned above my head. He held them there with one of his own hands. With the other, he dragged aside the skirt of my kimono. His hands became fastened in the silk of my underskirt and he abruptly lost patience with it, dragging it up and lunging into me without further ceremony. The thin silk of my underskirt was thrust into me along with Danjuro himself, and I screamed out loud at the incredible sensation of roughness and strength and heat combined.

His teeth were bared and he lunged at me, biting hard at the base of my throat. Sucking at the flesh as though he was starving and I was a feast laid out before him. I wriggled, not because I wanted to get away, but rather to try and force yet more of him inside me. Danjuro must have misread the signal as he raised his dripping mouth and smothered my lips, biting at them and my tongue savagely.

I cried out loudly as my body responded to him, but Danjuro had not finished with me. I might be finished, but he surely was not. He pulled away from me, almost leaving my body, and then slammed back, fastening me to the door as if I had been pinned by arrows. He worked at me, using me, caring nothing for me, for what I wanted, what I needed. My body and mind were in turmoil. I clung to him as if I was drowning, listening to his feral grunts, feeling the heat of his belly against me. And my body responded, whether I wanted it to or not. The roughness of the door behind me, the steel of Danjuro's grip on my pinioned wrists, the exotic sensation of both man and silk plunging into my sex all combined against me. And as Danjuro reached his own climax, my private parts roused to meet him and I felt the echoes and waves of another orgasm shuddering through me again and again and again.

When he finally let me go, I almost fell onto the floor.

It was only later, when the beast had fully left him, that Danjuro came to his senses enough to ask me what had happened to Suzume "She is not with you. Is she ill?"

"No, but she is no longer Suzume," I said sadly. "She has had her mizuage. She is now called Mineko. Because she is no longer a maid, she cannot accompany me. I have a useless lump of a new girl for a maid who is so shy she can't even speak."

He laughed at my pettishness and I smiled myself. "Is that why you were unhappy when you came in?"

Oh, he had noticed? I hid my surprise. I was going to lie, tell him it was nothing, but I saw him looking at me and knew he would see through the fibs. Before I realized it, I was pouring out my woes to him.

I told him all about Akira-san seeing me in the street and then turning up as Mineko's danna for her mizuage. I told him how Akira had insulted me. He listened silently, but I could feel the growing unease in my lover. And not just unease, anger. But a different sort of anger than I had expected.

When I had finished, he got to his feet and began to prowl around the room. "You must stay away from this man, Midori No Me."

I looked at him in irritation. Hadn't he heard a word I had said? Hadn't I just told him that Akira had taken great care to ignore me?

He stopped in front of me and crouched down so his face was level with mine. His stage makeup had become streaked and smeared during our lovemaking and now looked sinister and ugly. I felt as though I was looking at some being that was half Danjuro and half demon. It was... unsettling. And exciting.

"Listen to me." He gripped my shoulders for emphasis. "This man is dangerous. He is ignoring you for a purpose. He is doing it to insult me."

What? Had Danjuro taken leave of his senses? I was bewildered. Was I to be left with no self-esteem at all? It had been bad enough when I thought the yakuza was insulting me deliberately, but worse still to be told he was actually just using me to revenge himself on Danjuro. I shook my head and Danjuro shook me, hard.

"Akira came to the kabuki some months ago. He had money. Lots of money. He had always been interested in the kabuki, he said." Funny, I thought. I had never seen him there. And if he had been there, then surely I would have noticed that ugly face. "He wanted to buy a share in it. A large share. I and the other owners told him we were not interested. The kabuki was not for sale. He persisted, offering more money. We explained to him that it was the tradition of the kabuki that it stayed in the same families. That this had always been so. He became very angry. Probably because I was the spokesman for the families, he directed his anger at me. I would be sorry, he said. He was not used to being insulted, and I would find out that his revenge was painful. We showed him a stone face and he took his leave. Now he has appeared again, and this time he is using you as his tool."

I tried to reason with him. Akira-san could not know that Danjuro was my patron, I said. It was just a coincidence. But Danjuro would not listen to me. I must stay away from Akira, he insisted. I gave in and said that I would, confident that Akira-san would never look my way. In any event, I still thought that Danjuro was exaggerating, that the actor in him was looking for the lead part.

I made my way back to the Hidden House, Taneka a silent shadow at my heels.

16

Earth awakes at the
Touch of spring. Green shoots
Spring in my heart

There were some advantages to having Mineko as a fellow geisha. She could join us in the bath now and Auntie was happy – or at least unconcerned – that she often slipped into my room for a chat. Little Nekko liked her and played happily on the floor between us.

I told her what Danjuro had said about Akira-san, only afterward worrying that I had insulted her by diminishing the yakuza's attraction to her, but I need not have been concerned. Mineko had her head screwed on firmly and accepted what I told her with a shrug.

"I do miss going to the kabuki with you," she said. "I can't say I'm surprised about Akira-san. I thought he was too good to be true."

She laughed and rubbed her neck and I was shocked to see that her throat was badly bruised.

"Mineko! What's happened to your neck?"

"It doesn't hurt," she reassured me. Of course it didn't. But even so... "It appears that some of the patrons are greatly interested in a geisha who isn't supposed to feel pain. They all seem to want to see how far they can go before they make me shriek." I gasped in horror, but Mineko grinned. "It's alright, Midori-chan. I have it all worked out. They all start off in the same way. They give me a pinch or two, and then a slap on the bottom. I just stare modestly at the floor. Some of them pinch me a bit harder, and a few of them give me a punch." No! Although Mineko seemed unconcerned, I was furious for her. "At that stage, I start to pout a bit. When they get to the stage of wanting to strangle me or shove something odd in my sex – one of the old sods tried to put his whole foot in there yesterday, and looking at the state of his wilting tree, I'm not in the least surprised – I start to wail and moan and then they are happy. All puffed up with pride that they managed to hurt the geisha who cannot feel pain."

I looked at Mineko's beaming face and started to laugh. Who was using who? Mineko grinned, but an anxious thought sobered me.

"Take care, Mineko. One day one of them might go too far, then you will be dead."

She shrugged. "I know, there's always a risk. But is it really more of a risk than any of you take?" What could I say to that? She was right, of course. I shrugged. "I've got a good voice, I can always scream if I think there's any real danger. Anyway, tell me about the kabuki. What am I missing?"

We discussed the play, Mineko listening longingly. When I confided that I had told Danjuro about my dream of acting in the kabuki and he had said that it would never happen, she sighed deeply.

"I suppose it wouldn't be a dream if it could come true."

I found her words oddly comforting. But none of us had time to dwell on our hopes and wishes. The foreign Barbarians were no longer just in the streets of the Floating World, they were suddenly here, with us! Not in the Hidden House; Auntie said firmly that the Barbarians would be unable to appreciate our special nature. But she did allow them in the Green Tea House, and no doubt took their money happily. We all begged Auntie to let us take a peek at them. Was it true, Naruko asked, that they had tails? I said I thought not, as I had seen them in the streets and – at least in that respect – they appeared normal. She was greatly disappointed.

Auntie was so pleased at the thought of her strange, new guests that she eventually agreed to our pestering. We girls from the Hidden House would be allowed into the Green Tea House, but we must be discreet. We could walk casually past the open door where the visitors were being entertained, but only one at a time, and at discreet intervals.

We could hardly wait. I had been in the Green Tea House a couple of times, when Fumie had invited me to visit her, but the other girls had never set foot in the place, so that was an additional excitement. In spite of Auntie's firm instructions, we all went across the courtyard in a group. The day was warm and very sunny, and I almost ran across in case the sun made marks on my face again.

We heard the foreign devils before we saw them and paused and looked at each other. I reassured the girls that I had heard one of them speak before, and he had sounded like that, like an animal snuffling in the hay. The girls looked at me in awe. Suddenly, I was the fount of knowledge about the foreign devils.

We took our turns slipping past the wide open door. Mineko went last, and then we all gathered behind the large reception room, our eyes and mouths wide with excitement. The foreign Barbarians had brought one of their women with them! We could hardly believe it.

The foreigners – with the exception of the woman – were seated on the tatami. They seemed deeply uncomfortable. We could get a partial glimpse of them through the gaps in the screens. Although they were correctly seated, with their legs crossed, every minute or so one or the other of them would stretch out their legs and then refold them carefully. Their hands looked huge clasped around the tiny sake cups, and I could not help but think that they were not enjoying the samisen music. Their expressions looked almost pained, but perhaps that was down to their discomfort on the tatami. And two of them had hairy faces! The other girls were more shocked by that than anything, but I said casually that I thought it was quite common amongst the Barbarians.

In spite of everything, it was the woman who fascinated us most. She was seated on a Western-style chair, and I could see Auntie looking at it with deep interest. The woman could not have sat on the tatami, anyway. Her skirts were far too tight to allow her to bend, and the bodice of her dress was so stiff I thought she must be finding it difficult to breathe. She wasn't wearing a wig either, just a silly hat that looked as if it was going to fall over her eyes every time she turned her head. The woman was not drinking sake. She had a teacup in her hand, but she grimaced every time she took a sip from it.

What a rude person, I thought. If she didn't like the delicious tea, then she should drink sake like her men. And if she didn't like that, she could at least be polite enough to pretend she was enjoying the tea. Although, to be fair to her, she did not have the sort of face that looked as if it enjoyed a great deal at all.

The Barbarians had bought a translator with them. Judging by his accent, he did not come from Edo, but he was understandable enough when he spoke Japanese. I strained to listen, trying to match the Barbarians' voices with the translated Japanese words. It was very difficult at first, but gradually I began to get the rhythm of it and became sure that the translator was not translating exactly. It just did not sound right, somehow. And the questions!

Amazingly, it was the woman who asked the most. Even more amazingly, her men paused in their conversation and listened to her respectfully. Strange indeed, the ways of these foreign devils!

Was it true, the woman asked, that all the girls in the tea houses were slaves? That they were never allowed out of the Tea House except under guard? That they were forced to entertain men for money? The woman Barbarian's expression looked as if she was sucking a lemon. One of her men said something to her, very gently, and she frowned at him. I had no idea what she actually said, but I knew if any one of us had used that tone with a patron, we would have been thrown to the Boys for punishment. Except in the case of Mori-san, of course, but he was different.

The translator waited patiently for Auntie's answer. She replied honestly enough. Of course the girls were not slaves. They could buy themselves out if they made enough money or a danna could always take them for himself. That was hardly being a slave, was it? And naturally they were allowed out of the tea house, provided they were suitably accompanied by a maid or two. As for entertaining men for money, what did the Barbarians think the girls were doing now? I think perhaps Auntie's words were not translated exactly. In any event, the woman sucked in a deep breath and her ugly face looked outraged. Behind the screens, we pushed our fists into our mouths to stop ourselves from giggling out loud.

We couldn't leave until the Barbarians themselves had gone or they would have seen us, and that would never do. As soon as the ugly woman had stopped asking silly questions, she nodded to the men and they rose and filed out. Several of the men, I noticed, looked with interest at the geisha who had played and sung for them, but they still followed the woman.

None of us could talk about anything else for days. We dissected every detail about the Barbarians, from their trousers to their funny, tight jackets. Those with hair all over their faces made us giggle endlessly. Did they, we wondered, also have hair all over their bodies? And the way they had done what the ugly woman told them! We decided eventually that she must be a very high-ranking woman in Barbarian society and that the men were her servants.

The chair that the woman had sat on made its way to the Hidden House and Auntie used it every day from then on. She admitted it was not comfortable exactly, but it did make standing up so very much easier for her.

One even odder event happened on the day the foreign devils visited the Green Tea House. When we filed back into the Hidden House, I found Big waiting for me in my room. Nekko was nowhere to be seen, and I had to suppress a pang of worry that Big might have eaten him. I shouldn't have worried. Nekko came back as soon as Big left.

I bowed deeply to Big and smiled politely, trying to hide

my knocking knees. A visit from Big – or at least a visit that had not been ordered by Auntie – was unheard of, but at least on this occasion my conscience was clear. He grinned at me, lolling on the tatami as if this was his bedroom and I was the visitor.

"Come in, Midori No Me, come in. Been to take a look at the white Barbarians, have you?"

My throat was so dry I couldn't speak. I nodded instead.

"You will not find him, you know. I don't know why you're bothering to look."

I was bewildered. Find who? I cleared my throat and found a few words. "I was not looking for anybody, Big-san. I just wanted to take a look at the foreign Barbarians."

I stayed in a half crouch as Big laughed. A nasty, jeering sound. "Oh, you don't have to pretend with me, Midori. You were hoping that your father might have come to claim you, weren't you? That he had come back to find you, after all these years."

The idea was so similar to the thoughts I had had myself, I shivered. But it would never do, showing fear to Big. I kept my head low and murmured, "No, Big-san. That thought had not occurred to me."

"Well, don't bother thinking it." Big got to his feet and stretched luxuriantly, like a healthy animal waking from sleep. "Don't forget, I knew your mother. I knew her well. In fact, she relied on me as a friend. She forgot all about you as soon as she left the Floating World, and your red-haired Barbarian father never even laid eyes on you. Neither of them cared about you. Neither of them spared a single thought for their bastard half-breed. You take after your father, Midori No Me. He was ugly as well. The gods only know what your mother saw in him."

Big shouldered his way out and I sank to the tatami as

my legs refused to support me. I should have been deeply
upset by his spiteful words, but I was not. He had tried too
hard. He was doing his best to hurt me, and against all the
odds I felt a tiny flicker of pity for Big. He hated me, and I
suddenly realized that it was hardly surprising. He had
loved my mother, but she had fled from the Floating World
with her ugly lover, leaving me behind as a constant
reminder of her. And now, I had stolen Danjuro from him.
None of it was my fault, but Big did not see it like that.

If Big could hurt me in any way, he would do it. And he
would enjoy it. I shivered. But I was not unhappy for long.
Yet another sign of the changing times in the Floating
World, Mori-san was given permission to take me out of the
Hidden House. We were going to the river, to eat and float
up and down on one of the many pleasure craft. Would I
like that? I responded with unfeigned pleasure. I would
love it.

Once outside the Hidden House, the change in Mori-
san was remarkable. Although he barely came up to my
chin, he told me firmly that I was to walk behind him. He
strutted like a pigeon in heat, nodding regally to the many
murmurs of greeting that he received. The more people
looked at me, the prouder he became.

I struggled not to laugh at his posturing, hiding my face
modestly behind my fan. But I had to admit that Mori-san
came into his own on the boat. I had never actually been on
water before, and I hung onto the rail tightly, hardly able to
believe that this flimsy wooden vessel was not going to sink
beneath our very feet. Mori-san allowed me to cling on to
him and patted my arm reassuringly. I was even allowed to
sit beside him on the deck.

It was so peaceful, so beautiful floating down the river
that I forgot my initial fears very quickly and could not

conceal my delight in everything I saw. This, then, was Edo! To me, seen from the river, it was a fairytale place. Mori-san saw the awe and fascination in my expression and promptly tried to turn it to his advantage.

"This could all be yours, Midori-chan. You could be out of the Floating World. Mistress of your own house, with your own servants." He glanced at me sideway and added, "You could spend your days doing whatever you wanted, with no one to tell you to do this or do that."

I was tempted. The air was so very sweet, the motion of the boat so soothing. For the first time in my entire life, I was free. The thought of returning to slavery in the Hidden House suddenly made me feel sick. Then I thought of the true alternative Mori-san was offering: a life spent as *his* servant, caring for *his* needs. Alternatively bullying him and cajoling him when I wanted anything. Bearing his children and worrying if I did not produce a boy child. Worrying every day that he might grow tired of me and might put me aside. No, I would be just as much a slave as Mori-san's wife as I was as a geisha in the Hidden House. Suddenly, I was sure I caught a glimpse of Big, sliding into the crowd of people promenading along the river banks, and my mind was made up. I smiled as sweetly as I knew how.

"Ah, Mori-san. If it was up to me, I would be by your side in a moment. But alas, I am not free to make my own choice. You know that."

He sighed and blew out his cheeks. "I will persevere with Auntie. I know you are her favorite."

I was? Startling news indeed!

I was deeply sorry when we got off the boat. But more was to come. Mori-san had arranged for food to be served to us on the river bank and I lolled indolently as servants set out our food and drink. Even my new little maid Taneka was allowed to sit quite close to us and was served with food. She was so nervous I don't think she tasted anything at all, which was a pity as it was delicious.

If only, I thought. If only Danjuro was unknown to me. If only I couldn't feel my mother's presence beside me, urging me not to give in, to take from life what I wanted, not what life wanted to give to me. If only I was somebody else. If only I didn't know that a single day with Mori-san would drive me completely mad. If only...

They say that smugness is the one thing that is sure to annoy the gods. I had always thought that saying nonsense, but then I had never before had anything to be smug about. I was soon to find out that it was true.

We had barely finished our meal when a messenger ran up to Mori-san and handed him a scroll. He read it and tutted, but I could see that secretly he was pleased. An important client had arrived at his premises, he said, and had condescended to wait for him. He must leave immediately, but Taneka could escort me back to the Hidden House. I smiled and agreed. Of course, I understood. We were surely in no danger here in Edo.

I had had enough to eat and drink and the sun was seeking us out. I dreaded breaking out in brown marks again should it find us. I beckoned to Taneka and rose, brushing down my kimono. I was deeply reluctant to return to the Hidden House, so I decided we would walk alongside the river back into the Floating World. It was not the most direct way, but, oh, so very pleasant.

The assault was so professional that one moment I was sauntering, delighting in my freedom, and the next I was surrounded by men and was being hustled forward at a trot. I heard Taneka shriek and then nothing but the murmur of people going about their business on a sunny afternoon.

One man had hold of each of my arms. It took all my breath to keep up with them, but even had I screamed it would have done no good. I was a woman, not even a so-called free woman, just a geisha. Nobody would have bothered to look twice, still less come to my aid.

We were hustled along, *away* from the Floating World rather than toward it. I looked around when I could and realized very quickly that I was hopelessly lost. I had no idea at all where we were. Mineko might have known where we were being taken, but I did not.

"Look straight ahead. Don't bother gawping," the man at my right arm said. I did as I was told. I wondered if Mori-san was behind all this. Did he believe that Auntie would never give way and so had decided to take me by force? The idea was deeply reassuring. Mori-san I could cope with. Easily. I almost smiled.

After a minute or so, and innumerable turns and twists in the narrow streets, we paused before a high door set in a wall. I had seen nothing like this in the Floating World and was curious rather than frightened. After all, if it was only Mori-san who was playing tricks, what did I have to be afraid of?

One of the men banged on the door and a peephole popped open and closed quickly. The door opened and I was hustled through into a garden. The Hidden House had a garden of sorts, in the courtyard between us and the Green Tea House. I had always thought it beautiful, but it paled into something very commonplace next to this garden.

Most gardens in Edo were laid out on Zen principles. Some carefully raked gravel, boulders, shrubs planted here and there and pruned unmercifully. If the garden was large, a tree or two for shade. This garden spat in the face of Zen.

It was large and full of color. To my startled eyes, it appeared that every inch of space was filled with a riot of brilliant, flowering plants. Reds jostled whites, blues leaned companionably into pinks and yellows. It was breathtaking. I was breathless not just from the garden but also from a sudden, chilling knowledge.

This garden, this unconventional, truly beautiful garden, could never have anything to do with Mori-san. It would have made him ill with its colors and perfumes and sheer uncontrolled joy.

So if it was not Mori-san who had taken me, who was it?

Danjuro never entered my head. He had no need to snatch me off the streets. I was his for the taking, whenever and wherever he wanted me. Had I finally offended Big to the extent that he had decided to do something about me? Hadn't I seen him earlier? No, this was not Big's world. Whoever owned this house was a rich man. I had never seen anything like it.

I shivered with sudden terror. No one knew where I was. No one. Auntie would think me safe with Mori-san. If he did not deliver me back by the late evening, she might send one of the Boys to enquire after me. On the other hand, thinking me safe with Mori-san, she might simply get out her abacus and add more money to his bill.

I was breathless with fear as I was manhandled into the house, with Taneka behind me moaning endlessly in terror.

Once inside, our captors melted away. One moment they were all around us, the next we were alone. It was cool and shaded inside, and I began to shiver with cold as well as fear.

"Welcome to my home, Midori No Me."

The voice came from the shadows. I turned around and

at first could see nothing, nobody. He was standing so still, I couldn't make him out until he moved.

Akira-san, with his grey eyes, mustache, and swagger. Akira-san had taken me. The gods knew what he wanted me for, why he had bothered to kidnap me, but my fear ebbed a little. At least I knew him. At least it wasn't Big.

Taneka was bowing deeply to him, and I managed an unconvincing little bob. He laughed out loud.

"Ah, Midori No Me! Now I know that the wait will be worthwhile. Child," he nodded at Taneka and gestured toward a door behind him. "Go to the kitchen. They will feed you and give you something to drink. Don't be afraid, nobody will harm you here."

Taneka scuttled off as fast as her little legs could take her. I didn't blame her. Mineko, I knew, would have stood her ground at my side, but Mineko was not here.

"And me, Akira-san? Is any harm going to come to me?"

He was grinning. Everything I said seemed to amuse him. Anger slowly began to get the better of fear and I stared back at him defiantly as he walked around me, inspecting me from top to toe.

"Do you have only the one kimono? You never seem to wear anything else."

"I have dozens of them. I just happen to like this one," I lied.

"I will give you another dozen."

"Thank you, but I don't want anything at all from you. Except to let me go."

He was laughing at me. "I will let you go in my own good time."

I glared at him. I desperately wanted to pee. The sake I had drunk with Mori-san and fear combined in my poor bladder. His grin widened and I had a horrible suspicion that he saw my discomfort. "Auntie will search for me when I don't return," I said with the faint hope it was true. "She can be a troublesome woman. You will not be happy if Auntie is angry with you."

Pathetic, I thought. Here I was threatening a powerful yakuza with an old woman. It was partially true. Auntie was a great force in the Floating World. Greater men than this gangster had been cowed by her. But Akira-san was still grinning.

"Ah, but Auntie knows where you are. Or at least, she knows that you are with me. I sent her a message as soon as Mori-san was well clear. Don't worry about your patron. He really does have an important client willing and able to buy his gold. And by now, Auntie will be counting her fee and her blessings."

I clenched my teeth. Very well. If there was to be no escape for me, then Akira-san would be treated with exactly the same courtesy that I would offer to any other patron. See how much he liked that. With exquisite grace, I sank to my knees and bowed my head.

"I am at your feet, danna." I murmured.

He had stopped behind me. I could feel his stare, hot on the nape of my neck. I yelped with surprise as a cold, rough finger slid down my neck from my hairline to the collar of my kimono.

"You have a beautiful neck. Very long. Very slender."

And I just know that you would like to put your hands around it and squeeze until I screamed, I thought. I forced myself to remain motionless as that finger ran up and down my spine.

"But first things first." Akira-san sounded business-like. "You will take a bath. Then you will see." He clapped his hands and one of his thugs appeared immediately. Akira-san rapped instructions to him. I was to be taken to the bathhouse and shown every courtesy. The final command made me shiver. How would I have been treated otherwise?

The bathhouse was luxurious. Not as big as at the one at in the Hidden House, but bright, well appointed, and beautifully clean. A couple of little maids bowed me in and at my urgent request hurried to show me the lavatory. An indoor lavatory! Akira-san did himself well, to be sure. When I emerged, I was soaped and rinsed and allowed to wallow in the hot water. I lingered as long as I dared, but when the anxious faces of the maids began to hover over the edge of the bath, I climbed out with a regretful sigh.

They wrapped me in a drying robe and then a loose, thick silk robe in shades of the softest green and cream. There was no sign of my own kimono. I thrust my feet into the offered geti and followed yet another maid back into the house.

It was even larger than it appeared from the outside. Sparsely furnished in the traditional style, but even my inexperienced eyes could see that every single piece had been chosen for its beauty and harmony. And was expensive. I was finally shown into a reception room and I eyed the thick futons and bedding laid on the floor with something very like relief. If that was all Akira-san wanted, why on earth had he gone to all the drama of abducting me off the street? Unless, of course, it was simply to support his flamboyant reputation. Or to frighten me half to death, which seemed equally probable.

I made myself comfortable on the futon and waited. And waited. The afternoon had become warm, and I was drowsy from my bath. I could lay down for just a while, I thought. I could never sleep, of course. But the futons were thick and soft and inviting, and I sank into their comfort. I had barely closed my eyes, or so I thought, when I was awakened from sleep by the sound of the screen door opening and closing.

The afternoon had progressed. The shadows on the tatami were longer. Instinct made me keep my eyes almost closed, pretending I was still sleeping. I breathed slowly and evenly, relaxing my muscles. Even with my eyes barely open, I could sense Akira-san moving around. Hear his breath on the still air.

"Midori No Me." He spoke very softly and I knew that he did not believe that I was asleep. Perhaps I was not as good an actor as I thought. I opened my eyes.

Akira-san stood at the bottom of the futons. His shadow fell across the bed, and it felt warm. I stared at him, word-less with wonder. His clothes lay where he had discarded them on the tatami. My gaze ran up and down his body, wonderingly.

Every inch of skin, every part of his body from the base of his neck to his ankles and wrists was covered in tattoos. As soon as he was sure I was looking, he held out his arms from his body and turned very slowly. The tattoos looked like living things. There was no particular theme to them, no color scheme that I could see. Blossoms bloomed along-side exotic birds. A tiger stalked his belly, nuzzling between his breasts. A long snake ran down each leg to his knees. His lower legs were covered in swirling symbols, all color and curves. His arms bore more symbols. As he turned, on his back I saw a dog-fox, the eyes gleaming, the teeth bared. The bottom of his neck was tattooed with a collar, artfully executed to look like an intricate necklace. His ribs were decorated with larger-than-life-sized eyes, in all shapes and colors. I would have sworn that they were poised to wink at me. As he turned, the tattoos seemed to move with him, flowing into each other like the living works of art that they truly were.

Even his penis, his proud, jutting tree, was tattooed from the base to the very tip. Trailing vines with just-opening white blossoms covered the length while the glans bore a depiction of a pair of women's hands cupping the flesh. The work was so well executed that it actually looked as if the fingernails were denting slightly, nipping his skin.

I gasped out loud. Naked, Akira was very, very beautiful.

The last remnants of fear drained away and were replaced by gnawing desire. At the sight of the work of art that was his body, I forgot that he had insulted me. That I hated him. Even that Danjuro had warned me that I must stay away from him, that he was dangerous. Or perhaps it was just a combination of all those things.

I wanted him. Wanted to feel the heat from those tattoos – for surely, the colors had to be hot – rubbing against my skin. Wanted, above all, to feel the roughness of those blossoms on his erection as they opened themselves inside me. I shook the bedclothes aside and kneeled. Bowing my head on the futons, for once I meant it.

Akira moved toward me and bent down. He put his hands on each side of my head and licked the nape of my neck with a dry tongue. I hissed with pleasure.

"I shall put my mark on you, Midori No Me," he said. I was delighted to hear his voice was shaking slightly. "Not today, but soon. Now, look at me."

I raised my head. Moving without any command from me, my hand raised itself and ran my fingers down his belly, wrapping my fingers around his testicles. Even these had been decorated with concentric wavy lines. They tightened at my touch, and the lines parted, giving the illusion of a life of their own. Almost like ripples on water.

He took a deep breath. "I honor you with my body. No other woman has ever seen the whole of me. Does it please you, Kazuha-chan?" He had called me Kazuha – "Soft Leaf." A pun on the color of my eyes, but said tenderly. I was almost moved to tears. In the whole of my life, I had never had an affectionate name. I had always just been Green or Green Eyes. Even Danjuro had never given me a love name. I pushed the thought of Danjuro away determinedly. He had no place here.

"It pleases me greatly."

"Show me how it pleases you, Kazuha."

I shuffled forward the few inches that separated us and took his tree of flesh in my mouth. I had expected roughness from the tattoos, but there was none. His flesh was silken and very faintly perfumed. It excited me.

I ran my tongue around the bulbous head of his tree, forcing the hood back with my teeth. Akira stayed still, giving no sign that I was either pleasing or displeasing him. Slowly, I pushed him into my mouth until the tip of his erection was pushing against the back of my throat. Then, and only then, did I suck. Not just with my lips, but with the whole of my mouth and my throat. Then, I heard him give a groan of pleasure.

I allowed his flesh to slip slowly out of my mouth and my lips felt cold when it had gone. His erection was silver with my saliva, summer rain on the blossoms. I ran my gaze up his body to his face and simply waited. Whatever this strange man wanted from me, I would give. Whatever he wanted to give to me, I would take. Instinctively I knew I had no option. He radiated power. I was a prisoner in his house, at his command. And hadn't I been taught every day of my life that I had to obey? Only this time, obedience would be …easy. His whole aura demanded obedience. I felt like a well-trained dog, taking pleasure in following its master's word. Akira leaned down and ran his finger down from my between my breasts to my stomach. My robe parted beneath his touch. I shrugged the garment away from me and kneeled naked before him, the heavy silk pooling around my thighs.

For what felt like an hour, but was probably no more than a few seconds, he simply looked at me. Even his glance burned me. I bowed my head, looking at him from beneath my eyelashes.

"Lie down. No, on your stomach."

I did as I was told. For once from choice rather than necessity.

He kneeled behind me and pushed his hand beneath my sex. His nails were long and scratched slightly when they entered me. I shuddered with pleasure at his touch. All of his fingers rubbed me, and I lifted my bottom in instinctive response. He laughed.

"Like a cat when you tickle its spine," he whispered. His hand slid round from my sex to my anus, and a single finger slid inside. I tensed for a moment and then cried out in pain as the rest of his fingers followed.

"Shush," he whispered. "I am not hurting you. Not yet, Kazuha. Not yet."

I bit my tongue and felt the hot, coppery taste of blood. I would not cry out, no matter what he did. I would not.

His fingers slid out as surely as they had entered. I felt him pause, and then his erection was nuzzling the entrance to my anus. I couldn't help it. I was so desperate for him inside me, no matter where, that I pushed against him, forcing him into me.

He was a big, muscular man. His erection was not as obscenely freakish as Big, and certainly not as deformed as

Bigger's, but Akira was still handsomely blessed by the gods. I gasped as he slid into me. Any woman would have.

Very quickly, I remembered his remark that he was not hurting me – yet. As he thrust, trying to get more and more of himself into me, I felt as if I was being skinned from the inside out. Oh, he was not the first to want to split the melon with me, but generally the patrons who were interested in it were older men, ones who wanted to believe that there was some wickedness in doing it that way. But Akira was not an old man. He was young and vigorous and his tree of flesh was, quite literally, in full blossom.

"Tell me to stop, Kazuha," he hissed. He caught the nape of my neck in his teeth and bit. Hard. He turned the flesh in his teeth. I howled with pleasure, a bitch in heat that has enticed her mate and was being fully satisfied.

"No!" I shouted. "No, don't stop. Please."

I heard him laughing, his voice hoarse and deep.

Harder. Harder. And harder still. Every thrust, every plunge was an exquisite pain. A delicious hurt. I thought I wanted him to go on forever, and then I felt my orgasm beginning to grow and spread deep in my sex. It was as if Akira could read my body as if it was his own. He began to slow down, to take himself further out and then to shove in not quite as far. I almost wept with need.

"Please," I whispered. "Please."

He snickered, not quite a laugh, rather a sound from deep in his throat. "If I give you what you want, how will you repay me?"

I shook my head helplessly. I would offer him anything. But what did I have to offer that this rich, powerful yakuza did not either already have or could easily get?

"Anything. Anything. Anything you want."

"Remember that when the time comes, Kazuha."

He began to increase his pace, shoving at me so hard that I nearly fell onto the mat. I spread my knees for balance and discovered that the action meant I could grip him that much harder. The pain became fire, fire and ice together, and finally my body could take no more and I exploded in orgasm, screaming out loud with pleasure as the waves of my fruit bursting tore through me. Akira seemed to absorb some of my excitement, as I heard him begin to grunt deep in his throat. The animal sound was intensely exciting and raised me to a peak that left me shuddering.

Finally, he slowed and stopped, slipping out of me. I collapsed on the futon and Akira-san slid down to lie beside me. I couldn't help myself, I reached out and took his flaccid penis in my hand, rubbing the sticky residue from it with my finger and thumb. It must have been very tender, as Akira groaned and put his own hand on mine to stop me.

Every time I moved so much as an inch, I felt as if I had been torn in two, but the sensation was still a delicious reminder of what this man had done to me.

"You will bathe and then go back to the Hidden House, Kazuha. You will become Midori No Me again, until the next time I send for you."

I sighed and ran my fingers down his chest. Why had I ever thought him ugly? A sudden thought made me sit up straight, suspicion tingling in my spine. How had I come to forget? Danjuro had said that that Akira was only interested in me as a way of destroying him. Was that really true? And if it was, how had I come to take such pleasure in this man? In any event, the thought of Danjuro cast a cloud over my pleasure. How had I allowed myself to be taken with such pleasure by any man but my lover?

"What? Are you cold?" He sounded concerned, but now

I didn't believe anything he said. I shrugged, trying to appear casual.

"No, I am not cold. But," I paused, tracing my finger nail on the bedding, not looking at him. "But I don't understand, Akira-san. When you came to the Hidden House, you didn't so much as look at me. You were rude to me. And now you drag me off the streets and bring me here to take me. Why?"

He laughed at me. "I knew as soon as I saw you in the street that you were mine, Kazuha. You were beautiful and you looked at me so angrily, refusing to bow down to me. No woman has ever treated me like that. Any woman I want comes to me at a run. I was intrigued. So I asked around about little Midori No Me from the Hidden House. You were on the way to the kabuki, weren't you?"

I nodded. This was it, then. Was he going to lie? And if he didn't lie, would I like what he was about to say?

"I've been told that Danjuro is your danna. That you belong to him. Is that so?"

I considered my reply carefully. I was deeply uncomfortable discussing Danjuro with him. As my lust began to cool, more and more was I regretting pleasuring myself with this man. It was no good telling myself that I had had no option – that was only half the truth. A few minutes ago I would have crawled over broken glass to get to him. *That* was the truth.

Oh, Danjuro. I have betrayed you. I am so sorry.

"Danjuro is one of my patrons," I said. "He does not own me."

He remained quiet, turning my words over in his mind. Eventually he nodded, appearing satisfied. "Danjuro stood in my way when I wanted to buy the kabuki," he said finally. "If I can cause him hurt, then I will. But that is not the reason I wanted you, little Kazuha. I was determined to take you before I knew you had anything to do with Danjuro. Will you tell him you have been with me, here, in my house?" he asked curiously. I thought about lying, but what was the point? He would hear it in my voice.

"No," I said simply. "It would hurt him if he knew, and I am not part of your quarrel."

I was deeply relieved that my answer seemed to satisfy him.

Taneka walked back with me in the darkness to the Hidden House. Akira had allocated one of his men to walk back with me, and I was relieved. I had no idea how to find my way back, and to me Edo was more frightening than the Floating World.

It was very late, and the gate around the Floating World had been closed and barred before we got there. I heard the clink of coins being exchanged, and then the guard – an old samurai run to fat – was bowing us inside.

As Akira had said, he had obviously gotten word to Auntie that I would be late, as there was a light still burning in the entrance hall to the Hidden House. The door was locked, but when I tapped a maid quickly opened it.

My own bed was warm and comfortable. For my body, anyway, but not for my conscience.

Oh, Danjuro. What have I done?

17

Memories leave no shadows.
Yet I see you in
Each shade

I argued with myself in every odd moment. Should I tell Danjuro or not? When I was on my own, I found myself muttering out loud, asking myself "what if" questions and then answering them. Even Nekko began to look at me strangely.

It was not the simple fact that I had made love – if you could call it that – with Akira. For the first time, I thought bitterly that I might just as well be one of the poor women behind the lattices, out there in the Floating World. My purchaser had not even been a man of status and good reputation. He was a rich man, but a gangster, nothing more. My world tumbled around me as my proud illusions of being a geisha crumbled to dust. To make matters worse, I had enjoyed it. I had suddenly found the man I thought an ugly thug intensely attractive. Had the yakuza stripped all my pretensions away and revealed the real me? No longer the proud geisha, but the whore who was no better than her sisters in the gutter. Ah, but that hurt! I burned with shame as I thought of Danjuro. Oh, but I was sorry! I did not, for one moment, fool myself into thinking that I was in love with the yakuza. No, never that. But I yearned for him. Every fragment of my body wanted to touch him, my sex longed for him. Neither the love globes nor any patron could make me want him any less. It was not at all how I felt about Danjuro, who I wanted with not just my body but my soul. Even the knowledge that Danjuro could – and possibly did – take any woman that caught his fancy didn't make it any easier. He was, after all, a man, and in this man's world that was only to be expected. No, the simple truth was that I was terrified that when I saw Danjuro again, I might not feel the same about him. That I had lost something truly precious.

At least I was wrong about that.

Danjuro was absent for over two weeks. I fretted, convincing myself that somehow he had found out and was so angry that he no longer wanted to see me.

The girls teased me unmercifully, saying I had swapped one powerful danna for another and that I was greedy, mourning the absence of my first lover. I laughed with them, but ached for both men. Greedy? Perhaps so. But there was no telling my body that.

When Danjuro did turn up, he took me by surprise, for which I was intensely grateful. At least I had not had time to dither and worry. He came to the Hidden House at a bare hour's notice, Auntie said. She had to divert a patron to Kiku and, even worse, had to give him a discount.

I kept my eyes on the floor, sure he would read the truth

in them. But no, Danjuro had other things on his mind. He drummed his fingers on the matting, his whole body tense, and I realized quickly that he was almost as nervous as I was. Fear began to raise gooseflesh on my arms and the short hairs at the back of my neck stood up.

"Danjuro..." He silenced me with a gesture and glanced around as if he thought we might be overheard. He had no need to worry, I had developed a second sense as to when Auntie was crouched at her spy hole, and I knew that today we were alone.

"Midori No Me." His tone was formal. I flinched, expecting bad news as one might expect a blow from an uplifted fist. "I am sorry. I have ignored you shamefully. But there is a reason for this. I cannot tell you anything at the moment. I wish I could, but I don't know myself what is going to happen...yet. I have come tonight to tell you I am going away for some time. As soon as I return, I will send for you. I am sorry."

I stared at him aghast. This stumbling, almost incoherent man was not Danjuro. I knew him well enough to know that he was not acting. He simply could not find the right words. At least that was comforting, in an odd way. I shot questions at him: where was he going? How long for? What was so important that he couldn't trust me with it?

He simply shook his head and took my hand in his. It was such a tender gesture that I burst into tears.

"Midori-chan, no. No tears for me. For us. I will come back to you, I promise. And when I do come back, it will be to take you away from this place. Please, just remember that. As long as there is breath in my body, I will come for you."

He licked the tears from my face and laid me down gently on the futon. Our lovemaking was so tender, so sweet, it was like nothing I had ever known. Not even from Danjuro. And certainly not from Akira. Perhaps for the first time, I knew the difference between love and lust and realized with a heart that was fit to break that the two could be joined in the same person. Now, when Danjuro was about to leave me, I knew that he was the only man I wanted. Would ever want.

Suddenly, I needed to tell him about Akira. Not just that I had had sex with him, but that I had enjoyed every minute of it. If Danjuro no longer wanted me, then that was only fair. But I couldn't let him go with that blackness on my conscience.

"Danjuro, before you go, there is something I must tell you." I paused, trying to find the right words.

Danjuro shook his head. "I know," he said. My lips formed the word "no" silently. He did not know. He could not know. "I know. I know what happened. I can guess how the yakuza made you feel. If he was not my enemy, I would admire him. He is an extraordinary man. But take care while I am away, Midori-chan." His brow creased and when he spoke it was not the words I expected. "You will be safe with the yakuza. No one will hurt you whilst it is known that he is your danna. But wait for me, in your heart."

He kissed my lips softly, rose, and was gone. I lay down on the futon, huddling into the warmth left by his body, inhaling his clean, masculine smell from the bedding. I was bewildered and relieved. Danjuro did know. How, I had no idea. But at least he knew, and still he cared for me. I cried myself to sleep. But with Danjuro or without him, life had to go on at the Hidden House.

But not life as we had always known it. Not life as we had always assumed it would be. The foreign Barbarians were everywhere. Not in the Hidden House – yet! – but they began to appear regularly in the Green Tea House and were commonplace in the streets of Edo. Auntie claimed she could not tell one Barbarian from another, but I could, easily. Some had blue eyes, some brown. All had fair hair, but in so many different shades it was like looking at a tree in autumn. Some had hairy faces, some just mustaches. Others were clean shaven. And with just a little concentration, one could see the differences in their features, although those features were never as expressive as a Japanese face.

And they had money. Lots and lots of it. Some of them came to us to save our souls, they said. They wanted us to worship at the shrine of their god. We were bewildered by that. We had no problem adding one more god to those we already had, but that was not good enough for them. Rather, they wanted us to put aside our ancestral gods and worship only their god. The very idea! They obviously did not realize that this would not only lose our souls rather than save them, but would have been a gross insult to each and every one of our ancestors. But apart from the soul-stealers, many of them claimed to be in Edo to trade. They wanted silk, jade, porcelain, gold. Only the very best. Mori-san said his business was booming with them. And it was Mori-san that put a new idea into Auntie's head.

I was half foreign Barbarian, he pointed out. Could that mean that I would be able to learn the Barbarian language easily? That would be useful to both Auntie and Mori-san. They both looked at me with growing interest. I glanced from one to the other, worried. I had heard the Barbarians speak, and the strange, guttural sounds they made meant nothing to me. It was like listening to foxes bark at each other when the moon was full. Neither Auntie nor my patron would hear my protests. An appointment was made for me with the translator most of the Barbarians seemed to favor, and he set to work training my tongue. It was impossible at first. I could not get my lips around these strange sounds, and when I did, the words meant nothing at all. But Auntie indicated – with her stick – that I must persevere, and gradually it became easier. Once I had grasped a few words, Auntie allowed me to be present at the Green Tea House when Barbarians were present, much to the disgust of the tea house geisha! Not to speak, just to listen. It became much easier, once I could see the expression that went with the words. I soon realized that I had been correct when I had thought that the translator was not telling the whole truth when he translated. Many words and remarks were omitted. And I could see why!

It had never occurred to me that the foreign Barbarians found us as strange as we found them. That to them, our customs were crude and often revolting. Even the mixed bathing in the bathhouses, it appeared, was obscene to them. This did not, of course, stop them moving on from the tea house to the courtesans, but I was not surprised about that. That was the nature of men the world over.

Very soon, I could understand and even speak English much better than the translator. Auntie and Mori-san were delighted. Auntie dispensed with the expensive translator and even allowed Mori-san to use my services when he was negotiating with the Barbarian merchants – as long, of course, as the negotiations took place in the Tea House. It rapidly became obvious that the Barbarians themselves were both amused and pleased to have me as a translator. This in turn led to yet more customers for Auntie, as what they called "meetings" began to take place more and more often in the Green Tea House.

I was amazed to find that the Barbarians were interested

in me. They wanted to hear my story and were shocked when I told them that I had been abandoned by my mother, raised in the Floating World, and trained as a geisha when I was old enough. No mention, of course, of the Hidden House. Was it true, they asked, that young girls were often sold into slavery to please men? And that most geisha and courtesans were actually slaves?

I had great difficulty explaining all that to them. Didn't I mind, they asked. I explained that that was just the way things were, and it was normal. Didn't they have slaves in their country? That question made them deeply uncomfortable, and their answers were mumbled, so I guessed that they did. I steered the conversation into safer channels, and they relaxed again.

I was so busy helping Auntie and Mori-san that my services were barely called for by the patrons. I was faintly bewildered. My life had changed, certainly, but was it better? I did not miss the patrons, not for a minute! But I had no Danjuro. No lover to take me in his arms and make me feel whole. I missed my trips to the kabuki, deeply. Mori-san offered to take me, but I declined. It would have been so different. I would have spent the whole performance wishing I was watching Danjuro. The startling truth was that he had simply disappeared.

The whole of Edo was abuzz with the gossip. Danjuro had gone. He had left no message, nothing. An understudy had stepped into his robes, but it was not the same. The Floating World loved a mystery, and there were those who insisted that it was all a prank to gain publicity for the kabuki. That Danjuro would simply turn up unannounced and strut back onto the stage as if he had never left it. Others said he had been murdered. Or that he had run off with a nobleman's wife and was hiding in fear of his life.

I listened to it all, but said nothing. Instinctively, I knew that none of it was true, but along with everyone else, I had no idea what had really happened. I clung to Danjuro's last words, that he would come back for me, no matter what. I had nothing else to hope for. I was glad that Auntie was keeping me so busy. The translation work especially took all my attention and stopped my thoughts from wandering to Danjuro. When I was alone, it was different. I wept for him with silent tears that could attract no attention. I wondered endlessly if I had driven him away, if it was my behavior with Akira that had been too much. If only... The words echoed like a jeering ghost in my lonely thoughts.

And then Akira came back.

Auntie was nervous. It showed in her voice, in her expression. We all tensed, wondering what else was about to happen in this strange new world we were all living in? What was so momentous that even Auntie was uncomfortable? No announcement was made, no word circulated, but all at once, yakuza were lounging about the Green Tea House and the Hidden House. Lording it over the girls as if they owned the place. Even Big and Bigger seemed less themselves, less sure of their mastery of us all. Their normal sneers were replaced by scowls and sullen looks.

It quickly became obvious that I had been appointed spokesman. I was Auntie's favorite, the girls insisted. I was to ask her what was happening. Or if not Auntie, then Bigger. He would know. Bigger liked me, I must talk to him. Their nervousness infected me, and I trembled as I approached Bigger. I took Nekko with me to give me courage, and he grinned at the cat, which reassured me at least a little. I looked at Bigger – really looked – for the first time in months. He had lost weight, and his cheekbones pushed at his skin. Even his gums seemed to have receded, making his teeth appear long and pointed. I kneeled down and bowed quickly, before my knees gave way.

"So, Midori No Me, one of you girls has finally come to find out what is happening, have you? I wondered how long it would take."

I spoke to the tatami matting, not daring to raise my face. "Bigger-san. There seems to be so much happening. Not just in the Hidden House, but in Edo and the whole of the country. The girls are worried."

"And so they should be. Sit up, Midori No Me. I'm tired of looking at the top of your head. You've been translating for Auntie, haven't you?" I nodded. "And not even you have picked up any hints?"

What should I say? In truth, I knew nothing at all of Auntie's business. I simply shook my head.

"Well, dear Midori-san. I'm afraid I don't bring you good news. Or perhaps it is good news, for *you*." The emphasis he placed on "you" was unsettling. I risked an open stare and he smiled bitterly. "Auntie no longer owns either the Hidden House or the Green Tea House. She has sold them both. She is staying with the courtesy title of manager, but basically she is staying because Willow Road is her life. She has nothing else but the Floating World and would surely pine away and die if she left it. Your new master has a tender heart, it seems."

For once, I was very glad of the training I had been given over the years. Training in how to keep a straight face. How to smile when you wanted to cry. How to laugh in spite of pain. Truly, Danjuro had said I was an excellent actor! In spite of the fact that I was burning with curiosity, I simply smiled in polite inquiry.

Bigger laughed, not taken in at all. "You would sit there

all day before you asked, wouldn't you? Go on, guess who has bought Auntie out."

I considered. One of the patrons, I supposed. Mori-san? He was probably rich enough, but I doubted he would be able to bring himself to do it. Then, with a surge of hope, Danjuro? Bigger had said it was good news for *me*, hadn't he? The desire must have shown, or perhaps Bigger sensed it, as he shook his head.

"Danjuro is still missing," he said. There was anger in his voice and face. "Big is mad with worry. The fool has gone to search for him. Even if he finds him, Danjuro will not thank him. Whatever his mysterious business is, he will not return until it's finished. No, Midori No Me, the gods have not smiled on you quite that much. Or perhaps they have, for all I know. Your new master is Akira-san. You are now owned by a yakuza."

The afternoon sun on my face was suddenly hot. I stared at Bigger in disbelief. Akira had bought Auntie out? Why? Not just for my sake, no. In spite of what he had said, I wondered if part of it was really to take revenge on Danjuro. Or was it simply that he had seen an excellent business opportunity and decided to take advantage of it? Or was it simply the whim of a very rich man?

Bigger tired of me suddenly and waved me away. "Go tell the other girls. Give them the good news." He snickered and I scooped up Nekko and bowed my way out.

The girls were stunned. Quite literally, for it was the only time I had ever seen them all so quiet. Then they looked at each other and started firing questions, at both me and Mineko. Mineko simply shrugged. She knew nothing, she said. I could offer no more. Until Bigger had told me, I had known nothing either. Could Bigger be lying, just to be nasty? I thought not. And Big had really gone chasing after Danjuro? So Bigger said.

They all formed their lips into little purses, jingling the change of the gossip amongst themselves. What did it mean to them? What was to happen to the Hidden House? Would things change? I stared at them in exasperation. Certainly, I was privileged in that I was allowed to mingle with the Barbarians, but could they not see that the whole world was changing? That it was impossible for the Hidden House to continue as it always had? I tried to explain this, and was greeted with wails of fear. What did I think was going to happen? I had no idea. But whatever it was, this was only the start. They glared at me and accused me of trying to frighten them. I left them chattering amongst themselves like sparrows at dawn.

Akira took his own good time to turn up. For weeks, we expected each day that this would be the day he made his appearance. But no. Because of this, when he did enter the Hidden House it came as a shock. We had expected it for so long and it had not happened, I think we all had decided that nothing was going to change after all.

We were all ushered into Auntie's rooms by one of the yakuza who had taken to hanging about the Hidden House. It was late morning, and half of the girls were still yawning and stretching. Only Mineko looked alert. Akira was sitting in Auntie's chair. We were all shocked, and I heard Masaki mutter that he thought he owned the place. I elbowed her quickly, and she bit her lip in mortification at her silly mistake. Akira either did not hear or pretended not to. He greeted us all by name, me last, and waved his arm expansively, inviting us to sit down.

"My dear girls." He beamed. "You will no doubt have found out by now that I have bought the Hidden House and the Green Tea House. And all of you with it, of course. I have also bought a number of other houses on Willow Road. In fact, I now own a great deal of it."

We stirred, as if a breeze had trickled through the room. This was news indeed! The other girls looked at Akira with new respect. I could see the abacus working in each pretty head. Just how rich was our new master?

"As far as most of you are concerned, there will be no change to your lives. You will behave yourselves, and you will be as nice as you know how to the patrons. The patrons themselves will change. You will find that many of my business associates wish to buy your time. I think that you will find that they are very generous men, so I hope you will have nothing to complain about."

A chorus of "no, Akira-san" rippled the air like a hand through ripe rice. Only I remained silent.

"There will be one change. Midori No Me will be here some of the time, but will no longer work as a geisha. I will use her talents elsewhere. That is all. There is food for you all in the main room. Please enjoy." Numb, I rose with the other girls but did not leave. Akira's voice stopped me. "Midori No Me, you are to stay."

The girls filed past me as I stood, my heart beating so hard that I swear I could see the front of my kimono move with the force of it.

Akira stood and stretched from head to toe like a cat that had just woken up. I fixed my eyes on the floor and concentrated on breathing. So close, it was like being in the presence of a wild animal that one is not quite sure is properly secured. He walked around me and paused behind me. I felt his finger run down the nape of my neck and I shivered, cursing my body for responding to his lightest touch.

Oh, Danjuro. I am sorry! If you were back, this man

would mean nothing, nothing at all to me. But you are not here and I don't know if you are alive or dead. And this terrible man *is* here, and I am in his power.

"Kazuha." His voice was the whisper of silk, discarded prior to lovemaking. "I told you to wait. And now I am here."

I could not speak, my throat was too dry.

"I have taken you out of bondage. Never again will you need to smile for a patron. Now, you have no one to please except me. Does that please you?"

My mind was in turmoil, my thoughts autumn leaves blown by an unseen wind. Was I pleased? What could I say? I had never known anything but the Hidden House in the whole of my life. I had known from my first steps that my role in life was to please any man who wanted me, who could afford me. And now this almost unknown man was telling me that all that was to be no more. That I was no longer a geisha in the Hidden House. That in a single sentence, he had swept away the foundations of my world.

I was terrified. And told him so.

He listened, and then laughed out loud. "Any other geisha would be on her knees, kissing my feet with thanks. But not you, Kazuha-chan. Perhaps that is the reason I chose you. Or at least, one of the reasons."

Emboldened by his good humor, I asked, "What do you want me for, Akira-san?" It should have been obvious, I suppose. Akira was taking me as his mistress. But I sensed that there was more, and I was deeply curious.

"What a clever girl you are, Kazuha-chan. You are right to ask, of course. If I just wanted you to use, I could leave you here and take you whenever I chose and still get some income from you from the patrons. But you speak the foreign Barbarian language, don't you?" I nodded. "And I think you understand far more of their ways than the rest of us."

I considered. Yes, I suppose I did. They no longer seemed quite so foreign to me. Perhaps it was because I was half Barbarian myself, but something about them called to me. I loved being able to speak without thinking about what I was saying first. Loved actually being able to laugh without just pretending amusement. And above all, I loved that they treated me as a woman, a woman in my own right, not something to be bought and sold at will.

Akira was waiting patiently for my answer, and I nodded.

"Good. I want to do business with the foreign Barbarians. And to do that, I must have somebody I can trust. Not just to tell me what they are saying, but to tell me what the faces behind the words mean. You understand me?"

"Of course." I smiled. Every Japanese knows instinctively that words tell only half the story. The rest is expression and body language. But the Japanese could not understand their meaning when the Barbarians laughed and made jokes amongst themselves. They thought them deliberately insulting when I knew it was just their way of trying not to show nervousness. "I will help you, Akira-san."

"You will." His voice was suddenly cold, and I was reminded that no matter what, this man was my master. He owned me just as he owned the rest of the girls and could get rid of me any moment I displeased him. Tread carefully, I warned myself. Very carefully. "But for now, Kazuha-san, you will help me in a different way."

I trembled as he undid his robe and kicked it away. I felt the eyes tattooed on his body watching my every movement and was visited with the unsettling thought that he would still be watching me, even when he was asleep. I slid to my knees, less in obeisance and more because my legs refused to support me.

Akira swayed toward me and rubbed my lips with his tree of flesh. I opened my mouth to take him into me, but he tapped my head sharply with his extended fingers and pulled back. I kept my lips tightly closed as he rubbed back and forth, back and forth. Quite suddenly, he placed his hands on each side of my face and found the trigger point that forced me to open my mouth against my will, so my lips gaped wide in an involuntary silent scream. Then and only then did he thrust his tree of flesh in my mouth. He did so with such force that I nearly choked. His strong fingers continued to pinion my face. I could not close my mouth, not even a fraction of an inch, no matter how hard I tried. I heard him laughing, laughing, laughing and then he was exploding down my throat, almost choking me.

When he had finished, he simply walked away from me.

I was escorted away from the Hidden House that same day and taken to Akira's house. True to his word, Akira bought me a dozen new kimonos. All superb, all expensive. Even little Nekko was given a collar of braided silver. I had a suite of rooms all of my own. A bedroom, a sitting room, a roofed terrace that opened to the lovely garden. He took me to Mori-san and bought me a handful of expensive trinkets. I was immensely sorry for my poor former danna and wondered if Akira had chosen his establishment on purpose. It was only later that I realized that of course he had. He knew everything about everybody in the Floating World, and it was yet another way of showing his owner-ship of me. A trivial hurt, inflicted on Mori-san almost without thought, but vindictive all the same.

I should have been the happiest of women. No longer did I have to serve any man who clapped his hands. I had a rich, undeniably attractive lover. It did not take me long to notice the longing looks Akira received from other women. The courtesans behind the lattice, even the geisha promenading in the street, turned their heads to watch us go past, and I heard the wistful sighs trailing behind us. I had a home in one of the most beautiful houses in the whole of Edo. I had a half a dozen maids at my command. Anything I wanted was mine for the asking. I felt the way a baby bird must feel that has fallen out of the nest. For the first time in the whole of my life, I was on my own. I had no Auntie to tell me what to do, no Boys lurking in the background to protect me. Above all, I missed the companionship of the other girls. I missed our cozy gossips in the afternoons, the long sessions spent combing each other's hair, the delightful communal baths.

I was still deeply suspicious of Akira. And, oh, how I missed Danjuro. Being unable to utter a word about him was torture. I even made sure I shielded my thoughts of him when Akira was with me. He noticed everything. The slightest change of expression, the least gesture. There were those in the Floating World who said the yakuza was a demon in human form, all knowing, but at the same time caring for nothing. I came to believe that.

I had always imagined that it must be heaven to only have to be with one man. And if that man was deeply attractive and rich, why it would surely be heaven on earth! But I was wrong. So very wrong.

Akira would have none of the tricks I had learned at the Hidden House. He had to be in command, always. He knew in an instant if I was only pretending to enjoy what he was doing to me, and the inevitable outcome was a hard slap or even a punch. I learned very quickly to simply take what was given to me and to remain silent and inert if I didn't like it. In fact, I began to realize that he preferred it when he knew that I hated what he was doing to me. And increasingly, I did hate it.

He enjoyed my body often. If I was asleep when he came in, I was expected to be awake and alert within seconds of him coming to me. He took me when it was my time of the month and laughed at me when I could take no pleasure in his actions. Once, he woke me in the middle of the night and no matter how I tried, I remained dry and he could not enter me easily. He was angry. I expected a clout around my head – his usual form of reprimand – but no, he got up and wrapped his robe around himself and stalked out. I sent up a prayer of thankfulness, but it was premature. Akira came back with two of his men and set them on me while he watched. Afterward, he took me himself in the rear, the only part of my body that had obviously been forbidden to his men. I managed not to weep while he was with me, but when he had gone I cried myself to sleep. The next morning, he laughed at my swollen face and made me crawl on the tatami to him and then satisfy him with my mouth.

The only time I was allowed back to the Hidden House was when Akira was meeting clients at the Green Tea House. Being an astute businessman, he always ensured that my face was unmarked by either blows or tears on those days. Once business had been done, I was allowed to visit with my old friends until Akira was ready to go. I smiled for them and showed off my new kimonos, and it was only to Mineko that I whispered the truth. We sat with our arms around each other and comforted one another.

Mineko told me that it was not the same at the Hidden House. Since Akira-san had taken over, the clients had changed. Now anybody was allowed in, men who Auntie would not have let into the Green Tea House, never mind about the Hidden House. All that mattered was that they had the money to pay for the girls. Auntie herself was little seen, preferring to stay in her own rooms. Big appeared to have vanished altogether, and even Bigger was a pale shadow of his former self. The girls envied me deeply, and Mineko whispered that, bad as I thought it was with Akira-san, I was better off with him than here. I shuddered at the thought.

"Was there any word of Danjuro?" I asked. Mineko shook her head. Nothing had been heard of him these six months past. Nothing at all. Even the Floating World was beginning to forget him. I would never forget him, I vowed. Never. No matter what.

And then one of Akira's thugs was beckoning to me, and I had to go.

18

We touched the fallen
Leaves together.
I still feel them now

*T*he fire was the talk of not just the Floating World, but the whole of Edo.

The Floating World was no stranger to fire, of course. The whole of it was built of wood, and it took only a carelessly left charcoal burner or a flaring torch to start a fire. There were big ones every couple of years.

But this one was different. It took only the kabuki theater.

I heard about it from one of the maids while I was taking my bath. She was almost breathless to impart the news. I listened, and in spite of the heat of the water I felt my inner core turn cold.

She had been out shopping early that morning and

everybody was talking about it. The fire had been first noticed in the late evening, but by the time men had been roused to form a bucket chain to douse it with water, the heat was so extreme that nobody could get close enough to make a difference. By early morning, the kabuki was no more than smoldering ashes.

Akira was out and he had not been back all that night. I dared not venture out myself. If he found out – and he would – I would feel his anger. Instead, I encouraged the maids to pop in and out to bring me whatever gossip they could find.

It changed from hour to hour. At first, they said that part of the theater still stood. Then no, it had all burned to the ground. The theater people had gone back to the theater, they said, and were standing around, not knowing what to do. Then it was said that they had all been seen leaving Edo, carrying their goods on their backs with the richer ones leading mules and donkeys.

And then it rained. Not heavy, thunderous rain, but a good, steady downpour that dampened the ashes.

Then the news that I had half been expecting. A body had been found in the ashes where the stage had been. Enough of it was left to tell it had been a man. A tall man and probably a youngish man. The maid, eyes huge with excitement, said that everyone thought it was Danjuro, come to take his end in the place he loved. Or possibly his ghost. Who knew? Already the ballad makers were working hard on a special piece to mark the tragedy.

I waved her away and sat quite still, quite silent. I watched the sun work across the tatami matting, and still I waited. Suddenly, a bird came to rest on the open window – a rose finch, his feathers the entire palette of pinks and reds – and he opened his beak and began to sing. I smiled.

Akira was sad when he finally came in. He didn't bother to ask if I knew of the tragedy, he simply assumed that I had heard.

"You have heard about the body they found?" he asked.

"Yes."

"They say it is Danjuro. Do you think it is?"

I didn't bother to lie. What was the point? Akira would have known I was lying immediately, and that would have been very bad for me. "No. I don't know who it is, but I don't think it's Danjuro."

Akira simply looked at me, waiting for me to tell him why. So I told him about the finch, and he grinned.

"You think that was a good omen?" I nodded. "What if it was Danjuro's spirit, come to say goodbye to you?"

I tightened my lips to keep the tears back. It was not. I knew it was not.

"I'm sure it was Danjuro who died." He was smiling, rocking back on his heels. His expression was odd, almost dreamy. "A lot of people have been saying he died months ago. I thought so too, but now I wonder." Who had been saying that Danjuro was dead? I had not heard that rumor. I waited, silent. "He would never have wanted to just fade into obscurity. No, the great Danjuro would have wanted to go out with a grand gesture. And now he has. Even though he was my enemy, I admired him. If only the fool had let me buy at least part of the kabuki, this need never have happened. But no, he persuaded the rest of the owners that the kabuki could not fall into the dirty hands of a yakuza. As if my money is different from anybody else's!"

"What did you do to drive him away?" I had to ask, no matter what the consequences.

"Not a thing. What could I, a mere yakuza, do to a great, famous man like Danjuro? I suppose I might have encouraged a few of the better actors that life would be more promising for them in Kyoto. And there again, there may have been a few money-lenders who decided to call in money owed to them by the kabuki. And I did hear that Danjuro himself had received a number of death threats. Surely, none of that could have driven the great man to take his own life? You don't think for a minute that the loss of the woman he loved could have anything to do with it, do you?"

Akira rose. He was whistling happily. I watched him leave, showering blessings on his head. Strange that it should take another man to tell me that Danjuro loved me. I was still convinced that my lovely finch had come to sing to me of good news, not bad.

Akira came to wake me himself next day. He had risen early and gone out, and I had turned over and gone back to sleep. Now he was prodding me with his toe, telling me to go and take a bath. His mood was so good that I was instantly suspicious. But I did as I was told. He watched me while I bathed, still whistling. Once I was dry, he told one of the maids to bring a loose robe for me and then escorted me back to my bedroom.

"Pin your hair up," he commanded. "As tightly as you can."

As I worked at the unruly curls, he walked round me, rather as if he was viewing a sculpture he might want to buy. I kept my face blank.

"How long ago did I tell you I was going to put my mark on you?" I paused, suddenly wary. "Didn't you ever wonder what I meant? Or were you so clever that you thought if you didn't mention it, I would forget? I wonder about you, some-times. Are you really so much brighter than I think you are?" What was I supposed to answer to that? He was still smiling when a man bowed himself into my room and began unpacking a wooden box. I stared at the contents and my stomach churned. Now I knew what the yakuza had meant.

It took the artist the whole of the day. Akira allowed him to pause once, to take a drink and a bite to eat, but it wasn't until dusk fell that he stood back and announced he had finished.

"It will take perhaps a week for the swellings to go down, Akira-san," he said hurriedly. "You will not really be able to see what it is like until then. It will be better covered completely for a few days, with some salve to keep it moist."

The nape of my neck, from the hairline to between my shoulder blades, was screaming in pain. I was stiff and cold from being made to sit still for so long, but that pain was nothing compared to how my neck felt.

Akira arranged for a doctor to come and see me, and to apply something soothing to my skin. He came every day and changed the dressing. It would be fine, he assured me. Absolutely fine. I tried not to move my head, as every movement was sheer agony.

I expected Akira to share my futon as usual, to gloat over my pain. To rub it in that he had absolute power over me. But to my relief, he did not. I could sense his excitement building, day by day, but I when I saw him, he was almost formal with me. I was bewildered.

On the seventh day, the doctor came and removed the dressing but did not put a fresh one in its place. As soon as he had gone, Akira came and stood behind me, staring so hard at my neck that I swore I could feel his gaze.

"You are very beautiful, Kazuha-san. And I have made you even more beautiful. Do you want to look?"

He didn't bother waiting for my answer, but walked me across to the mirror. He stood behind me again, and held up another, smaller mirror behind me so that I could see both my front and back at the same time. At first I was puzzled. The mirror he was holding showed me the small of my back, which appeared as normal. I shrugged my shoulders, relieved that it no longer hurt, and he grunted, adjusting the mirror he was holding carefully.

When I saw my neck, I screamed out loud.

You must understand that to a Japanese man the nape of a woman's neck is the most erotic part of her body, more so even than her breasts or her black moss. My neck was long and slender, very white and very beautiful, and had always been complimented by my patrons.

Now, the nape of my neck was no longer white. From my hairline to between my shoulders, a dragon rioted in reds and yellows and oranges. Its nostrils flared fire, its talons curled ready to rip and plunder. To my eyes, the tattoo was hideous and I burst into tears.

Akira capered around me, crowing like a cockerel at dawn. "So, there is something that can make you cry!" He laughed. "But why the tears? I have made you a living work of art, my Kazuha-chan. Now, every time I look at you I will be further enthralled by your beauty. And it is mine, and mine alone. When you are outside this house, you will cover my dragon. No other man's eyes will ever see it."

I was thankful for that. I put my hand to my neck and was surprised when my flesh was cool. The colors of the tattoo were so vivid, I had expected it to be hot.

"You should be honored, Kazuha-chan. The dragon is the mark of my clan. You are the first woman ever to be given it. It is a great mark of respect."

I stared at him and realized in amazement that he meant it.

He approached me slowly and leaned over, tracing the

outline of the tattoo with his lips. "You are truly mine now. Does that please you?"

"No. You've made me hideous. No other man would look at me twice now."

It was a brave reply, but stupid. It was a miracle that he did not knock me to the floor for insolence. But instead, he laughed out loud.

"You were not like any other woman in Edo before I honored you, Kazuha. Now you are truly unique." He walked away, still laughing.

I hated the tattoo, both because it marked me as being Akira's possession and because I thought it disfigured me. It was a bitter potion to swallow. Having spent the whole of my life thinking of myself as a freak, I had just begun to believe that I had some worth. That I was not, perhaps, as ugly as I had always thought myself to be. Now that faint tremor of self-confidence had been knocked away. Now, I knew that I was truly different. Forever. And that I could do nothing at all about it.

I hated the tattoo, and I hated Akira even more for forcing it onto me.

Akira's attitude changed toward me subtly once the disfigurement was on my body. He seemed to want me to be with him more, not just in private, but in public. Even in Edo itself, rather than just the Floating World. If he had a meeting with foreigners, then I had to go with him, of course. But he also began to take me out more. We strolled down the avenues, the cherry-blossom petals falling on our faces. Occasionally, he would take me to the river and we would stop at an inn for food and drink. He told me with a cheerful grin that once the kabuki was rebuilt, he would take me to a performance. Anybody watching us would think us a perfectly normal couple. A man promenading with his mistress. I was always to walk a few steps behind him, of course, with my maid following behind me. In public, I was expected to keep my eyes on the ground and only speak when he spoke to me.

But I knew none of it was normal. Not at all. Before we left the house – the gilded prison I had come to hate almost as much as I hated Akira – he would inspect me. I was always to wear my newest kimono, my best obi. He bought me several sets of the hated kingfisher-beak combs, and they were always to be in place. They made my head itch as though I had fleas, but I never told him how much I disliked them. If I had, he would have made me sleep in them. Opulent rings adorned my fingers. A wide necklace encircled my throat.

And always, before we left the house, he made me tip my head forward so that my chin bit against my breast so he could check that under no circumstances did my tattoo show. Because that was his private joke. No matter how much the clothes on my back cost, no matter how richly I was decked out, the hated tattoo was his mark. The thing that made me his. The one thing that nobody else could ever see. Just him.

If I could have scratched it off with my nails, I would have tried. At first, I tried to soak it in the bath, and then scrubbed at it with a hard brush until my skin was sore. It did no good, it was still there. And anyway, Akira took to sharing the bath with me, so I had to stop. He became particularly fond of turning me to face the wall of the bath and pushing himself into me from behind. Whenever he did this – and it was often – he would bite, hard, at the tattoo, rolling my flesh between his teeth and scraping his teeth on the ink. It was, apart from anything else, his way of showing me that no matter what I did, it would never come off.

I hated the tattoo. And I hated Akira.

As much as I hated Akira and the life he made me lead, I equally longed for the company of my old friends in the Hidden House. I even enjoyed the meetings with the foreign Barbarians simply because it was somebody else to talk to. And sometimes – not every time, but sometimes – if Akira wanted to talk to Auntie after his business with the foreign Barbarians was done, he would allow me to wander into the Hidden House for a snatched few minutes to chat with the girls. Oh, how I lived for those days! The maids in Akira's house were too timid to dare to talk to me. It was all, "Yes, Midori No Me-san" and, "If it pleases you, Midori No Me-san" until I wanted to scream. So lonely was I that sometimes even Akira would have been welcome as a companion, but other than when he took his bath with me and slept with me, he was rarely in the house during the day. I wandered through it like a wistful ghost, Nekko at my heels as my shadow.

Nekko was, in truth, my constant companion these days. Even when we went to the Hidden House, Nekko came with me, following alongside me like a faithful dog. He amused the Barbarians immensely, and so Akira encouraged his presence.

I would have committed suicide if it was not for the certain knowledge that somewhere Danjuro was still alive. That one day, perhaps a long way in the future, he would come back and claim me. If, that was, he wasn't so repulsed by my hideous tattoo that he could no longer bear to look at me. I prayed daily before the household shrine that that would not be the case.

Every now and then, Akira would taunt me. "Still think

he's alive, do you?" he would jeer. I refused to answer and just stared into space until he became bored.

Akira regarded me as lucky. Since I had come to him, his business interests had multiplied three-fold. Nothing, it seemed, could now go wrong for the yakuza. He even deigned to tell me that one day, and I decided to seize my chance. After all, what could he do to me? He already pinched and nipped and bit me regularly. If he was in a bad mood, he added in a good slap and even a punch for good measure, tugging my hair until my scalp screamed. He could set a couple of his thugs on me while he watched, but he had already done that, and I had survived. He could beat me until I was black and blue, break a few bones perhaps, but I would heal. I was beginning to wonder how far he would really go without worrying about damaging his all-important luck.

So I decided to ask him. "Akira-san." I kept my head down, but watched him from beneath my lowered lids. He had drunk a lot of sake, and – although he could hold his drink – it seemed to me that he was in as jolly a mood as he ever was. "May I ask something from you?"

He paused, his sake cup not quite at his lips. He seemed positively startled, and I realized that this was the first time I had actually asked him for anything. His lips peeled back in a feral grin, and I could see his mind working. Did he really think he had tamed me at last? Apparently he did, and the idea obviously gave him great pleasure.

"Ask away, Kazuha. Is there some trinket you want? Would you like to visit Mori-san again? Do you want another kitten for Nekko to play with?"

I tittered politely. "Nothing, Akira-san. I have everything that any woman could want." Was I piling it on too thickly? A glance at his face assured me I was not. He was practically purring. "It's just that I miss my friends, master. Until you took me out of the Hidden House, I was with the other girls day and night. You are often absent on business. I cannot talk to Nekko. Please, master, may I visit the Hidden House now and then, just to gossip and chat for an hour?"

It was the first time I had ever called him master. He drained his sake cup, and I hastened to refill it for him, right to the brim. With a sweeping gesture, he indicated that I should get some for myself. I sighed hard, staring at the tatami, my expression woeful.

"I do not like you associating with those freaks. Those harlots."

I kept my eyes down, but inside I burned. I was just the same as the other girls. We were what we were. I tightened my mouth to stop myself saying so and suddenly felt a wave of despondency. What was the use? If Akira's mind was made up, then I was wasting my time. Tears blurred my vision. I blinked to hide them. I would not cry. He would not make me cry. And if I could not stop myself, he was not, under any circumstances, going to see he had made me cry.

"I am pleased you do not try and defend them, Kazuha. Are you learning some sense, at long last? Are you actually beginning to realize how well off you are with me?"

"Yes, master," I said dully. What was the use? If I persisted, Akira was quite likely to refuse to let me see them at all, even for the precious five or ten minutes I had at present.

Akira sucked at his sake. I poured him another cup.

"Is it true, Kazuha, that somehow the girls in the Hidden House find out all the gossip of the Floating World without ever setting foot in it?"

I nodded. Patrons talked as if we were not there or were

deaf. The maids gathered tittle-tattle on their many errands. We heard, even if we could not see.

"Perhaps, then, we could come to an arrangement." I stiffened, hope making my heart thud. "You are always discreet, Kazuha. I appreciate that. But I would like to know if there is anything happening in Edo that I don't know about. Would it be possible for a woman to listen, and remember, but not chatter back?"

"I would never, ever tell anybody anything about your business, master." And that was true enough. My life depended on my discretion. By now I knew too much about the many grains of rice in Akira's dish. If he even suspected that he could trace an indiscretion back to me, then rightly or wrongly, I would be dead.

"It could be useful, then. But tell me, what would you do for, say, an hour a week to chat and gossip to your old friends?"

"Anything," I said simply. After all, what was there left to inflict on me? What remained that he hadn't already done? I almost smiled at the thought. Nothing. Nothing at all.

"Ah, be careful what you say, little one."

Even though my gaze was fixed on the tatami, I heard the amusement in his voice and the hairs at the back of my head rose in response. But I had gone too far to back out now, so I repeated, "Anything."

"Let me see then." He was gloating. He already had something in mind, I knew. I waited silently. "Ah, I have it! You know I am greatly attached to you, Kazuha. You are the only woman on earth who has ever seen the full glory of my body. Now, just so that I am sure that you are equally fond of me, I suggest that you give me a little wash. With your tongue."

Not so bad, I thought. Not so bad at all. There was surely

not an inch of his body that had not already received my attentions. I almost smiled in relief. "Of course, master."

Then I realized what he wanted me to clean. Not his body at all. His feet.

He had leaned back, lolling at his ease on his elbows. His feet were stuck out, not dirty, exactly, but dusty from the street. He wiggled his toes at me. At any other time, the gesture would have been funny. But not now.

I swallowed hard and licked my lips, trying to find some saliva. He clapped his hands and pointed at his feet.

"Clean, Kazuha. As clean as if I had just climbed out of the bath. If I am pleased enough with you, then you shall have your trips to the Hidden House. You have my word on it."

I shuffled across the tatami on my knees and when I thought my head was dipped sufficiently so that he could not see, I closed my eyes tightly.

In spite of the bile that rose in my throat, leaving a sour taste in my mouth, I did it. I gripped his right foot in my hand, and, starting with the toes, licked and nibbled every last bit of skin. Akira said nothing, but I could feel him watching me. I thought I really was going to vomit when he spread his toes in invitation to my tongue to go between them, but I forced it back. The left foot got the same attention. Finally, when I was absolutely sure that there was not a single bit of either foot that was not spotlessly clean, I sat back on my heels, my head bowed, and waited.

"Very good, Kazuha." He grinned and stretched and got to his feet. "I think I shall have a bath now. You don't want to join me? Suit yourself."

I could hear him laughing as he walked down the corridor.

As soon as he had gone, I asked one of the maids for tea.

I drank three cups, scalding hot, but still my mouth tasted vile. I drank sake, but still I could taste him. I went to the lavatory and poked my fingers down my throat until I vomited and then drank so much water my stomach swished. Although I could never have imagined it at the time, it was worth it. For in the Hidden House, I found my mother. And my father.

19

There is a storm, overhead.
But no matter.
It will pass.

*A*kira was so confident in his power over me that he let me go to the Hidden House on my own, with just a maid for company. Even without the tattoo on show, it was as if the world knew that he had put his mark on me and that it was not safe to try and interfere with the property of the most notorious yakuza in Edo. I had learned, all too quickly, that Akira-san was feared throughout Edo. And why. By now, I knew where the bodies were buried. And there were many. On that particular afternoon, I set out with a light heart. I was going home! Nekko walked beside me, with his tail held high, and the maid trotted behind me.

I trembled as I slid open the door of the Hidden House. It was a warm, pleasant afternoon and bees buzzed drowsily about the honeysuckle growing in the courtyard. I could hear an equally lazy murmur of voices from the main room, but I never got that far.

Mineko's door was half open, and I was about to call out a cheerful greeting when she saw me and jumped to her feet. In a second, she had pulled me through the door and shut it, though she had to open it again when Nekko yowled to be let in. She dismissed my maid with a nod, telling her kindly to go to the kitchen for some food. This particular maid was notoriously greedy and she nodded with a gleam in her eye.

"Midori No Me, what an unexpected pleasure!" Mineko spoke so formally, I stared at her in surprise. She opened her eyes wide and jerked her head at the screen. In the hazy sunlight, I was sure that I could see the shadow of some-body on the other side. My maid? I raised my eyebrows and Mineko nodded. For a few moments, we exchanged nothing but trivialities until we were sure that she had gone. Mineko blew out her cheeks in a sigh of relief and we hugged each other with delight.

"I have waited and waited for weeks in the hope of catching you," Mineko said very softly. "Akira-san is not with you?"

I explained he had kindly allowed me to visit alone. The sarcasm must have shown in my voice, as Mineko nodded her understanding, her expression tight.

"How long do we have?"

"One hour. But I hope that will be every week. Probably not always on my own, though."

I watched in astonishment as she got to her feet and poked her head into the corridor. Even Nekko, who was washing his back leg in the contorted gesture only a cat can manage, paused and stared at her.

She slid the door quietly and then darted to her little

cupboard, coming back to lay a bulging silk furoshiki – the traditional square of cloth used to carry items in Japan – at my feet.

"Listen, for I have a lot to tell you, and it's important that you visit with the rest of the girls. If you don't, that maid will tell your yakuza, and it will be bad for you." I smiled tightly. If only Mineko knew how bad. "This is for you."

I stared at it in surprise. The furoshiki was old, the silk faded along the creases. It looked as if it had been knotted in a hurry and then left untouched for many years. Mineko spoke quickly.

"I have kept that for you for months. A priest brought it to the door and handed it to one of the maids along with a good tip. He told her to give to me, nobody else, and not to speak of it. She said he was a very venerable monk, with piercing eyes, and she was afraid of him, so she did as she was told. There was a note with it, asking me to give it to you as soon as I could, but to make sure you were alone when I passed it to you. I burned the note as soon as I could - anything out of the ordinary is dangerous here, these days."

I held out my hands in bewilderment. I didn't know any monks. I had never seen the furoshiki before.

"Open it!" Mineko urged.

I did so. Inside were a small box and a folded and re-folded packet. I lifted the box. It was surprisingly heavy and jingled when I shook it. Intrigued, I pried at the tight fitting lid and gasped as it flew off suddenly. Inside were ten coins, each a gold koban. A fortune. A koban was worth three *koku* of rice. Just one koku of rice could feed one person for a whole year. In my hands, I had enough money to feed myself for thirty years. I stared at Mineko, my jaw sagging foolishly. She stared back. Nekko yawned, stretched, and wandered over to pat the coins. Quickly deciding he couldn't eat them, he lost interest.

"The letter," Mineko whispered. "Read it, quickly. Tell me what it says."

I turned the package in my hands. I had no idea why, but I was frightened of it. I was shaking so much I had trouble focusing on the inscription on the front. When I did, I trembled still harder.

To my dear daughter

I held it out to Mineko to show her, desperate for her to confirm what is said. She shook her head in bewilderment.

"It's for you, Midori No Me. Not me. Oh, open it, do. Read it out loud. Quick!"

I dropped the folded pages twice before I could hold it still enough to read. The writing was cramped and looked to have been written in a hurry.

My Dear Daughter,

I am sorry you must read this. I have no idea how long it has taken to get to you, even less idea of what has happened to you, what sort of life you have led away from me. I can only hope that my dear friend Big…

I paused and stared at Mineko in disbelief. She waved her hands frantically at me to continue. I cleared my throat and tried again.

I can only hope that my dear friend Big has been able to look after you, as he promised he would. Has he spoken to you about me, dear one? Explained why I had to leave you? I pray so. But now I can tell you in my own words.

You must know that I ran away with my Barbarian lover, your father. His name, if you do not know, is – or at least the nearest I can get to it in Japanese – is Seemon. He came to the Green Tea House for months before you were born. The other girls thought him ugly, but I could see nothing but his gentleness. He made me laugh, made me feel as if I was the most beautiful woman in Edo. Made me feel as I was human, not just a slave who sang and played and danced to order for any man who had her price in his pocket. I fell deeply in love with him, and to my joy, he loved me. I felt it said much that he not only tried to learn to speak Japanese, but also learned to read and write it. He taught me a few words of English as well.

Seemon tried to buy me off Auntie, but she would have none of it. At that time, I had several patrons who were interested in buying me for a mistress, but it was not really the money that mattered. Auntie felt that to sell me to a Barbarian would bring shame on the tea house and told Seemon that no matter how much he offered, it would not be enough.

So I took him as my lover. We were very happy for a time, but then I discovered that I was pregnant with you. Apart from my mizuage, I had had no lover other than Seemon, so I was proud to tell him that he was your father. He thought that it would force Auntie's hand, but I knew that would not happen. Ever. She would have killed me – and you – first.

So we decided that we would run away together. I was perhaps slightly more than seven months pregnant at the time. I was always very slim and by tying my kimono and obi very tightly, and making sure I always bathed alone, I managed to hide you. Only Big knew, but he was my friend and I knew I could trust him. We made our plans very carefully, your father and I, but you, my dearest daughter, were in a very great hurry to get into the world, and you decided to arrive while I was still at the tea house.

At least you had the sense to arrive on a night of the festival of the cherry blossom, when Auntie had taken the rest of the girls out to see and be seen. I pleaded a stomach ache and insisted I could not be parted from the lavatory. Auntie wasn't happy to leave me, but the other girls nattered at her and she gave in.

We were going to slip away as soon as everybody left. Your father had a carriage standing by, which was to take us to a ship moored in Edo. But fate did not like us. I had felt ill all day, my stomach really was painful. I had no idea what childbirth felt like. When everybody had gone, Big let Seemon into the tea house, and he knew at once what was happening. We were frantic. I wanted to go anyway, but Seemon said no, it was impossible. I could not be moved. He would stay, he said, and face Auntie at my side. But you, daughter, you had other ideas! You were born shortly after midnight. Big said that if I could walk, he would help me to the carriage, which was still waiting. I wanted to take you with me, dear one. I said I would not go without you, but Big said it was no use. You would never survive the journey, you were too young, too fragile. I said I would stay in that case, but Big said if I did, then Auntie would have all three of us killed before morning. And she would have, you know. Nobody would have known.

I had just given birth. I was very young and I was terrified. I was in no state to argue. Big promised he would look after you, that he would tell you about me. I hoped that it would not be long before I sent for you. Big took you from my arms. He gave me a few moments to scribble this note to you, and I put all the money I had saved in a casket for you. He promised that if I did not get you back by the time you were old enough to understand, he would give them both to you. And I have to be satisfied with that.

So, my dear daughter, don't let anyone tell you that your

father and I did not love you. For that is not true, and never will
be. You are the most beautiful baby I have ever seen, and your
eyes are the exact color of your father's eyes. We both love you
and will think about you every day until we are together again.

Trust Big, for he has been a good friend to me.
Your loving mother,
Terue

I finished with a gasp. Mineko and I stared at each other, both unable to speak. I realized I was holding my breath and took a deep gulp of air. "All these years," I said. "All these years, I thought she had abandoned me because I was so ugly. Because I was deformed. Because she was ashamed of me. And it wasn't that at all. She wanted to come back for me. Oh, Mineko!"

My voice choked. I could find no more words. I was not ugly. My mother did not hate me. I even had a father who loved me. I shook my head in disbelief. Mineko had tears in her eyes. She did not speak, but reached out and took my hand, and we sat in silence for a few minutes. It was sensible Mineko who came to life first.

"Come on, we have to go to the other girls. You need to be with them when your maid comes to take you home." I nodded, shaking myself to regain my wits.

"Mineko, will you keep the gold, here? I have nowhere I could hide it that Akira would not find. I will keep the letter," I folded it as if it was the most precious thing, and hid it in my obi. "I think I can just slide it under the shrine at Akira's house. He will not look there, he is not a religious man."

Mineko nodded briskly. "Of course. I have somewhere where it will not be found." Of course she did. We all had our secret places in the Hidden House.

The other girls welcomed me happily, and I sat down to be immersed in the gossip. I could barely concentrate, I was so happy, but I made sure I had a few juicy tidbits for Akira. There were two new girls in the room, and I stared at them in astonishment. They were identical twins. The girls glanced at me without interest and did not speak. They simply sat, hand in hand, and stared into space.

Kiku was openly rude about them, but they either didn't notice or care.

"Just look at them," she sneered. "They do that all the time. If you talk to one, the other one answers. Then the first one finishes off the sentence. When they talk to each other, it sounds as if they are speaking Japanese, but when you listen it's just nonsense. Only those two understand it. And they sleep together on the same futon. There's something really...unnatural about them. I don't trust them for a minute. Auntie's over the moon with them, though. She's going to offer the patrons two for the price of one once they've had their mizuage. She has to. They've no talents at all. They can't sing or dance or play the samisen, nothing. They're courtesans, not geisha." She sniffed her disapproval.

"Tell Midori No Me your news, Kiku." Masaki giggled.

Kiku simpered, the expression so unlike her that I was startled. "I've been bought out." She grinned.

I congratulated her and then looked at the other girls, who were all giggling. "Who?" I demanded.

"Mori-san."

I broke into a broad grin. Dear, dear Mori-san! Kiku would make a wonderful wife for him, much better than I ever would. I congratulated her heartily, and meant it.

"Something else, as well." Masaki was bursting to bring me up to date with the gossip. "The Green Tea House has a new patron. We don't know who he is, but he's an important nobleman. Not from Edo. He's been coming for the last month, once or twice a week. He always asks for a different geisha each time, and he's very generous with his presents. You should see his carriage and his robes! All the geisha are mad to take their turn with him, but so far he's not expressed a real interest in any of them."

"He doesn't come here, then?" I asked. The girls shook their heads in unison. All except the twins, who simply sat and stared into space, although I had the distinct impression that they were listening to every word that was said. I knew what Kiku meant. There was something about them that left me uneasy. I decided I would make sure I said nothing at all in their presence that I would not be happy for Akira to hear.

"I wish he would," Mineko said cheerfully. "I could do with the sort of presents he hands out." She grinned slyly and all the girls laughed. Except the twins, whose faces remained expressionless. I could feel them watching me as I rose to go.

Akira interrogated me over supper. I was intensely grateful for the acting skills I had learned in the Hidden House. I kept my tone of voice light and amused, and at the same time made sure that my body language was deferential, obviously grateful to him for allowing me to go to the Hidden House.

He nodded when I told him about the twins. He knew about them, of course. I ventured to say that they seemed a little strange. He grinned and said they were fine girls, that there was nothing at all wrong with them. I was right, then, they were his creatures and would report every word that was said in the Hidden House. It was the first time that Akira had made the slightest slip, and I was careful to pretend I had not noticed. He also knew about Kiku, but pretended to be surprised.

He was most interested in the gossip about the noble-man. Had I seen his carriage? Did the girls say what he looked like? Did they know anything about him, at all? I shook my head. No, he never strayed from the Green Tea House. I had not seen him, I apologized.

He shrugged. "No matter. I will find out. I believe he is an important man from Kyoto. I wonder what has bought him all the way to Edo for his amusement."

I frowned. It was hardly unusual. Many wealthy men made the pilgrimage to Edo – to the Floating World – once a year. I would try and find out, I said. Akira nodded.

He seemed distracted and went out with his henchmen in tow as soon as he had eaten. I retired to my bedroom and forced myself to wait until I was sure beyond doubt that he really had gone. Nekko was a good indicator. Whenever Akira was in the house, he would not settle but prowled around growling to himself. Now, he came and sat on my knee and curled up.

I took the letter from my obi and read it and re-read it. I was deeply reluctant to let it out of my sight, but eventually I decided I had to hide it somewhere safe. If Akira found it, he would not be pleased. Not pleased at all. As I thought, the household shrine sat in a slightly indented base. I could only lift it with a huge effort, but it was enough to slide the letter underneath. Once the shrine was in place again, it looked as if it had not been moved in a hundred years. It would be difficult to get the letter out again, but no matter. I already knew it by heart.

I lay down to sleep in a contented haze. I was so joyful, I could not get comfortable but wriggled until the futon and bedding was a wrinkled mess. It didn't matter. I could have slept on the tatami and been happy. I went over the letter in my head, over and over and over. I was on the verge of sleep when something occurred to me and I bolted upright. Annoyed, Nekko dug his claws into my arm, but I barely noticed.

Suddenly, the thing that had been submerged by my joy at discovering my mother surfaced. Big. Mother had said that Big was her true friend. That he had helped her to escape. Had promised to look after me. Big. Bigger had said that Big loved my mother, hadn't he? If he truly loved her, then why had he gone back on his promise to her to look after me? Why hadn't he given me her letter and the money years ago? And now that the train of thought was in motion, it ran on with its own steam. Why had the letter arrived *now*? Had Big sent it? Who was the priest who had delivered it? Why, why, why? I had no answer to any of it. Bewildered and exhausted by the sudden knowledge that had erupted in my life, I lay down, sure I would never sleep. Nekko cuddled up on my stomach and before I knew it, it was morning.

20

Each new day with you
Is a Journey into the
Unknown

*W*hether by accident or design, I was not allowed back to the Hidden House on my own for the next six weeks. Akira said he had much business with the foreign Barbarians, so he accompanied me. I sometimes wondered if he spoke more English than he pretended, so I was always meticulous in my translations. After the business was done, I was allowed to visit with my friends while Akira went to chat with Auntie. It wasn't the same with him there, and I certainly never dared to go aside with Mineko, but it was better than nothing.

Kiku was near her time to leave and was as giggly as a young girl. The other girls looked at her with envy. To my surprise, I realized that they envied me even more. They plied me with questions constantly. Was it true that Akira-san had one of the most splendid houses in the whole of Edo? Was I wearing yet another new kimono and obi? How many had he given me? How many maids did he keep? And – time and time again – what was he like as a lover? I kept half an eye on the silent twins when I answered, but knew my responses were satisfactory when the girls sighed and looked at me jealously.

The unknown nobleman was still visiting the Green Tea House, they said. He seemed to favor two geisha in particular, and they were ready to tear each other's hair out in jealousy. Gossip had it that he was either known at the once-again important Imperial Court itself or at least had connections there. Perhaps he was looking to ingratiate himself with the emperor. In any event, money seemed to be no object to him, and with each visit he became more handsome, more desirable. The only strange thing about him, they whispered, was that he never asked for any courtesan to be bought to the Green Tea House for him, nor did he ask for directions to one. Where he went when he took his leave from the favored geisha of the day, nobody seemed to know. Still, who knew what went on in men's heads? Who cared, as long as they were rich and young and handsome!

I passed the gossip on to Akira, who told me to find out more. I guessed he, also, had no idea who the mystery man was and that it both irked and worried him. Nothing was allowed to go on in the Floating World that Akira did not know of and approve.

He was solicitous that day when I was ready to set off for the Hidden House. The afternoon was overcast and he said it might rain. Was I going to wear my new cloak and my high geti? I was relieved. He had been strange to me for the past few days, and it worried me. Even in the midst of my new happiness, I wondered if he was tiring of me. I was under no illusion. If he was, then I was dead. It would be below Akira-san's dignity to let me go back to the Hidden House. Certainly not to any other house, respectable or not, in Edo. Nor would he simply pay me off and let me go. I not only bore his mark, but I knew far too much about him. No, if he had had enough of me, I would simply disappear from the face of the earth. And nobody – except, possibly, Mineko, and I prayed she would have more sense of her own self-worth – would dare to even comment, still less ask.

Akira had taken to coming to my futon later and later. For almost a week, he laid beside me in the darkness, silent and still. I lay awake with him, counting the minutes and hours until his breathing told me he was asleep. This was what terrified me. If he had no use for me in his bed, how long would my usefulness with the Barbarians keep me alive? Although I hated his very touch, I decided I had to take the chance. I had to find out. A couple of days before, I waited until he was still before leaning across and pulling the bedding back. He did not move. I placed my hand on his bare chest, running my fingers down his body. In the pitch darkness, I was certain I could feel the slightly raised outlines of his tattoos, feel the heat of the colors.

Instead of finding his erection, I stroked his chest and ribs, tickling him as if he was Nekko. He moved slightly, and I paused immediately, waiting for some sort of direction. Nothing. Very well, I would finish what I had started. His arms were straight beside his body. I ran my tongue down the inside of his arm, sliding over his wrist and finding his palm. That, I nibbled and licked. Nothing. I grimaced in the darkness, finally forcing my lips to find the tips of his fingers. I took each one in turn in my mouth, sucking gently. I closed my eyes and made myself take the stump of his little finger between my teeth.

Akira loved that. Months before, when I had found how much it aroused him to have his fingers caressed, I had dared to ask him how he had come to lose most of his little finger. He had laughed at my ignorance.

"I chopped it off myself," he said. I stared at him in shocked disbelief. Why? Akira grinned. "Many years ago, when I was a very lowly yakuza, there was some question of my loyalty to my master. I cut the finger off to prove my loyalty to him."

Ever after that, I hated even touching the stump of the finger. And the more I hated it, the more Akira loved me taking it between my lips. But today, he was unmoved. Letting his finger slip from between my lips I placed my palms flat on his chest and began, very gently, to massage him, moving lower and lower with each stroke. I heard him sigh, and guessed he was finally enjoying my attentions. My hands moved lower and lower, finally finding his tree of flesh. I was relieved to find that that, at least, was very much awake. I lowered my head to his belly and began to lick his flesh, running my tongue down from his navel to his black moss. Before I could reach his erection, Akira-san put his hands on my shoulders.

He was tremendously strong. With just the power of his hands and arms, he pushed me up and held me in the air at arm's length. I dangled like a boneless doll, unable to move as he pushed me higher and higher, until only my knees were on the floor, barely supporting my weight. With a sudden, almost careless flick, he jerked me upward and then lowered me so that I half fell, half sat, on his tree of flesh.

And there he left me. That night, I used every trick I had ever learned in the Hidden House. I gripped him with my internal muscles until my thighs cramped and my belly hurt. I rode him fast, slow, barely moving. I kissed and licked and bit every inch of his body I could reach. I whipped him with my hair. When I was almost so exhausted I could barely move, he suddenly rolled over, taking me with him. He rode me as if he was an automaton, silently, with not even a grunt. As he reached orgasm, he took my hair in both hands and pulled it until I screamed. And then pulled it harder until my breath ran out and I was forced to stop in order to breathe.

I was terrified that I had over-stepped the mark, but it appeared I had not.

As we lay in the moth-colored darkness, I could feel he was smiling.

"There is no other woman like you in the whole of Edo, Kazuha. I chose wisely when I chose you. Did you miss me so much?"

I mumbled something that he hoped he would interpret as "yes." He seemed satisfied, for in minutes he was asleep.

So now here I was, with my little maid at my heels, and Nekko trotting beside me, tail held high. I was eager for the friendship and the gossip of the Hidden House. This would be the last time I would see Kiku, for she was leaving the next day for her new life. I was desperate to talk to Mineko, too, to see if she had any thoughts on the conundrum of Big and my mother.

But I never saw Kiku. Never got to talk to my dear Mineko. I still hope that one day I may see Mineko again, if the gods are very, very good to me.

It started to rain, just as we turned onto Willow Road. It was not a heavy downpour, but a thick, chilly, grey drizzle that made people shiver and turn off the street for cover. The unknown nobleman's carriage was parked outside the Green Tea House again, I noticed. I supposed I would have to ask the girls about him, yet again. Akira was certain to ask, and he was becoming increasingly impatient when I had nothing to tell him.

I glanced down, lifting my foot to avoid a puddle. I heard the maid scream, a sound that was cut off quickly, and I thought she must have tripped and fallen. I turned my head to see if she was all right, and then there was a figure at my side, a man, but I could tell nothing at all about him for he was lifting his arms and a bag was thrown over my head before I could even shout. The cloth was pressed into my mouth and held firmly in place. Another pair of arms clipped around my breasts and upper arms, pinioning me effortlessly, clutching me. I tried to kick out, but was hampered by my kimono. A second later, my feet were churning in the air and I was thrown over somebody's shoulder and a moment after dumped – although quite gently – onto a soft bench. An indignant yowl informed me that Nekko was with me. I was pushed onto my side, and a body flung itself alongside me, keeping me both still and imprisoned.

There was nothing I could do. In truth, it took all my effort to breathe through the silk that was still around my head. I felt the bench begin to move beneath me and realized I was in the carriage that had been waiting outside the Green Tea House. Oddly, the carriage was not hurrying at all. The horses were moving at what sounded like a brisk walk, but without any urgency. I lay still, terrified beyond either moving or trying to fight.

I was certain that this was all Akira's doing. I was right. He had tired of me. But it was not enough for the yakuza to dispose of my quietly, oh no! It had to be in a flamboyant gesture, to show the world that he cared nothing. That he was above everything and everybody else. That he would do what he wanted.

Tears leaked down my cheeks and I started to pray silently. I felt an overwhelming relief in knowing that I had received my mother's letter. At least I would go to my death knowing that she had loved me. That I had been wrong all these years. Suddenly, I was sure that I had been wrong about Danjuro. He *was* dead. Perhaps he was waiting for me on the other side of death. The thought gave me courage, and I lay still. Oddly, Nekko had settled down on my back and was purring quietly to himself. Contrary cat!

The coach rolled on. I felt it stop at the gate to the Floating World, but the pause was brief and it must have been waved through quickly. Once outside the walls, the pace picked up, and I could hear and feel the movement of the fine horses pulling the coach pick up, first to a trot, then a fast canter. Even in my distress, I was puzzled. Why on earth was Akira taking me out of the Floating World? Did he intend to kill me in full view of the whole of Edo? Was his vanity that great? Probably.

We rolled on for an interminable time. It could have been ten minutes, it could have been nearer an hour. I had no way of telling. I was cold and deeply uncomfortable and terrified. Apart from the noise of the coach, everything was silent. Plucking up a little courage, I tried to speak to whoever was sitting against me, but I received no reply. I decided to save my voice for one last scream when I was finally taken out of the carriage. Nobody would pay any attention, of course, but at least I would feel better.

I was not even given the chance to do that. The carriage slowed and finally drew to a halt. I tensed, wondering if I might have the chance – the smallest chance would do – to wriggle free and make at least an attempt to escape. I heard somebody opening the door from the outside, but before I could move so much as a finger, I was scooped up in somebody's arms, one arm beneath my shoulders and one beneath my knees. I had been cramped and still for so long, I felt my bones creak when I was moved. I did manage to scream, though. Long and loud. And repeatedly. But I had been right. Nobody came to see what was happening. As far as I knew, nobody even noticed. I was, after all, just a woman.

I didn't matter. I had never mattered.

The thought suddenly raised fury in me. I did matter. I did. My mother had been the greatest geisha in Edo. My lover had been the greatest actor in the kabuki. Even the man who was about to kill me was the most powerful yakuza in Edo. I might matter to nobody in the whole world but myself, but I did matter.

I wriggled and screamed and thrashed. I caught the man who was holding me a blow on the nose and I was delighted when he grunted in pain. If I had to go, then I would go out fighting. Nekko joined in with gusto. He shrieked and yowled and – from the noises – I guessed he was digging his claws into somebody's leg.

None of it did us any good. I was carried over uneven ground and then my captor tilted backward as he began to climb a steep slope. A steep slope that seemed to move beneath his feet. Fury gave way to renewed terror, and I clutched at his shoulders in fear that he would drop me. Whatever was happening, it was bitter for me.

Even through the fog of terror, I wondered who had taken me. Akira? No. If he wanted to harm me, and there was no saying that he did not, he would have done it as publicly as he possibly could. I had heard whispered tales of his cruelty to those who dared cross him. Men who had

had their testicles sliced off and then treated with huge care to ensure that they lived to tell the tale. A business rival who had been found spitted on a long stake right in the center of Edo. A courtesan who had displeased Akira in some way and had had her hair shaved off and her lips sewn together. The tales went on and on. This was flamboyant enough for Akira, certainly, but it was too private. Had he wanted to humiliate me for some imagined slight, he would have made it as public as possible. After all, he had his reputation to maintain.

Perhaps it was simply fear of the unknown, but the idea popped into my head that a business rival of Akira's was behind this, and that frightened me more than anything. If this rival yakuza wanted to get revenge on Akira, who knew what he might stoop to? I shuddered and bit my lip so hard to stop myself screaming out loud that I tasted blood on my tongue.

I was on flat ground again, but the earth was still swaying. I heard a door latch snick and then my captor was putting me down. Or at least trying to, as I still clung on for grim death. My hands and arms were detached firmly yet with an odd gentleness, and then I heard the door open again and the soft murmur of voices. I was weeping, tears running down my face into my ears. I sent up a prayer, *Let it be done quickly, please.* I was sure I could hear Nekko purring and cursed the faithless beast heartily.

"Midori No Me."

Then I knew then that I was already dead. That the worst was past and I could begin my journey into the next life. Even through the muffling hood, even through the strange noises that were gathering all around me, I knew who that voice belonged to. I would have followed it to the inner reaches of hell. Perhaps I had.

Gentle hands unwound the hood from my head and a slow hand wiped the tears from my face. As fast as they were wiped away, then faster still did they fall.

"I am so sorry, my love. So very sorry. It had to be this way. Nekko, get off."

I scrubbed at my own face with my hands. My eyes were so bleary with tears I could barely see. But I had no real need of sight. I would have known him anywhere by his voice, by the feel of his body.

"Danjuro," I whispered. For answer, he put his face into the hollow above my shoulder blade and kissed me gently. So very gently. Nekko shoved his whiskers into my ear and said, I am sure, "Told you so!"

I clung to Danjuro, incapable of saying anything. Although every one of my senses told me it was true, I dared not believe it. Was I asleep and dreaming? No, the bed I was lying on – and it was a bed of some sort, not a futon – was moving under my body. I could not dream a movement I had never felt before. The hood that had been over my head was beside me. I rubbed it between my fingers. Suddenly, I was coldly, furiously angry. I yanked my way out of his arms – and felt the lack of them immediately – and hit him, hard, across the face with the back of my hand.

"I thought you were dead!" I wailed. A lie, but only half a lie. I had worried he had been dead. There had been days when I was *sure* he had been dead. "And now you have me kidnapped. How dare you! Oh, Danjuro!"

My anger turned to relief and I sat and bawled. He wiped my face with a silk handkerchief and patted and stroked me, as if he feared something might be broken. He murmured my name over and over and I realized that he was as worried and distressed as I was myself. When my tears dried, he held me in his arms and said nothing, as if the mere touch of our bodies was enough.

"Midori No Me, I am so sorry. It had to be this way. If I could have gotten to you sooner, I would have. But it was impossible. We would both have been killed."

Questions crowded my mouth. I started to speak, then stopped. When I could find words, the question that popped out was not the one I wanted to say at all. "Where am I?"

"You are on board a ship. We have left Edo harbor behind us. You are safe."

Safe? I had never been on the sea in my life. This was his idea of safe? But at least the constant movement of the floor was explained. I paused, cautiously wondering if I liked the strange motion or not. I decided I did.

"Tell me." I was exhausted. Suddenly, my whole body was limp. I craved sleep. But first, I had to know. Everything.

"It's a long tale." Danjuro was smiling at me. Did he know about Akira, I wondered? How he had kept me by his side like a chained dog? Used me like an animal? If he did not, then I would tell him. Everything. And if he decided to throw me overboard as a result, then so be it. I prayed that I was right.

"Why did you leave Edo?" At that moment, it seemed the most important question. After all, hadn't I just heard him call me "my love"? Nothing mattered more than that.

He held me close and spoke softly into my ear. I struggled to keep sleep at bay at first, but as his story went on, I became more and more alert. If only I had known. If only.

"I told you I had stopped Akira from buying the kabuki?" I nodded, snuggling against the silk of his robe. I could feel his heart beating against my face. He had told me, a lifetime ago. "I knew then that I had made a terrible enemy, and that I would have to be careful for a long time. But then I heard that Akira was taking an interest in you, Midori No Me."

I mouthed the word "no" against him. It had not been like that. Akira had wanted me because Danjuro was my lover. I tried to explain that to him, but he shushed me.

"No. He wanted you because you are beautiful and you are spirited and there is no other woman like you in the whole of Edo. He wanted to tame you. To make you his creature. Did he try?"

I shuddered and nodded. Oh, yes. Akira had tried.

"And did he succeed?" Danjuro's voice was very gentle, but also compelling. He wanted the truth, at any cost. I did not even have to think.

"No," I said exultantly. "No, he did not. You always said I was a wonderful actor, Danjuro. Toward the end, he thought he had me where he wanted me, but he was wrong."

Silence fell for a moment, and I could feel him smiling as he stroked my hair. A thought occurred to me abruptly and I sat up, away from him. For the first time, I looked fully at his dear face. He looked older, I thought. I touched the wrinkles at the corner of his eyes that had not been there before. His face was...naked to me. No longer Danjuro the great kabuki actor, this was simply my man. My lover. He was staring back at me with the same intensity. I relaxed, and reached up to my hair, finding the hated kingfisher beak combs by touch. I pulled all four of them out and threw them on the floor, allowing my hair to fall past my shoulders.

"He gave them to me," I said. "I always hated them. As soon as I get a chance, I will throw them into the sea. Akira did not tame me, Danjuro. But he did put his mark on me, and it will be there forever."

I had to show him. Had to show him that no matter how long the gods gave us together, I could never lose the mark of the yakuza. I had to make sure that he could – not forgive me, as I had had no choice in the matter – but that he could live with it. I lifted my hair from my neck, lowered my kimono, and turned my back to him.

His fingers traced the pattern lightly. I waited until he had taken his hand away and turned to face him.

"I must live with that," I said quietly. "You do not have to."

He nodded and stood. "Akira has done us both great wrong." He undid the sash of his robe and pulled it aside, and I gasped with horror and empathy. It was as if Danjuro had tried to commit seppuku. A great scar ran across his belly from left to right, starting high up on his ribs and running almost into his black moss. I closed my eyes in sick horror. Just as he had done with my neck, I ran my fingers across the scar, and then – unable to even comprehend the pain he must have felt when this was inflicted – put my lips to it and planted a row of tender kisses on the entire length. I laughed out loud when Danjuro responded, his penis thrusting toward me.

Nekko was pushed aside as all questions were put away for the time. I opened my arms to him and my lover entered me immediately, sliding into my wetness as if I was the scabbard to his sword. He belonged there, and always would.

Our lovemaking was almost unbearably tender, and short. We were hungry for each other, and this would have to do. For the moment at least. Satisfied and – at last! – sure I was not dreaming, I lay back on the strange bed with

Danjuro at my side. He threw his robe over both of us for warmth, and Nekko slid himself comfortably in the small of my back. When I could speak again, I asked, "Akira did that to you?"

"He did. It was supposed to kill me. He didn't do it himself. He had two of his thugs hold me down and a third wielded the sword while he watched and grinned. I often wondered why it wasn't he who actually did it, and I still don't know why. Perhaps it was one thing he couldn't stand to have on his conscience, who knows? When my body was found, it would have been thought that I had committed suicide. There would have been no connection with Akira. But it did not kill me. I have very good friends who came to find me. They got a physician to me and I healed." Danjuro paused, and I wondered if he was remembering the pain. I shuddered as I recalled Akira-san telling me casually that Danjuro had received death threats. How that must have amused him! "It took a long time for me to recover, but I was determined that Akira was not going to win. That he was not going to kill me and keep you. I told you there was danger for me, before this happened... Afterward, I had to disappear, I was supposed to be dead. If Akira had found out that I had survived, he would have gone to any lengths to finish me off. That is why I couldn't get word to you, dear one. You are a good actress, but if you had known what was going on, there would have been a time when you let your guard down. You would not have been unhappy enough. He would have sensed it. And Akira would have done anything to get the information out of you, no matter how he felt about you. "

"He didn't care about me," I protested. "I was useful to him, and he liked the idea that he had taken me away from you. That's all."

"No, you're wrong." Danjuro smiled. "It was the talk of the Floating World. The great yakuza had been bought to heel, by a woman at that! Did you never wonder why he let you roam about Edo, just accompanied by a maid? It was because you were never in any danger. Had anybody so much as spoken to you, they would have been a dead man. Even Akira's rivals dared not hurt you."

I shook my head in amazement. "Was it Akira who burned the kabuki?"

"Yes. If he couldn't have it, then nobody else was going to."

I rubbed my hand against my lips. Something did not make sense. "There was a body found in the ashes of the theater. Everybody said it was you. Akira tried to make me believe it was, but I never believed him. But if he thought you were already dead, why did he put somebody else in there?"

"He didn't," Danjuro said quietly. "He thought he had killed me with this," he said, rubbing his hand on the terrible scar. "He thought with me gone, he could buy the kabuki easily. But he didn't reckon with the spirit of those who were left. They would still not sell to him. So he decided if he could not have the theater, then nobody would. That is why he set fire to it."

I nodded. Knowing Akira as I did, that made perfect sense. Who, then, was the poor soul who burned with the kabuki?

"It was Big," he said softly. I put my hand to my mouth in disbelief. "I was told that he was haunting the theater, waiting for me to come back. Sometimes, he sat in my dressing room for the whole of the performance. Other times, he mingled with the crowd, never looking at the play, but searching for me in the audience. He loved me, you know. Just as, a long time ago, he loved your mother."

"You're sure? You're sure it was Big?" It all made perfect sense, but I had to be convinced. Danjuro nodded.

"I know. When I heard the theater was burning, I went. I had to see it with my own eyes. I was wearing a merchant's robes, nobody noticed me. I could probably have gone without any disguise and in the excitement nobody would have seen me. I helped throw water on the flames, even though I knew it would do no good. I had to. This was my life, burning in front of me." He hesitated, and I could see that there were tears in his eyes. I waited in silence for him to continue his tale, frightened that if I spoke it would halt the flow of words. There was so much I still needed to know. He drew a deep breath and continued. "I waited until the next day, when the ashes were cool enough to walk on. It was me who found poor Big's body. He must have been in my dressing room at the side of the stage and was caught by the flames. I guessed it was him, but when I looked carefully," he pulled a face, and I swallowed as I thought of the courage it must have taken to examine the badly burned corpse, "I found the amulet he always wore. I broke it off and took it with me. I was deeply sorry for my poor friend, but I had to make sure that people would think it was me. I knew Big wouldn't mind. If he thought he was helping me, his spirit would be appeased. There was nothing else that I could see to identify the body. I would have dropped something of mine – a ring, perhaps – but somebody saw me bending over Big and obviously thought I was looting. When they shouted at me I had to run."

"My mother thought Big was her friend," I said sadly. "She thought he would look after me."

I was shocked when Danjuro laughed. "Mineko made sure you got your parcel, then." I stared at him in disbelief, my mouth sagging open. All the questions I wanted to ask crowded on my tongue, bumping into each other so that no sound emerged except an inarticulate croak. Danjuro took my face in his hands and smiled, putting his finger to my lips to silence me.

"I know. So many questions, little one! Wait, and I will tell you. When I found poor Big, I felt I had to do my best for him. Too little, too late, I know. He had lodgings in Edo, away from the Floating World." I raised my eyebrows in surprise. I – and all the other girls – had assumed he lived the whole of his life between the Green Tea House and the Hidden House. Danjuro nodded his understanding. "I went to pay any rent that he owed, and to tidy away his things. He had few possessions, and what there was I gave to the Shinto shrine to distribute to the poor. Two things only I kept. One was a letter to me, from Big. He said in it that he knew I was not dead, and that he would keep searching for me. That if he didn't find me, he prayed that I would one day read this letter. That he loved me, and always would. He knew I thought of him only as a good friend, and could never respond to him as he wanted, but it made no difference to him. He loved me, and that was that." Poor Big. Always doomed to love those who did not love him! And at the same time, I felt a pang of pity for Bigger, who in his turn had loved his fellow geisha. What a miserable tangle! "In that letter, he told me to look in his cupboard where I would find an old furoshiki. He asked that I would make sure that it got to you. I glanced at the letter, and realized that it was from your mother, that it must be important to you. There was money as well. A lot of it, but I knew that it was the letter that would be important to you. I had to get it to you, so I took a risk and bribed one of the old priests from the temple to deliver it to the Hidden House, with strict instructions that it be given to Mineko for you. I had no way of knowing how long it would take to reach you, so I just waited."

Tears came to my eyes and I brushed them away. Danjuro was watching me, his expression tender.

"All these years," I managed to say. "All these years, Big had that letter. I've grown up thinking my mother didn't care about me, that she left me because she hated me because I was a freak. He knew, but he let me carry on." My voice choked and I could not go on.

"I know," Danjuro said softly. "It should never have happened. Never. Big should have told you as soon as you were able to understand. But he adored your mother. He wanted her for himself. It would have been bad enough if she had chosen somebody of her own race to fall in love with, but a foreigner. A white Barbarian! And to bear his child. I think it was too much for him. He took it as a personal insult, as a huge loss of face. That's why he hated you so much. But you owe him your life, you know." I stared at him in disbelief. Danjuro nodded gently. "Poor Big sealed his own fate when he invited me to the Hidden House. I think he thought I would be amused by you girls, but I knew as soon I saw you that you were special. That the gods had bought us together. Big saw my interest immediately, and perhaps it was in hopes of finding favor with me, but he told me that after your mother left, he persuaded Auntie to keep you. Convinced her that if she got your mother back, you would be a bargaining point. And if your mother was never found, then you could be an attraction in the Hidden

House. He even persuaded Auntie to get a wet nurse for you."

"Big did that?" I asked. He nodded. Suddenly, Big was no longer important. I had to ask him. "You never said you cared for me. Never. I thought I was just some sort of distraction to you. Nothing that mattered."

He shrugged. There was a long pause as he searched for words. The right words.

"All my life, little one, I have lived for the theater. Never did I feel that I was good enough. Never worthy of the honor of my name. I have spent my life mouthing other people's words. Never my own. It didn't matter, nobody looked beyond the mask of the makeup and the costumes. Nobody ever thought about the man underneath. But you did. You looked straight through me, into my heart. And I was bewildered. I didn't know how to respond to you, what to do. So I did what any man of Edo would have done. I treated you badly. I treated you as if you were less than me. As if you didn't matter. And it didn't work. I couldn't even convince myself." He drew a deep breath. "I love you, Midori No Me. More than life itself. If you wish it, we will spend the rest of our lives together."

If I wished it! I stared at him, blinking hard as Danjuro the actor and Danjuro my lover blurred together and became one. Became the man I loved. All I could do was nod.

"Then it will be so," he said. "Shall I finish my tale? Or is it irrelevant now?"

"Finish. I want to know everything." I was floating – not on water, but on air – but still my curiosity lingered.

"As soon as I found out Akira had taken you into his house, I started to make my plans. I was frustrated at first, when he only allowed you back to the Hidden House with him, but I prayed that you would find a way to come back, alone. I was nearly mad with waiting. I saw you, you know." He smiled and I stared at him in astonishment. "I told you, I have many very good friends. My patron from Kyoto was kind enough to help me. It didn't take a lot of persuasion to get him to become a regular client of the Green Tea House. Nor to get him to take me with him on his visits. I disguised myself as his servant, and waited in the carriage for him. Waited and watched. I caught a glimpse of you from time to time when we visited the Tea House. Only from a distance, across the courtyard, but it was enough to give me hope. At least I knew you were alive, and allowed to go to the Hidden House now and then."

"I knew you weren't dead," I said. "I knew it. I felt it."

"Of course you did. Was life with Akira very bad?"

"Later on, yes." I had to tell him. I could not live with it on my conscience. "At first, I thought he was exciting. Attractive." I stared at him, trying to see what he was thinking. "Even though I was betraying you, I couldn't help it. If I had known what he had done to you, I would have killed myself before I let him touch me, but I didn't know."

"Many women have felt the same about Akira. When he wants to be, he can be a very attractive man indeed," he said. "But you were the only one he wanted. He has hurt you, he has hurt me. But he is the past. He is gone. I, also, have hurt you, and for that I am deeply sorry. Forgive me, Midori No Me?"

Forgive him? *He* was asking *me* to forgive him? I was caught between tears and laughter. I could do nothing but shake my head.

"I even hurt you bringing you here," Danjuro said. "You must have been terrified, but I had to do it this way. If something had gone wrong and Akira had found you – and he has eyes and ears everywhere – it was essential that you were innocent. That you could tell him nothing except that you had been kidnapped in the street. Until our ship was well out of harbor and I knew we were safe, I had to make sure you knew nothing at all about what was happening to you. If he thought for a second that you had been mixed up in it, he would have killed you. It would have been too much loss of face for him to do anything else."

I shuddered, knowing that he was right.

"And now?" I asked. "What now? We can't go back to Edo."

"Now, we go to America." I gasped, sure I had misheard him. "Whilst I was gone from Edo, I was not idle. My patron in Kyoto has strong links with America. He is a shrewd man. He says that is where the future lies. Some of the actors who fled from the kabuki in Edo have already gone to America to find their fortune. I am not a poor man, even with the loss of the kabuki. In any event, my patron wants to sponsor me. Us. He has spoken already to friends of friends in America. There is a welcome assured for us there. We will find my actors, and we will make a new kabuki theater. In America."

He paused, waiting for me to speak. I could see the need for reassurance in his face, but even so, I thought carefully before I responded. The time for lies was long gone. And yet, the more I thought about it, the more attractive the idea became.

"Many of the foreigners..." I was careful not to refer to them as foreign Barbarians anymore. "Many of the foreigners who came to the Green Tea House were Americans. They were very interested in our culture and seemed to enjoy the geisha's singing and dancing."

Danjuro smiled. "And many more found their way to the kabuki. I have spoken to them often." I stared at him in surprise. Danjuro spoke English? "I do not speak English as well as you do. But I will learn more, if you will teach me. Already many Japanese have found their way to America. We will bring memories of home to them, and something new to the foreigners. I think – and my patron thinks – that we will do well."

Amongst the bewildering rush of new ideas, one word struck me. "We?"

"We. We are going to a new world. Why should a woman not act in the kabuki there?"

I thought I might die with pleasure, then. But one shadow fell across my dreams. "Danjuro, for us, this is a future to welcome. But what of my poor Mineko? She has been a true friend to me, and I have left her in the Hidden House."

"You left your mother's money with her?" I nodded. "There is more than enough there for her to buy herself out. Even Auntie will be unable to resist that much. Akira will be too worried about what has happened to you to care, I think. I will get word to her that the money is hers, if that will make you happy. And in time she could even come to us in America. A good friend for you and another fine actress for the kabuki!" The tears came then and would not be stilled. I cried for my lost mother and my father. For myself. For all the years that I had wasted, without even knowing that there could be anything better. Danjuro held me in his arms until I had no more tears to shed, and then he kissed me.

"Do not weep, my own one. Do not weep, for we will be together now until the gods choose to part us by death. We have always been together, in this life and the lives before it.

We will be together in the life to come. No more tears, for what is done is done."

I felt the ship rock beneath us, speeding us on to our new life. Eventually, I fell asleep in the arms of my lover, safe in the knowledge that I had come home.

At last.

THANK YOU

Thank you for reading *The Geisha With the Green Eyes*. I hope you enjoyed it! Don't forget to read the next book about the women of the Hidden House, *The Geisha Who Could Feel No Pain*.

Subscribe to my mailing list so you never miss a new release.
https://indiamillar.com/contact-me/

THE GEISHA WHO COULD FEEL NO PAIN
SECRETS FROM THE HIDDEN HOUSE BOOK 2

https://books2read.com/u/4EkO5e

Out of all the geisha, only Mineko's strangeness was hidden from the world.

Mineko was the geisha who could not feel pain. She was the geisha that no man could hurt, no matter how hard they tried. And not only was Mineko unable to feel physical pain, she was also unable to feel the emotions of love and longing and need. Until she met the Samurai who became her lover; the man who—just as she was—was owned body and soul by Mineko's master, the terrible yakuza Akira.

As her desires were awoken by Ken, her Samurai lover, Mineko begins to dream of another life, one of freedom.

In this, the second in the "Secrets from the Hidden House" series, the terrible mysteries that lie at the heart of the Hidden House are revealed. Past and present twist together, each secret deeper and darker than that which has gone before. The enigma that is the Hidden House unfurls the petals of its history here, in Mineko's story.

The story of the Geisha Who Could Feel No Pain.

WILD IRIS: DAUGHTER OF THE YAKUZA
BOOK 1

https://books2read.com/wildiris

In a world built on lies, one woman's quest for truth and freedom begins.

Life is never easy for a rebel, especially one determined to forge her own path in a society that demands conformity. Ayame has always felt at odds with her place in the world, her spirit yearning for freedom. Her parents' latest decree—to marry her off to a repulsive suitor—becomes the final straw, pushing her to the brink of despair.

In a desperate bid for autonomy, Ayame turns to her new friend in Kyoto's infamous pleasure quarter. Amid the vibrant chaos and shadowy corners of this sleazy district, she makes a startling discovery: her entire life has been built on a foundation of lies.

The truth about her origins, hidden from her for so long, emerges, revealing that her past is not what it seems.

Determined to break free from the shackles of her fabricated existence, Ayame embarks on a perilous journey back to her unknown beginnings. As she delves deeper into the mysteries of her past, she must navigate a treacherous path filled with unexpected allies and dangerous enemies. Along the way, Ayame discovers a strength she never knew she possessed and learns that true freedom comes not just from escaping one's circumstances, but from embracing one's true self.

ABOUT THE AUTHOR

 With a literary journey spanning more than a dozen captivating novels set in historical Japan and a collection of evocative haikus, India Millar has embarked on a diverse career. Her professional odyssey commenced amidst the machinery of British Gas's heavy industry, eventually culminating within the hallowed halls of the British Library, where the tapestry of knowledge and storytelling merged seamlessly.

Now, India finds herself in the idyllic embrace of early retirement on the enchanting Costa Blanca. As she continues to explore the realms of history and poetry, India remains deeply grateful for the winding path that has led her to this peaceful and creative haven. Each word written, each page turned, is a testament to the enduring passion for storytelling that continues to shape her life's narrative.

Learn more about India and her books and sign up for her mailing list at https://indiamillar.com/.

ABOUT THE PUBLISHER